She looked so brittle—vulnerable almost. Adam felt an unwanted stirring of sympathy, but pushed it ruthlessly aside.

"There's no point fighting this," he said, hoping Reggie would see reason. "They are all good men, but different enough to give you a real choice. I'm certain you'll decide which you find most compatible in that period of time."

"Are you, now?" The vulnerable air evaporated to be replaced by the scorching look and frigid tone she'd brandished before.

So much for that stirring of sympathy. Obviously, Miss Nash could hold her own in any war of words.

"As for this contract—" her chin tilted up at a militant angle "—I'm sure I'll need time to study it, perhaps have a lawyer look it over, before I sign it."

Adam stiffened. *He* was a trained lawyer, which she knew quite well. And he was here to help her through this. "I'd be glad to explain any—"

"I'd as soon ask the devil to explain a scripture."

Winnie Griggs

Handpicked Husband
&
The Bride Next Door

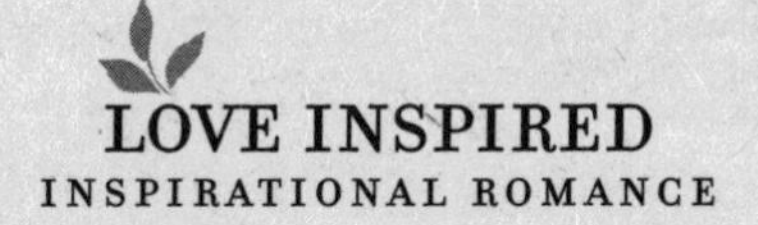

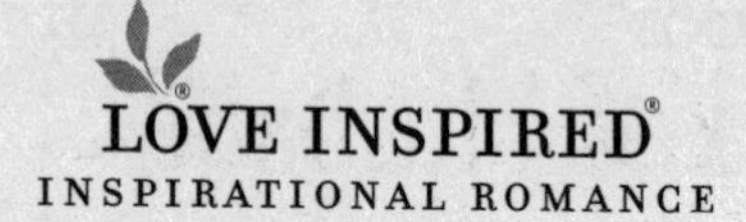

ISBN-13: 978-1-335-23988-4

Handpicked Husband & The Bride Next Door

This edition published by arrangement with Harlequin Books S.A.

For questions and comments about the quality of this book, please contact us at CustomerService@Harlequin.com.

Love Inspired
22 Adelaide St. West, 40th Floor
Toronto, Ontario M5H 4E3, Canada
www.Harlequin.com

Printed in U.S.A.

CONTENTS

Winnie Griggs is a multipublished award-winning author of historical (and occasionally contemporary) romances that focus on small towns, big hearts and amazing grace. She is also a list maker and a lover of dragonflies, and holds an advanced degree in the art of procrastination. Winnie loves to hear from readers—you can connect with her on Facebook at Facebook.com/winniegriggs.author or email her at winnie@winniegriggs.com.

Books by Winnie Griggs

Love Inspired Historical

Texas Grooms

Handpicked Husband
The Bride Next Door
A Family for Christmas
Lone Star Heiress
Her Holiday Family
Second Chance Hero
The Holiday Courtship
Texas Cinderella
A Tailor-Made Husband
Once Upon a Texas Christmas

Visit the Author Profile page
at Harlequin.com for more titles.

HANDPICKED HUSBAND

Remember ye not the former things,
neither consider the things of old. Behold, I will do
a new thing; now it shall spring forth; shall ye not
know it? I will even make a way in the wilderness,
and rivers in the desert.

—*Isaiah* 43:18–19

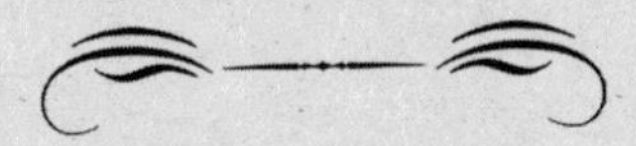

To my editor, Melissa Endlich, whose faith in me
and sincere efforts help me make my writing
the best that it can be, and who has been
a source of encouragement, inspiration and joy
during the years we have worked together.

Chapter One

Northeast Texas, 1894

An ear-splitting shriek ricocheted through the forest, startling a raucous cloud of blackbirds from the roadside trees.

"Easy, Trib." Adam Barr patted the horse's neck as the animal shied. *What now?*

The buggy behind him slowed to a stop, but Adam ignored it, along with the uneasy questions from the three men seated inside. He'd promised to escort the men from Philadelphia to Texas, not be their nursemaid.

The wailing continued and Adam fought the urge to tilt back his head and answer with a wild, full-throated howl. He'd gritted his teeth so often these past few days the muscles in his jaw hurt. Taking on this job when more important business waited for him in Philadelphia had him in a foul mood, as his companions could no doubt attest.

After six years of biding his time—six years, two months and thirteen days to be exact—he'd thought he could finally pursue his goal without distraction.

If this assignment had come from anyone but Judge Madison…

Adam scanned the brush-skirted hardwoods lining the trail. Whatever the source of that eerie sound, it was headed their way.

He eased his rifle from the scabbard. Anticipation stirred his blood. He might have to employ his "company manners" with his three charges, but this bellowing beast was another matter.

No telling what manner of creature roamed this forsaken backwoods. The wail was too high-pitched to belong to a bear. A large cat maybe?

He urged Trib closer to the trees. There seemed to be a pattern to the sound, a certain mangled cadence. Almost as if—

Well, what do you know?

He leaned back. Not a wild animal after all. Too bad.

"Do you think it's a wolf?"

Adam glanced over his shoulder. Chance's expression, like his tone, held more eagerness than worry. Did the kid think it would be some kind of lark to face down a wolf? Of course, from what Judge Madison had told Adam, the twenty-one-year-old was on this expedition precisely because he *was* prone to seek out trouble.

"Sounds more like an infernal wildcat." Everett adjusted his shirt cuff with exaggerated care, doing a creditable job of appearing unconcerned. But his British accent was more pronounced now, something Adam noticed happened when anything rattled the dandified cynic.

Mitchell, who controlled the skittish carriage horse with ease, refrained from comment. Nothing unusual in that. The loose-limbed bear of a man had spent most of the trip west with a sort of sleepy-eyed disinterest. What *was* different, however, was the subtle alertness that radiated from him now, as if he were a cavalryman waiting for the enemy to appear over the rise.

Another strident note drew Adam's focus back to the roadside. He didn't bother to disabuse them of the notion that it might be a wild animal. It'd do the pampered trio good to have something to worry about besides the unorthodox plot they'd gotten themselves embroiled in.

"Perhaps you should get the carriage moving," Everett said. "I'm sure our escort can handle this better without us to distract him."

"We shouldn't abandon Mr. Barr," Chance shot back. "He might need—"

"This is about common sense, *Junior*, not courage," Everett interrupted. "Besides, I do believe Mr. Barr is more interested in getting rid of the lot of us than having us guard his back."

"I told you before—the name's Chance, not Junior."

Adam's jaw tightened. Everett was right. Even if it had been a grizzly headed this way, he'd rather face *that* than listen to more of this petty bickering. This assignment couldn't be over soon enough to suit him.

A heartbeat later, the source of the ear-grating racket stepped onto the roadside. As soon as the creature caught sight of them, the discordant warble ceased.

"It's a man!" Chance's tone carried as much disappointment as surprise.

"Not quite." Adam didn't blame the youth for the mistake. The party responsible for that unmelodic braying wore baggy overalls and an equally oversize shirt, both of which had seen better days. There was even a smudge of dirt on one cheek to match those on the clothing.

But this was no man.

From Adam's closer vantage, he spied a frizzy brown braid long enough to brush the seat of the overalls. That, along with the slender neck and hint of curves below, proclaimed this person as most definitely female. He hesitated, though, to use the word *lady.* She appeared more a disheveled forest waif than a civilized being.

The girl seemed as startled as the men in the carriage. But a flicker of something else—disbelief? wariness?—shadowed her surprise.

Remembering he still cradled the rifle, Adam resheathed it and tipped his hat. No point scaring her more than they already had.

Besides, she might be a good source of information.

He dug deep for the polite pleasantries that had grown rusty with disuse. "Good afternoon, miss. My apologies if we startled you."

"Good heavens, it's a girl." Chance's whispered-but-easily-heard comment only served to heighten the color in her cheeks as she broke eye contact with Adam.

"Or what passes for one in this barbaric wilderness." Everett didn't bother to lower his voice. "Do you think she speaks English?"

Adam narrowed his eyes in annoyance. Did the men think just because she looked like an uncivilized rube she didn't have feelings?

But before he could say anything, the girl snapped out of her slack-jawed immobility. Her lips compressed and her eyes flashed daggers. So, there was more wildcat than rabbit in her, was there?

Instead of baring claws, however, she bent down to

pluck a stem of grass. Straightening, she favored them with a broad, neighborly grin as she stuck the weed between her teeth.

But something in her stance told Adam the claws were there, merely out of sight for now. He also noticed she didn't step away from the protection of the trees.

This girl was no fool. He mentally saluted her precaution, then leaned back in the saddle, ready to enjoy whatever performance she had in store for his companions.

"Howdy, gents." Her words were drawn out in a thick, rustic drawl. "I reckon I *was* a mite surprised at that, but no harm done. We don't get many strangers out this way, especially fancy-lookin' gents like you 'uns."

Her gaze flickered to Adam's again. Some trick of the light lent a luminosity to her irises, made them appear to change from green to blue and back again. The image of a statue he'd admired in a museum years ago shimmered through his memory. The scales of the dragon had seemed to glow, had rippled with a fluidity of color that was mesmerizing.

This girl's eyes were just like that.

She turned to the men behind him, and the spell was broken. Adam collected himself, annoyed at the fanciful turn his thoughts had taken. This trip must have worn on him more than he realized.

Mitchell remembered his manners first. "Are you all right, miss?"

She slid the stem of grass to the other corner of her mouth with bucolic nonchalance. As she did so, Adam saw her size up the speaker, no doubt weighing Mitchell's intimidating size against his concerned gaze.

She finally flashed a friendly grin. "Fit as a filly in a field of clover. Why'd you ask?"

Let it go, Adam silently advised. But Mitchell apparently hadn't figured out what was all too obvious to Adam.

"It's just, well, that screeching we heard. I thought maybe something had frightened you."

Adam watched for her reaction with interest. Would she dissolve into tears of mortification, or give Mitchell a blistering set-down for his innocent blunder?

To his surprise, she did neither. Instead she winced and gave a rueful smile. "My kinder friends call what you just heard a 'joyful noise.'"

Adam tilted his hat back with one finger. A female who could laugh at herself? Now *there* was a novelty.

Ruddy color crept into Mitchell's face along with the belated light of understanding. "I beg your pardon. I didn't mean any disrespect. I—"

She smiled and raised a hand. "Don't fret none, mister. No offense taken. Why do you think I wait 'til I'm out in the woods to really give it my all?"

She looked around, including each of them in her gaze. "You fellas lost? There's not much out this way but trees and critters. If you're looking for the road to Bent Willow, you passed the turn about three miles back."

"Actually, we're looking for Miss Regina Nash." A flicker in her expression told Adam she knew the name. "I understand she's staying somewhere out this way." He'd hand it to the judge's granddaughter, she'd taken great pains to make it as difficult for him to find her as possible. But she obviously didn't know who she was dealing with if she thought a trek through the woods would deter him.

The girl nodded, pulling the stem from her mouth and waving it in the direction they'd been traveling. "Her place is about a twenty-minute ride farther on. Can't miss it." She rolled the stem between her fingers, eyeing him speculatively. "I was by there a bit ago, though, and it didn't seem like they was expecting company."

He swallowed a sour laugh. "No, I don't imagine they are." He watched her toss the blade of grass away, still intrigued by her in spite of himself.

Goodness knows it didn't have anything to do with her looks. In that grubby getup and with smudges on her face, and her hair indifferently tamed into a bushy braid, she lacked anything resembling sophistication or feminine wiles. No, it was more the glimpse of personality he'd seen in her eyes, and the complete lack of apology for her untidy appearance, even after the tactless comments from the men in the carriage. The girl seemed a product of her environment, completely lacking artifice or slyness.

"Do you live nearby?" he heard himself ask. "Can we give you a ride?"

Now why had he made such an offer? It wasn't like him to act impulsively. Too late to retract the offer now, though.

"No, thanks. I'm headed that'a way." She waved toward the trail behind her.

Adam nodded with more relief than disappointment. As interesting as this backwoods miss was, he didn't have time for distractions right now. The sooner he found Regina Nash, the sooner he could be done with this mess.

"Then I suppose we'll be on our way." He gathered the reins. "Good day."

"Nice talking to you fellas." She hooked her thumbs under the straps of her overalls and rocked back on her heels. "Tell Miz Nash I said hello when you see her."

Adam raised a brow. "Who shall I say sends her greetings?"

"She'll know."

Being coy, was she? He'd already decided the girl wasn't quite as guileless as she seemed. That drawl was a bit too thick, that gleam in her eyes a bit too knowing.

Not that he thought the worse of her for it. Under the circumstances, she probably felt safer pretending to be simple. Living down to their expectations, as it were.

He turned back to the carriage. "All right, gentlemen. Time to move on." But as he set Trib in motion, Adam felt her gaze on him, like a prickle between his shoulder blades.

A moment later when he glanced back, however, she'd disappeared.

He mentally offered a salute. It was as if, by getting him to look back, she'd managed to have the last word.

Mitchell's gaze followed Adam's. "Who do you suppose she was?"

Everett clapped Mitchell on the back. "So, you like an earthy quality to your women, do you?"

Mitchell shot him a contemptuous glower. "The kind of woman I like is none of your concern."

Adam faced forward again, wondering why Everett took such pleasure in needling his companions. Did he think his polished manner somehow made him superior?

"Oh, she wasn't so bad," Chance offered. "Seemed a bit simple, but she was friendly enough."

Chance saw her as simple? Adam shook his head. Was he the only one who'd glimpsed the intelligence in those changeable eyes?

"What does it matter?" Everett's question had an irritable edge. "Until Miss Nash makes her selection, none of us has any business looking at another woman."

A pall descended on the trio. The clink of harness and the rattle of carriage wheels suddenly seemed unnaturally loud. The question of who would be selected as the sacrificial lamb in this unorthodox lottery rode alongside the carriage like a black-clad specter.

Would the man who drew the short straw *really* follow through with his end of the bargain? Adam shrugged off any feelings of sympathy for their predicament. They'd known the terms before they signed the contract. *His* only concern in this matter was to see everything settled according to the judge's wishes, and the sooner the better.

For six eternal, nightmarish years, he'd waited for the day he would be free to pursue the truth, to clear his reputation and unmask those who had blackened it. The proof he needed was almost within reach now, he could feel it. Soon, very soon, he'd be able to exonerate himself, to reclaim the life that had been stolen from him.

But he couldn't do it from Turnabout, Texas.

His frustration over being forced to put his own plans on hold for even a day, much less four weeks, was burning a hole in his gut.

Not that he'd let on as much to anyone else. His ability to maintain an unperturbed demeanor through any situation was a matter of pride to him. And a major source of annoyance for his opponents.

It was an ability that had served him well in his years as a trial lawyer. The drive to hold on to that one piece of himself, to not let them take it away from him along with everything else, had helped keep him sane the last six years.

That, and the burning need to see justice done.

He nudged his horse to a slightly faster pace.

It would be nice if Miss Nash acted sensibly and dispatched this business with as little fuss as possible.

It would be nice, but given the situation and his own run of bad luck, he didn't hold out much hope.

Reggie sprinted down the overgrown trail, grateful for the freedom the overalls gave her. The road the men were taking meandered through this hilly woodland, twisting and turning without a discernable pattern. On foot, she could cut a much more direct path. With any luck, she'd reach the cabin a full ten minutes ahead of the riders.

Thank goodness she'd decided not to take her photographic equipment with her this afternoon.

Reggie winced as her boot caught on a root. Reluctantly, she slowed to a trot. Spraining an ankle wouldn't be in her best interest.

Adam Barr.

Now *there* was a face she hadn't expected to ever see outside of Philadelphia, much less in the backwoods of Northeast Texas. The last time she'd seen him had been in Grandfather Madison's home seven years ago. A lifetime ago.

Back then, her grandfather's dashing young protégé

had been an up-and-coming lawyer, a man who seemed to have the world at his fingertips.

Until his spectacular fall from grace.

She wasn't the least bit surprised he hadn't realized who she was. In fact, she doubted he'd have recognized her even if she'd been all gussied up in her Sunday best. She'd been only a girl back then, fifteen years old. And he'd mostly seen her in the company of her stepsister. Next to Patricia she might as well be invisible. Reggie had always thought of herself as shadow to Patricia's sunlight.

But she'd recognized him immediately. A woman rarely forgot the object of her first romantic schoolgirl fantasies—even if she'd dusted her hands of the fantasy as she matured.

Not that he hadn't changed. He'd aged of course, but it was more than that. He still had that heart-stopping dimple in his chin and bluer eyes than any man had a right to. But now those eyes held a flintiness, and that dimple seemed incongruous rather than endearing.

He'd also got himself a faded but new-to-her scar on his cheek. A souvenir, no doubt, from the kind of life he'd lived since she saw him last.

Well, she might have been young back then, but her wallflower status gave her lots of time to observe without being caught out. She'd sensed the charming, save-the-world idealist had some shadowy secret lurking behind his easy smile. In fact, it was one of the things that had drawn her to him, had caused her to moon over him with such private, embarrassing-to-remember enthusiasm all those years ago.

Now, though, those shadows seemed to have taken stronger hold, giving his smile a cynical twist.

Seeing him through the eyes of a woman rather than a child, Reggie was relieved to discover his glance no longer had the power to set her pulse aflutter. To the contrary, her heart-thumping reaction to the sight of him had been due to surprise—that was all.

Of course, that was neither here nor there right now.

What in tarnation was he doing in Texas? What possible reason could he have for seeking her out? And who were the three city dudes he'd brought along? Surely, if Grandfather Madison had sent them, he'd have sent word ahead of time. Of course, the old fox hadn't told her of his plans to donate a new wing to Turnabout's schoolhouse, either.

Maybe that was it. Maybe they'd come to check on the progress of her grandfather's newest project. But why had they come out *here* when the schoolhouse was back in town?

None of this made sense.

Could it have something to do with the letter she'd written Grandfather last month asking for guidance on how to formally adopt Jack? Were these men here to give her legal advice? But surely the matter was nothing more than a simple formality.

As far as Jack was concerned she was practically his mother already. Jack had been only three months old when her stepsister Patricia passed on. She'd been helping her brother-in-law, Lemuel, care for him ever since. Now that Lemuel was gone as well, she wanted to make certain Jack knew how special he was to her.

Her gut clinched. Surely there hadn't been a problem with her request? What obstacle could there be to her adopting Jack? In the eyes of the law she was only his step-aunt, true enough, but he didn't have any close blood kin, save the judge. No, there had to be some other reason they were here.

Ignoring the stitch in her side, Reggie picked up speed again as the cabin came into view. She had preparations to make before her callers arrived.

The Adam Barr she'd known all those years ago had been a pleasant, witty charmer, a self-made man who, after years of paying his dues, was just coming into his own. Certainly not a man to be afraid of.

But time could change a person, especially considering where the zealous ex-lawyer had spent the past six years.

Reggie wondered just when he'd gotten out of prison.

Chapter Two

As Reggie sprinted the last few feet to the cabin, Mrs. Peavy stepped out on the porch, wiping her hands on her apron. "Goodness, what's got you in such an all-fired hurry?"

Reggie grabbed the porch rail, struggling to catch her breath. "Company's coming." She inhaled deeply then tried again. "Be here...in about five minutes."

"Company?" The housekeeper looked more puzzled than alarmed. "Who'd be coming out all this way?"

"It's Adam Barr." Reggie climbed the steps, finally able to speak without panting. "He's a friend of Grandfather's I met in Philadelphia ages ago. And he's brought three men with him."

"Land sakes. Someone's come all the way from Philadelphia to see us? Did the judge send him?"

"I'm not sure. But until I find out, I'd rather keep Jack busy elsewhere. Would you step down to the lake and let Ira know he and Jack should stay put until I signal it's okay?"

Mrs. Peavy gave her a considering look. The squarely built woman was shorter than Reggie and had more salt than pepper in her hair, but she could assume a commanding presence when she wanted to. "You expecting trouble?"

Reggie shrugged. "Hard to tell." For now, she'd keep the information about Adam's jail time to herself. She didn't want to alarm Mrs. Peavy. Still, it wouldn't hurt to let the housekeeper know caution was in order. "I'd just prefer to find out what this is about before introducing them to Jack."

Their reason for seeking her out might be perfectly innocent, but she didn't believe in taking chances. Four able-bodied men versus herself, a six-year-old and an elderly couple—the scales seemed weighted in the visitors' favor if trouble erupted. But there were a few things she *could* do to even the odds until she learned their reasons for being here.

She gave Mrs. Peavy a level look. "Ira *does* have his hunting rifle with him, doesn't he?"

The housekeeper straightened, then nodded. "I won't be gone but a few minutes. Think I'll bring Buck back with me. You go get yourself cleaned up."

Oh, she'd clean up all right. By the time the handsome lawyer-turned-convict and his friends arrived, there'd be nary a trace of the ragtag tomboy they'd met earlier.

If Adam Barr remembered anything at all about her from her long ago visits to Philadelphia, then he'd learn he wasn't the only one who'd changed. She wasn't the tongue-tied wallflower she used to be.

In Philadelphia she'd always felt like some critter put on a leash and made to heel. Here, she was free to be herself.

She marched into the cabin, her hands already on

the buttons of her overalls, her mind planning her next moves.

If she remembered right, her old blue dress had pockets large enough to hide her father's derringer.

Adam bit off a groan as Chance cleared his throat. He should have known the silence wouldn't last.

"Do you really believe Miss Nash came out here to avoid us?"

The question hung in the air a moment, then Everett swatted at something on his neck with an irritated oath. "Can you think of any other reason a sane person would choose to hide out in this ghastly wilderness?"

Adam refrained from comment. Arriving in Turnabout to discover the judge's granddaughter had retreated to an isolated cabin had only added to his sense of time—and opportunities—slipping away. The plan had been for Miss Nash to receive her grandfather's letter of explanation before the four of them arrived so she would have time to come to terms with the arrangement in relative privacy.

Instead, she'd apparently used the time to enact this childish stalling tactic. Did she think they'd get tired of waiting and go back to Philadelphia? Or was she using the time to devise some clever scheme to outmaneuver them?

Well, he had no intention of cooling his heels in Turnabout while waiting for her to reappear. Over the grumbling protests of his companions, he'd immediately set out to find her.

Judge Madison had cautioned that his granddaughter would do her best to thwart his plans. He'd also said she was shrewd and not one to take being manipulated with good grace. In other words, much like the judge himself, even if the two didn't share a blood tie.

Adam had expected a more direct assault, however, not this cowardly retreat. But, then again, he *was* dealing with a woman.

Of course, the judge also had good things to say about the step-granddaughter he obviously loved. He'd assured Adam that beneath her tough exterior was a kind-hearted, vulnerable woman. The old schemer had made Adam promise to do his utmost to see that she wasn't unduly embarrassed by the situation. Although, considering the "situation" was instigated by the judge himself, and deliberately orchestrated to force her hand, Adam wasn't certain how he was going to pull off that part of his assignment.

But he'd given his word to try. It was the least he could do for the one person who'd stood by him through everything.

And it wasn't as if he didn't feel some sympathy for Miss Nash. He could imagine her reaction to that letter. She no doubt felt as if she were being backed into a corner.

And he, of all people, knew what it was to feel trapped and betrayed by those you trusted.

"I still think the three of us should have stayed in town while you approached Miss Nash alone." Mitchell's words held an accusatory edge. "I can't imagine Judge Madison would approve of the lot of us descending on his granddaughter's privacy this way."

"It's *my* job to decide what the judge would or wouldn't want," Adam answered shortly. He might owe the older man a debt of gratitude, but that didn't mean he couldn't look out for his own interests as well.

"Do you think that's Miss Nash's place?"

Adam raised up in the saddle at Chance's words. They'd topped a low hill, and ahead of them, barely visible amidst the trees, was a log structure.

"Only one way to find out." He nudged Trib into a trot.

The others didn't appear to share his impatience. Not only didn't they increase their pace, Adam sensed a definite slowing of the carriage. The closer he got to the cabin, however, the less certain he was that they'd reached their destination. He studied the place while the carriage caught up.

"The judge's granddaughter is staying *here?*" Everett's words echoed Adam's thoughts.

They'd all been inside Judge Madison's stately home. Adam had assumed the granddaughter lived in a comparable level of luxury, albeit a more countrified version. Of course, this wasn't the household's primary residence, but even so…

"This is a hovel." Everett sounded horrified.

"I wouldn't go that far." Chance's response lacked conviction. "It's plain, but—"

"Look at it." The British undertones in Everett's voice sharpened. "The walls are unfinished logs and the whole lot isn't much bigger than a respectable parlor. Those benches on the porch—bah! They look as if they were put together with odd bits of scrap timbers by a drunken carpenter. There aren't even glass panes on the windows."

Adam turned to face them. "We don't know for certain that this *is* Miss Nash's place." He narrowed his eyes and added a flintiness to his tone. "But even if it is, she's Judge Madison's granddaughter and is to be treated like a lady. Is that understood?"

He might be as irritated as a picnicker in a rainstorm by Miss Nash's delaying tactics, but he'd given his word to protect her honor, and these men better remember that.

He waited for their reluctant nods, then faced forward again. Now that he'd had time to get a good look at the place, he found he didn't agree with Everett's assessment. True, the structure was rougher than he'd expected. But the swing hanging on one end of the porch held calico cushions, and the whole area seemed well-tended. Maybe it was because of the years he'd spent in that iron-barred rat hole, but this place had a simple, homey appeal.

Wisps of smoke curling from the chimney and an abandoned checkerboard on the porch assured him someone was in residence, but was it Miss Nash? It seemed more likely this was home to the girl they'd encountered earlier. Not that she'd had time to make it here. Still, there might be someone else about.

Sure enough, a stocky, older woman appeared from the side of the cabin. The banshee's mother perhaps?

Whoever she was, she eyed them with as much suspicion as the muddy yellow cur padding along beside her. The dog had a feral quality that didn't bode well for anyone the creature took a dislike to.

Chance gave a low, appreciative whistle. "Look at that mutt, will you? He's big as a pony, and those teeth are like spikes. Do you suppose he's part wolf?"

"Given our surroundings, I wouldn't be surprised," Everett responded. "I, however, don't intend to get close enough to examine his features."

"Afraid?" Chance's tone matched the sneer on his face. "Are you a coward as well as a dandy?"

"Listen, *boy*." Everett flicked a spot of dust from his sleeve. "I have no intention of rising to an adolescent dare just to prove I can live up to your idea of manly valor."

The dog watched the men without blinking. The woman's expression was even less welcoming than that of the cur.

Doing his best to ignore the squabbling men, Adam tipped his hat. "Good afternoon, ma'am. We're looking for Miss Regina Nash. Can you tell me where I might find her?"

"Who's asking?"

The lack of warmth in the woman's tone was punctuated by a low growl from her companion. She lowered her hand to stroke the creature's head, never taking her gaze from Adam.

What did it take to get a straight answer around here? Adam tamped down his impatience. "My name is Adam Barr. Miss Nash's grandfather sent me."

She nodded acknowledgment, but remained stone-faced. "Funny, the judge didn't send word about your coming."

Did that mean this *was* Miss Nash's place? In which case, was the female major domo bluffing, or had Miss Nash kept the letter a secret?

Not that it mattered. Adam would play along, as long as it got the judge's granddaughter out here. "As a matter of fact, he did. Perhaps his letter arrived after you left town."

Her manner remained stiff. "I see." She gave the dog's head another pat, then moved to the steps. "Miss

Reggie's inside. I'm Mabel Peavy, the housekeeper. If you gents will make yourselves at home out here, I'll let her know we have company."

A housekeeper for *this* place? It was almost laughable, if he'd been in the mood to be amused. If Regina Nash was inside she'd doubtless overheard them. Why didn't she come on out? Surely she knew it was futile to continue hiding?

As Mrs. Peavy reached the door, she glanced back. "Don't worry about Buck. He won't bother you as long as you don't make any sudden moves toward one of the family members. He has a strong protective streak. Otherwise, he's just a big overgrown puppy."

The dog's baleful glare seemed to contradict her statement.

Adam dismounted, glad to stand after sitting in a saddle for so long. He moved toward the porch, but only climbed the first two steps before lounging back against a support post. No shaded bench for him. He preferred to feel the sun on his face. He couldn't seem to get his fill of fresh air and open spaces ever since he shook off the dust of prison two months ago.

Besides, from here he had a clear view of the door.

Everett climbed onto the porch, giving Buck a wide berth. He dusted a chair with his handkerchief, then sat down with the air of royalty stooping to grace a mud hut.

Chance paused in front of the dog. When the beast bared his fangs, though, Chance continued up the steps. Glowering at Everett's smirk, he sauntered to a bench on the other side of the porch and slouched down on it.

Mitchell remained on the grass in front of the porch, his hands stuffed in his pockets. He kept a respectful distance from the dog, but otherwise seemed more concerned with watching the front door than the animal.

Adam thought about who these men were and what they were being offered, and he still couldn't find the logic in the judge's selections. Everett—an officious dandy who'd destroyed an entire family with his sloppy reporting. Mitchell—a man who'd let his bottled rage get the better of him and killed someone in a gunfight. Chance—the spoiled younger son of a politician who'd gotten into trouble one too many times for the law to continue turning a blind eye.

As a prosecuting attorney, Adam would have had little trouble convicting any of them. Sure, there had been extenuating circumstances in all three cases, but that was neither here nor there. In Adam's view, there was right and wrong, good and evil, black and white. Trying to see shades of gray only resulted in confusing the issues of guilt or innocence.

He himself, an innocent man, had spent six years in prison, and was still struggling to pull his life back together. Yet these three self-proclaimed wrongdoers not only remained free, but were being given a generously funded opportunity to start over.

Where was the justice in that?

Adam heard the murmur of voices from inside and pushed away his sour thoughts. Had Miss Nash finally decided to join them? His three companions were strung so tight he could feel the tension crackle in the oppressively still air.

A deerfly buzzed by and landed on his cheek. Swatting it away, he stared at the door, barely controlling the urge to march up and demand Miss Nash show herself.

When the door finally *did* open, his three companions snapped to attention. The dog also stiffened, eyeing them as a predator would its prey. But it was only Mrs. Peavy.

Confound the woman, was she deliberately keeping them waiting? The judge hadn't painted her as either mean-spirited or a coward. But perhaps he didn't know his granddaughter as well as he thought.

Mrs. Peavy held a tray containing a pitcher and glasses. She quieted the dog with a word, then turned to the men. "It's a long ride from Turnabout," she said as she set her burden on a nearby bench. "I imagine you'd all be glad of a nice, tall glass of apple cider while you wait."

Mitchell, ever the gentleman, was the first to step up. "Thank you, ma'am. That does sound inviting."

The housekeeper responded with a smile. "Help yourself." When she turned to Adam, though, she was all business. "Miss Reggie will be out in a moment."

Adam nodded, refraining from comment.

It irked him that he couldn't remember much about Regina Nash. He was usually good with names and faces. True, he hadn't seen her often, but that was no excuse.

He remembered her stepsister in exquisite detail. And it wasn't just that he'd known Patricia longer—it would be hard for anyone to forget such a delicate, feminine creature. Not only was she a beauty, she had the willowy grace of a ballerina and the gentle sweetness of a lamb. Being on the receiving end of one of her smiles had made a person feel special.

But Miss Nash's image was elusive, a wispy shadow he couldn't bring into focus. She was younger than Patricia, and different in appearance and personality.

He remembered a dark-haired girl with a coltish awkwardness about her, a girl who preferred to keep to the fringes of gatherings rather than mingle. She'd seemed a wren in the presence of the elegant swans that were her stepmother and stepsister. That was all he remembered—impressions more than real memories.

His thoughts drifted to the less than musically talented miss they'd encountered earlier. Something about her hinted at earthiness and fire and a quixotic vulnerability. Perhaps, if the opportunity materialized, he'd ask Miss Nash about her.

Adam stroked the brim of his hat between his thumb and forefinger as his thoughts circled back to his reason for being here. "I don't see the judge's great-grandson about," he said, catching the housekeeper's gaze.

Mrs. Peavy stiffened, and the dog's lip drew back as he gave a low, throaty growl. The beast seemed to be waiting for word to attack.

"Just why would you be interested in Jack's whereabouts?"

Adam mentally counted to ten, maintaining his smile by force of will. Why did the woman treat every question he asked with suspicion?

He was spared the need to answer as the door opened once more.

Their hostess had finally deigned to join them.

"Now Mrs. Peavy, there's no need to be impolite." The speaker, a tall, slim woman, stepped out onto the porch.

Adam took a minute to size her up. He'd always been proud of his ability to read an opponent—it was another of those skills that had served him equally well in the courtroom as in prison.

If she'd kept them waiting so she could primp it didn't show. While he could find nothing wrong with her appearance, he saw nothing particularly special about it, either. Her dress was a nondescript blue frock and her coffee-brown hair was secured into a serviceable knot at the nape of her neck.

Yet something about her commanded attention. Perhaps it was the way she looked you straight in the eye, as if trying to take your measure. Or perhaps it was the way she carried herself, as if the world would have to meet her on her own terms. Or maybe it was the healthy glow she projected, like a freshly picked and polished apple.

Miss Nash might not be the beauty her stepsister had been, but he definitely couldn't picture this confident woman meekly fading away in anyone's shadow. As for the coltish awkwardness he remembered, the years had replaced that with an air of self-assurance and composure.

This woman was one he would definitely remember.

"Hello, gentlemen." She included them all in her polite smile. "Sorry to keep you waiting. I hope you took the opportunity to enjoy a glass of cider."

She extended a hand toward Adam. He noticed she kept the other hidden in the folds of her skirt. "Mr. Barr, how nice to see you again."

Adam took her hand and nodded acknowledgment, wondering what she concealed in her other palm. "Miss Nash."

Something about her appearance and voice *did* seem familiar, but not like something from his distant past. It gave him a nagging, I'm-missing-something feeling.

She laughed. “You don’t recognize me, do you? Not surprising—I looked very different last time we met.”

He straightened abruptly. Those eyes! That vivid, translucent blue-green of a dragon’s scales.

This woman, with her air of country gentility, was the backwoods hoyden with the banshee voice they’d encountered earlier. *Now* he knew what had delayed her. But how had she managed to get here ahead of them?

And what had she been doing out in the woods earlier, alone and attired in castoff men’s clothing?

Her gaze registered surprise at his reaction, then she nodded slightly, acknowledging the connection he’d made. Was she embarrassed at having been found out? If so, she didn’t show it. She merely eyed him expectantly, waiting for his next move.

Should he call her hand? She’d toyed with them, pretending to be something she wasn’t, pretending not to know him. Had she been watching for them? Perhaps hoping to turn them back?

As for him unmasking her, if the others weren’t observant enough to see through her disguise, it wasn’t his job to point it out to them.

“To the contrary,” he said, replying to her earlier remark, “I remember our last meeting quite well.” He released her hand. “Before I forget, I promised to relay greetings to you.”

“Oh?” Her voice held a wary note.

“Yes.” He gave her a mock-innocent smile. “We encountered a grubby, barely civilized girl down the road who claimed to know you.”

A flash of indignation crossed her face. Then her lips twitched. “An unflattering but accurate description of my friend.” Then she waved toward the others. “Please, introduce me to your friends.”

"Of course."

As he made the introductions, he tried reading her mood. But she didn't appear at all discomposed that they'd called her bluff and followed her out here.

Once the amenities had been satisfied, Miss Nash turned back to him, raising a brow in question. "I hope my grandfather was in good health when you saw him last." Her tone was polite, but contained a hint of something else as well.

"He was his usual irascible self when we left Philadelphia."

She nodded, and Adam was puzzled by the flash of relief in her expression. It seemed her question had been more than a casual inquiry.

"Then if you gentlemen will excuse my directness, may I ask what brings you to this remote location?"

Adam stilled, studying her expression carefully. Was this another delaying tactic?

But all he saw was puzzlement and suspicion. Did she truly not know what was going on?

"Are you telling me you never received your grandfather's letter?"

"I'm afraid not."

Either she was a very good actress or she had no idea what she was about to face. It appeared he owed the lady an apology for the unflattering thoughts he'd entertained about her these past few hours.

Then the full import of the situation hit him, and Adam swallowed several choice oaths. He'd have to explain the judge's Machiavellian scheme to her. That wasn't supposed to be part of his duties.

But this wasn't her fault, either. "Then please forgive our intrusion. It's unfortunate you didn't receive proper warning of either our arrival or our purpose."

Not sure what else to do, he reached into his pocket and retrieved the missive Judge Madison had entrusted to him. "Your grandfather asked me to give you this before we began serious discussions, so perhaps it would be best for us to start there. Then I can explain things to you in more detail."

She took the paper from him, a crease marring her forehead.

Adam rubbed the back of his neck. This didn't feel right. How much had the judge put in the second letter? Would it make any sense to her if she hadn't read the first? Maybe he should explain—

Everett cleared his throat. "While Miss Nash is reading the letter and Mr. Barr is making his explanations, perhaps the rest of us could take a look around. A walk would be welcome after that long ride."

Adam wondered cynically if Everett's offer came from a gentlemanly urge to give her some privacy to absorb the news, or a cowardly urge to distance himself from her reaction to it.

Whatever the man's motives, he was immediately joined by the other two.

"Good idea," Chance agreed hastily.

"My legs could do with a bit of stretching, too," Mitchell added.

Their eagerness to exit the area was so obvious, Adam wasn't surprised to see Miss Nash's brow raise.

Uh-oh. Her visitors suddenly seemed like critters fleeing a brushfire. Reggie figured that meant only one thing.

They knew she wouldn't like whatever she was about to learn from her grandfather's letter.

"Of course," she answered smoothly. She actually welcomed the chance to read the letter in private since she wasn't known for having a poker face. "Mrs. Peavy, why don't you escort them on a little tour of the area. I believe the *south end* of the lake would offer the best view."

Not to mention keep them away from Jack. "Oh, and I think Buck would enjoy the walk as well."

Reggie did her best to ignore the knowing look on Adam's face. If only he wasn't so perceptive. How could he have seen through her disguise so quickly? She was certain none of the others had. It would be better all the way around if he went along on that little walk.

But as Mrs. Peavy and the other three men headed away from the porch, Reggie stared at his I'm-not-budging demeanor and knew it would be wasted breath to even suggest he leave.

She sat on the porch swing, feeling his gaze on her. She couldn't help but remember that little jolt of connection she'd felt when she realized he recognized her.

Forcing that thought aside, she opened the letter. Scanning quickly over the greeting, she searched for the promised explanation. Her gaze paused at the third paragraph.

Your desire to adopt Jack came as no surprise. However, though you have been like a mother to him since his infancy, we both know the bonds that unite you are those of affection, not blood. I am, in truth, the only blood relation Jack has left.

Reggie flinched. Regardless of what others thought, she was closer to Jack than *anyone* else—he was truly the child of her heart. She'd thought her grandfather understood.

I do not want Jack to grow up without a man in his life. It is important for a boy to have someone to teach him the proper lessons on his road to manhood, something you could not do on your own. My first impulse was to ask you to send him to me.

Reggie's heart thumped erratically. Surely Grandfather wouldn't take Jack from her.

I admit, however, that this solution has drawbacks. I'm no longer young. It is quite probable I won't be around long enough to guide Jack into manhood.

Reggie breathed easier. She wasn't overly concerned about the judge's health—he'd used that bluff to get his way more than once. Even though he must be in his seventies, the old codger would probably outlive them all.

My next thought was to send him to boarding school. There are some fine institutions that would provide wonderful experiences for a boy such as Jack.

How could Grandfather consider such a thing? Those places were impersonal, sterile. Jack was too young—he still needed her. And she still needed him.

Of course, there is another option—to find you a husband.

Reggie sat up straighter, a different kind of dismay flooding through her as an inkling of the men's mission sank in.

Surely she was mistaken. Even the judge wouldn't—

Reggie glanced at Adam, then wished she hadn't. That sympathetic glint in his expression was unnerving.

She swallowed hard and stared back down at the letter, hoping she'd misunderstood.

> *Naturally I am not suggesting you marry just* any *man. It must be someone worthy of you and Jack. Since you seem to have no interest in any of the eligible men there in Turnabout, I've taken it upon myself to find someone for you.*

Grandfather was trying to play matchmaker.

Chapter Three

Reggie's thoughts raced, skittering in several directions at once.

How *could* he? This was a farce, a disaster. It was too manipulative for even a schemer like her grandfather.

Didn't he know that if she'd *wanted* a husband, she could have landed one a long time ago? Didn't he trust her to raise Jack right and properly on her own?

Why would Adam agree to such a harebrained scheme? Did he think she was the best he could hope for since his conviction? Or was it more that he thought he owed the judge a debt of some sort?

Merciful goodness, did he or Grandfather know she'd once been infatuated with him?

Her cheeks flamed at the thought. Oh, why hadn't Adam gone away with the others?

Pull yourself together. You will not *fall apart in front of him.*

Reggie forced herself to relax her grip on the letter, commanded her racing pulse to slow.

She continued reading, trying to grasp what this meant. But her mind kept circling to the men her grandfather had sent. Adam's reasons for wanting to start over in a place where he wasn't known were obvious, but what could induce the others to take part? Did they also have something they were running from?

Another paragraph snagged her attention. Grandfather was *bribing* them to court her. They would each get a nice little prize for their part in this farce.

How could Grandfather humiliate her this way?

She barely had time to absorb that when she got her next little jolt. Adam was *not* one of her suitors after all. Instead, he'd come as her grandfather's agent.

But *why* wasn't he a candidate for her hand? Not that she wanted the ex-lawyer for a suitor. But still—did he think she wasn't good enough for him? Or was Grandfather not as certain of the man's character as he pretended?

Flicking the paper with a snap, Reggie read on. Grandfather had tasked Adam with escorting her "beaus" to Turnabout, making sure everyone understood the rules of the game, and then seeing that the rules were followed.

It was also his job to take Jack back to Philadelphia if she balked at the judge's terms. Her grandfather would then pick out a suitable boarding school for the boy, robbing her of even the opportunity to share a home with him in Philadelphia.

Reggie cast a quick glance Adam's way, and swallowed hard. She had no doubt he would carry out his orders right down to the letter.

No! That would *not* happen. Even if it meant she had to face the humiliation of a forced wedding, she wouldn't let Jack be taken from her.

And hang Grandfather, he knew it.

One last surprise was buried in the closing. It seemed the forewarning she was supposed to get had been Adam's idea and the judge had only pretended to go along. There never *had* been another letter. Grandfather freely admitted this, saying he knew better than to give her time to begin plotting a way to avoid her fate.

It took every ounce of control she had not to crumple the letter and fling it as far as she could. Of all the emotions boiling through her right now, the strongest was a deep frustration that Grandfather wasn't standing here so she could give him a piece of her mind.

Gathering her outrage about her like battle armor, Reggie stood. Her gaze locked with that of the man who suddenly wielded so much power over her life.

She would *not* let him know how deeply betrayed, how humiliated she felt. "I assume you know about this scheme of my grandfather's?" The flicker of relief in his expression wasn't lost on her.

Happy not to have to explain things, was he?

He crossed his arms and leaned back. "Yes."

She stalked closer, displeased with his one-word answer. "Then you know how completely irrational he's being."

"The judge has never struck me as an irrational man." He shrugged those broad shoulders of his. "Autocratic and overbearing perhaps, but not irrational."

Reggie was no longer in the mood for word games. She shook the letter in his face. "You don't think playing matchmaker in this heavy-handed fashion irrational?"

He didn't even blink. "I'm sure he has his reasons."

"Reasons!" Realizing she'd shouted, Reggie took a deep breath and tried again. "He's asking me to choose between hog-tying myself to one of these strangers or losing Jack."

He remained unmoved. "Arranged marriages happen all the time. At least you get three to choose from."

Reggie wanted to scream, to pound her fists against his chest, to claw his eyes out. Was the man made of stone? She hadn't expected an overabundance of sympathy, but his calm attitude was infuriating. "Would it surprise you to learn that Grandfather lied to you about sending me word ahead of time?"

His brow drew down, but there was no other visible reaction. "And how would you know this?"

She shoved the letter toward him, pointing to the pertinent paragraph. "Because he told me."

Adam glanced at the letter and she saw a flicker of something cross his face. But when he looked up, his expression held that same unshakable determination. "As I said, I'm sure he has his reasons."

Reggie was determined to cut through his indifference. "So what do *you* get out of this blackmail scheme?"

His eyes narrowed. "What do you mean?"

She moved closer. "According to the letter, your companions are getting nice incentives to participate." She fisted her hands on her hips. "What form does your thirty pieces of silver take?"

His ice-blue eyes stared at her with irritating dispassion. "Not that it's any of your business, but I'm doing this mainly because the judge asked me to, and I owe him." He tipped his hat back and crossed his ankles. "It's as simple as that."

"You *owe* him?" Reggie lowered her arms and

glared. How she itched to wipe that calm expression from his too-handsome face.

The fact that he could still stir something in her besides anger only made this whole mess more maddening.

Reggie sniffed. "Because he stood by you during the trial, you mean?"

If she'd wanted to get an emotional reaction from him, she'd finally succeeded. He stiffened, his jaw clenched, and he looked as if he'd like to throttle her.

Adam felt that sense of injustice, of being branded unclean, of honor lost, wash over him again. He'd expected to be the target of her emotions once she read the letter, could even admire her for reacting with outrage rather than helpless tears.

But her disdain gnawed at him.

Foolishly, he'd assumed Miss Nash shared her grandfather's opinion on his conviction. The exchanges they'd had up until now had only reinforced that assumption. They'd been heated and challenging, but had seemed tempered by a degree of mutual respect.

Apparently he'd read her wrong.

So be it. He'd quit trying to change people's minds about his innocence with mere words long ago. It was proof he needed, and proof he was determined to get. Just as soon as he finished this business and could get back to Philadelphia.

"The relationship I have with the judge," he said evenly, "and what it's based on, is also none of your business. As I'm sure it states in that letter you're waving around, he trusts me enough to send me here to preside over this arrangement."

"But not enough to be completely honest with you."

He tightened his jaw, but let that barb pass. "What *does* concern you are the terms the judge outlined, and my duty to see them carried out as he intended."

She narrowed her eyes. "So, just like that, I'm supposed to line up three strangers, look them over, and pick one to be my husband."

If only she'd get it over with that quickly.

But an adversarial attitude wouldn't help him. Time to use the two main tools he'd learned as a lawyer—reason and persuasion. "I understand this is not the best situation to find yourself in. But you must know your grandfather would never send you a man he didn't have complete confidence in."

She raised a skeptical brow and he hurried on. "That being so, it's a given that any one of them should to make you a good husband. And they won't be strangers forever. After all, you have two weeks to get to know them."

The thought of having to cool his heels here even that long was frustrating. He'd already had to wait for what seemed an eternity.

"Two weeks," she repeated, her voice ending on a squeak.

He grimaced as the color drained from her face. So, Judge Madison hadn't put everything in his letter after all. Hang the old conniver for his sly games.

"According to the terms your grandfather has laid down," he explained, "you have two weeks to select your groom, and then another week to plan your wedding."

"All the time in the world," she said bitterly.

She looked so brittle—vulnerable almost. He felt

an unwanted stirring of sympathy, but pushed it ruthlessly aside.

"There's no point fighting this," he said, hoping she would see reason. "They're all good men, but different enough to give you a real choice. I'm certain you'll decide which you find most compatible in that period of time."

"Are you now?" The vulnerable air evaporated, replaced by the scorching look and frigid tone she'd brandished before.

So much for his stirring of sympathy. Obviously, she could hold her own in any war of words.

"As for this contract—" her chin titled up at a militant angle "—I'm sure I'll need time to study it, perhaps have a lawyer look it over, before I sign."

He was here to help her through this. "I'd be glad to explain any—"

"I'd as soon ask a heathen to explain a scripture."

Adam tightened his jaw. Taking a slow, deep breath, he decided to let that one pass as well. She'd been backed into a corner and it was only natural that she'd lash out.

"Have it your way. But don't think by putting off signing you can delay the deadline. According to the judge's instructions, your two weeks start when you meet your suitors."

Suspicion flashed in her eyes. "Tell me, Mr. Barr, why *did* you drag those men out here rather than leave them in Turnabout and deliver the news alone? Or better yet, wait for me to return, since someone in town likely mentioned I'd be back inside of a week?"

She pointed a finger at him and he could almost see it tremble with the urge to poke him. "It was because you wanted to start the clock ticking on this ridiculous scheme as soon as possible, wasn't it?"

The woman was too perceptive for her own good.

She must have sensed her words had hit their mark, because she tore into him again, this time her finger actually jabbing his chest to underline her words. "Of all the insensitive, ungentlemanly actions. You just couldn't *wait* to deliver this little ultimatum."

She gave his chest another jab. "You had to come racing out here to spoil our outing just so you could hurry things along."

The woman presumed too much. Adam captured the offending finger. "Miss Nash, I haven't claimed to be a gentleman in quite some time."

Her eyes widened and a flush blossomed on her cheeks. Her reaction told him her aggressive contact had been unintentional. After another moment to make his point, he released her.

She snatched her hand back as if stung.

"What's done is done," he continued. "As you so eloquently stated, the clock *has* started ticking, and there's no setting the hands back."

It didn't take her long to recover. Her shoulders drew back before he'd stopped talking.

"Doesn't it matter that I don't *want* a husband?" She flung the words like rocks. "That I think turning control of my life and possessions over to someone else simply because he's a man is akin to slavery?"

She threw up her arms. "Why does every male think the sum total of a woman's ambition should be to find someone to marry so she can go straight from her father's care to her husband's?"

He'd never met a female like her before. No wonder

the judge felt compelled to take such a drastic step. "I personally don't care a jot whether you marry one of these men or not. In fact, my *only* concern in this affair is to see that Judge Madison's wishes are carried out."

He leaned back again. "Now, part of his instructions was that I make certain your interests are protected—within the scope of his plans, of course. But that doesn't mean I can let you ignore the rules. On that score I'll be scrupulously, might I say *ruthlessly*, single-minded."

By the stiffening of her spine, he knew she'd gotten the message.

"In other words, I'd advise you not to use any of your feminine wiles on me. It'll do you no good to try to play on my sympathy. I have none. It'll do you no good to try to bribe me. There's nothing you could offer to make me betray the judge. And as for trying to seduce me—" he shrugged "—let's just say it'd be wasted effort."

From the way her hands curled, he'd guess he was lucky she didn't have a club handy.

My, but the lady did have a temper.

"Mr. Barr." She enunciated each word clearly. "I have no intention of using *wiles*, feminine or otherwise. I intend to be forthright in my dealings with you and the other gents, and I expect the same in return."

She impatiently tucked a lock of hair behind her ear and his focus shifted to the soft wisps framing her face. How long had it been since he'd stroked a woman's hair?

He straightened abruptly and swallowed an oath. There was no room in his life right now for thoughts like that, especially when it came to the judge's granddaughter.

Pushing away from the rail, he stepped down, wanting to put distance between them. "I'll get the contract."

He wondered, not for the first time, why Judge Madison hadn't considered *him* as a suitor for his granddaughter. Not that Adam wanted to tie himself down with a wife right now—but it stung that he hadn't been on the list of candidates. What did her grandfather see in the others that was missing in him? Had the time he spent in jail tarnished him in the judge's eyes as well?

He had to clear his name soon. Only then would he have any chance of living a normal life.

"Grandfather actually expects me to sign a contract agreeing to his addle-pated plan?" The words bristled with outrage, a hint of the banshee they'd encountered earlier coming through.

"All parties to the contract are required to sign." Adam jerked the packet from his satchel. "The other three signed it, I signed it, even your grandfather signed it. Now it's your turn."

She accepted the papers as if he'd handed her smelly rags. "I've never heard of the livestock being haggled over signing the bill of sale along with the buyer and seller."

Her tongue was as sharp as any knife he'd wielded. She'd make a good lawyer. Adam was beginning to believe the judge had decided not to come for reasons other than the ones he'd stated. "If you refuse, then Jack and I board the next train to Philadelphia."

She snapped the papers with a *humph* and started reading.

If she was looking for loopholes, she'd be disappointed. The judge had drawn up the document and then had Adam review every syllable. Adam would bet the horse he rode in on that it was ironclad.

Adam wondered which of the men would end up escorting the reluctant bride to the altar.

Everett seemed the best equipped to deal with her lethal tongue. The educated cynic would give as good as he got in that department. Then again, he might consider himself too sophisticated for a lady who appeared equally comfortable in overalls as a dress.

Mitchell, on the other hand, wouldn't mind her provincial ways. He didn't let much rattle him. Always searching for the middle ground, Mitchell had defused several tense moments during their trip. But did he have the determination required to deal with the overbearing Miss Nash? His size not withstanding, the woman would likely ride roughshod right over him.

If a peaceful life was what Mitchell wanted, he wouldn't get it hitched to this virago.

That left Chance. The boy was younger than the potential bride, and rebellious enough to stand up to a riled bear, so Adam didn't think she would intimidate him. Adam suspected, though, in a battle of wills, Miss Nash would come out the winner.

Besides, would it be fair to shackle the kid to a wife before he'd had a taste of the independence he so obviously craved?

Judge Madison had been adamant, though, that one of the men he was sending here was the perfect match for his granddaughter. He also insisted she would realize it herself, as soon as she bowed to the inevitable and got to know them.

Adam watched the emotions flash across her volatile features as she poured over the contract.

He wouldn't want to be in the position the three

others found themselves in, and he certainly wouldn't want to be the one to have to do the picking.

Reggie stared at the contract, the words blurring into a meaningless jumble. There had to be a way out of this. Marriage wasn't an option for her. It hadn't been for a long time.

If only her grandfather had come himself so she could talk to him, could read his expression, hear the shades of meaning in his voice as they discussed this.

He'd never understood her easy acceptance of maiden aunt status, but she never dreamed he'd take things this far, even if he did believe it was "for her own good."

Clearing her head from the useless what-ifs, Reggie forced herself to read the contract. It appeared to say the same thing as the letter, but in more formal terms. One thing she did learn, however, was exactly what each of her suitors stood to gain from the arrangement.

Everett Fulton would be set up with his own newspaper press, a first for Turnabout.

Mitchell Parker would be given a house in town and a job as teacher, thanks to the new wing the judge was having built onto the schoolhouse. Ahh, so that was the motive behind Grandfather's unexpected altruism.

And, oddly enough, Chance Dawson was being given the burned out Blue Bottle Saloon and money to renovate it.

Plump carrots indeed. No wonder the men had agreed to take part in this backward marriage lottery. Not only were they being given fresh starts, but they would come into the community as men of consequence.

She glanced up to see Adam leading his horse to the

shade of a nearby tree. At least he'd quit watching her with that unnerving stare.

He stretched and corded muscles strained against the confines of his shirt, muscles he'd no doubt acquired while in prison. A powerful reminder that this was not the same man she'd known all those years ago. This man was both powerful and dangerous.

Abruptly, Reggie turned her focus back to the contract. She had no reason to fear Adam—Grandfather would never have sent him here if he hadn't trusted him completely.

Quickly finding her place, Reggie skimmed over the next few paragraphs. What it all boiled down to was that, in exchange for her grandfather's generosity, the trio agreed to "court" her, to truthfully answer any questions about their past and their aspirations, and ultimately, each of them agreed to abide by her final selection without hesitation.

Reggie paused and reread that part. Now here was something she could use. She was no prize catch to start with. The fact that her grandfather had offered such extravagant bribes showed he thought so, too.

Best not to dwell on the sting of that right now.

Instead, she explored how she might take advantage of the small chink in the contract's armor. If she could hone in on which of her would-be suitors was least enthusiastic about marrying her, and play up whatever would most intensify his reluctance, she might manage to get out of this yet. She just had to make sure, when she made her choice, the man in question would decide he was better off without the judge's bribe than hitched to her.

Tricky, but she *could* pull it off. She had to.

Surely the judge wouldn't follow through with his threat

if she'd done her part? If nothing else, it would serve as a delaying tactic while she planned a countermove.

There was an interesting catch to the agreement—exactly the sort of stipulation her deviously-minded grandfather loved to impose. If the man she picked balked at the idea of marrying her, the deal was off for all of them. The trio were in this together.

If her plan worked, she would squash the dreams of not one but three men.

Reggie refused to feel even a smidgeon of guilt. If they truly wanted to start a new life in Turnabout, they didn't need her grandfather's backing to make it. They'd just have to do it with the sweat of their own brows rather than with handouts.

From what she'd seen, a stretch of hard work and diet of humble pie wouldn't hurt any of them.

If they chose to turn tail and head back to Philadelphia rather than dig in and try to make a go of it on their own, well then, they deserved just what they got.

Reggie read the section that addressed Adam's duties with returning indignation. She glanced up and caught him watching her, an admit-you're-beaten expression on his face.

The earlier attraction she'd felt was extinguished as if it never existed. What had Grandfather been thinking to entrust this heart-of-stone man with so much power over her and Jack's future? If the arrogant Mr. Barr thought he held all the cards, let him. She had no intention of showing her own hand just yet.

Feeling better now that she had a plan, Reggie lowered the contract and faced Grandfather's henchman.

"Do I need to explain any of the legal terms to you?" he asked.

She shook her head. She'd changed her mind about hiring a lawyer. Given her options, she'd have no choice but to sign anyway. And there was no point risking having this humiliating situation made public. "I believe I understand the terms. Given my choices, I will, of course, sign the document."

Seeing his satisfied smile, she couldn't stop herself from adding, "But I must say, it proved interesting reading."

His eyes narrowed suspiciously. Let him wonder what she had up her sleeve. It would work to her advantage if she could keep him off balance.

He nodded. "There are copies for each of us. Everyone has signed them but you."

She would sign the contracts, all right. But Adam was sadly mistaken if he thought she would give in without a fight. Her take-no-prisoners campaign was just beginning.

Adam didn't like the battle-ready expression Regina wore as she signed the papers. She'd seen something in the contract to raise her spirits, and that didn't bode well for the judge's plans. But what had she seen?

He'd have to take a closer look when he had a moment.

She handed the packet to him, holding one copy back for herself. Her fingers brushed against his—not drawing-room-smooth skin but feminine nonetheless.

"I imagine your friends have had enough time to stretch their legs." She slid her copy into her dress pocket. "Shall I call them back?"

"Call them?" Surely they'd traveled too far for a simple hail?

With a schoolgirl grin, she placed two fingers between her lips and let out a piercing whistle, immediately followed by a second blast.

He winced at the shrill sound. "Are you in the habit of calling your people as if they were dogs?"

In the blink of an eye the schoolgirl transformed into an indignant woman. The heat in her cheeks complimented her dragon's eyes.

"I do *not* treat people like animals." She waved a hand. "We tend to scatter when we're out here. The whistles are signals we've worked out to get each other's attention."

She took a deep breath and her expression lost its high emotion. "Mrs. Peavy knows two whistles means she's wanted back at the cabin, and Mr. Peavy and Jack know they can ignore the call."

As if to support her words, two answering blasts came from the distance.

"There," she said, "that's Mrs. Peavy signaling she heard me." Dusting her skirt, she flounced down the steps. And promptly tripped on her hem.

Adam reacted on instinct, catching her before she could land at his feet. With his arms around her, their gazes locked. Her eyes widened and she gave a breathy little gasp that shot through him. Suddenly the world shrank around them as if they were figures in a water globe, the very air swirling around them.

He'd almost forgotten what it was like to hold a woman—to feel her softness, to breathe in her subtle fragrance, to watch the rosy flush of emotion bathe her cheeks.

An unexpected urge to tighten his embrace, to protect her, to kiss her, took hold of him. Not that he would do so—that would be madness.

But what would she do if he tried?

Chapter Four

Sharp barking shattered the glass of their water globe, bringing Adam back to earth with a crash.

Regina started and the color in her cheeks deepened.

He turned away, as much to regain his own composure as to allow her to regain hers.

What was wrong with him? She was the judge's granddaughter and he was supposed to be looking out for her interests, not taking advantage of her. Even if he'd been interested in pursuing her—which he wasn't—his whole reason for being here was to make sure she married one of the other men.

"Are you going to signal for Jack and Mr. Peavy also?" The question came out more sharply than he'd intended and he moderated his tone. "I'm sure the men would like to get to know the boy as well. After all, the one who wins your favor won't just be gaining you as a wife, but also a son."

"Not yet." The steel was back in her voice. "I need to reach an understanding with you all on a few things before I bring Jack into this."

Adam didn't care for her tone. Did she think she was running this show?

Then he gave a mental shrug. She was probably as disconcerted by what had just happened as he was. Besides, he was merely an observer and enforcer. The three suitors would be the ones required to deal with her bossy ways.

And regardless of her posturing, she couldn't get around the judge's terms. She could toy with them all she wanted, he wouldn't stop her. But in the end she'd have to submit to her grandfather's dictates.

It would be interesting, though, to see what she meant when she said they needed to "reach an understanding."

A few moments later, the hikers came into sight. Adam hid a grin as he got a good look at them. While Mrs. Peavy seemed totally composed, the trio trailing behind her did not.

Chance's step lacked its usual bounce. Not surprising, given that his left leg, from the tip of his boot, to about six inches up his trouser leg, was damp and muddy.

Everett was red-faced and breathing heavily, as if unused to whatever exertions he'd just been through.

Mitchell had his sleeves rolled up and was vigorously scratching his left arm. Even from here Adam could see the angry red welts forming. Insect bites? Stinging nettles?

In any case, if it had been the housekeeper's intent to take the visitors down a notch, she'd certainly succeeded.

Behind him he heard a softly uttered, "Oh, dear." When he glanced back, he saw as much sympathy as amusement in Regina's expression.

She stepped forward. "I hope you gentlemen enjoyed your walk."

"Oh, we had a grand time," Mrs. Peavy answered for them. "Did run into a bit of unpleasantness, though." As she reached the porch, the housekeeper turned back to her entourage. "You gents have another glass of cider while I get something for Mr. Parker's rash. Mr. Dawson, if you'll slip off your boot, I'll get it cleaned up."

As Mrs. Peavy disappeared inside, the three men trudged onto the porch.

The judge's granddaughter waved her hand in a lady-of-the-manor gesture. "Please be seated. There's no need to stand on ceremony out here."

Without further prompting, the men plopped down onto various benches and chairs. The wind had definitely been taken out of their sails.

But when Regina joined them on the porch, Adam was amused to note they all came to wary attention.

"Well, gentlemen," she began, "now that I've read my grandfather's letter and accompanying contract, it's time we talked."

Mrs. Peavy opened the door just then and hesitated. "Should I step back inside until you're finished?"

To Adam's surprise, Regina shook her head.

Not that it really mattered. With no panes on the window, the housekeeper would still be able to hear every word.

"I think it best you know what's going on," the soon-to-be bride said. "It seems these three were sent by my grandfather to start a new life in Turnabout. He's generously providing each of them the means to join our little community as men of influence. All they have to do in return is participate in a marriage lottery, with *me* as the prize."

Her tone was pleasant enough, but Adam watched each man shift uneasily under her stare. At the moment it was hard to believe she wasn't Judge Madison's blood kinswoman.

"For my part," the self-proclaimed lottery prize continued, "all I have to do is select a groom and marry him within three weeks. Otherwise, Mr. Barr will take Jack to Philadelphia so Grandfather can ship him off to a boarding school."

Mrs. Peavy's reaction was an indrawn breath and a glare directed toward Adam.

"Did I sum the situation up correctly, gentlemen?" Regina crossed her arms across her chest and stared them down.

"I believe you covered the relevant facts," Everett answered. The dandy had apparently recovered his aplomb.

"Thank you, Mr. Fulton. From a reporter, I'll accept that as a compliment."

Mrs. Peavy approached Mitchell and motioned for him to hold out his arm. She slathered her ointment on the rash with perhaps more vigor than was necessary, but the man bore it without flinching.

The judge's granddaughter ignored this bit of byplay. "First off, to put things baldly, you should know I'm not happy with this situation. I'm not interested in getting married to anyone, much less a stranger who's been bribed to offer for me."

Her tone remained pleasant. Her expressive eyes, however, carried a different message.

"Grandfather couched his letter in polite terms, assuring me any one of you would happily step into the role of my husband. However, I have the distinct impression that the only vying you'll do over the next few days is to see how best to avoid drawing the short straw."

She met each of their gazes in turn. "Would any of you care to dispute that?"

When no one spoke up, she nodded and her tone hardened. "Well, it seems our wishes in this matter don't amount to a hill of beans. My grandfather wants me hitched, and since he knows I'd do anything to keep Jack with me, it looks like wedding bells are in my future. But I want to make it plain from the get-go that I intend to call the shots in how we run this farce."

Adam watched the men's reactions.

Chance glared with sullen belligerence.

Mitchell, his forearm still an angry red, twisted his hat uneasily.

Everett, surprisingly, met her gaze with a condescending smile. "My dear Miss Nash," he said with exaggerated deference, "there's no need for such dramatic posturing. We are all agreed that the selection lies squarely with you, and we are firmly committed to abide by your decision. In fact, you can make the selection right here and now if you like."

Everett shrugged. "Or you can keep us all guessing by drawing it out the full two weeks." He half rose and executed a mocking bow. "We are entirely at your disposal."

"Yes, you are." Her expression conveyed quite clearly that she had something specific and very likely unpalatable in mind.

Adam tried not to grin. The lady had obviously learned a thing or two from the judge. If she had her way, these three would pay a steep price for their part in this scheme.

"Now that we've agreed who's in charge," she continued, "let's get down to business. First and most importantly, under no circumstances is Jack or anyone else outside of this group to learn about our arrangement. As far as everyone in Turnabout is concerned, you are here as friends of my grandfather."

She nodded as if making up the story as she went along. "I will, quite naturally, wish to see you comfortably settled, and you'll return my neighborly attention with courtesy calls. My subsequent engagement to one of you will appear as a delightfully unexpected result of those calls."

She tucked a stray hair behind her ear. Did her finger tremble slightly or was that his imagination?

"I read the contract," she continued, "and it clearly states that you are to court me, and I intend to see that you do it properly. I want it all, gentlemen—attention, pretty words, love tokens, flowers and gewgaws."

Her gaze sharpened. "And I expect a good faith effort from you. No just going through the motions, no begrudging attentions. You have to actually *vie* for my favors."

Her color heightened, but her tone never faltered. "It has to look and feel real to everyone who sees us. And I'll not have a reluctant martyr for a husband. If I get even a hint that any of you are holding back, I'll cry foul, and Mr. Barr here will have no choice but to tell my grandfather you failed to abide by the terms of the contract."

She swung around and met Adam's gaze. "Isn't that so?"

Adam had labored over that contract to get exactly the nuances Judge Madison wanted, and he had it all but memorized by the time they were both satisfied. He mulled it over in his mind now, and slowly nodded his head. "One could interpret the terms that way."

Was that her plan? Well, she'd have to come up with some pretty convincing proof to get him to disqualify anyone, unless that suitor out-and-out refused her selection.

Besides, the judge had done a thorough job of interviewing candidates before settling on these three. They all knew what was expected. Adam would be more than a little surprised if anyone backed down at this point.

But he was an observer, not a confidante. If they couldn't figure out she was all bluster, that was their problem.

She clearly intended to extract her pound of flesh in terms of their pride. And she wanted pretty words and showy trinkets, even if they were insincerely offered.

A typical woman.

Well, he'd be watching her. With the power the judge had given him, he wouldn't hesitate to whisk Jack away to Philadelphia if she gave him reason to. But the judge had made it clear that wasn't the outcome he desired.

Regina nodded. "Okay gentlemen, then let's open the curtain on my grandfather's ridiculous play. I'll call Jack, and I expect you to honor your word. You're friends of my grandfather visiting from Philadelphia and are here paying your respects."

At some point, Mrs. Peavy had slipped into the cabin to put away her ointment. Now she stepped back outside and set Chance's freshly cleaned boot next to the door.

Regina gave her housekeeper a quick nod, then

turned back to the men. "It's too late for you to return to Turnabout today, so you'll be spending the night here. We'll head back together in the morning."

She lifted her chin. "We're not set up for visitors, though. Mrs. Peavy and Ira sleep in the alcove off the kitchen and Jack and I share the loft. That means you can either spend the night on the cabin floor or here on the porch.

Adam failed to detect any sympathy in her tone. It seemed she intended to make sure the hapless trio jumped through some unpleasant hoops over the next few weeks.

He had to hand it to her, she wasn't one to wring her hands and bemoan her fate when faced with unpleasantness. Instead, she showed amazing determination.

If he wasn't in such a hurry to get back to Philadelphia he could find himself amused by her performance.

Reggie paused, reluctant to take the next step. But she'd put it off long enough. "I suppose it's time for you to meet the rest of my household."

She stepped off the porch. Taking a deep breath, she blasted out a long, drawn-out whistle, followed by two shorter ones.

The answering whistles confirmed Ira and Jack were headed their way. Reggie forcibly relaxed her hands at her sides, but she didn't turn back to her visitors.

She had to fight the urge to tense again when Buck stood, his tail wagging in anticipation. For Jack's sake, she must pretend nothing was wrong, that these men were welcome guests. But if they did anything to upset Jack…

Grandfather, you're going to have a lot to answer for next time we meet.

Ira and Jack appeared a moment later, and the dog bounded forward to greet them. Jack danced around with Buck for a minute, trying to keep the string of fish he carried out of harm's way. Not an easy task for a slender six-year-old. "Look at all the fish we caught, Aunt Reggie," he said rushing forward, his brown eyes sparkling with excitement.

"My goodness!" Reggie smiled down at the light of her life. "It looks like we're going to have some mighty good eating tonight."

"I caught more'n half of them myself."

Ira, hunting rifle slung over his shoulder, hefted the two cane poles he carried in his other hand. "Our boy is turning into quite a fisherman, all right." His words were addressed to Reggie but his gaze was fixed on the men behind her.

Mrs. Peavy joined them and reached for the string of fish. "Here, let me have those. I'll get them cleaned and ready to cook." She bobbed the string, as if gauging the weight. "Yes, sir, add a few potatoes and that cobbler I baked this morning and we'll have more than enough to feed everybody."

Jack seemed to notice the visitors for the first time. "Hello."

Adam stepped forward. "You must be Jack."

"Yes sir." Jack seemed more curious than concerned.

Reggie stepped behind Jack, pulling him against her skirts with a hand on each shoulder. "Jack, these men have come all the way from Philadelphia for a visit." She managed to keep her voice friendly enough. "This one is Mr. Barr. The others are Mr. Fulton, Mr. Parker and Mr. Dawson."

Each man nodded acknowledgment as she called his name.

"Gentlemen, this is Jack." She nodded over her shoulder. "And the other fisherman is Mrs. Peavy's husband, Ira."

"Hydee, fellas," Ira welcomed. "You all are a ways from home, aren't you?"

Reggie smiled as she saw a few brows go up. If they had expected the wiry old handyman to act like one of her grandfather's servants, they now knew better. Ira and Mrs. Peavy were like part of her family.

"Do you know Grandfather Madison?" Jack asked before anyone could respond to Ira's question.

"We sure do." Again it was Adam who spoke up. "And he wanted us to make certain we told you he said hello and that he wishes he could have come."

Reggie barely swallowed her snort of disbelief. The old coot had never set foot in Turnabout before. And she sure as sunshine knew this particular trip was one he hadn't wanted to be along on.

"Is that why y'all came all the way out here?"

"Jack," Reggie warned. "It's not polite to pester our guests with questions."

"That's all right." Adam brushed Reggie's concern aside and met Jack's gaze again. "How's a fellow to find out anything if he doesn't ask. And yes, Jack, that's one of the reasons we came out here. I promised your great-grandfather to deliver that message just as soon as I arrived in Turnabout."

Jack glanced up over his shoulder. "Are they staying here with us, Aunt Reggie?"

"Just for tonight. We're all going back into town tomorrow."

That brought a frown to the boy's face. "But I thought we were gonna stay another two days," he protested.

She ruffled his sandy red hair. "I know. But you don't mind leaving a bit early, do you? This cabin wasn't built to hold more than a few folk. As it is, our guests are going to have to sleep on the floor tonight." Not that she gave a fig for the four men's comfort. She was more concerned with the wagging tongues back home.

"Besides, our visitors are eager to get settled in town, and we wouldn't want to send Grandfather Madison's friends off without our help, would we?"

"No, ma'am." He turned back to the men. "If you like, you can go frogging with me and Ira tonight."

Pride shimmered through Reggie. That was her boy—quick to get over his disappointment and generously willing to include the troublemakers in his fun.

"Frogging?" The question came from Mr. Fulton.

"Yes, sir," Jack said with a nod. Then, apparently realizing an explanation was in order, "You know, hunting bullfrogs. If we catch enough, Mrs. Peavy promised to fry up some frog legs for lunch tomorrow."

Reggie didn't bother to hide her grin at the sight of the dandy's horrified expression.

"Sounds like fun." The young Mr. Dawson was obviously not as squeamish. "I've never hunted frogs before."

"Don't worry. Me and Ira'll teach you," Jack promised.

Reggie gave Jack's shoulders a light squeeze then stepped back and dropped her hands. "You go along and help Ira put away the fishing gear. Then see if Mrs. Peavy needs any kindling brought in."

She turned to the others. "I'm afraid we live a pretty

simple life out here. Not much to offer you in the way of fancy amenities, and everyone pitches in to help with the chores. There's a place around back where you can feed and tend to your horses. Then you can get washed up down by the lake if you've a mind to."

"I'll take care of the horses and the buggy," Mr. Parker volunteered.

Adam straightened. "Thanks, but I'll take care of Trib myself."

"Come along then," Ira instructed. "Jack and I'll show you where we keep the feed."

Reggie watched them disappear around the corner, then turned to her two remaining guests. "You'll find some buckets on the other side of the porch. I'd appreciate it if you'd each grab one and go down to the lake to fetch some fresh water. We'll be needing it to clean the dishes and the like later."

"Yes, ma'am." Chance immediately stood and reached for his still-damp boot.

Mr. Fulton didn't respond right away, but at her unblinking stare, he finally gave a short, mocking bow and turned to grab the bucket.

As the two headed down the trail, Reggie found herself alone for the first time since the men had swooped into her life like hounds on the scent of game.

Feeling suddenly tired beyond reckoning, she sagged down on the porch step and put her chin on her knees.

It wasn't fair! The pieces of her life had just started to fall into place. With Lemuel's passing, God rest his soul, she was independent, answerable to no one for the first time in her twenty-three years. Her grandfather had known how restricted she felt living in her brother-in-law's household, and how she'd only stayed there to be close to Jack.

Now, to have that sweet, newfound freedom snatched away before she'd had time to truly savor it was more than cruel. It was downright spiteful.

Grandfather, why did you do this to me?

Chapter Five

As Adam followed Ira and Jack around the cabin, he studied the older man, trying to sort through the jumble of contradictory impressions he presented.

Though nearly bald and sporting a chin full of gray whiskers, the housekeeper's husband was as spry as a schoolboy. His leathery skin and crow's feet were offset by eyes that shone as blue and clear as a newborn's. Slightly built and a head shorter than Adam, he had a puckish quality about him. Maybe it had something to do with that glint of a gold tooth Adam had spotted earlier, or with the abundance of laugh lines bracketing his mouth.

A flash of color distracted Adam from his musings.

What in the world...

He stopped dead in his tracks, blinking at the exotic contraption perched beside the small feed crib.

It was a wagon, he finally decided. But he'd never seen its like outside of a circus parade. To call it gaudy was doing it a kindness.

From this angle, only the back and part of one side was visible, but it was enough. *More* than enough.

Not only was the caravan-style conveyance painted in garish shades of green, maroon and gold, but it was constructed in an overblown design, complete with exuberant scrollwork and elaborately carved panels.

"What kind of rig *is* that?"

Adam tore his gaze away from the flamboyant sight long enough to glance at Mitchell over his shoulder. The man wore a bemused, dumbfounded expression. Adam realized his own was probably similar.

"Looks like a circus wagon," he said, stroking Trib's nose. "Though what it's doing out here—"

Ira, dusting his hands after sliding the fishing poles up under the eaves of the crib, grinned. "I see you spied Reggie's photography wagon. She's a beauty, ain't she?"

Photography wagon? Adam led Trib forward with a click of his tongue. "Did she inherit it from her father?"

The balding leprechaun cackled. "You didn't know Reggie's daddy, did you? Warren Nash would never have been caught driving such a fanciful contraption as this. Plain and simple was more his style."

Ira Peavy patted the wagon as if it were an old friend. "No, Reggie designed this herself after one of them traveling circuses passed through here."

She'd actually *intended* it to look like this? Miss Nash was either as bereft of taste as she was of singing ability, or she had a wicked sense of humor.

"It's the fanciest wagon in all of Turnabout," Jack announced proudly. "Everyone stops to stare when we pass by."

"That I'll believe," Mitchell muttered.

"So, your aunt's a photographer, is she?" Adam asked Jack.

"Yes, sir. Photographs people mostly. But she does

plants and animals, too. Some of 'em turn out real pretty." He gave Adam a big smile. "I'll bet she'd be glad to take a picture of you and your friends if you wanted."

"I'll keep that in mind," Adam responded noncommittally. He knew her father had been a photographer, and Judge Madison had mentioned something about her following in her father's footsteps. But Adam had assumed it was a slightly eccentric pastime of hers, something she toyed with when she was bored, the way other women did with watercolors or the piano.

But if she'd gone to the trouble of designing her own wagon…

"You'll find feed for the horses over here," Ira said, interrupting Adam's thoughts. "You can water them down by the lake and there's lots of good grazing there as well. I'm afraid the lean-to is only big enough for our two horses, so you'll have to tether yours under the trees tonight. Weather's fair, though, so that shouldn't be a problem."

Mitchell set to work unhitching the horse from the buggy. "We appreciate your hospitality," he said over his shoulder.

Before Adam could unsaddle Trib, he found Jack at his elbow. "Mighty fine-looking horse you got there, mister."

The youngster's words might mimic something he'd heard an adult say, but the look on his face was pure wide-eyed, little-boy awe.

"Thanks." Adam offered Jack a friendly smile. Winning the boy's trust was important right now. It might make things easier on both of them later on if this marriage scheme fell apart. "Maybe I'll let you ride him sometime before I head back to Philadelphia," he added.

Jack's face split in a wide grin. "Jiminy! Did you hear that, Ira? Dewey Jenkins is gonna be toad-green jealous when he sees me riding this horse."

"I heard," Ira answered. "But don't forget you've got to get your Aunt Reggie to agree first."

Adam frowned, studying Ira's expression. Had he said that because Miss Nash was overly cautious where her nephew was concerned? Or had the older man picked up on the fact that she distrusted Adam and wouldn't think highly of any plan he put forward that involved Jack?

Jack, however, seemed unworried. "Aw, Aunt Reggie won't mind. She was talking the other day about how I was the man of the family now and all."

Ira squeezed Jack's shoulder. "We'll see." Then he gave the boy a mild swat on the seat of his pants. "Now off with you and fetch that kindling like your aunt asked. Don't want to be holding up supper."

With a nod and a wave, Jack headed for the wood stacked near the cabin's back door.

Ira waited until the boy was out of earshot, then turned to Adam and Mitchell. Nothing puckish about him now. His arms crossed unyieldingly over his chest, and his expression gave him a surprisingly dangerous look. "I'm not sure what's going on here, but Reggie obviously didn't want it talked about in front of Jack. Either one of you fellas care to fill me in?"

Adam shrugged. "We're here at Judge Madison's request. Other than that, I think it would be best if you hear the story from Miss Nash herself."

"Fair enough," Ira answered. "But there's something

you need to know. I went to work for Warren Nash over thirty years ago. I was around when Reggie was born and I helped Warren take care of her after her momma died. When Warren lay on his deathbed, I gave him my word I'd look after her as if she were my own." He paused a moment. "And I'm still keeping my word, to this day."

Adam met his gaze levelly. "Understood."

Their gazes remained locked for several heartbeats. Then Ira uncrossed his arms and the friendly, amused-at-the-world grin returned. "Well, now that we've got that out of the way, I'll leave you to care for your animals." With a wave, he headed around to the front of the cabin, whistling a jaunty tune.

"Did that little gnome just draw a line and dare us to cross it?" Mitchell's expression was a mixture of disbelief and admiration.

Adam bent to work the straps on Trib's saddle. "It seems he's as protective of Miss Nash as his wife is." He gave Mitchell a sideways glance. "A man could look for worse in a wife than one who inspires such loyalty."

It was a lesson he himself had learned the hard way.

"Amen." Jack finished his prayers and clambered onto his pallet.

Reggie drew the bedsheet up to Jack's chin, ruffling his soft brown hair as she did so. She'd tried not to roll her eyes when he'd included their four visitors in his litany of people and things to be thankful for.

"So, how did the frogging go tonight?" she asked.

"We bagged a whole sack full of big ole' bullfrogs." Jack snuggled down on the pallet. "Mrs. Peavy's gonna have more'n enough to feed us all tomorrow."

"And were our visitors much help?"

"Mr. Barr got the hang of it pretty quick and caught his share. And I think maybe Mr. Parker has gone frogging before." Jack paused and looked at Reggie with wide eyes. "He sure is a big one, isn't he?"

"That he is," she said carefully. Did the man's size intimidate Jack?

Jack, however, merely yawned. "Mr. Dawson seemed to really have fun, but Ira said he had a bad case of the flibbertigibbets."

"And Mr. Fulton?"

"He just took care of watching the sack for us." Jack frowned. "I don't think he likes getting his hands dirty."

Reggie hid a smile. Only a few hours in their company and it seemed the six-year-old already had the men accurately pegged. "Mr. Fulton probably hasn't had much experience with outdoor life."

She patted the covers. "Settle down and get some sleep. I'm going to see if Mrs. Peavy or Ira need any help settling our guests in."

Reggie gave Jack a quick peck on the cheek, then turned and climbed down the loft ladder. "Well," she said as she stepped off the bottom rung, "where are our visitors?"

Mrs. Peavy set down a bundle of sheets and blankets on the dining table. "Mr. Barr herded them outside. He insisted they allow us some privacy to settle in." She gave Reggie a questioning look. "They're not used to roughing it the way we are. It don't feel neighborly making them sleep on the floor while we take the ticking."

Reggie shrugged. "It's not as if we have much else to offer." She raised a hand. "And don't even think about offering up your and Ira's bed. It's not big enough for all of them anyway." She pulled the pins from her hair and shook it free. Ahh, that felt good. "Besides, it's just for one night. They'll survive."

"Confound it!"

The British-accented exclamation, accompanied by the sound of a slap, easily penetrated the netting-covered windows.

"Hang propriety, Barr," Mr. Fulton grumbled. "These mosquitoes are as big as bats and thick as an English fog. We're getting eaten alive out here."

"For once I agree."

That sounded like the young Mr. Dawson.

"Take a step toward that door before I say you can," Adam replied pleasantly, "and I'll see that you sleep out here with your winged friends tonight."

Reggie raised a brow. She hadn't expected such gallantry from Adam.

"Sounds like your grandfather picked the right man for the job," Ira remarked.

Reggie reluctantly agreed.

Mrs. Peavy tsked and made shooing motions. "Now stop this dawdling, both of you. We may not be able to offer them more than a floor tonight, but there's no need to make them suffer more than necessary."

Reggie nodded and climbed back up the ladder. She could tell by the sound of Jack's breathing he was already asleep. Changing for bed, she lay down on her own straw-stuffed ticking. A second later, Ira dimmed the lamp and invited the men back inside.

Reggie stared at the rafters in the shadowy moonlight and listened to the men bedding down on the floor just scant feet below her.

If her grandfather had his way, one of these strangers would soon be her husband, would have the right to share her life.

Reggie rolled to her side and cradled her cheek on one arm, trying to encourage her weary body to relax enough for sleep to overtake her.

Unbidden, the memory of being caught up in Adam's arms as she tripped tiptoed into her thoughts. For a few moments this afternoon she'd once more been that moonstruck schoolgirl who considered him a white knight.

Stop it! Remember what's at stake.

Reggie flopped over and fluffed up her pillow. She closed her eyes and forced herself to remember Adam saying *I'll be scrupulously, might I say ruthlessly, single-minded.*

She didn't doubt for a minute he'd meant every syllable of his vow.

Some masculine grumbling drifted up from below. If the unimaginable happened and she had to actually make a choice, which man would she end up with?

Heavenly Father, I know I've been mostly a disappointment to You, but please help me figure out how to handle this. If not for me, then for Jack's sake. I couldn't stand to see him hurt by any of this.

As Reggie finally drifted off to a troubled sleep, her three suitors whirled through her dreams, twirling her in a dizzying square-dance.

And above it all stood Adam Barr, playing the fiddle and calling the moves.

Adam trailed behind Chance as they climbed the footpath from the lake to the cabin in the early morning light. The kid had more of a spring to his step now than when they had headed down just past dawn. Apparently the night spent on the cabin floor hadn't done any permanent damage.

Chance had even perked up enough to whistle.

Adam tightened his grip on his shaving gear, sourly wondering what his companion had to be so cheery about. *He* certainly didn't find the situation any more palatable today than yesterday. In fact, if anything, he was more eager to get this assignment over and done with than before.

The members of this unorthodox household had been unfailingly polite to their guests last night. But all through the simple supper and homey conversation, Adam had felt like a boorish trespasser, an infidel invading a peace-loving land. It was as if Regina had gone out of her way to show the four "Easterners" just what a happy home they were about to invade and destroy.

Adam nearly slammed into Chance as the young man halted in the middle of the trail.

"What—" Chance's bit off exclamation ended in a long drawn-out whistle.

Adam, peering past the startled young man, grinned wryly. While they were down at the lake getting cleaned up for breakfast, Ira had driven the gaudy wagon around to the front of the cabin.

Here in the bright morning sunlight it presented an even more startling spectacle than it had in the evening shade yesterday. For one thing, he could see the front now. The wagon's roof extended over the seat, shading a pale pink upholstered bench. The sides extended past that same seat in a double set of quarter-moon-like scallops. It made the driver's box appear to be the inside of some exotic seashell. Combined with its other flamboyant features, the vehicle had all the finesse of a clown at a funeral.

"I see you've noticed my studio on wheels."

Regina, arms wrapped around a small crate, stepped down from the porch. She handled her awkward burden with more ease than Adam normally expected from a woman. It should have made her appear mannish. Instead, it gave her a sort of stately grace.

"Quite striking, don't you think?"

It took him a heartbeat to realize she was talking about the wagon. Clearing his throat, he reined in his wayward thoughts. And realized her eyes glinted with the hint of mischief.

She was baiting them.

Chance, however, missed the signals. "Um, yes, quite striking." Then he tilted his head as if he wasn't sure he'd heard correctly. "Studio?"

She smiled sweetly. "Yes. I'm a photographer." She made as if to step past them. "Now, if you gentlemen will move aside, I'd best put this away before I drop it."

"Here." Chance reached for her burden. "Let me give you a hand."

"No!"

At her sharp tone, Chance's hands froze inches from the crate, then slowly withdrew.

Adam frowned. What was wrong with the woman? Couldn't she see the kid had only been trying to help? She seemed to be going overboard trying to prove she didn't need a man in her life.

"I'm sorry." Chance stumbled over the apology, his confusion obvious. "I was just—"

Her eyes rolled and she gave a deep sigh. "Look, Mr. Dawson, I appreciate your gesture, but this box contains fragile photography plates representing many, *many* hours of work. No one but myself or Mr. Peavy handles them."

"Yes, ma'am."

"If you want to help someone." She paused to blow a strand of hair off her forehead. "Mrs. Peavy is getting breakfast ready. I'm sure she could use a hand setting the table."

Looking none too happy with the mundane chore he'd been assigned, Chance nodded and headed inside.

Adam fell into step beside Regina as she resumed her trek to the wagon. He didn't make the mistake of offering to take the box from her. "A bit hard on the boy, weren't you?"

She cut him a sideways glance. "I have too much invested in these to take risks." She blew at that obstinate lock of hair again. "Besides, Chance doesn't strike me as the careful type."

Adam couldn't fault her there. Changing the subject, he pointed to the wagon. "So, is the understated look your idea?"

She tried hard to appear affronted, but Adam saw the slight twitch to her lips. "I prefer a touch of flair over the mundane." She moved to the back of the wagon, where a stubby ladder led up to an open door. "As for the colors, I figured such a fancy design cried out for a truly resplendent treatment."

"Resplendent? Don't you mean gaudy?"

Before she could offer a retort, Ira appeared in the wagon's doorway. "Here, just slide those in." Ira's sleeves were rolled up and his gold tooth glinted in the sunlight. "I have the camera and equipment already stowed away."

The judge's granddaughter, huffing out a feminine grunt, hefted her load onto the ledge at the top of the ladder. "Thanks, Ira. I have one more set of plates. We can load the rest of our baggage and supplies later."

A strangled oath, uttered in British overtones, signaled Everett's return from the lake. Adam stepped to one side to see the dandy, hair still damp and a towel flung over one shoulder, staring at the wagon in absolute horror.

"You don't think she expects us to ride in that atrocity, do you?" Everett's mouth was set in a belligerent line. "This is just too much. First we spend the night on the kitchen floor, then we have to hike down to a lake this morning just to wash and shave. I will not—"

His words ground to a halt as Regina stepped out from behind the wagon. Placing a fist on her hip, she tilted her chin up. "Rest assured, Mr. Fulton, *she* doesn't expect any such thing. I only extend that privilege to my friends."

Everett had the grace to flush.

"Now if you're finished praising my hospitality, you may avail yourself of more of the same by joining us for breakfast." With a decided flounce, she headed back to the house.

Mitchell, who'd been a step or two behind Everett, met Adam's gaze with a barely perceptible twitch of his lips. He slapped his towel on Everett's shoulder. "You might want to follow Miss Nash inside and see if you can make amends."

Everett shot him a dark look, then spun on his heel and headed for the front door. Mitchell followed at a more sedate pace, as unruffled as ever.

Adam glanced toward Ira to find the man grinning broadly.

"Consider all this amusing, do you?"

Ira chuckled. "Things are sure gonna be interesting around here the next few weeks." He gave Adam a conspiratorial wink. "I always did think highly of Reggie's granddaddy."

Adam wasn't quite certain how to respond, so he changed the subject. "Mind if I take a look inside?" He nodded toward the wagon. "I've never been in one of these before."

"Suit yourself." He gave Adam a tongue-in-cheek grin. "Just don't touch anything. Reggie'll have my hide if you break something."

Adam nodded and climbed inside, ducking under the short doorway. It only took a moment for his eyes to adjust. With the open door and a window on each side, the interior wasn't as dark as he'd expected.

He just barely had room to stand upright, though, and if he stretched out his arms he could probably touch both sides of the wagon at once.

"Not very roomy for someone your size," Ira commented. "Ain't much of a problem for me though."

The gnome of a man bent over and slid the newly-delivered crate into a cubbyhole sized exactly right to accommodate it. Then he deftly fastened a leather strap across the front. That box wouldn't budge from its slot, no matter how bumpy the road.

The whole left wall, from floor to ceiling, was covered with similar niches and cabinets. A good many of them were already snugly filled with odd-size crates. "All these boxes contain photography equipment?"

"Yep." Ira straightened. "Cameras, flash pans, chemicals, glass slides—everything a photographer might need, along with spares for emergencies."

"So, she's pretty serious about this hobby of hers?"

The older man winced. "I wouldn't let her hear you call it a hobby if I were you, son. Reggie considers herself a professional, with good cause."

Interesting. Was the man just being loyal, or was Regina really that good? She certainly seemed to have the determination to make a go of something like this if she put her mind to it.

"Hand me a strap from that pile, would you?"

Adam turned to face the other side of the wagon. Along this wall was a long, well-padded, benchlike structure running more than half the length. Adam guessed it probably doubled as a cot when needed.

Cabinets made good use of the space below, and hooks hung above it for storing odds and ends, many of them unrecognizable to Adam.

He grabbed the requested strip of leather and handed it to Ira. "Did you construct all this?"

Ira nodded. "Yep. Every bit of it—at least on the inside. Reggie designed it, though." He shook his head. "You should have seen her measure and fuss. She wouldn't let me touch a thing until she was sure she had it all figured just right."

Adam had no trouble believing that. Regina Nash was obviously a woman who liked to be in control.

"Set a spell, if you like," Ira said over his shoulder.

But Adam had seen enough. The enclosed space was beginning to feel too much like the prison cell that had been his home for over six years. "Thanks, but I think I'll see if there's anything I can do to help get everyone packed up."

He climbed out of the wagon and drew in a lungful of the fresh woodsy air. His eyes drank in the view of open sky and rolling woodlands, unobstructed by fortified walls or armed guards.

As he stepped around the wagon, he was greeted with another sight that had been absent from his life behind bars. Regina Nash pushed through the cabin door, her arms wrapped around another of those small crates. Several more wisps had escaped her hairpins, giving her a not unattractive look of disarray. Such an intriguing mix of confidence and vulnerability.

Adam decided it would be an insult to offer her a hand since she had been so insistent earlier that she could handle things herself. Instead he stood where he was, crossed his arms and enjoyed the view.

As she stepped from the porch, Regina's gaze met his and she paused mid-stride. A what-are-you-up-to-now look crossed her face.

When he broadened his smile, she jutted her chin up and stepped forward with an almost convincing air of nonchalance.

She'd only progressed a few paces when Jack dashed around the side of the cabin on a direct collision course with her.

"Whoa, there, son." In two steps, Adam had snagged the boy, lifting him off the ground with legs still pumping.

Jack squirmed a minute longer, then seemed to realize what had just happened. "Gee, Mr. Barr, I'm awful sorry. I—"

"Put him down!"

Adam, who'd been in the process of doing just that, stiffened. What had put the flint in her tone now? He'd just averted a catastrophe involving her precious photographic plates. Instead of gratitude, though, she looked at him like a lioness whose cub had been threatened.

"I said, put him down," she repeated.

Adam set the boy down and raised his hands, palms out.

Jack scuffed his foot in the dust. "I'm sorry, Aunt Reggie. Didn't mean to come barreling around like that."

Regina took a deep breath and smiled at her nephew. "Of course you didn't. Just try to be a little more careful next time." She hefted her load. "Now, go on inside. Mrs. Peavy has your breakfast ready."

"Yes ma'am."

As the boy sprinted up the porch steps, she turned back to Adam, her expression more defensive than apologetic. "If you'll excuse me, I have to finish loading the wagon."

Adam watched her walk stiffly by, and wondered what had set her off.

Reggie could feel Adam's gaze follow her all the way to the wagon. She knew she'd overreacted, but she wasn't about to apologize.

Seeing him hold a squirming Jack in his clutches had reminded her of what his mission was. If things didn't go the way she'd planned, he could very well haul Jack away, kicking and screaming in protest, stealing him out of her life forever.

She would do well to keep that in mind over the coming days.

Reggie handed the box to Ira, then turned to find Adam still watching her.

"What time would you like to head back to town?"

Surprised and relieved he hadn't mentioned her earlier outburst, Reggie smoothed her skirt. "I was thinking we'd pack up right after lunch. I want to get back before dark, but I don't want to get there too early."

"Why's that?"

"Well, for one thing," she said with a smug smile, "I want to make sure you stalwart hunters don't miss the opportunity to feast on the wild game you bagged last night."

He grimaced, but Reggie noticed the amused glint in his eye.

She pushed a lock of hair off her brow. "Mainly, though, it's because I'd prefer it if you four would go straight to your quarters this evening and not mingle with the townsfolk more than necessary."

He raised a brow. "If you're planning to keep us sequestered for the duration, I'm afraid you might have a mutiny on your hands."

Reggie waved a hand airily. "Don't be silly. I'm just talking about today."

He didn't seem reassured by her statement.

"Tomorrow is Sunday," she explained patiently, "and I'm thinking we can all go to church together." She paused and raised a brow. "I trust that won't be a problem for anyone?" Any man who wanted to be a part of her and Jack's life would have to do more than give lip service to his faith.

"We'll be there."

Was that annoyance in his expression aimed at her question or her insistence on taking the lead?

Not that it mattered. "Good. At least when we formally introduce you as friends of my grandfather, they'll be seeing you all in a charitable, God-fearing light." She pointed at him. "But it's important that we present a united front, that we all tell the same story."

Adam raised his hands. "You won't get an argument from me on that score. I'll make certain everyone follows your lead."

She nodded. "Now that that's settled, shall we join the others for breakfast?"

Six hours later, the cabin was closed up and they were headed toward Turnabout.

Reggie watched Adam as he rode ahead of their three-vehicle caravan. His horse was an impressive animal, with a powerful frame and an arrogant demeanor.

Not unlike the man astride him.

She'd give him this much—Adam *did* know how to sit a horse.

Forcefully turning her focus away from Adam Barr's distracting back, Reggie smiled at the man seated beside her. She had suggested one of her suitors ride with her, so they could get to know each other better. Chance had gallantly stepped forward.

Behind them, Mrs. Peavy rode in the carriage the men had arrived in with her two other suitors. Jack and Ira brought up the rear in the photography wagon. Reggie had made sure the boy was safely insulated from the influence of her less-than-eager suitors.

She flashed Chance a neighborly smile. "So, Mr. Dawson, tell me something about yourself."

"Please, call me Chance, ma'am." He shot her a roguish look. "We're supposed to be friends, remember?"

Was he flirting with her? "Of course, Chance. But you must stop calling me ma'am. It makes me feel so old."

He flushed at this reference to the difference in their

ages, just as she'd figured he would. This would likely be the Achilles' heel she'd want to attack with him. But would it be enough to make him throw in the towel on this ridiculous scheme?

Chance recovered quickly. "So, what would you like to know?"

She could see Adam from the corner of her eye. What would it be like to question him, to ask whatever she wanted and have him be obliged to answer?

What would she ask?

The carriage bounced over a rut in the road, pulling her attention back to her companion. "Well, for one thing," she said, gathering her thoughts, "Chance is an unusual name. Is there a story behind it?"

"Actually, Chance isn't my real name." He shifted uncomfortably. "My given name is Chauncey, but I never did care for it much. One of my brothers started calling me Chancey as a joke, and it eventually got shortened to Chance." He shrugged. "I think it suits me better."

"Oh, you have brothers?"

She caught the barely perceptible stiffening of his spine. Was his family a tender subject with him as well?

"Yes, ma—" He slid her a guilty sideways look. "Um, yes. Four of them."

"Any sisters?"

He rubbed his neck with his free hand. "No. Just the five of us boys."

"Just?" Reggie let out a genuinely wistful sigh. "I always dreamed about having a house full of siblings to play with."

Chance lifted a brow. "You had a sister, didn't you? I mean, that's her son you're raising."

"Patricia was my stepsister." She watched Adam lift his hat and wipe his forehead with his sleeve. The motion stretched his shirt tightly across broad, well-muscled shoulders.

Clearing her throat, she determinedly focused on Chance. "I was three when my father married her mother. Patricia was ten. We grew to be close friends, but not exactly playmates."

Time to turn the conversation back to him. "I imagine you and your brothers were a rowdy crew when you put your minds to a bit of mischief."

She'd expected a reminiscent grin. Instead he gave the reins a casual flick. "I was a late arrival. Michael, the closest in age to me, is six years older. I guess that's something we have in common."

"So, you're the baby of the family?" She didn't give him time to respond to her deliberate barb. "Your mother must have had her hands full keeping up with six men."

His jaw tightened. "Mother died when I was born."

"Oh." Reggie felt a twinge of unwanted empathy, seasoned with a dollop of guilt. She'd touched a nerve again, but this time she wasn't so pleased with herself. "I'm sorry."

He flashed her a smile that didn't quite reach his eyes. "No need to apologize. It wasn't your fault."

It was her turn to shift in her seat. She decided to ignore her protesting conscience and go on the offensive again. "So, tell me, why did you decide to sign on for my grandfather's matchmaking scheme?"

"Let's just say my father thought I needed a change of scenery, and I agreed."

From his tone, it didn't sound like it had been an

amicable parting. “Ready to shed the family traces and strike out on your own, are you?”

“Something like that.”

Reggie pounced again. “Only you’re not striking out on your own. My grandfather is staking you.”

He shot her a level look. “I plan to earn my stake, one way or the other.” He turned his gaze back to the road. “If I don’t end up sharing my earnings with you and Jack, I’ll pay Judge Madison back a bit at a time.”

Now he’d surprised her. “But that wasn’t part of the contract.”

“Doesn’t matter.” The set of his jaw had an uncompromising hardness. “I might accept a generous loan to get started, but I don’t take handouts.”

“I see.” He sounded sincere. This unexpected glimmer of nobility, however, didn’t keep her from pursuing the opening he’d provided. “And that grub stake is in the form of a half-burned saloon building and cash to renovate. Seems a rather *unusual* payment, especially from my grandfather. I wonder why he’d think it suitable?”

Chance didn’t glance away from the road. “You’ll have to ask *him* that question.”

“And do you fancy yourself a saloon owner?”

He shrugged. “I haven’t decided what kind of business I’ll open yet, but I haven’t ruled out a saloon.”

“But that doesn’t answer my question. Is running a saloon something that appeals to you?”

This time he did look at her, and she was surprised by the fire in his expression. “Owning my own business, in a town where no one has ever heard of my father and never met my brothers, appeals to me a great deal.” His voice vibrated with determination.

Then he took a breath. “If that business happens to

be a saloon, so be it." He gave her a mirthless smile. "Believe me, I've been inside more than my share of saloons."

"Have you?" He'd just revealed a great deal about his life. She'd file it away and analyze it later. Right now, she wanted to keep pressing. "And do you think a saloon keeper would make a good father and husband?"

He met her gaze levelly. "That's for you to decide, isn't it? Besides, as I said, I haven't decided yet."

Chance had more intelligence than she'd given him credit for. "How do you feel about being father to an active six-year-old?"

He shrugged. "Raising kids is more the mother's job. Of course, I'd teach him the things a father should—like how to hunt and fish, how to defend himself, how to transact business."

She should have expected an answer like that from someone who'd barely reached manhood himself. "That's your idea of the involvement a father should have in his child's upbringing?"

"Oh, I know there's more to it. I'll do what's necessary when, and *if*, the time comes." Something unreadable flashed in his eyes. "If I become Jack's stepfather, he won't ever be made to feel he doesn't measure up."

Now *that* was an interesting statement. Reggie was getting a picture of what had turned Chance into such a rebellious, cocky young man.

As if afraid he'd said too much, Chance changed the subject. "Mind if I ask you a few questions of my own?"

"Not at all. I just don't guarantee I'll answer them." As she said the words, Reggie realized Adam had moved alongside them. She deliberately kept her back turned, but the tingling along her nape kept her acutely aware of his presence.

"How'd you end up being a photographer?" Chance asked, recapturing her attention.

"My father was a photographer. One of the finest in Texas. I used to help him when he'd let me. When I was eleven, he purchased a new camera and gave me his old one. After that, you couldn't hold me back. Then, when Father died, it just seemed natural for me to take over the business."

She smoothed her skirt. "I couldn't have done it without Ira, though. He likely knows more about photography equipment than any man alive."

The tingling on her neck was more pronounced. What was Adam doing? Was he watching them? Her whole body strained to turn and take a quick peek over her shoulder. But she fought the urge, refusing to let him know how aware she was of his presence.

"But why did you bring your equipment *here?*" Chance asked. "There's no one for miles around except your household, and you could take their pictures back in town if you wanted to."

Reggie leaned forward. "I don't just photograph people. I've always been fascinated by plants, ever since I first buried a seed and watched it sprout. I've read every botany book I could get my hands on, and regularly scour the area looking for new plants to add to my collection." She gave Chance a self-deprecating smile. "When Father gave me my own camera, I started shooting studies of my finds as a way to both practice photography and preserve the images."

Those had been some of the happiest days of her life. Her family had still been intact—her father and stepmother still alive, her stepsister, Patricia, not yet married. She'd roamed the woods, delighting in her discoveries, proud when she captured images good enough to earn her father's praises.

"A few years back I learned about a scientific journal back East specializing in botany. The publishers are willing to pay for quality photographic plates of plants native to this region."

Reggie paused. She hadn't intended to do so much talking about herself, especially with Adam listening in. She kept forgetting others didn't share her passion for this particular merger of art and science.

At least Chance's eyes hadn't glazed over. But it was time to turn the conversation back around to her inquisition. "I'm sure that's more of an explanation than you were after."

"On the contrary," Chance said gallantly, "I find it quite fascinating."

"As do I," Adam agreed.

So, he was tired of being ignored, was he?

Reggie turned and narrowed her eyes, refusing to be distracted by the incongruous dimple in that uncompromising chin. "Are you in the habit of eavesdropping, Mr. Barr?"

"Just doing my job, ma'am." At her raised brow, he continued, "Keeping an eye on how things are progressing, that is."

The man was insufferable. Did he enjoy reminding her of the power he held over her future? "As you can see, things are progressing just fine and dandy. Why, I already feel like I know Mr. Dawson here like an old friend."

She gave him her most haughty look. "Was there anything else we could do for you?"

He tipped his hat back, apparently unaffected by the lack of warmth in her tone. "Just wanted to check my memory. The road skirts an open meadow about halfway between here and town, doesn't it?"

Reggie nodded, annoyed that he appeared not to notice he'd just been put in his place.

"Good." He straightened, leaning back in the saddle. "We'll stop there to rest the horses for a bit and stretch our legs."

This time she had to bite her tongue. He seemed to think *he* was in charge of this expedition.

But she believed in choosing her battles carefully. This wasn't a point worth quibbling over, especially since his plan had merit. She'd save her verbal ammunition for the more important battles she knew were bound to come.

Turning back to Chance, she dismissed Adam from her view.

But not from her thoughts.

Chapter Six

Adam suppressed a grin at Regina's would-be snubbing. The woman didn't acknowledge authority easily. He was surprised he hadn't gotten more of a rise out of her than he had.

Almost disappointing, really.

He dropped back to inform the other members of the plan to take a break shortly. But his thoughts remained on how vibrant, almost glowing, her voice and manner became when she spoke about her photographic and botanical interests. The woman actually seemed approachable when she didn't have her back up over something.

Once he'd passed the word along, Adam nudged Trib with his knees, quickly moving forward again. But he didn't immediately take the lead. Instead, he found himself studying the judge's granddaughter. Watching how she used her hands when she talked, noticing how she smiled ever so sweetly when she asked one of her more probing questions, observing how she fiddled with collar of her dress when she paused to think through some point.

In life, as in court, it paid to learn as much as possible

about your opponent's "tells," those little unconscious movements that gave away state of mind.

Not that he necessarily saw Regina Nash as an opponent.

But it wouldn't hurt to be prepared.

Adam dismounted and dropped the reins to let Trib graze.

He watched as the carriages and the wagon turned off the road into the meadow. Before he realized what he was doing, he'd stepped to the first carriage and offered his hand to help Regina climb down.

She hesitated a split second before placing her hand in his.

Why? Certainly it wasn't fear—he couldn't picture this woman afraid of anything. But what did she see when she looked at him?

The man she'd met in her grandfather's home years ago?

A convicted felon?

Or merely the agent of her grandfather's manipulations?

Her hand felt so small in his. Not baby-smooth, but gently work-tested and surprisingly firm.

She climbed down with a no-nonsense assurance. A far cry from the awkward schoolgirl hiding in the shadows of her grandfather's parlor. Who would have believed then that she would grow into this confident, independent-minded woman?

As soon as her feet touched the ground, Regina withdrew her hand. "Thank you," she said with stiff politeness. Without another word, she turned and headed toward the photography wagon.

Adam watched her walk away, watched how the gentle sway of her hips softened the stiffness of her back, watched the way the sun painted glints of roan in her brown hair, watched the way her whole bearing seemed to radiate energy and purpose.

Then he turned away, his hand still pulsing with the warmth of her touch.

Reggie smiled as she watched Jack and Buck race across the open ground. Jack had lots of energy to work off after sitting in the wagon for so long. Best to let him get as much exercise as he could before they set off again.

This past week at the cabin had been good for him. For them both. Patricia's husband hadn't been a bad father to Jack, but to Reggie's mind he hadn't been the most loving one, either.

Lemuel and Patricia were so deeply in love, so wrapped up in each other, that they'd built a bubble around themselves that excluded everyone else. When Jack entered their lives, that bubble had expanded to include him.

But when Patricia died three months later, the bubble burst. It was as if, without Patricia, Lemuel lost all capacity for such gentle emotions. He walled himself off, never really returning to the man he'd been before. Their household in Turnabout had transformed into a somber shell of what it had once been, a perpetual air of mourning hanging over everything, and everyone.

Reggie did what she could to give Jack a mother's love, but she knew she hadn't been able to compensate for the indifference of his father. While Lemuel's death was something she had never wished for or welcomed, now that it had happened, Reggie hoped she could bring more laughter and joy into their household.

Lemuel had been gone four months now, and already she saw changes in Jack. The boy truly mourned the death of the only father he'd ever known. She still saw an occasional sadness in his eyes that nearly broke her heart. But he was more exuberant now, more willing to run and laugh and just plain be a boy, than she'd ever seen from him before.

It would be a different household now.

Or at least that was the plan before her grandfather turned everything upside down.

Some sixth sense, or an indefinable stirring of the air, raised the hairs on her nape, alerting Reggie that someone had stepped up behind her. She didn't have to turn to discover who stood there. The tingling in her palm hadn't yet gone away from his earlier touch. His large hands had enveloped hers—assisting, protecting, reassuring.

Her shoulders fluttered in memory.

"I never would've pegged that dog as a child's playmate." Adam stepped to her side, his gaze following Jack and Buck as hers had.

Had he noticed her involuntary reaction?

"Buck can be fierce when it comes to protecting the family." She watched Adam from the corner of her eye, trying to assess his mood, his motives for approaching her. "But when it comes to Jack, he's just an overgrown puppy."

"So I see." Adam finally turned his unreadable blue eyes toward her. "Let me ask you something. Now that Jack's father is gone, don't you find raising him alone a heavy responsibility? I would think you'd welcome the opportunity to marry a man who was willing to share that burden."

She rounded on him, her earlier distraction forgotten. "Burden? Jack's not a burden. And there is absolutely no way I would welcome any man into my life who looked at him that way."

He held up a hand. "Whoa. That's not what I meant. Of course you care for him. I only meant that you must feel tied down sometimes."

Was he trying to convince her to play along with her grandfather's scheme, or did he really believe what he was saying? "Let me explain something, Mr. Barr. Jack was only three months old when Patricia died and I stepped in to help. I feel like he's my own son. And a mother doesn't look at her children as burdens, but as precious gifts from God. A mother puts the interest of her child before her own."

"Not all mothers."

Though his tone was matter-of-fact, the words and the sentiment behind them chilled her. He must have dealt with all manner of ugly things in his work as a lawyer.

"All mothers who truly love their children," she insisted.

Something flickered in his expression, something that made her wonder if this was a more personal matter than she'd assumed. But before she could say anything, he changed the subject. "I came over to let you know Mrs. Peavy's laying out a small picnic."

"More frog legs?" she inquired, forcing a light tone.

An answering grin tugged at his lips. "I think she's going to spare us a repeat of that delicacy. She mentioned something about cheese and berries."

Reggie nodded. "Thank you. I'll tell Jack." She headed across the meadow, trying to remember what she'd heard about Adam's family.

He'd been raised by his Uncle Phillip, a bachelor. She knew that because Phillip Barr had been her grandfather's secretary for a great many years.

Other than that, she knew…nothing. What had happened to his parents? Had her words opened old wounds?

Reggie caught Jack's attention and told him about the picnic. Then she headed back.

Mrs. Peavy and the three suitors-for-pay were setting out the foodstuffs while Ira and Adam watered the horses. The two men were laughing, as if sharing a joke.

So much for worrying about having stepped on his feelings. She turned to Mrs. Peavy. "How can I help?"

"Set that down here," Mrs. Peavy instructed Mitchell. Then she turned to Reggie. "Would you fetch an extra jug of cider from the wagon? I imagine everyone is good and thirsty after that dusty ride."

In addition to cheese and blackberries, Mrs. Peavy pulled out a large jar of pickled tomatoes and a loaf of bread. A simple but appetizing spread.

Everett was the first to dig in. Reggie grinned, remembering how little he'd eaten at lunch. He'd barely nibbled on the beans and completely ignored the frog legs, claiming lack of appetite.

Later, as Mrs. Peavy lifted the now much lighter hamper, Reggie waved her away. "I'll take care of the blanket."

Before she could lift more than a corner, however, Mitchell stepped forward. "Here, let me help."

"Thank you, Mr. Parker. If you'll give it a good shake, I'll fold it and put it away."

As Mitchell shook the crumbs and leaves from the blanket, Reggie finally realized what it was about him that bothered her. He seemed the most pleasant of the three men, was unfailingly polite, and was the first to step forward to lend a hand. Yet there was a wall around him, a standoffishness that made one hesitant to approach uninvited.

She offered a smile as he handed her the large cloth. “Thanks. You don’t seem a stranger to domestic chores.”

His expression shuttered immediately. “My wife liked picnics.” With a nod, he turned and walked away.

She’d forgotten he was a widower. How long had his wife been gone? The pain was obviously still raw. But if he hadn’t managed to put the past behind him, why was he looking for another wife?

More to the point, what in the world was such a man doing in this marriage lottery?

Regina folded the blanket, her gaze focused on Mitchell’s stiff back.

Hang it all! She didn’t want to feel sympathy for any of these men. She couldn’t afford to soften toward them, not if she wanted to have any chance of getting out of this fix.

She had to remember what was at stake, had to get the fire burning in her gut again.

Reggie glanced across the meadow toward her grandfather’s sergeant-at-arms, and tilted her chin up.

Pulling the blanket firmly against her chest, she marched toward her quarry.

Adam heard her approach, but continued grooming Trib, waiting for her to speak.

“Mr. Barr.”

Her tone held a note of challenge, a sound he was becoming familiar with. Straightening, he gave her his full attention. "Yes?"

She planted a fist on her hip. "Thanks to the way you headed out here almost before your train left the station, there's probably been speculation in town about who you are and why you're here."

They'd covered this ground already. "Most likely."

"Your concern over the notoriety you've heaped on my household is truly touching." Her color rose and her voice took on that caustic edge that signaled he'd riled her again.

He was finding it an entertaining pastime.

"I'll likely receive more than my usual share of welcome home visits this evening and tomorrow after church."

He idly slapped the reins against his free hand. "Which I'm certain you'll deal with admirably."

She didn't appear amused. "I aim to try to put the best face I can on a bad situation. Just introducing you to folks at church isn't enough. So, tomorrow afternoon I'll host a garden party in my backyard."

Her eyes flashed with purpose. "This will give everyone a chance to talk to you and ask all the questions that have been simmering since yesterday. They can also see from the get-go what good friends we all are."

"Fine with me," he said, ignoring her sarcasm. How far could he push her with his show of unconcern?

"I wasn't asking for your approval, only your cooperation," she snapped. Then she took a deep breath. "I'll introduce you as friends of my grandfather who are looking for investment opportunities. You all have come to Turnabout at his recommendation, and want to look the place over for yourselves."

"Seems as good a story as any." It appeared the judge wasn't the only one in this family who had a knack for planning ahead.

She batted away an errant bumblebee without blinking. "It has the benefit of being the truth, as far as it goes. Remember, it would be best if you four keep to yourselves as much as possible this evening." She frowned as if she'd just discovered a hitch in her plans. "Are you staying at the hotel or Mrs. Ortolon's Boardinghouse?"

"The boardinghouse."

She grimaced. "Eunice Ortolon won't be bashful about asking questions. And she's not easily ignored."

Not unlike another woman he knew. "Don't concern yourself—we'll handle it." He lifted a brow. "Now if there's nothing else, I need to check Trib's saddle."

She glanced at the horse and some of her stiffness eased. "He's a magnificent animal. Did you bring him with you from Philadelphia?"

Adam was surprised by her softening. He'd expected her to stalk off. "Yes. He was sired by a stallion I owned before—" He caught himself, then pressed forward, refusing to sugarcoat what had happened. "Before I lost everything."

During those years he'd spent caged in that bleak prison, he'd dreamed of galloping across rolling hills and meadows, with only open ground and endless sky around him. When the judge had paid him for this assignment, Adam had used the money to buy Trib. He hadn't even considered leaving the animal behind.

He gave her a cynical grin. “In fact, this was my ‘thirty pieces of silver’ from the judge you inquired about yesterday.”

“Oh.” Instead of meeting his gaze, she shifted the blanket she carried to her other arm and patted the horse with her free hand. “Trib is an unusual name.”

“The man I bought him from named him Lancer’s Tribute. Sounded too pompous to me, so I shortened it.” He bent to check the cinch straps. “Besides, Trib can stand for things that have more meaning to me, like ‘Retribution’ or ‘Tribulation.’”

He didn’t realize he’d actually said that last aloud until he heard the slight hitch in her breathing. Her head came up and shock widened her expressive eyes. Her gaze locked with his, and something strong and elemental flashed in the air between them.

A butterfly shiver fluttered her shoulders.

That tiny quiver cleared the fog from his brain and brought him back to the present. Taking a deep breath, he smiled. “Time to round everyone up and get moving again.”

She nodded and turned without saying a word.

Adam watched her go, wondering what it was that had just passed between them.

He rubbed the back of his neck. Three weeks seemed an eternity. He didn’t have time for this distraction, didn’t want to lose his focus, his edge.

Jack ran up to Regina as she neared the carriages. She bent down and straightened his shirt collar. Then she gave him a hug and ruffled his hair affectionately.

Adam reached back in his mind, trying to dredge up a memory of his own mother doing something similar.

Nothing came.

He'd been four years old when his mother abandoned him. His only memories of her were of a tired, unhappy woman. She'd clothed and fed him, but he couldn't remember one time when she'd given him a motherly kiss or even an affectionate pat.

Her dumping him on his uncle's doorstep without a backward glance had widened the hole that already existed in his life.

Well, his uncle had made up for that. Philip Barr hadn't been an openly demonstrative man, but he'd always treated Adam well. Adam had known, as long as he did as he was told and followed all the rules, he'd have a home and a family.

Shaking his head to clear his thoughts, Adam led Trib toward the road. He watched Regina organize the group, making certain everything was packed properly and all were accounted for.

Then, as they moved toward the carriages, she touched Everett's arm. "Mr. Fulton, why don't you join me in my carriage?" She smiled at Chance. "You won't mind trading places, will you?"

So, she was ready for a new victim, was she?

Chance gave her an elegant bow. "Whether or not I mind, I graciously concede the seat of honor to Everett."

She touched a hand to her chest. "Why, Chance, I didn't realize there was the touch of the gallant in you."

It was the young man's turn to give her a pointed look. "There are a lot of things you don't know about me, Miss Nash."

Adam hid a grin at her nonplussed look. Regina was a resourceful woman, one who seemed accustomed to steering her own course, and perhaps that of the others around her. It probably wasn't often she was forced to question her own perceptions.

"All right, folks," he called out. "Time to get back on the road."

Regina shot him an affronted look, just as he'd known she would. But her momentary self-doubt was gone.

He wasn't sure why that mattered to him.

As soon as they left the meadow behind them, Reggie began her interrogation of Everett. "Tell me, Mr. Fulton, are you truly British, or is that accent just part of your carefully constructed image?"

"No need to sound so disdainful." He gave the reins a flick. "We all construct facades of one type or another. Some of us are just better at it."

"That's a rather cynical attitude, don't you think?"

"Not at all. For instance, the facade you wear of being reluctantly cooperative, while you are plotting how to have your own way is quite convincing."

She wasn't sure how to respond to that one.

"And to answer your question," he continued, "my parents were both British. I lived the first twelve years of my life on an estate about an hour's ride from London."

"And what brought you to America?"

"A ship called the *Lucky Star,* if memory serves me," he replied blandly.

Reggie's lips twitched in spite of herself. "You may consider me impertinent, sir, but if I'm to make the choice my grandfather saddled me with, then I should be armed with as much information as I can gather."

"I only thought to spare you a sordid, embarrassing story."

"Embarrassing for whom?" When he didn't answer she pressed further. "Remember, by the terms of the contract, you are obligated to answer my questions truthfully."

His lips compressed into a tight line, then he gave a short nod. "Very well. My father is a prominent member of the British aristocracy, my mother was an actress. They were not married, either before or after my birth."

So, he was the illegitimate son of an English lord. That explained a lot.

"When I turned twelve, Father finally decided to take a wife. Unfortunately, it was not my mother, and his new bride took a dim view of his continued closeness to her." Everett shrugged. "So we were shipped an ocean away to start a new life."

Reggie felt her heart go out to the boy he had been and the hurt that had been dealt him.

She must have made some sound of sympathy because he gave her a cynical smile. "No need to feel sorry for me. That was a long time ago. And Father gave my mother enough money to ensure that we could make a nice place for ourselves when we arrived."

Slamming the lid on her sympathetic feelings, Reggie jumped at the opening he'd just given her. "Just as Grandfather did when he sent you here."

Her companion stiffened. "Nobody *sent* me here. This time it was my choice."

"Was it? Why would a man who so obviously appreciates the finer things in life, willingly come to a place like Turnabout?"

"Are you saying your fair town has none of life's 'finer things'?"

He was good at turning her words back on her. But she wasn't about to let him get away with it. "Don't play word games with me. I'm quite happy with the life Turnabout offers. But I've visited Philadelphia several times and I know what so-called amenities are lacking here by comparison."

He stared straight ahead. "You might want to be careful, your facade is slipping. A bit of the single-minded bulldog is showing through."

An unflattering comparison, but not completely inaccurate. She'd have to watch this one.

"Well?" she pressed, ignoring his comment.

He gave her a you're-not-fooling-me look. Then he acknowledged her question with a nod. "It's no coincidence your grandfather is setting me up with a printing press. I worked for a prominent newspaper for over ten years, the last seven as a reporter."

"Why did you leave?"

"Because I was asked to," he said bluntly. Without waiting for her to prompt him, he expanded on his surprising revelation. "I wrote a sordidly sensational piece about one of our local politicians that stirred up quite a furor."

"And they fired you over that?"

His smile was mirthless. "Oh, no. That they liked. Sold lots of newspaper for them. The trouble came when the story turned out not to be true." His jaw tightened. "Seems I wasn't very diligent in checking my sources."

"Oh." Ran him out on a rail, did they? "Given your,

shall we say, colorful, background, what makes you think you'd be a good father to Jack?"

He speared her with a searching look. "Interesting that you should focus on the role of father rather than that of husband."

Reggie straightened. "Nothing odd about it. I'm a grown woman, quite capable of dealing with whatever unpleasantness may come my way." She took a smidgeon of satisfaction at his wince. "I'm much more concerned that Jack doesn't suffer from this ridiculous matchmaking scheme."

"To answer your question, I consider myself a man who learns life's lessons quickly. I don't make the same mistakes twice, and I don't knowingly betray others' trust." He shrugged. "Never having been a father before, that's the best answer I can give you."

"Well, that's an honest enough response, I suppose."

Reggie caught a movement from the corner of her eye and turned to watch Adam, who'd been talking to Ira, ride past and take the lead again. There was something commanding about the easy grace with which he sat in the saddle, about the way he automatically assumed leadership of their group, not only in terms of physical position but in looking out for their welfare.

Even back when he'd been her grandfather's protégé, he'd carried an air of quiet authority. Surprisingly, his time in prison appeared to have honed and tempered that part of his character rather than leeching it from him.

No doubt, that was one reason her grandfather had chosen him for this job.

She remembered listening to Adam and other young men argue points of law in her grandfather's drawing room. Adam had always been so passionate, so articulate, it had seemed to her that he talked rings around everyone else.

She hadn't been able to take her eyes off him back then.

Reggie gave herself a mental shake. Surely she was a stronger person now.

Resolutely, she turned her attention back to Everett.

Chapter Seven

"...Newspaper would be an absolutely wonderful thing for Turnabout, Mr. Fulton. In fact..."

"...to have such polished, *eligible* gentlemen, looking to make Turnabout their home..."

"...tell us about Philadelphia. Is it really..."

Adam skirted the edges of the gathering, catching snippets of conversation here and there. He was doing his level best to keep from being collared by any of the dozens of Turnabout's finest now crowding Regina Nash's lawn.

Once upon a time he'd felt at home at gatherings such as this. He'd prided himself on how far he'd come from his humble beginnings. He'd thrived on the interaction with the educated and social elite of Philadelphia.

All that had disappeared, of course. The only respectable home in Philadelphia that still opened its doors to him was Judge Madison's. Old friends, when they bothered to acknowledge him at all, did so with frigid politeness or uncomfortable nervousness.

Would the people currently strolling around Regina's back lawn still offer friendly smiles, warm welcomes and open invitations to visit if they knew his history? Even though he knew himself innocent of the charges against him, he still felt like a fraud, as if he were here under false pretenses.

It would always be that way, until he cleared his name. Which made this little expedition more than just an irritant. Every day, every hour he was away from Philadelphia meant that much more of a delay in clearing his name.

He shook off those thoughts. No point chafing at things he couldn't change.

Regina's friends had welcomed them all with open arms. His three companions were at least putting on a good show of enthusiasm for the town and its citizenry. Even Mitchell had relaxed enough to smile and chat with the other guests. Now that the game was on, they all seemed serious about wanting this "fresh start" to work.

Adam scooped up a ball that had escaped from Jack and his friends. He tossed it back to them, then moved on before the pair of matrons walking purposefully his way could corner him.

No doubt about it, Regina's garden party was a success. The adults chattered with the "honored guests" or each other in ever-shifting clusters. The food table was visited frequently and the punch bowl refilled at regular intervals. Even the children seemed to be enjoying themselves as they played on one end of the lawn.

"...having a party so soon after Lemuel's death is pushing the bounds of propriety."

Adam paused, frowning at the three ladies standing nearby. Was this the opinion held by most of Regina's neighbors?

"Oh, for goodness sake, Eula Fay, it's no such thing," one of the other women said.

"Lemuel's been gone for four months now," the third woman added. "He wasn't even Reggie's blood kin. Besides, she has an obligation to her grandfather to see..."

Adam moved on, satisfied the self-righteous Eula Fay was in the minority. He wouldn't want to be responsible for setting tongues wagging any more than necessary.

He'd marked this Eula Fay though. If he remembered right, she was Mayor Sanders's wife. He'd do some digging to find out if she had a particular axe to grind with the judge's granddaughter. Not that it would be hard to imagine the outspoken Miss Nash making a few enemies among her acquaintances.

"There you are, Mr. Barr."

Adam looked around to find the subject of his thoughts approaching with a man, woman and young lady in tow. As if to confirm his earlier thoughts she had a wicked glint in her eye that belied her otherwise bland expression.

"I believe you met Reverend Harper after the service this morning," she continued in her best hostess voice.

Adam gave her a long, steady look, then bowed to the inevitable. He offered his hand to the gray-haired, scholarly-looking gentleman. "Good afternoon, sir. That was a fine sermon today."

The reverend took his hand and pumped it vigorously before releasing it. Where Adam had expected an air of dignified solemnity, he spied an unexpected trace of good humor in the cleric's expression. "Thank you, Mr. Barr. That's most kind of you to say. Please allow me to introduce my wife, Anna, and my daughter, Constance."

Adam greeted the sweet-faced woman on the reverend's arm and the spectacle-wearing adolescent at his side.

Regina gave him a my-job-is-done-here smile. "I'll leave you to get acquainted while I check on some of the other guests."

Adam watched her walk away, sourly amused by her skillful manipulation. She didn't go far, though, pausing to speak to a group standing just a few feet away. Did she plan to keep an eye on him? Was this a test of some sort?

"So, Mr. Barr, what is your interest in our town?"

Adam turned back to Reverend Harper, though part of his attention remained focused on Regina. "Sir?"

"Mr. Fulton is looking into the possibility of starting a newspaper. Mr. Parker is considering the position we have for a new teacher. And young Chance seems interested in the Blue Bottle Saloon building." He waved a hand. "I just wonder where your interests lie."

This wasn't the first time today Adam had been asked that question. He trotted out the response he'd used earlier. "I'm afraid I'm just along on this trip for the company. I'm not looking to relocate at this time. There's too much unfinished business waiting for me in Philadelphia."

"Ah, our loss, I suppose. But I hope you enjoy your visit. How long do you plan to be here?"

"About a month, give or take." He watched Regina from the corner of his eye. "Actually, I made the trip more as a favor to Miss Nash's grandfather than anything else. He asked me to check on how she and Jack are faring since Mr. Willis's death. Judge Madison is naturally concerned since there's no man to look out for them now."

Regina's back stiffened as if an invisible string had jerked her upright. So she *was* eavesdropping.

"Mother?" The girl pushed her glasses higher on the bridge of her nose. "Is it all right if I go visit with Rosie?"

The reverend's wife nodded indulgently. "Run along, dear." Then she turned to her husband and Adam. "If you gentlemen will excuse me, I want to ask Doris Greene how her son is doing." She smiled at Adam. "Mr. Barr, it was very nice to meet you."

Adam bowed. "My pleasure, ma'am." Now if he could disentangle himself from her husband as easily.

But Reverend Harper seemed in no hurry to move on. "If I may be so bold as to ask, what sort of work do you do in Philadelphia?"

Adam hesitated a heartbeat, very aware of Regina's within-earshot presence. Then he carefully schooled his features. "I'm a lawyer by profession."

Regina had half turned in his direction as he spoke. Had she been on the verge of rescuing him? Or unmasking him?

Her gaze met his briefly, then she turned back to the woman at her side. Regardless of her original impulse, it seemed Miss Nash had decided to let his story stand.

"Ah," Reverend Harper reclaimed his attention. "I see why Reggie's grandfather entrusted you to check on matters here. You may rest assured, she and Jack are well taken care of. That's one thing about a small town, folks look out for their neighbors." He gave Adam a just-between-us smile. "And Reggie is quite a resourceful young lady. I'm sure she'll manage things with ease."

Resourceful—Adam supposed that was one way to describe her.

The reverend stroked his chin. "You know, Turnabout could certainly use a lawyer. A shame you're not looking to make your home here." He held up a hand. "Not that we have a lot of crime, mind you. Turnabout's a peaceful community. But there are always legal matters to settle—land claims, contract interpretation, that sort of thing."

Adam refrained from comment. Until he managed to clear his name, he didn't figure he'd be anyone's choice as an advocate on legal matters. Which only drove home again how much better he could be spending his time if he were in Philadelphia.

Reverend Harper gave a self-deprecating smile. "Sorry. I didn't mean to go on with all that arm-twisting. I'm sure you have a much more exciting practice back in Philadelphia than what we could offer here."

Thankfully, the reverend was hailed just then and excused himself from Adam's side.

Adam moved toward the refreshments, carefully sidestepping groups of chattering guests, and helped himself to a glass of punch.

Regina appeared at his elbow and refilled her own punch glass. Was she going to chide him for his evasiveness?

"Enjoying yourself?" she asked instead.

"Best party I've attended in the last six years," he replied dryly.

She arched a brow, but didn't take advantage of the opening he'd handed her.

So, she really *was* going to let the subject lie. Was it consideration for his feelings?

He grimaced. More likely she held off because she knew any public notoriety heaped on him would reflect on her.

Adam turned and motioned toward the crowd with his glass. "Quite a turnout for such short notice."

He had to give her credit, her plan had worked masterfully. In one bold stroke, she'd introduced the men to the town, explained their purpose for being here in a way that seemed perfectly logical and actually had the townsfolk excited about the addition of three relative strangers into their community.

"I can tell you're not familiar with small town life," she said with a smile. "The arrival of not one but *four* strangers is news. The fact that three of you are considering moving here and that you went to such lengths to seek me out immediately is downright gossip-worthy."

She took a sip from her cup. "Why, there's not a soul in town who wasn't already dying to meet the four of you before we even showed up."

Her knuckles whitened as she tightened her hold on the glass. "Even if I'd given only an hour's notice, the turnout would have been the same. In fact, this will probably go down as *the* social event of the year."

Her bitter tone reminded him just how little she wanted them here. He'd forgotten for a moment she was doing this because she had no choice, not because she wanted to.

"Isn't that every hostess's dream?"

Regina shot him a look that would have chilled a flame. Then she produced a mock-sweet smile. "Now, let's see. Who haven't I introduced you to yet?"

He groaned inwardly, knowing she'd just put an end to his attempt to remain on the fringes of the gathering. She definitely wasn't afraid to attack a man's weak spots.

"Ah, yes," she said with suspicious glee, "there's Thomas Pierce. You'll definitely want to meet him. Thomas and Lemuel shared ownership in the bank, and he's currently seeing after Jack's interests."

She placed her now empty glass on the far end of the table. "As Grandfather's agent, you'll want to have Mr. Pierce open the books to you, something he'll be more than happy to do." She gave him a sugary smile. "You'll find he's quite enthusiastic when it comes to explaining the finer points of the bank's operations. Why, I imagine he'd be glad to give you *hours* of his time discussing it."

She placed a hand over her heart. "And, after all, a mere woman like myself can't be expected to understand such matters."

There it was, the burr under her saddle, the thing she couldn't let go. He knew his comment had only exacerbated her irritation. But why couldn't she believe the judge was concerned for her welfare, not doubting her abilities?

Regina brushed at her skirt as she turned to face him. "Now, take my arm and smile as if you're having a grand time."

"How about I just take your arm and try not to glower?"

"An improvement, to be sure." With that, she placed her hand on his arm and faced forward with a polite smile.

Moving across the lawn, she paused twice to greet guests along the way, before finally leading him to a rotund, balding man with a sonorous voice and a commanding presence. "Mr. Pierce, I'd like to introduce you to Mr. Adam Barr." She released Adam's arm. "I was just explaining to Mr. Barr that you and Lemuel were partners and that you're helping me watch out for Jack's interests."

"Mr. Barr." The banker offered his hand with a jovial smile.

"It's a pleasure to meet you, sir." Adam let the man pump his hand enthusiastically twice and then firmly withdrew it.

"What do you think about Turnabout so far?"

"Seems a nice, friendly town." One he'd be glad to shake the dust of from his feet as soon as possible.

Pierce beamed as if Adam had just praised him personally. "Oh, it *is* that, all right. Although I imagine it seems small and provincial by Philadelphia standards."

Before Adam could respond, Regina spoke up. "I'm sure Mr. Barr will agree that Turnabout has a certain charm all its own."

Pierce nodded. "Quite right. And don't let looks fool you. We're a very forward-thinking community." He leaned back on the heels of his feet. "Ever since the railroad came through here we've made all sorts of improvements. Did you notice the fancy streetlights on Main Street?"

Regina met Adam's gaze with an amused glint in her eye. "Mr. Pierce was the driving force behind many of our town's recent modernizations," she said in an ingenuous tone.

Adam took her cue and made the appropriate "very impressive" noises.

Which seemed all the encouragement the banker

needed. "I think you gentlemen will be wonderful additions to our community."

Regina nodded solemnly. "My grandfather assures me that to him, they're like part of the family."

Adam bit back a smile at her dry observation. But the undercurrents seemed to sail right over the banker's head.

Pierce nodded affably. "Well, that's a good enough endorsement for me. A newspaper is just the thing our town needs. And the Blue Bottle Saloon has been closed down for far too long. It'll be good to inject new blood, not to mention new businesses, into our town."

"That's very welcoming of you, sir," Adam said, trying to stem the gentleman's effusiveness, "but I'm afraid I'm just visiting, and none of the others have made up their minds to stay just yet."

The older man clapped him on the back. "Just give us time, son. We'll win you over, I'm certain of it."

"And you're the man to do it," Regina said enthusiastically. "Mr. Barr just needs the right kind of encouragement."

Adam shot her a warning look.

But she smiled and turned back to the banker. "Adam is also here as Grandfather's agent."

Surely she wasn't planning to tell this man about the judge's marriage scheme? Not after her repeated insistence that they all keep it secret.

"He's going to be taking a look at how the construction on the schoolhouse is coming along," Regina continued.

"Excellent." Mr. Pierce gave Adam a beaming smile. "I'm confident you'll like what you see. As a member of the town council, I had a hand in approving those plans myself."

"I'm certain everything is in order." Adam gave Regina a pointed look. "But as a businessman, you know how important it is to follow up on these things. Judge Madison didn't want Miss Nash to have to bother trying to keep up with all the nagging little details."

She took a sip from her cup. "Grandfather is so very thoughtful of my welfare." She smiled at Mr. Pierce again. "I was thinking it might be a good idea for Mr. Barr to take a look at the books while he's here. I'm sure Grandfather would rest easier if he had another man's word for their soundness rather than just mine."

Mr. Pierce's smile stiffened a bit as he looked at Adam. "Does Judge Madison believe there's some problem with my handling of the funds? If he'd prefer to have his own man come in and act in Jack's stead—"

"No, no, nothing of the sort," Adam reassured him. "Again, just good business practice."

The man relaxed. "Of course. We'll have to make an appointment for one day next week."

Before Adam could respond, a young woman strolled up. She was pretty in a flashy sort of way, the type of woman Adam thought of as a socially acceptable Jezebel. While there was nothing overtly immodest about her, she dressed and moved in a way calculated to command the attention of every man there. And she had a pretty, pouty smile. Her artless appearance was likely the result of endless hours of practice.

No doubt her words would drip honey when she spoke. Emma, his former fiancée, had been just such a woman.

Too bad he hadn't seen through her facade sooner.

"Thomas, dear," she said, claiming the banker's arm, "you mustn't hog the company of one of Reggie's honored guests."

Yep, her voice was as sweetly pitched and the words as flirtatiously delivered as he had guessed.

The banker's chest puffed out visibly as he patted the woman's arm. "Sorry, my dear." He turned to Adam. "Mr. Barr, allow me to introduce you to my wife, Eileen."

This was Pierce's *wife?* Why, she must be a good fifteen years younger than her husband. "Mrs. Pierce." Adam bent over her proffered hand, as much to hide his reaction as to be polite.

"How do you do, Mr. Barr?" She flashed a coy smile. "I do hope my husband hasn't bored you by extolling the virtues of our little backwash version of paradise." Her gaze studied him like a cat eyeing a bowl of cream.

"Not at all. I find your husband's enthusiasm quite refreshing." Adam took Regina's arm. "I hope the two of you will excuse us, but there's a matter I need to discuss with Miss Nash."

Mrs. Pierce's eyes flashed with surprised displeasure. Apparently she was used to a very different reaction from the men in her circle.

Her husband, however, smiled and waved a hand. "Of course. But I insist on having you and your friends over to our home for supper soon."

Adam bowed again. "I'm sure I speak for my friends as well as myself when I say it will be our pleasure." With that he gave Regina's arm a squeeze and turned her firmly toward a less crowded part of the lawn.

Reggie allowed Adam to lead her toward the large oak that shaded a quiet corner of her backyard. The determination in his expression hinted at some pent-up emotion. What was it? Irritation? Outright anger?

Deciding not to let him get in the first word, she stopped and turned to face him. "What was it you wished to discuss?"

His smile was polite, but his eyes conveyed a different emotion. "I wanted to make certain you fully understand I'm not one of your suitors." He enunciated each word with a chisel-hard precision, echoed by the flinty glare in his eyes. "I am under *no* obligation to jump at your bidding."

That's what *he* thought. If he was trying to intimidate her, he had failed miserably. She lifted a hand to her heart. "Why Mr. Barr, is that what you were doing—jumping to my bidding? I had no idea."

He didn't seem amused by her light treatment of his attempted scold. It was fascinating to see how the dimple in his chin deepened when he clenched his jaw.

"Miss Nash, why do you insist on treating me like I'm the enemy? I assure you, I'm not."

Reggie's own amusement died. "On the contrary, sir," she said grimly, "I consider any person who has both the power and the resolve to take Jack from me my enemy."

He raked a hand through his hair. "You know perfectly well that isn't the outcome either your grandfather or I wish for."

"But I also know *you*, Mr. Barr, and I know that you'll do what you believe to be your duty, whether you wish to or not."

He stiffened and his face reflected some dark, bitter emotion. "You *know* me? I think not. Until two days ago we hadn't even seen each other for seven years. Before that, you were barely out of the schoolroom and I was an adult. I doubt we spoke two words to each other during any of your many visits to Philadelphia."

His jaw tightened. "And even if you had some inkling of who I was back then, that man no longer exists." He turned his glower full on her. "No, Miss Nash, you might know something *of* me, but you don't *know* me."

She met his gaze levelly, her own emotions rising. "I may have been little more than a schoolgirl, but I spent many hours eavesdropping on the conversation in my grandfather's parlor. You and your friends debated everything from law to politics to social issues."

She saw he still didn't believe her. Very well. "I know you are passionate about not just the law but about seeing justice done. I know you pride yourself on owing nothing to anyone. I know you set high standards for yourself and for those around you."

She placed her hand on his arm again, looking straight ahead as they resumed their stroll. "You have a soft spot for strawberry teacakes, you show the same consideration to servants that you do to peers and you don't really like Grandfather's favorite port, though you drink it anyway to be polite."

She felt him looking at her. Did he believe her now? "I know you place great store on loyalty, but like most men you set a different standard for women and can be taken in by a sweet face and honeyed words."

She lifted her chin. "I also know you view things as either right or wrong, black or white. You don't have much use for the middle ground. You would rather take a bullet than compromise your values or beliefs. And because I know all of this, I know you could not have committed the crime you were convicted of, because no amount of money would tempt you to break the law."

His step faltered the merest bit at that, but he recovered quickly.

She turned and met his gaze once more. "And that, sir, is why I fear you. Because my world is filled with compromises and shades of gray, which you will never understand or accept. And also because I know with absolute certainty that you will take Jack from me if you feel you must in order to keep your word to my grandfather."

Please tell me I'm wrong, that I have nothing to fear from you.

Chapter Eight

Adam stepped through Regina's front gate, the need to escape her perceptive gaze driving him forward.

He felt as if she'd stripped him bare and flayed him for good measure. His mind was spinning in an attempt to take in all she'd said. He only hoped whatever excuse he'd given before he made his exit had been coherent.

She had been *that* intuitive at fifteen?

She'd even figured out what a blind fool he'd been when it came to sweet-mannered, lovely, fickle Emma.

It wasn't enough Regina had reduced him to a set of faults and virtues. Within a space of seconds she'd graced him with her belief in his innocence and cursed him with her fear of his intentions.

How in the world was he supposed to respond to such a speech?

Stuffing his hands in his pockets, Adam turned left, toward Turnabout's Main Street. Might as well do a bit of exploring, scout out whatever there was to see here.

Thirty minutes later he found himself on the edge of town, near the railroad depot. He had studied every storefront, explored every side street the town had to offer.

He shook his head at the sparseness of the offerings. For most people here, Turnabout was all they knew of the world. But Regina had spent a great deal of time in Philadelphia. She'd experienced theater, libraries, elegant shops, museums. How could she willingly choose to live here when she *knew* how much more the world had to offer?

Was the freedom to live her eccentric lifestyle so important to her? What about the cultural experiences she was denying Jack?

What had she meant when she said her life was filled with compromises?

Adam shook off his musings, not wanting to think about that conversation just yet.

What decision she made or why she made it wasn't really his concern. He was just here to carry out Judge Madison's wishes.

Adam rubbed the back of his neck. Now what? He was tempted to saddle Trib and head out for a good gallop. Might clear his head a bit. But he probably should return to the party, just to make certain everyone was still playing their parts properly.

Not to mention that he'd been one of the guests of honor.

Squaring his shoulders, Adam turned and retraced his steps. In much too short a time he had Regina's house in sight again.

"Hello." Eileen Pierce, her arm linked through her husband's, stepped through the front gate. "We wondered where you'd gotten off to."

Adam assumed the easy smile that had once been

second nature to him. "I needed to stretch my legs a bit." He included Thomas Pierce in his glance. "I took the opportunity to make a tour of your fair town."

"Well, I certainly hope you liked what you saw," the banker responded. "I haven't given up trying to convince you to make your home here."

"Yes indeed." Mrs. Pierce looked up through her lashes. "We would all be very happy to welcome you into our midst."

"That is most kind of you both, but as tempting as it sounds, I'm afraid that won't be possible." Adam shook his head as if disappointed. "I'm afraid there's just too much business I left unfinished back in Philadelphia." He stepped aside to wave them on. "Please, don't let me hold you up."

Adam nodded a farewell and strode forward. He paused to exchange pleasantries with another group of departing guests before he reached the back lawn. Perhaps the party was finally breaking up.

He rounded the corner of the house to discover he was in luck. The only people in sight were Regina's household and her "suitors."

Regina had her back to him and was busy handing out assignments.

He paused, watching the commander address her troops.

"Since you three are like members of the family now," she said, "I'm sure you won't mind helping clean up."

Mitchell rolled up his sleeves. "Of course not. Just tell us what you need done."

Adam noticed Everett and Chance didn't look quite so agreeable, but neither did they refuse.

"To start, the three of you can move the chairs back inside. Mrs. Peavy will show you where everything goes."

She turned to Ira. "Would you take care of the punch bowl and tablecloths please?"

Then she looked at Jack. "And as for you, young man—" her voice softened as she ruffled the boy's hair "—you can help me gather up the glasses and the napkins."

Adam stepped forward. "And what job do you have for me?"

Regina turned and her gaze searched his warily. But she gave no other sign she remembered their earlier conversation. "So, you decided to grace us with your presence again."

He shrugged. "It's my job to check in on the players of this little game periodically."

Jack tugged on Regina's skirt. "What game is he talking about, Aunt Reggie?"

She shot Adam a displeased schoolmarm look before she smiled down at her nephew. "Mr. Barr was teasing, Jack. He didn't mean a game the way you think of one. Don't pay him any mind."

Laying a hand on Jack's shoulder, she faced Adam again. "If you're really interested in helping, you can disassemble the table once Ira clears it. Ira can show you where we stow the boards and sawhorses."

"Of course," he said. But he was talking to her back. She'd already started gathering the discarded dishes.

Twenty minutes later, Adam unrolled his sleeves. Under Regina's watchful eyes, the cleanup had been completed in less time than he would have imagined. Other than a few trampled flowers near the porch, the large backyard no longer showed any traces of the festivities that had taken place earlier.

Everett sat on one of the steps of the wraparound porch, leaning lazily back against the rail. Mitchell stood by the back door, helping Mrs. Peavy fill a large washtub on the kitchen porch. Chance, with Jack at his side, had finally managed to approach Buck on civil, if not friendly, terms.

Regina marched toward the back porch, toting a large basket loaded with dirty dishes.

Adam moved to intercept her. "Here, let me take that."

He thought for a moment she would refuse.

Then she nodded. "Thank you." She handed him the basket and immediately moved away. "Let me grab those two cups from over there and we can take them inside."

A large kettle of water simmered on the stove. It filled the small, cozy kitchen with a humid heat that pounced on them as soon as they entered the room. Adam saw the stray tendrils at her nape slowly but defiantly coil into springlike curls, saw the moisture sheen on her face like a damp mask.

She glanced his way and nodded toward the kettle. "If you don't mind, could you pour that into the basin here? Then we can set these dishes to soaking."

Adam nodded and set the basket on the table. This stiff formality had him on edge. He felt he should say something, but he couldn't for the life of him figure out what.

As soon as he emptied the kettle, Regina placed the two glasses she held into the hot water. She reached for the basket to take care of the others, but Adam stopped her. "Here, let me hand them to you."

She nodded and without a word, they emptied the basket.

This is ridiculous. This isn't a two-person job. I should just get out of the way and let her finish up, or send her away and do it myself.

But for some reason he couldn't bring himself to say anything. Besides, they were almost done now.

When she reached for the final dish, though, her wet hands failed to get a good hold. As she bobbled the cup, Adam reached over and grasped both the cup and her hands between his own.

Her gaze jerked up to his and for a moment they stood there, frozen. Her dragon's scale eyes darkened until they were almost deep purple, and a small muscle quivered at her throat.

She'd said she believed him innocent.

She knew he liked strawberry tarts.

His grip tightened on her hands. Was the rapid pulse beat he felt coming from his veins or hers?

"What do you think you're doing?"

At Mrs. Peavy's sternly uttered question, Adam jerked his hands back and the cup went crashing to the floor.

Regina bent to pick up the pieces, but not before he saw the flush climb into her cheeks.

"I thought I'd help clean the dishes." Her voice sounded almost composed.

"So I see," Mrs. Peavy said dryly. "Now, you two get out of my kitchen before you break the rest of the china." She emphasized her words with shooing motions. "I'll take care of this mess. You have guests you should see to."

Reggie was more than happy to escape the too-close confines of the kitchen. With a nod, she deposited the broken bits of china on the counter and wiped her hands on a dry dish rag. "If you don't want our help, we'll leave it to you. But you know very well those gentlemen out there are not really my guests."

She moved to the back door that Adam already held open for her. "As it happens, though, there *are* a few things I'd like to discuss with our friends from Philadelphia."

Reggie stepped outside and immediately put some distance between herself and Adam.

She drew a deep breath, trying to clear her senses along with the humid air from her lungs. What had happened in there a moment ago? It had been the same as the time Adam caught her in that near-fall back at the cabin two days ago.

She might as well face the truth. Something about Adam Barr still touched her on a level she couldn't fight. He remained the white knight of her dreams, a knight whose armor was tarnished but who continued to fight the good fight.

Any unexpected touch from him did something to her, scrambled her senses in a way she didn't like at all. She could not afford to feel those things.

Especially not now, when she needed her wits about her more than ever.

What had she been thinking? She should never have said all those things to him. It gave him an unfair advantage over her, revealed too much about how she felt.

Well, if he tried to use that against her, he was going to be disappointed. She was no simpering debutante. She might be attracted to him, but that attraction wasn't so potent that she couldn't resist.

Reggie lifted her head, feeling more in control.

Mr. Fulton and Chance were just as she'd left them. Mr. Parker had strolled over to the oak tree and was deep in conversation with Ira.

"Mr. Barr," she said, careful to keep her tone formal, "I'd be obliged if you'd gather up Chance and Mr. Parker and join me and Mr. Fulton on the side porch."

"Of course."

Everett stood as she approached.

His movements conveyed a practiced ease, his smile a cynical humor. "Allow me to compliment you on the success of your soiree. I suppose this is the kind of social highlight I can look forward to reporting on in upcoming editions of the *Turnabout Gazette*."

Reggie took a seat on a comfortable chair and arranged her skirt. "Don't worry, Mr. Fulton. There will be all sorts of news to fill your society pages—barn raisings, church socials, quilting bees, the monthly dance in the town square." She paused a moment. "And then, of course, there's the occasional wedding to look forward to."

Was that a wince? If so, he recovered quickly. "It sounds like Turnabout is veritable whirl of social activity."

Before she could respond, the other men joined them.

"Well, do you think we passed muster with your neighbors?" Chance asked.

"They seemed quite impressed," Reggie responded. She placed a finger to her chin as if remembering something. "Of course they had that same reaction when a medicine show came through with a trained bear last month."

Far from taking offense, Chance's eyes lit up. "Now that must have been something to see."

Reggie resisted the urge to roll her eyes. Mercy, but this one really was young.

Her gaze met Adam's and she saw that same sentiment in his expression.

"Ah, yes," Everett drawled, pulling her gaze back to him, "another of the cultural delights one can look forward to as part of life in Turnabout."

"Very true. If my grandfather led you to believe otherwise, I'm afraid you were misinformed. No one would blame a man of your obvious refinement if you just packed up your bags and returned to Philadelphia."

He raised his brow and gave her a knowing smile. "On the contrary, I will consider it part of my service to this community to introduce an element of sophistication and artistic enlightenment to their lives."

Oh, but it was going to be satisfying to take this one down a peg or two. "How charitable of you to take us heathens under your wing."

Mitchell cleared his throat. "Perhaps we should discuss what our next steps are."

Adam leaned back against the porch support. Regardless of what had passed between him and Regina, he still had a job to perform, and as she had so eloquently pointed out, he *would* do it.

"Excellent idea," Regina said, answering Mitchell's suggestion. "I think we've made a good first impression. Still, for this whirlwind courtship to be convincing, it's important that we be seen spending as much time together as possible without causing an outright scandal."

Adam found her attitude amusing. "I assume you have something specific in mind."

"Of course. Starting tomorrow, you are all hereby invited to take your suppers here with us. That will allow us to be in each other's company at least once each day. It will also give Jack a chance to get better acquainted with you, and you with him."

She glanced Adam's way. "That includes you. Even if you're not a participant in this lottery, we should keep up appearances that we're all one happy group of friends."

Adam nodded. "I'd be honored."

She gave him a searching look, then turned back to the others. "And in case you were wondering, I was being polite when I said this was an invitation. I expect you to be here unless we agree to different plans ahead of time." Then she smiled. "But don't worry, you'll find Mrs. Peavy sets a much better table than anything you'll get at Mrs. Ortolon's."

"Is that it?" Adam knew it wasn't, but he wasn't above giving her the cues she needed.

"Of course not. That only covers our group time. I'll also need to be seen with each of my beaus individually so it appears there's some actual courting going on."

She spread her hands. "Folks'll naturally make allowances for a bit of strangeness since you all are from back East, but we need to make your actions seem as reasonable as possible. I've given this a great deal of thought."

I'll just bet you have, Adam thought.

"What I've come up with isn't perfect, but I trust you'll all do your part to make it work. It's the best I could do with such short notice."

The look she threw Adam's way seemed to blame him for her lack of adequate planning time.

She turned to Mitchell. "I'm guessing you're not a

stranger to hard work. There are a number of repairs that are needed here at the house—shingles need replacing, the workshed needs painting, the fence needs work. I've been meaning to have it all taken care of for some time. I've even gotten the needed supplies. But Ira gets insulted every time I mention hiring it out."

She stroked her chin with her forefinger. "However, should a friend of the family volunteer to lend a hand, I'm sure Ira would be grateful for the help. As, of course, would I."

Everett spoke up before Mitchell could respond. "Miss Nash, were you under the impression that we were sent here to be slave laborers for you?"

Adam suspected Everett wasn't so much outraged on Mitchell's behalf as he was worried he'd be assigned a similar role.

"I'm under the impression, Mr. Fulton, that my grandfather sent you here to impress me with your ability to provide for myself and Jack. Fancy back-east manners, pretty words and even a plum position in the community aren't enough—at least not for me."

She lifted her chin. "But, please wait your turn. I believe I was speaking to Mr. Parker."

Mitchell nodded. "I'll be glad to help. I'm not much for just sitting around anyway. I'd welcome some physical activity to keep me occupied over the coming days."

"Good."

Regina swung around to face Chance, and the young man drew himself up as if facing a judge in court.

Adam caught an annoyed expression on Everett's face. Was she deliberately making him wait until last?

"The members of our congregation are trying to raise funds to replace our church organ. One thing we're planning to accomplish this is a fair. Among other things, I'm working with the committee that's planning activities for the children. I would be pleased to have you volunteer to lend a hand with that."

Chance frowned. "Why certainly, if you want me to. But I don't know anything about entertaining children."

"Don't be modest," Everett said in mock-camaraderie. "It hasn't been all that long since you were playing tag with your chums yourself."

Chance's eyes narrowed and his hands clenched, but before he could do more, Regina intervened. "Don't worry about lack of experience, Chance," she reassured. "Others will do most of the planning. You'll just be there to help out."

With a firmly planted smile she turned to Everett. "Now, Mr. Fulton, shall we discuss your role?"

"Saved the best for last, did you?" The bravado in his tone would have been convincing but for the apprehension shadowing his smile.

"You might say that. As a reporter, you're going to develop a keen interest in my photography work. So much so, that you're going to volunteer to accompany me and lend a hand on several outdoor sessions I have scheduled over the coming days."

Immediately the apprehension disappeared to be replaced by relief. "An admirable plan," Everett agreed.

"Is that it?" Chance asked in disgust. "Seems to me he's getting off mighty easy."

Reggie raised a brow. "Do you find my plans for you unpleasant, Chance?"

The would-be businessman flushed. "No, ma'am. It's just that—"

She wagged a finger at him. "Don't concern yourself with the assignments I've handed out to the others. As I said, I've given this lots of thought and I'm certain you'll find it's pretty evenhanded in the end."

Adam suspected Everett wouldn't be getting off as lightly as he imagined.

She included them all in her glance again. "Now, does anyone have questions?"

Mitchell raised a hand. "When would you like me to get started, and what do I tackle first?"

"Your enthusiasm is commendable, Mr. Parker, but there's no need to start right away. Check with Ira and see what works best for him. In fact, I'd like to take you down to the schoolhouse tomorrow morning and let you see how the construction is progressing."

He nodded. "It would be my pleasure. Shall I meet you here at, say, nine-thirty?"

"Nine-thirty would be fine."

Regina turned to Everett. "I'll be visiting the Keeter family at their farm east of town tomorrow afternoon. I believe that would be an ideal time to have you begin assisting me."

He executed a theatrical bow. "My time is yours to command."

She stood. "Chance, we'll discuss your role further after supper tomorrow evening. Now, if you will excuse me, it's been a long day. I'd like to change out of these fancy duds and spend some time doing something I actually enjoy this afternoon."

Nothing equivocal about that dismissal. Adam took his leave with the others, but parted company with them at the front gate, heading toward a country lane he'd spied earlier.

He had some thinking to do and it was best done alone.

He'd come close to letting things get away from him

in the kitchen. No doubt his slip was due in part to their earlier conversation.

She wasn't even the kind of girl he was normally attracted to. There was nothing polished or refined about the judge's granddaughter—in fact, just the opposite.

But as contrary and infuriating as she was, that can't-keep-me-down spirit appealed to him in spite of himself. And her efforts to hide those flashes of vulnerability that occasionally showed through touched him in a way that weepy, hand-wringing, damsel-in-distress tactics never would.

But he had to remember that he was here to see her married to one of the others, not entangle his own life with hers.

Adam bent to pick up a pebble, then flung it with as much force as he could summon. Why had the judge picked him for this assignment?

Then he straightened. "Why" didn't matter. The judge *had* selected him and that was that. There was no way that he was going to betray the trust of the one man who had stood by him these past six years.

He'd endured squalid living conditions, back-breaking forced labor, sadistic guards and dangerous cellmates without letting it crush his spirit or his body.

Surely he could survive a few weeks spent with this one spirited female.

Couldn't he?

Chapter Nine

Reggie, now comfortably attired in a worn but serviceable dress, stepped inside her studio to find Ira there ahead of her.

"That was quite a shindig you threw," he said, opening the curtains to let more light into the spacious ground floor room. "Folks'll be talking about it for days to come."

"They'll be talking about our friends from Philadelphia, you mean."

Ira cut her a probing glance. "They all seem nice enough. You could do worse in a husband."

Reggie groaned. "Not you, too? You know as well as I do that it has nothing to do with what sort of men they are. Even if Grandfather had sent Prince Charming himself, I'd still refuse. Marriage just isn't for me."

"Seems your granddaddy has a different opinion. Can't say as I disagree with him, either."

Why was Ira talking this way? He knew how she felt about this and why. "I'm not marrying anyone, and that's that."

Ready to change the subject, she glanced around and

wrinkled her nose. "This place could do with the services of a broom and dust rag."

Ira gave her a hard look, then followed her lead. "We *were* gone for over a week."

Relieved that he'd backed down for now, Reggie set her handbag on the counter. "True. Which do you want—broom or dust rag?"

Ira shook his head. "It's still Sunday. The cleaning will keep 'til tomorrow." He made shooing motions. "Get yourself on upstairs. You know good and well you won't be no good for anything else with your mind on them photographs."

Reggie laughed and held up her hands. "All right." But instead of going upstairs immediately, she stood there, chewing on her lower lip.

"So," she said casually, "what do *you* think of our visitors?"

Ira cocked a shaggy eyebrow. "Well now, that depends. Do you mean as individuals, as perspective fathers for Jack, or as perspective husbands for you?"

She fiddled with a button on her dress, not quite meeting his gaze. "All of the above, I suppose."

"Well, they all four show potential, though each in a different way."

"Four?" She glanced up in surprise. "You forget, Mr. Barr is only here as an observer."

Ira shook his head. "I didn't forget. You just asked me what I thought of the visitors, not of your suitors."

She looked away, nudging her purse until it was centered on the counter. "Did you know Mr. Barr spent time in prison?"

"Something about stealing company funds, wasn't it? If I recollect right, your granddaddy came out solidly on Mr. Barr's side." He gave her a pointed look. "And I also seem to remember a certain young lady following the case about as close as anyone could from hundreds of miles away."

"He was found guilty."

"True. Served his time, though. Paid his debt to society. Seems like he deserves a fresh start."

She straightened. "Be that as it may, he's not one of the suitors, nor does he seem to want to be."

Forcing a cheerful smile, she crossed the room. "Don't feel you need to stick around here on my account. I know the way home."

Ira nodded. "Okay. But if you're not back at the house by supper time I'm coming back to fetch you."

With a wave Reggie headed upstairs, shaking off the unexpected flash of moodiness. As she stepped into the mostly open second floor, the old feeling of anticipation hit her.

Most folks wrinkled their noses at the chemical scent permeating the place, but not Reggie. To her it was the smell of coming home, of the childhood she'd spent watching her father at work.

Humming, she reached for the thick, stained smock she wore over her clothes. She couldn't wait to see how her latest batch of photographs turned out.

Sometime later, Reggie stepped back and studied her work laid out on the drying trays. All in all, not a bad collection of work. The pictures ranged from passing fair to downright wonderful, if she did say so herself.

And one in particular—Reggie stepped over to study it again. Yep—absolutely stunning. The main focus was a prickly vine adorned with three flowers. The plant itself didn't appear remarkable, but Reggie had never seen one like it before. She always felt a rush of excitement when she stumbled on a new find. The slender vine, twined around a woody stalk of grass, was displayed to perfection, perfectly posed by nature itself.

This was the kind of shot she lived for. It would be hard to part with it.

With a satisfied nod, Reggie rolled her neck and shoulders, easing the stiffness from her muscles.

She opened her workroom door, glanced at the next box of plates waiting for her, and chewed her lip indecisively. Her fingers itched to unpack the box and she actually took a few steps toward it before calling herself to task. It was getting late and she didn't want Ira to trouble himself with coming after her.

Humming, she began putting away the chemicals and trays she'd used. Before she'd finished, she heard the sound of footsteps on the stairs. Oh, dear, she'd made Ira come after her after all.

"I'll be done in just a minute," she called over her shoulder.

She heard Ira cross the outer room. "Since you're here, come take a look. I think this is the best lot yet. There's one I'm particularly proud—"

Her smile froze as she looked around and saw Adam in the doorway. "What are you doing here?"

He raised a brow. "Nice to see you again, too."

Reggie lifted her chin, refusing to let him bait her into a response.

He shrugged. "I was out for a stroll and saw Ira headed this way." Adam leaned a shoulder against the doorjamb, managing to fill the space with his very masculine frame. "He asked me to stop in and send you home."

Adam looked around the small workroom, as if curious about what she did up here.

Relieved that he'd broken eye contact, Reggie took a deep breath. *Don't think about that intense moment in the steam-filled kitchen.*

"I'm surprised. Ira knows I don't allow gawkers up here." Hang it all, she hadn't meant to sound so shrewish.

Adam gave her another of those infuriatingly amused smiles. "Apparently Ira doesn't consider me your everyday gawker. In fact, he asked me to escort you home when you get done."

She'd have Ira's head for this. "Thank you, but that's not really necessary. I'm able to find my way home on my own."

"Sorry." Adam sounded anything but. "I gave my word, so it looks like you're stuck with me, whether you like it or not." He crossed his arms and managed to appear both at ease and as immovable as a well-rooted tree at the same time.

Arguing with him would not only be pointless, but would make her seem churlish. Changing tactics, she shrugged. "All right. But be careful. These chemicals can ruin your clothes or worse if you get it on you. In fact," she waved toward a chair on the far wall, "it would be best if you take a seat over there while I finish up."

Naturally he ignored her. Straightening, he moved farther into the workroom. "You mentioned something about a photograph you were proud of?"

"Stop!" She stepped forward, blocking his progress. Too late she realized how close together that placed them. Her first instinct was to step back and put some distance between them, but instead she stood her ground. "If you're not concerned for your own clothing or person, please have some consideration for my work." She fervently hoped he wouldn't notice the slight tremble in her voice.

Adam stared into her eyes without speaking for what seemed forever. What was he thinking? If only she could believe her face reflected the same lack of emotion.

"You think me such a clumsy oaf?"

His mild tone threw her further off balance. Surely he wasn't bothered by her words? "I believe this room is my domain and that you should abide by my wishes," she said firmly.

His lips twitched. Whether that mocking smile was directed at her or inward she couldn't tell.

"Very well." Bending in a too-polite bow, Adam turned and crossed to the chair she'd indicated. Once seated, he folded his arms across his chest, stretched his legs out negligently, and crossed one booted foot over the other. Settling down, he proceeded to watch her with an air of an adult humoring a contrary child.

Reggie turned back to her work, but she was no longer humming. She refused to glance his way, but she could feel his gaze following her every movement. It made her self-conscious, clumsy.

It was a wonder she didn't make a mess of things, but at last all the chemicals were properly stored, the implements cleaned and put away.

Reggie stepped into the outer room and closed the workroom door. "Just let me put this smock away," she said, untying the belt, "and we can go."

He stood, but there was nothing impatient in the

gesture. "No need to rush on my account. I've nothing else to do."

Still he watched her with those penetrating eyes. Reggie was suddenly aware of how stained and ill-fitting her smock was, how mussed her hair must be, how her clothing reeked of the chemicals she had been working with.

Then she put the steel back into her spine. What did she care? She certainly wasn't trying to impress him with her appearance—or anything else for that matter.

Crossing the room with firm, confident steps, Reggie hung the smock on its peg and rolled down the sleeves of her blouse. "I'm ready."

Adam waffled between amusement and irritation with Regina. At least she'd quit blaming him for this heavy-handed matchmaking scheme. Now when she looked at him he didn't see accusation and resentment, only starch and a challenge for control.

He certainly couldn't fault her for that.

When they reached the staircase, instead of escorting her down, Adam motioned to the flight leading to the floor above. "What's up there?"

"My *private* office," she replied "There's not a thing there that would be of interest to you, I'm sure. Now, if you don't mind, I don't want Mrs. Peavy to hold up supper waiting on me."

His curiosity was definitely piqued, but he let it go for now. "Of course. Lead the way."

He followed her stiff back down the stairs, then waited while she fetched her handbag from the counter before moving to open the door. "So, how much business do you actually do here?" Had her father managed to make a living at this before he died? Turnabout seemed much to small a town to make that viable.

"Not afraid to ask personal questions, are you?"

He smiled at her haughty tone. "Just following your lead."

She gave an indignant huff. "If you must know, I do well enough. Father traveled a lot, going where there were more clients, but that isn't an option for me. So I tried a different approach. Every chance I get, I hammer home how great it is to capture special moments with a photograph. Not only for themselves, but as mementos to pass on to their children and grandchildren."

"Hammer home" seemed an apt phrase. Regina Nash wasn't a subtle woman.

"My campaigning has paid off," she continued. "Folks don't even think twice anymore before asking me to take photographs when there's a wedding or christening, or even a barn raising. And I have a few folks who contact me every year, regular as clockwork, for family sittings so they can mark the changes in their children."

Interesting how animated she became when she was talking about this subject.

"And then there's my work with plants," she continued. "The botanical journals pay nicely for the plates they use."

Her voice held a touch of pride. And why not? She had found a way to support her household on her own terms.

"What about you?" she asked. "Have you reopened your law practice?"

Was she trying to get in another jab? But there didn't

seem to be any meanness behind the question, just open curiosity.

"Not much point in it right now." He tried to keep the bitterness from his tone. "No one in Philadelphia wants to be represented by a convicted criminal."

She glanced sideways at him. "There's nothing that says you have to stay in Philadelphia. Why not start over somewhere else?"

"Now you sound like your grandfather."

She smiled. "I'll take that as a compliment. But you didn't answer my question."

"I'm not ready to leave Philadelphia yet. Not until I take care of some unfinished business."

"Unfinished business?"

He gave her a direct look. "Clearing my name."

"Oh."

She didn't say anything else for a moment, and he wondered what she was thinking.

"I'll pray for your success," she said finally.

He decided a change of subject was in order. "What do you think of your suitors so far?"

Her lips compressed. "They seem nice enough. But, as I said before, I'm not in the market for a husband."

And just like that, they were out of the murky, uncomfortable quagmire her question had landed them in and back to that verbal sparring he was more comfortable with.

Reggie rose and set her book aside as Mrs. Peavy led Mitchell into the parlor the next morning. "You're prompt, Mr. Parker. An admirable quality in a man."

Mitchell executed a short bow. "Nine-thirty was

what we agreed on. I don't give my word unless I intend to keep it."

"Another admirable quality. Shall we go?" She moved forward with a breezy smile and he allowed her precede to him from the room.

As they stepped out onto the front porch, Reggie turned her face up to the sunny sky and inhaled deeply. She loved being outdoors. Especially on a day such as today. The only thing that would be better was if she were still at the cabin, where she could dress as she pleased and really enjoy herself.

She *would* still be there if it weren't for the hounds her grandfather had let loose on her.

Before she could stop herself, Reggie cut Mitchell a resentful look.

He responded with a raised brow. "Have I made a misstep already?"

Reggie shook off her sour thoughts. Black moods didn't fix anything and only served to make one more miserable than they already were. "I'm sorry, just a stray thought."

She deliberately changed the subject as they stepped from the porch. "A perfect day for a walk, don't you think?"

"Couldn't imagine a nicer one."

They strolled in silence for a while.

Reggie was acutely conscious of her escort's size. He was such a *large* man. Not big in a beefy way, just tall and broad-shouldered. She felt absolutely dwarfed in his presence but, strangely enough, not threatened. He'd adjusted his steps to match hers and his demeanor was both attentive and polite. Before long, they turned off of her quiet street and onto Main Street.

Mitchell took her arm as they crossed the road. "So, when do you begin quizzing me?"

His directness caught her by surprise and she almost missed a step.

"That *is* why you suggested we walk over to the schoolhouse this morning, isn't it?"

Reggie quickly regained her composure. "So, we won't mince words then. Let's start with your profession. Do you have any experience as a teacher?"

"Actually, yes. I taught for a short time, many years ago."

"Why did you give it up?"

"I joined the army."

"The army?" Reggie didn't know why that revelation surprised her. He had the disciplined bearing of a military man, and he certainly would make an impressive and intimidating soldier. But somehow she couldn't picture him thirsting for battle.

His nod was choppy. "A youthful folly on my part. The call to adventure lured me away from the mundane world of the classroom."

Youthful folly? This solid-as-a-rock man? "Why do you consider that a folly?"

He gave a tight smile she was certain hid some deeper emotion. "I'm afraid military life was not as noble and heroic as I'd imagined." He shrugged. "Or maybe I just didn't have it in me to follow orders unquestioningly."

There was a story there, but Reggie wasn't quite up to pursuing it just now. "How long ago did you return to the life of a civilian?"

"About three years ago."

He certainly wasn't volunteering much information. "And what did you do between that time and now?"

"Purchased a piece of land to farm. Married a fine, peace-loving woman. Buried her. Lost my farm."

"Oh." He might not be talkative, but he certainly could pack a wallop in what few words he did volunteer. His baldly stated history left Reggie momentarily at a loss for what to ask next.

Fortunately, a diversion in the form of the reverend's wife served to fill the silence.

"Reggie, Mr. Parker," Anna Harper said, stopping to greet them. "Good morning to you. A beautiful day, isn't it?" Settling her shopping basket more comfortably on her arm, she seemed ready for a nice, neighborly chat.

"Mrs. Harper." Mitchell tipped his hat, returning the greeting. "Yes, it's quite pleasant out today."

"Is Reggie giving you a tour of the town?"

"Actually," Reggie intervened, "I'm taking him over to the schoolhouse so he can have a look at the facilities."

"Splendid idea." Anna beamed at Reggie's companion. "I'm certain you'll be pleased with what you see." She hefted her basket again. "Well then, I'll get on with my shopping and let you be on your way."

By the time they resumed their walk, Reggie was ready to continue her questioning. "What made you return to teaching now?"

He stared straight ahead. "Even though I didn't stick with it very long, teaching seems to be the one thing I can do well. If I'm going to start a new life, this seemed a good first step."

Why did she get the feeling he was leaving something out? "Why come to Turnabout? Why not start over in Philadelphia?"

"Because there was nothing left to hold me there." He adjusted the tilt of his hat. "Besides, starting fresh means no reminders of past follies or of things that are lost forever." He met her gaze levelly. "I think we've probably covered enough on this particular subject, don't you?"

Reggie couldn't bring herself to take exception to his blunt words. She didn't really enjoy all this probing and digging into the men's private lives. But she didn't have much choice.

"Very well." She'd let the matter drop for now. But she would file this bit of information as something to come back to at another time, in another way. Then she pointed to the left. "The school is this way."

They turned the corner, and she shifted the conversation to a new subject. "How do you feel about becoming the father of a six-year-old?"

He didn't answer immediately, as if he was wrapping his mind around the question. "I've always liked children," he said finally. "Sarah and I had hoped to have a large family." That closed off look crossed his face again and she could almost see the mental shake he gave himself. "Jack seems like a fine boy. I would do my best to raise him proper."

His mention of wanting a large family startled Reggie from her single-minded probing. The heat climbed into her cheeks as she thought of what that might mean. Did he expect—

She scrambled for a new topic to fill the awkward pause. "I saw you speaking to Miss Whitman at the party yesterday. Did the two of you decide how you will divide up the students?"

"Not definitively." He smiled dryly. "After all, I can't commit to taking the position until you've made your selection. However," he continued, "what Mayor Sanders proposed yesterday was that Miss Whitman teach the younger children, say ages six to ten, and I take the older ones."

She nodded. "That makes sense." Janell Whitman, a petite twenty-one-year-old, seemed to have more affinity for the little ones anyway. Some of the older boys had several inches and more than a few pounds on her. Discipline had never seemed to be a problem, but one never knew. And she couldn't imagine Mr. Parker being intimidated by any of the boys, or their fathers either for that matter.

"There it is." She pointed to the schoolhouse. It was July, so there were no classes in session. But even so there was plenty of activity around the building. The sounds of hammers and saws, along with the conversation and grunts of the men wielding the tools, drifted to them as they neared.

Reggie was surprised at the progress made since she left town. The new room was nearly complete. By the time they finished, the schoolhouse would be double its original size.

Word that her grandfather planned to provide money to build a new wing to the schoolhouse had surprised Reggie, but it hadn't raised her suspicions. After all, he had said the donation was in memory of his daughter and granddaughter, and it seemed just the kind of gesture he would make. Especially now that Jack was old enough to start attending.

In hindsight, it was obvious the wily old goat had been scheming this little marriage lottery all along.

"Hello, Calvin," Reggie hailed one of the workers. "Is your father about?"

The young man paused with his hammer in mid-swing, and smiled. "Oh, hi, Miss Nash. Pa's around back discussing the work with someone."

Reggie waved to her companion. "Calvin, this is Mr. Mitchell Parker. He's thinking about taking on the new schoolteacher position."

Then she turned to Mitchell. "Mr. Parker, this is Calvin Hendricks, and that's his brother, James, over there." She pointed to another youth up on the roof. "You met their father, Walter, at the reception yesterday. The three of them are doing most of the construction on the schoolhouse addition."

After the two exchanged greetings, Reggie waved a hand. "Come on, we'll check in with Calvin's father and then you can take a look around inside."

Without waiting for his answer, she led the way to the back of the building, then halted abruptly. The person Walter Hendricks was "discussing the work" with had his back to her. But there was no mistaking the man for anyone but Adam Barr.

What was *he* doing here? Just looking after her grandfather's interests? Or was it that he knew she planned to accompany Mitchell here this morning?

Mr. Hendricks looked up. "Why, hello there, Reggie. I was just telling Mr. Barr how grateful the town is for your grandfather's generous donation."

Adam turned and nodded a greeting.

She returned his nod, then focused on the carpenter. "I'll be sure to pass along your kind words, Mr. Hendricks, but I assure you, Grandfather got as much pleasure in the giving as our town did in the receiving. I'd even guess more so in *this* particular instance."

She couldn't resist sending a pointed look Adam's way, but his expression remained as bland as ever.

Deciding it would be better to ignore the presence of her grandfather's agent, she turned back to Mr. Hendricks. "I believe you met Mr. Parker at the party yesterday."

The workman stuck out his hand. "Good to see you again. I hope you like what you've seen so far."

Mitchell took his hand. "Yes, sir. It appears you and your sons are doing a fine job."

"Yep, them boys of mine are hard workers." The builder's voice was heavy with pride. "Let me show you around a bit. I reckon this'll match anything you have back in Philadelphia. We've spared no expense, just like Judge Madison requested."

As the two men moved ahead, Adam fell into step beside Reggie. She held her tongue, determined not to be the first to speak, but as the seconds ticked away, she changed her mind. "Checking things out for your report to Grandfather?" she asked.

"Something like that."

The distance between them and the two others widened.

Adam slid her a sideways glance. "So, did you manage to get much information out of Mitchell this morning?"

His tone made it sound as if she were some mean-spirited busybody. Or was that her own conscience?

"We had a very nice discussion, thank you," she answered. "Mr. Parker seems a true *gentleman*."

"As opposed to present company, you mean?" He sounded more amused than insulted.

When she only shrugged, he shook his head. "Don't worry about offending me. As I told you once before, I haven't aspired to be a 'true gentleman' in quite some time."

"I understand." She nodded, pasting on a friendly smile. "No sense setting goals you can't possibly reach."

His lips quirked. "Exactly."

In spite of her determination not to, Reggie found herself unbending. Why did the man have to have a sense of humor so well matched to her own?

Time to turn the conversation to something less personal. "And does the Hendricks's work meet with your approval?"

"It does. The judge shouldn't have any complaints on this project."

"At least that'll give you one positive item to put in your report."

"Contrary to what you seem to think," he said evenly, "I'm not here to find fault with anyone or anything. I'm only here to do the job Judge Madison assigned me."

"Regardless of whose life you have to ruin to do it?"

He speared her with a challenging look. "You've spent time with each of the men. Do you honestly think any of them would be a terrible husband?"

"They all have good qualities, and I'm sure they'd each make some lady a fine husband. But that doesn't mean any of them are right for *me*." She tossed her head. "I have eleven days left to make my choice, and I intend to use every bit of that time, so if you're angling to get back to Philadelphia ahead of schedule, you can just forget it."

From the set of his jaw she knew she'd hit a sore spot.

"I need to get to know them better before I decide," she continued. "For one thing, I want to make sure they're able to provide a good influence for Jack. That will play a big part in my decision."

"So why didn't you bring Jack along today?"

"Patience, Mr. Barr. All in good time."

His jaw tightened again, but he gave a short nod. "So, what's next on your list of hoops to jump through?"

"Tsk, tsk, there's no need to take that tone." His irritated frown only sweetened her smile. "This place is much too public for us to discuss such matters."

As if to emphasize her point, Mr. Hendricks hailed them. "Come look at the supply closet and mudroom we're putting in. I think you'll like the way we've laid it out."

"We'll be right there," Reggie answered. Then she turned back to Adam. "Anyone can put on a good show in polite company. The next step is to see how they handle the little assignments I've given them."

Yep, she intended to see just what each man was *truly* made of.

Chapter Ten

Ten minutes later, Adam leaned against a beam, only half listening to Hendricks point out the amenities of the nearly completed classroom. He'd gotten this tour earlier and was already satisfied that the work was going well.

He watched Mitchell and Regina, trying to picture them as a married couple. The more he thought about it, the more he concluded the schoolteacher was the best hope for a compatible partner. Mitchell had a solidity about him, a quiet strength that most women would find reassuring, perhaps even attractive.

As a schoolteacher, he should also be the best one to satisfy her concerns about fatherly interaction with Jack.

As for Mitchell, dealing with the blunt, determined Miss Nash might not be a job he'd give his right arm for, but Adam believed the widower just might be up to it.

All in all, it would be a good match. No doubt Mitchell was the one the judge had in mind when he'd planned all of this.

And yet…

Adam shifted, some niggling dissatisfaction nagging at him.

Mitchell had come to the judge's attention because he'd gotten himself involved in a land dispute and ended up killing someone. The action might have been justified, but was that the sort of person Judge Madison wanted looking after his granddaughter and great-grandson?

Surely she deserved better.

He straightened and shoved his hands in his pockets, swallowing an oath. He needed to get away from here, away from this assignment. Already he'd gotten himself too involved in these people and their troubles. He should be focusing on his own affairs, not theirs.

Regina gave him a searching look, as if sensing his mood.

Then she tugged the strings of her handbag. "If you'll excuse me, I'll leave you to discuss the finer points of construction. I'm headed for my studio."

Adam pushed away from the beam. "Mind if I walk with you?"

She eyed him suspiciously, hesitating a moment, then smiled. "Not at all."

They walked in silence until they'd left the schoolyard. "So," he finally said, "tell me what it is you like about being a photographer?"

Regina cut him a sideways glance, as if trying to gauge his intent. "I imagine it's the same sort of thing you liked about being a lawyer."

What would she know about his passion for arguing a case?

He thought she would leave it at that. Then her expression softened. "My father considered photography a special calling, an art form. I guess some of that feeling rubbed off on me. He used to say, when a person asks you to take a picture, they're entrusting a bit of history to you. They're asking you to capture a special person or event in their lives, to preserve that moment for them and for those who come after them."

Regina moved one hand, fingertips closing, as if plucking the words she needed from the air. "When you can arrange it so the lighting, the setting and the subject all work together just exactly right, it's an almost mystical experience."

She blinked and smiled self-consciously. "I suppose that sounds silly."

"Not at all. A person *should* feel passionate about the work they do. It adds zest to your life, gives you something to fire your imagination and stretch your abilities." She'd been correct. It was the way he used to feel about his own work.

It was how he now felt about his quest to clear his name.

"Exactly!" Her smile was genuine this time.

For once it seemed they were in perfect agreement. "How about when you photograph plants?" he asked, wanting to keep her talking. "I don't imagine that's the same. I mean, you don't have to worry about posing and capturing expressions."

Regina frowned. "You're right, it's not the same. In a way, it's even more challenging." She fiddled with the collar of her dress. "With people, I have to work within their vision of how the photograph should look. And usually the customer is more concerned with projecting who they want to be rather than who they are."

Her hands were in motion again, as if she needed

more than words to explain. "With plants, though, I can experiment however I like. I'm free to capture both the flower and the thorn, the beauty and the harshness. In the end, I only have to please myself, and I'm my own most demanding client."

She laughed. Was there the trace of a blush on her cheeks? "There I go, chattering on. I don't expect you to understand what I'm talking about. I barely understand myself."

Actually, he did understand, at least to a certain degree.

"Hello, Reggie, Mr. Barr. How are you this morning?"

Adam looked up, annoyed at the interruption. He was even more annoyed to find Eileen Pierce smiling coquettishly at him. The banker's wife was attired in a surprisingly fashionable frock for such a provincial town. The frilly parasol she carried was tilted at an angle that both shaded her face and framed it at a calculatedly fetching angle.

"Hello, Eileen." Reggie's smile was polite but not overly warm. "Out doing your morning shopping?"

Mrs. Pierce gave a tinkling laugh. "Oh, Reggie, you are so droll. You know Mrs. Coffey runs all my household errands." She slanted her eyes at Adam. "I just felt the urge to enjoy a bit of sunshine this morning."

"It is a nice day for a stroll," Adam commented politely.

"If you'll excuse me," Regina interjected, "I need to get on over to my studio."

The banker's wife gave another of those laughs. "That's our Reggie. Always busy with some task or other." She paused and then her eyes widened. "Why,

I just had a thought. Since Reggie is so busy, why don't I show Mr. Barr around town?"

Adam took Regina's hand and tucked it over his arm before she could move away. "As attractive as that offer sounds, I already made a prior commitment to accompany Miss Nash to her studio. Perhaps another time."

The woman's smile slipped for a moment, then returned brighter than before. "Of course. I look forward to it." With a regal nod, she sailed past them.

Regina glanced at him as they resumed their walk. "Prior commitment?"

"I agreed to accompany you, didn't I?"

Her face split into a wide grin. "I don't think Eileen's favors have been rebuffed so firmly in quite a while."

He shrugged. "I don't care for the kind of games her type likes to play."

"I see."

Her voice held that hard-to-interpret tone again.

They strolled in silence for a while. She finally halted in front of her studio. "Here we are," she said unnecessarily. "Thanks for the escort, but you really don't need to come in." She glanced through the large front window. "I see Ira is already here."

Adam reached for the doorknob. "I don't mind. Unless you'd rather I didn't?"

She hesitated, then lifted her chin in that you-don't-intimidate-me way she had. "Suit yourself."

He opened the door, setting the bell mounted above it jingling. He allowed Regina to flounce past him before following her inside.

"Hi there." Ira paused in the act of setting up a ladder. "I see you brought some help."

Regina's only response was an unladylike noise.

"You just missed Patience Bruder," Ira continued. "She made an appointment for tomorrow morning."

While they spoke, Adam studied the framed photographs gracing the walls. He'd only glanced casually at them yesterday. Most of the pictures were standard fare—stiffly posed subjects, some in groups, some alone, all looking about as cheerful as if they were attending a funeral.

One of the photographs, though, was different. It depicted a woman and child sitting side by side on a sofa. The little girl snuggled against the woman, while the woman held an open book of fairy tales.

What made this one stand out, though, was not the pose but the expressions on the subjects' faces. Neither seemed aware of the camera. Their eyes were focused on each other and the child's innocence and the woman's tenderness was almost real enough to touch.

Regina stepped up beside him. "I wish I could get more clients to relax like that," she said wistfully. "Most of them prefer more traditional poses."

"It probably makes them feel less vulnerable, more in control of the outcome."

She gave him a surprised look. "I never thought of it that way." Then she tilted her head. "What about you? Have you ever been photographed?"

He shook his head.

"Well then, perhaps we'll have the chance to remedy that before you leave Turnabout."

"I don't think I'll need a souvenir to remember this little adventure," he commented sardonically.

That drew her brow up again. "Is that how you think of this? As a 'little adventure'?"

Adam mentally winced. He hadn't intended to get

her riled again. "Poor choice of words," he said by way of apology, then quickly changed the subject. "I don't see any of your botanical studies here."

She shrugged. "Those aren't what bring in the business."

"But you do have some around? The description you gave of the difference in technique was interesting. I'd like to see what the finished product looks like."

"As I said, I do most of those for a scientific journal. I ship them off in lots almost as soon as they're developed."

"But not all of them."

"She has a portfolio up in her office," Ira volunteered.

Regina shot the older man an irritated glance. "I'm afraid my office is in no shape for visitors right now."

"What about those photographs you developed last night?" Adam wasn't sure why he pressed her on this. Somehow it seemed important that she allow him into this part of her world.

Regina fingered her collar as she nibbled on her lip. For a moment he saw the girl she'd once been in the woman standing there.

"Oh, very well." Her tone conveyed a decided lack of enthusiasm. "Though why you should be interested in seeing some pictures of flowers, I can't imagine."

She turned and stalked toward the stairs.

Adam followed at a slower pace, meeting Ira's gaze as he passed. The gold-toothed handyman had a grin as wide as a melon slice.

Adam topped the stairs to find Regina already halfway across the storeroom. Without turning to see if he followed, she opened her workroom door and stepped inside, lifting the window shade to let in some light.

By the time he caught up, she stood with her hands primly clasped in front of her. "There they are." She nodded toward a set of racks. "Look all you like, just don't touch anything. I'll be in the storeroom."

Adam stepped aside to let her pass, wondering why she seemed so nervous. It hadn't bothered her when he'd looked at the photographs on display downstairs.

More curious than ever, he moved to the pictures. And discovered a whole new side to Miss Regina Nash.

Even in the low light, he could tell these had been taken by a true artist. Each plant had been captured at its prime, with the light shining on it at just the right angle to showcase its shape and texture. Some of the specimens were growing in areas that must have required her to work in unpleasant conditions.

One photograph in particular caught his eye. Adam took a closer look and barely stopped himself from picking it up. Something about this one reminded him of Regina herself.

A prickly vine that one normally wouldn't give a second glance to had somehow found a way to lift itself off the ground and boldly stand upright. The three nondescript blossoms set amid the briars were just enough to soften its appearance without taking away from its feisty defiance. Then there was the use of a glittery backdrop, a spangled spider web of all things, to make the world sit up and take notice.

A smile tugged the corner of his mouth. Oh, yes, this was Mother Nature's own version of Regina Nash and her can't-ignore-me wagon.

Adam stepped out of the workroom a moment later to find Regina staring at the contents of a lower cupboard. He cleared his throat to make his presence known.

She straightened abruptly. “All done?”

“Yes. Thanks for letting me have a look. A remarkable collection.”

“I’m glad you approve,” she said uncomfortably, before turning away again.

“In fact,” he said impulsively, “I’d like to purchase one of them.”

She glanced over her shoulder and he could tell she was as startled as he by the offer. “You want to buy one of my photographs?”

“Yes, I do.” Suddenly he was quite certain he had to have it. “I’m interested in the one of the prickly vine and spider web.”

Something flickered in her expression. “Why that one?”

He shrugged. “It reminds me of something.”

“You have a good eye—that’s the best of the lot.” She turned to face him fully. “But I already have a buyer for those.”

Her reluctance only made him more determined. “I’m certain you don’t send them every photograph you take.” He waved a hand. “I only want the one, and I’ll pay you the same price as your other buyer.”

She hesitated a moment longer, then nodded. “All right, if you’re so set on it. I’ll have it ready for you when you come to supper tonight.”

Adam leaned back on his heels, feeling as if he’d won a victory of sorts.

He’d have a souvenir to take home after all.

* * *

The next day it was Everett who Mrs. Peavy escorted into the parlor.

"Ah, there you are." Reggie laid the book aside and stood. "I trust you're ready to get underway?"

Everett's jaw dropped as he took in her appearance. "Surely you're not going out dressed like that?"

Reggie glanced down at her clothing—an old blue striped shirt of Lemuel's and a green calico skirt that had seen better days—then looked back at Everett. "Why? Is there a tear I can't see?"

Everett shook his head. "No. But… I mean, surely you have something more suitable to wear in public."

"Suitable? I did mention that we would be doing *outdoor* photography today, didn't I?"

"Yes, but—"

"Well, these are my outdoor work clothes. Not my most presentable ones, I'll allow, but serviceable enough. Surely you're not embarrassed to be seen with me?"

"I—" He paused and swallowed audibly.

"Yes?" She laced her voice with sugar.

His eyes narrowed and he stared at her as if just realizing something. He tugged the cuff of his shirt and executed a polite bow. "Not at all. You look lovely as ever. I await your pleasure."

Reggie smiled. He'd obviously just realized she'd deliberately dressed this way to annoy him.

So, he thought he was ready to meet the challenge, did he?

Time for part two of her plan. "It's a thirty-minute ride to the Keeter place, so we'd best get started. I told Ira we'd meet him at the studio."

Everett offered her his arm and escorted her from the room.

The studio was normally a five-minute walk from the house, but it took a bit longer today since Reggie made a point of calling out greetings to everyone they passed.

Not that she needed to make an effort to call attention to herself. *This* getup was extreme, even for her.

She had to admit, though, Everett took it well. He hadn't winced more than once or twice at the looks they attracted as they walked down the sidewalk.

When they reached the studio, however, he paled visibly. Parked in front of the building was her wagon, in all its colorful glory.

"There you are," Ira said cheerfully. "I was beginning to wonder if I'd have to fetch you."

Regina turned to Everett. "I hope you don't mind taking the reins. I told Ira he could have the afternoon off."

The man looked like he'd just bit an unripe persimmon. But he nodded gamely. "Of course."

Reggie met his determined smile with one of her own. If he thought she'd thrown her worst at him, he'd soon learn different.

Once he'd helped her board, Reggie settled back in her seat. "I'll give you directions as we go. For now, just head east, right through the middle of town."

Everett's jaw tightened, but he obediently set the wagon in motion. "It won't work," he said stiffly.

"What won't work?" Reggie used her most innocent of tones.

"No matter how big a spectacle you make of yourself, I won't back down."

Hah! We'll see about that. "Don't you mean how big a spectacle I make of *us?*"

He gave her a sour look before facing forward again. "As I said, it doesn't matter. I gave Judge Madison my word, and I plan to keep it."

Reggie nodded approvingly. "A man of your word, are you? That's one of the qualities I'm looking for in a father figure for Jack."

Reggie's lips twitched as Everett's face paled. He definitely didn't want to contemplate the idea of "winning" their marriage lottery.

She turned her face upward and inhaled deeply. "It's a lovely afternoon, don't you think?"

He made a noncommittal sound.

She smiled. "Do you know any songs, Mr. Fulton?"

That won her a startled, somewhat apprehensive glance. "A few."

"Sing one for me, please."

"Sing? You mean *now?*" He looked as if she'd asked him to dance naked in the street.

"Of course. This is the beginning of our public courtship, after all. I've always thought being serenaded by a beau would be quite romantic." She raised a brow in challenge. "Unless you no longer consider yourself a suitor for my hand."

Everett remained silent for a moment, but from the way his jaw worked she could tell he wrestled with some inner emotion. Finally, he nodded. "Very well." He took a deep breath and began signing.

The song was more spirited than loverlike, but Reggie had no desire to quibble with his choice. It would serve her purpose nicely. Predictably, however, his voice was pitched to reach her ears only.

She folded her hands in her lap and stared at him with a rapt expression. "Very nice," she whispered, "but do try to put more enthusiasm into it. We want everyone to know you're enjoying my company."

Looking none too happy, Everett nevertheless increased the volume a notch.

By now they were attracting a fair share of attention. Reggie even noticed a few strollers calling into shop doors and motioning others to come out.

Everett reached the end of his little ditty, and Reggie clapped appreciatively. "Well done. I've never heard that song before, but I like it. Do you suppose you could sing it again, and this time I'll join in on the chorus?" She gave him a coy smile. "I find singing is so much more fun when you have someone to share it with."

With a decided lack of enthusiasm, Everett nodded. He opened his mouth to begin, then stiffened and snapped it shut.

Reggie followed his gaze to see Adam and Chance standing in front of the boardinghouse, making no attempts to hide their grins.

"Don't pay them no nevermind." She patted his hand. "It's me you're trying to please, remember?"

Encouraging the horse to a faster pace, Everett nodded and started into his song again.

She noted he focused straight ahead, a stony expression on his face.

As soon as he finished the opening verse, Reggie was ready. Head high, she took a deep breath and enthusiastically joined in the chorus.

Before she could get out more than a few notes, Everett stopped mid-lyric and his head snapped around to stare at her. Reggie continued another two lines then stopped as if just noticing she was singing alone.

"What's the matter? Did I get the words wrong?"

"It was hard to tell," he said tightly.

She clicked her tongue in a tsking sound. "Come now, that wasn't very gentlemanly."

"You're her, aren't you?"

"Her?"

"Don't play coy. You know very well I'm referring to that hoyden we encountered on the way to your cabin."

Reggie grinned. "Oh, *that* her. Yep, that was me."

"Did you enjoy playing us for fools?"

"If I recall, you gents assumed from the get-go I was nothing but a bumpkin. I just chose not to disagree."

Reggie laughed as if greatly amused and gave him a none-too-gentle nudge. "Now if you don't mind, pretend I just told you something funny and share a laugh with me. Then we'll start singing again so everyone sees how well-suited we are."

Everett's laugh had a bite to it. Then, visibly bracing himself, he started into the song's refrain once more.

Reggie joined in, mentally patting herself on the back.

If things continued the way she'd planned, by the time they returned to town, Everett would have trouble conjuring up even a fake smile, much less a laugh.

Adam stepped out of the livery several hours later just in time to see Regina and Everett roll back into town.

And what a woeful sight it was.

He tilted back his hat and shook his head.

Whatever the two of them had been up to, it had definitely taken the wind out of Everett's sails. Not only was the fastidious dandy dirty and disheveled, but he had a queasy, dazed look about him, as if he'd experienced something too horrible to endure.

What had the clever Regina been up to?

Adam stepped off the sidewalk. "Hold on a minute."

The wilted dandy obediently halted the vehicle.

"It appears you could use a rest and a bit of freshening up." Adam tried not to let his amusement show. "Why don't you climb down and allow me the pleasure of driving Miss Nash the rest of the way?"

Did he detect a glint of gratitude in Everett's expression? Regina really must have put him through the wringer today.

"Thank you." Everett quickly set the brake. "I—" He paused and turned reluctantly to Regina. "If Miss Nash doesn't mind, that is?"

She waved him aside. "Of course not. And thank you again for all your help today. I'm sure we'll have some very nice photographs from this session."

Everett grimaced, then nodded. A moment later he had hopped down, exchanged stiff pleasantries with Adam and turned toward the boardinghouse.

"Oh, Mr. Fulton."

At Regina's hail, Everett paused and turned back to face her.

"I have an appointment to take photographs at Milford Conners's place Wednesday. I trust I can count on you to assist me again?"

Everett executed a curt bow. "Of course."

"Good. We'll talk about it more at supper tonight."

Another nod and Everett again turned, this time making his escape with quicker steps.

Adam climbed up and took the reins. He watched Everett's quickly retreating form, then raised a brow

Regina's way. "And just what torture did you put your escort through this afternoon? Outside of singing for him, that is."

She laughed. "That was a most unkind thing to say. And, Mr. Busybody, all I did was get Everett to help me pose Cletus Keeter and Lulu."

"Don't try that innocent tone on me. I'm not buying it. There's bound to be more to the story than that."

Reggie absently twirled a tendril of hair around one finger. "Did I forget to mention that Lulu is Cletus's pig?"

Adam let out a startled laugh. "Everett helped you pose a pig?"

"Oh, this wasn't just any pig," she assured him with a straight face. "Lulu is Cletus's pride and joy. She won him two blue ribbons at the county fair last month."

"Impressive."

"Yes, it is. But I'm afraid Mr. Fulton didn't see it that way." She waved a hand. "Of course, Lulu wasn't at her best today. The camera flash upset her, so she took quite a bit of calming down after the first shot."

"Let me guess. That was Everett's job."

Reggie nodded. "Mr. Fulton was a bit squeamish at first, but he finally got enough dirt on him to realize a bit more wasn't going to make a jot of difference. I think he began to see it as a sort of personal challenge toward the end."

She gave an unconvincing sigh. "I'm afraid Mr. Fulton didn't have nice things to say about pigs in general, and Lulu in particular, on the way back to town."

Adam shook his head. "I'd have given a pretty penny to see him work with that pig."

"You'll get your chance," she said smugly. "I got a

shot of him and Lulu together, though I don't think our friend plans to ask for a copy." She tapped her chin thoughtfully. "Maybe I'll hang it in my studio."

The woman was downright devious. "He'd buy it from you first."

She raised a brow. "He can't buy what I'm not selling."

By this time they'd reached her studio. "Where do you keep this circus wagon when it's not in use?"

She pointed to a side street. "There's a storage building around the corner that Ira converted into a carriage house. But stop here first so I can unload my things."

Before Adam could set the brake on the wagon, Ira stepped onto the sidewalk.

"How did it go?" he asked as he handed Reggie down.

"Exactly as planned," she replied with a satisfied smile. "I don't think your job is in any jeopardy from Mr. Fulton."

Chapter Eleven

Reggie pushed back from the table with a smile. "An excellent meal as usual, Mrs. Peavy."

The men pushed back their chairs as well, politely standing as she rose from her seat.

"Lemuel usually stepped out on the back porch after supper to smoke a cigar." Reggie moved toward the parlor. "I trust, however, that none of you share that smelly habit."

"If any of us do," Adam said diplomatically, "I'm sure he can refrain while we are guests in your home."

Reggie nodded and sat down on the small sofa that occupied the place of honor in the parlor. Jack settled beside her and the four men arranged themselves with a minimum of fuss in nearby chairs.

A moment of silence ensued, which Chance finally jumped in to fill. "Everett was rather closed-mouthed about your little outing today, Miss Nash. Perhaps you'll be more forthcoming on how he managed to acquire that generous and rather aromatic spattering of dirt."

Everett did his best to appear bored, though Reggie detected a slight stiffening of his spine.

She cast a quick glance Adam's way. So, he hadn't filled the others in on the story. Did he feel compassion for Everett? Or was it more he wished to keep his distance from the lot of them?

Reggie smiled at Chance. "Taking photographs, especially outdoors, tends to be messier than most folks credit. Especially when you're new at it the way Mr. Fulton is. I'm sure he'll get better at maintaining his footing with practice."

She managed to hold back her grin at the sight of the wince on Everett's face. Just wait until he found out their trip to the Conners's farm on Wednesday was to photograph a pair of goats.

Amazing how many folks had taken her up on her offer to photograph the animals that had taken ribbons at the county fair.

Jack yawned and she gave his shoulder a squeeze. "Now, young man, run along to the kitchen and see if Mrs. Peavy needs help with the dishes. Then it's off to bed. I'll check in on you when I come up later."

"Yes, ma'am." He gave her neck a generous hug before he said goodnight to the others. Reggie's heart squeezed in response. Those little signs of affection seemed more precious than ever now.

Once Jack had exited, Reggie crossed back to the sofa. "Well, gentlemen, I suppose we should discuss what we want to accomplish this week."

"I thought I'd begin those repairs tomorrow," Mitchell volunteered. "What would you like me to tackle first?"

"I think replacing the damaged shingles is the most pressing need," Reggie answered. "When should I expect you?"

"I'd like to get started early, before the heat gets so bad." He tilted his head deferentially. "However, I don't want to rouse the household before you're up and about."

"Any time after six o'clock will be fine."

Mitchell nodded. "A few minutes after six it is."

She turned to Chance next. "The committees for the fundraiser are meeting at the town hall tomorrow at two o'clock. Can I count on you to escort me?"

"Of course."

Then she faced Everett. "And I assume you're prepared to accompany me to the Conners's farm on Wednesday."

Everett gave a short nod. "What time shall I come by?"

"I promised Milford we'd be there by ten. If we left at nine-thirty that should give us plenty of time."

"Very well."

His tone reflected a decided lack of enthusiasm. Perhaps her plan was already bearing fruit.

"We'll discuss other outings another time. For now, it's growing late and I have a busy day tomorrow."

She escorted them to the front porch, then turned to Adam. "If you don't mind, I'd like a word with you."

His brow raised in surprise. "Of course."

The other three exchanged glances but left without comment.

Reggie leaned against the porch rail, studying the bushes that flanked the steps. "Jack told me about the bag of marbles you brought him while I was out with Everett today. And how you spent time teaching him to play."

He leaned beside her, resting his forearms across

the rail. If she moved just a finger's width closer their shoulders would touch.

"Hope you don't mind," Adam said. "I saw them at the mercantile this morning. Thought Jack might enjoy them."

"Of course I don't mind. In fact, I wanted to thank you for the gesture. Jack is proud as can be of both the marbles and his newfound skills." She'd never seen Jack so pleased with a gift. In her heart she knew that it was more than the marbles themselves. Adam had given him something today that Lemuel never had, the gift of his unbegrudged time and undivided attention.

"No thanks needed. Jack is a good kid. And I know what it's like to lose your parents when you're young."

Regina wanted to take exception to that. Couldn't anyone get it through their heads that to Jack, she was a parent?

But she saw the look on Adam's face and let go of her irritation. "Tell me about your parents."

He gave her a startled look, then stared out at the fireflies on her front lawn. A mirthless smile twisted his lips. "It's not an edifying story. Are you certain you want to hear it?"

More now than ever. "Only if you want to tell me."

He was silent for a time, then he leaned forward. "I never knew my father," he began. "My mother was an actress, but she had to quit that and work as a seamstress when I came along. She worked long hours, resenting everyone and everything that kept her from the life she loved."

Did that extend to her son?

"Finally, she worked her way back into the theater. Then, about the time I turned four, she met a man who wanted to marry her." A muscle near his mouth twitched. "Problem was he only wanted *her*. The proposal didn't include another man's castoff. So, Mom dropped me off at her brother's house and never looked back."

Anger fired Reggie's veins. How could that woman have done such a thing?

She laid a hand on Adam's arm, wanting to comfort that little boy who'd endured such painful rejection. "I'm sorry," she said softly.

"You have nothing to apologize for." His smile was firmly back in place. "It happened a long time ago. Besides, you're doing your best to see that Jack never experiences anything similar."

He lifted his arms from the rail as he straightened. "I just wish I understood why you don't want to give him the benefit of a father as well."

Reggie stiffened. She'd forgotten for a moment they were on opposite sides of this battle.

"I have my reasons." She nodded dismissal. "Thank you again for your kindness to Jack. I won't keep you any longer."

Reggie watched Adam saunter down the front walk and out the gate. She rubbed her upper arms, feeling a sudden chill in the night air.

If only things could be different....

"Mr. Parker, how is it going?" Reggie shaded a hand over her eyes as she stared up at the man on the ladder. He'd been hard at work for two hours now. Though he seemed to have worked up quite a sweat, he showed no signs of tiring.

"I should have the roof finished soon," Mitchell answered, wiping his brow with the back of his hand.

"Why don't you take a little break. I've brought out a pitcher of Mrs. Peavy's lemonade."

He nodded. "Let me hammer in these last two nails and I'll be right down."

Reggie stepped back onto the porch and filled two glasses. When Mitchell joined her, she handed him one, then took the other.

"I appreciate your dedication," she said. "But I didn't intend for you to work yourself quite so hard."

He shrugged. "I like working with my hands."

"Yet you've chosen to be a teacher?"

He took a sip from his glass. "A person can find pleasure in more than one thing," he said finally. "For instance, as much as you enjoy photography, you wouldn't give up being surrogate mother to Jack in order to pursue it."

"I see. One's personal passion as opposed to professional satisfaction." She gave him a considering look. "And which is which for you?"

"An interesting question."

Was he being deliberately evasive or was he unsure how to answer?

Not that it mattered, other than satisfying her curiosity. She'd already decided Mitchell wasn't the best target for her campaign. The schoolteacher seemed too controlled, too solid to have an Achilles' heel she could successfully attack.

No, Everett or Chance would be easier to manipulate.

But she was curious about one thing. "Mr. Parker, do you mind if I ask a personal question?"

The hint of a smile crossed his face. "I haven't noticed our feelings on the matter playing a big part in your asking," he said dryly.

She grimaced. "True. Circumstances have called for more than my usual bluntness lately. But this is different. You don't have to answer if you don't want to."

His expression immediately closed off. "Very well."

"Why did you agree to participate in this farce? Surely you could have found a teaching position on your own."

He stared into his glass, as if it somehow held the answer to her question. Finally, he looked up. "I went a little crazy after my wife died and did some things I'm not proud of. Judge Madison helped me through a tough situation and brought me back to my senses. After that, I couldn't tell him no."

He set his glass down. "Thanks for the refreshment. If you don't mind, I'll get back to my work."

Reggie nodded and let him pass. "When that's done, I think you should call it a day. The fence can wait 'til tomorrow."

She watched him climb back up and return to work. What had he meant when he said he "went a little crazy"?

Reggie shivered, convinced she'd made the right decision when she'd eliminated him from her plan. Somehow, she didn't think this was a man she'd want to try to manipulate.

"Ah, it looks like we're late." Reggie, her hand tucked onto Chance's arm, scanned the nearly full room. Folks were gathered in clusters, vigorously discussing various aspects of the upcoming fair.

Reggie indicated a group across the room. "There's

our committee." She allowed Chance to escort her through the maze of chairs, pausing frequently to greet friends and neighbors.

She stopped in surprise, though, when she spotted Adam in deep discussion with Mr. Pierce.

Why was he here? Surely he didn't plan to help with the fair. He'd be back in Philadelphia before it was even held.

Should she say something or keep moving?

Then Mr. Pierce took the decision from her when he spotted her. "Hello, Reggie. It took a bit of arm-twisting, but I've convinced Mr. Barr to help with some of the paperwork for the fair. You don't mind if he delays looking over the files on Jack's behalf a little longer, do you?"

Reggie smiled. "There's no need to ask me. That was Grandfather's idea."

Pierce clapped Adam on the back. "That's settled then. We may just persuade you to extend your stay here yet."

Adam merely smiled without answering.

The banker, however, had already turned to Chance. "What about you, Mr. Dawson? There's plenty of work to go around. Can we convince you to lend a hand?"

Reggie laughed. "You're too late. I've already talked him into helping our group." She waved toward the far corner.

Mr. Pierce blinked in surprise. "Children's activities? Surely we can find something more suited—"

Reggie raised a hand. "Oh, no you don't. As I said, you're too late." She patted Chance's arm with her free hand. "He's already promised to help me and I'm not giving him up."

Mr. Pierce eyed that bit of byplay with raised brows.

Then he gave a knowing smile. "I see. Well, there's nothing wrong with a man wanting to help a lady in need. Welcome aboard, Mr. Dawson."

Chance shifted uncomfortably. "Thank you."

Reggie tugged lightly on her escort's arm. "If you'll excuse us, I see the rest of the committee is waiting."

Adam watched them cross the room. Chance stiffened slightly as he got a good look at the group he'd just become a part of. Regina's committee appeared to be composed of a sweet-faced grandmother, a shy-looking brunette who seemed barely out of the schoolroom and Reverend Harper's studious-looking daughter, Constance.

As the introductions were made, the trio welcomed the hapless Chance with a mix of emotions. The white-haired matron patted his hand fondly as if he were a favorite grandson, the brunette blushed and gave him a moon-eyed smile, and Constance seemed to be reserving judgment. Chance held a chair out for Regina. Then, after casting a wistful glance at the group of men discussing some sort of construction project, took his own seat between Regina and Constance.

Poor Chance. Just as she had with Everett, Regina had found his weak spot and was exploiting it mercilessly. Adam was glad she hadn't turned her clever mind to discomfiting him.

If she had been so inclined, though, what weakness would she have latched on to? What sensitive spot would she have probed and prodded until she had him squirming like the others?

Reggie drummed her fingers on the desk in Lemuel's study—hers now, she supposed. Today was the day. Her grandfather's deadline had arrived, and she still wasn't sure if her plan had worked.

She looked down at the contract spread before her and sighed wearily. She'd gone over it so many times, looking for even the slightest loophole, that she practically knew it by heart.

For all the good it did her.

She'd pushed Everett and Chance as hard as she could these past two weeks. Both were showing signs of strain. And she made a point of taking buggy rides and casual strolls with Mitchell just so he would believe he was still in the running.

But the three were obviously made of sterner stuff than she had first supposed. It was time she faced facts. She might actually have to marry one of them.

Reggie shoved away from the desk and began pacing.

If it *did* come to that, if she had to risk humiliation to keep Jack with her, which man would be the better choice?

Chance was young, but that wasn't necessarily a bad thing. It meant he'd be more likely to defer to her judgment, especially where Jack was concerned. But a possible saloon owner? Was that really the example she wanted Jack to grow up with?

Mitchell was well-educated, steady, reliable. As a teacher, he would obviously be comfortable around a young boy. And while not much of a talker, he also wasn't one to stir up conflict. But there was a sadness in Mitchell, a perpetual pall that shadowed him no matter the circumstances.

Perhaps he would do a better job controlling his emotions than Lemuel had, but Jack had spent his first six years in the shadow of a man who had no joy or laughter to share. Reggie didn't want that happening to her sweet boy all over again.

That left Everett. Not someone she'd consider ideal husband material. But she'd gained a new respect for him the past few days. Although he grumbled and complained with that biting tone he had, he'd met every challenge she threw at him. And she'd actually begun to enjoy his caustic wit, his cutting but on-the-mark comments on absurdities surrounding them.

He was also the most worldly of the three, something to consider given the situation.

She paused in front of the window, staring out without seeing anything beyond her own troubled reflection. What if she could convince one of them to agree to a platonic arrangement? To marry her and share her home, but not her bedroom?

She wouldn't even consider asking Chance. He was too young and spirited to saddle with such an arrangement.

Mitchell might agree. In fact, he might welcome a name-only marriage if she chose him. After all, he obviously still mourned his first wife. But should she take advantage of that? And what kind of impact would his moodiness have on Jack?

Which brought her back to Everett.

Heaven help her. It seemed she had only one choice.

A knock on the door broke the silence and she spun around, her heart suddenly pounding.

No. I'm not ready.

At the second knock she took a deep breath and moved back to the desk. "Come in."

Mrs. Peavy stepped inside, a sympathetic half smile on her face. "The gentlemen are here to see you."

Reggie tried to project an unworried air. "Show them in." She held up a hand. "Oh, and please see that Jack is kept occupied elsewhere."

Mrs. Peavy nodded and allowed the men to enter.

Reggie waved toward the chairs in front of the desk. "Please, have a seat."

As Mitchell, Everett and Chance sat down, Reggie was relieved to see they appeared as edgy and uncomfortable as she felt. Even Adam, who stood with arms folded, leaning negligently against a bookcase, seemed affected by the wary anticipation crackling through the room.

Of course, he probably felt more relief than dread. After today he could plan his return trip.

She studied the faces of her beaus and mentally groaned. It was obvious each one was fervently hoping he would not be chosen—a mortifying thought in itself. But there was also a determination in each of their expressions, a sort of grim, martyr-like set to their jaws that told her they wouldn't shirk their duty if they drew the short straw.

"It's time," Adam said when the silence had drawn out painfully long. "What's your decision?"

She was surprised by the sharp edge to his voice. Was he so impatient to have this over with? She admitted to herself that it bothered her that he could view her marriage to someone else with such detachment. Apparently the connection she'd felt between them wasn't as strong as she thought.

"Actually," she said, stalling for time, "I have until midnight tonight."

"No," he countered. "If you'll remember, we arrived

at your cabin around three o'clock in the afternoon. That means you only have another thirty minutes."

Reggie glared at him, resenting being cornered this way.

Perhaps she should just give in, let him take Jack back to Philadelphia. She could tag along, confront her grandfather when they arrived, somehow make him see reason.

But what if she gambled and lost? She couldn't bear the thought of losing Jack.

She studied the faces of the her suitors again, but nothing had changed. The only man in this room she could say with any certainty would refuse to walk her down the aisle was Adam.

Too bad he wasn't one of the contenders.

Reggie froze. A shiver shimmied up her spine. Could it be—

Not trusting her memory, she grabbed the contract, leafing through it for the right paragraph.

There it was.

She read it twice, her mind tumbling over itself with a mixture of giddy relief, smug self-approval and triumph.

Her prayers had been answered!

Adam straightened as Reggie snatched up some papers from her desk. Was this another delaying tactic? Hadn't she put them all through enough already?

Then he saw the relief light up her face, saw the confidence return to her expression and posture. Something was up. Whatever she'd discovered, it didn't bode well for the judge's plan.

Why did he feel a stirring of anticipation rather than irritation?

She finally looked up and met his gaze with a certain-of-victory smile.

"Very well," she announced. "I've made my choice."

From the corner of his eye, he saw the three men tense. But his gaze never wavered from Regina's challenging one.

He braced himself to face whatever new trick she had up her sleeve.

She leaned back in her chair. "I choose you, Mr. Barr."

Chapter Twelve

Adam snapped upright, ignoring the confused exclamations from the other men.

What did the infuriating woman think she was doing? "Come now. Enough of this nonsense. As flattered as I am," he infused as much sarcasm as he could into his drawl, "we both know I'm not a valid choice."

"Oh, but you are." She held up the papers which he now recognized as the contract they had all signed. "It says so right here."

Despite himself, Adam felt apprehension creeping like a spider up his backbone. He marched forward, rounding the desk to look at the contract. "Show me."

She pointed to one particular paragraph.

By affixing his signature below, each man who is party to this contract agrees that, should he be selected by Miss Regina Nash as her husband-elect, he will accept the honor and duties entailed therein, fully, with utmost respect, and without reservation. Should said party refuse to do so, it will render this entire contract null and void.

Was that it? "You're grasping at straws. This paragraph obviously refers to the three gentlemen seated before you. It does *not* include me."

She raised a brow. "Doesn't it? Don't you have specific obligations set out under this contract that make you a party to it?"

He frowned. "Yes, but those obligations don't include—"

"What those obligations are," she interrupted, "doesn't matter. By your own words, you agree you are a party to the contract. And isn't this your signature?"

The ground suddenly shifted under Adam as he took in the possibility that she might actually have a case. How in the world had he let this get by him?

Did she actually *want* to marry him? Was it possible she preferred him over the men her grandfather had handpicked?

Adam met her gaze and tightened his jaw. Of course not. How could he have imagined anything so ridiculous for even a moment? She fully expected him to refuse. That's what this was all about—her weaseling out of the trap her grandfather had set.

Quite a clever miss, this one.

"Is it true?"

Adam glanced up. The question had come from Chance but all three men wore identical expressions—a mixture of confusion and hope. A muscle twitched at the corner of his mouth. If she was right, he now had their futures to worry about as well.

He stared down at the contract again, his mind whirling over the implications. "I suppose one could argue in favor of that interpretation," he said slowly. That was the closest he could come to admitting she was right.

"Which means my choice stands," she said, pouncing on his admission.

"What does this mean for us?" Chance asked.

"It means," Everett responded dryly, "that our prizes are at the mercy of Mr. Barr's response."

Adam noticed Regina had the grace to look sympathetic.

Four pairs of eyes focused on him, waiting for his answer. The same way they'd focused on Regina while she took her time announcing her selection.

He straightened his shoulders. This might not be the duty he'd had in mind when he gave the judge his promise, but that didn't mean he was any less bound by his word. Feeling his well-laid plans crumble around him, Adam knew he didn't have any choice.

He turned to Regina and trapped her gaze with his for a long moment. Slowly her smile faded.

"Very well," he finally bit out. "I accept your proposal."

It gave him only the tiniest jot of satisfaction to see the look of horror on her face.

Reggie felt the blood drain from her face. For a moment she couldn't see anything. Her eyes just plain refused to focus.

She hadn't heard right.

He couldn't have agreed.

He didn't want to marry her.

He wanted to get back to Philadelphia right away.

She blinked, trying to focus on his face. His tight, I-called-your-bluff expression erased any lingering doubts she held.

No, no, no! This was a disaster. Somehow she had

to undo this, had to call her words back. If she had to get married, any of the other three would be better. She could *not* marry Adam. Not like this, not under these circumstances.

She could read in his eyes that he hated her for doing this to him. Mercy, she'd made a royal mess of things.

He finally released her gaze and turned to the others. "Rest assured, you'll all receive the bonuses the judge promised you. Now, if you'll excuse us, Miss Nash and I have matters to discuss."

Reggie watched the men spring up from their chairs like prisoners suddenly released from their shackles. She wanted to call them back, to tell them it had been a mistake, that she was prepared to select someone else.

Don't leave me here alone with Adam, not while he's looking so cold and forbidding.

But the words stuck in her throat. She watched helplessly as the door closed behind them, leaving her alone with the man who, unbelievably, was now her fiancé.

She stared at her hands folded in her lap, suddenly fascinated by the tiny scratch on her right thumb.

"Miss Nash."

His voice was calm. Too calm.

"Yes." She didn't quite meet his gaze. How could she? What would she see there?

"You are many things, but I never figured a coward to be one of them."

Reggie's gaze snapped to his, outrage stiffening her spine.

"That's better." His smile was anything but warm. "Let's be honest. Neither of us is pleased with this situation. You picked me because you thought I'd say no."

He raised a cynical brow. "Whereas, if you really

knew me as you once assured me you do, you'd understand that I don't renege on a promise, even one given unwittingly."

Reggie tried to control her panic. He was angry, but he was also being realistic. Perhaps she could find some way out of this yet. "You're right. Neither of us wants this. If we put our heads together, surely—"

His eyes narrowed. "You weren't listening. I said I don't renege on promises. And I certainly don't intend to start with a promise made to your grandfather. Whether either of us wants this is now irrelevant. You've made your choice and we're both going to have to live with it. So start planning the wedding. It appears we're getting married within the week."

With that, he gave her a curt bow and exited in long, swift strides. It seemed he couldn't get away from her quickly enough.

As soon as the door closed behind him, Reggie folded her arms on the desk and plopped her forehead down against them. She'd taken a bad situation and made it worse. The man she still thought of as a slightly flawed but nonetheless heroic white knight, now hated her.

And unless she did something quickly, he would soon learn her deepest, darkest secret.

Adam walked to the livery stable, looking neither left nor right. He needed to work off the pulse-pounding emotions churning through his gut right now. A breakneck gallop sounded like just the thing.

In a matter of minutes he had Trib saddled. Another minute and he was mounted and headed out of town. There was an open field just outside of town. That ought to do the trick.

Trib tossed his head and strained at the bit, seeming to sense Adam's restlessness. Adam patted the animal's neck. "Easy, boy. We'll be there in just a minute."

His hands tightened on the reins as his mind replayed that scene in the study. How could matters have turned out so horribly wrong?

Engaged, and to the judge's granddaughter no less.

It might be easier to swallow if she hadn't looked so horrified when she realized he was going to call her bluff.

She didn't want him for a husband. In fact she'd seemed ready to change her mind and choose one of the others, *any* one of the others, rather than actually marry him. She'd actually looked physically ill before he marched out of the room.

Why? What was he lacking that made women shy away from him so forcefully?

He grimaced at the turn his thoughts had taken. Why was he so concerned with that aspect? He should be thinking about what this meant for his plans to clear his name.

He *could* move back to Philadelphia after the wedding, he supposed. He was certain Regina wouldn't have any objections to that arrangement. They could put it out that he had some business to take care of before moving here permanently—not a lie.

But that meant facing the judge, a friend who'd trusted him to see that his granddaughter and great-grandson had a husband and father at hand to look out for them. He couldn't disappoint him that way.

It appeared he was stuck here for the foreseeable future. What was he supposed to do in this bucolic backwater? Take care of Jack's interests certainly. But would that be enough to keep him occupied, make him feel useful and valued?

Or would it merely be a prison of another sort?

Adam finally reached his destination and nudged Trib with his knees. It was all the encouragement the spirited horse needed. They made two circuits around the field, riding as if the devil's own hounds were on their heels.

He gradually slowed the lathered horse to a more sedate pace. His mood hadn't lifted, but he knew the time for railing at his fate was over.

Besides, there was Jack to think about. Regardless of how he and Regina felt about each other or this marriage, he was certain they would agree on one thing. Their feelings should not spill over onto Jack.

The boy deserved a home with parents who cared for him and would look out for his welfare. He'd make sure Jack's childhood would in no way mirror his own.

Adam turned Trib back toward town. Judge Madison would expect a telegram from him today.

How would Regina's grandfather feel about the unexpected outcome of his little matchmaking scheme? Would he be disappointed that his granddaughter hadn't chosen one of his handpicked suitors? Would the judge welcome him into the family, or would he feel his former protégé had overstepped his bounds?

Adam admitted his life had been a mess before, but at least he'd had a focus, a goal to keep him going. Now that had been stolen from him as well.

Reggie pulled the covers up to Jack's chin. She'd dreaded this moment all evening. But she had to tell him.

She still clung to the hope that she could turn the

situation around. If she succeeded, then telling Jack now and recanting later would upend his world twice in one week.

But word was spreading. Already, two callers had dropped by this evening to find out if the "happy news" they'd heard was true, and to offer congratulations. By now the rumors would be all over town.

Better for Jack to hear the announcement from her than from someone else.

She smoothed the covers and took a deep breath. "I have some news for you," she said, forcing a light tone.

"Something good?"

"I hope you think so. How would you feel if I got married?"

Jack squirmed into a sitting position. "Would I still live with you?"

She gave him a fierce hug. "Of course. No one is ever going to take you away from me."

"Is it one of those men from Philadelphia?"

"Uh-huh. Mr. Barr."

"Oh." Jack looked thoughtful for a minute. "Will that mean we have to move to Philadelphia?"

Reggie shook her head. "We wouldn't even have to leave this house. He would move here to live with us."

Jack gave an approving nod. "Then, if you like him, that's okay. Mr. Barr seems like a nice man. He's not fussy like Mr. Fulton, or sad like Mr. Parker."

He snuggled back down. "And I really like his horse," he added as if that settled the matter.

"We're still talking it over," she said, preparing him for what she hoped would be the outcome. "But if we do decide to get married, it will be pretty soon."

"Okay," he said with a yawn. Then he opened his

eyes wider. "If you marry him, do I still call him Mr. Barr?"

"I suppose you could call him Uncle Adam, if that's all right with him."

"Uncle Adam," Jack repeated. "I like that. I never had an uncle before."

Reggie tousled his hair. If only things were different…

Planting a kiss on his cheek, she left.

She had to start planning how to derail this wedding scheme before she became Mrs. Adam Barr.

Chapter Thirteen

Two days later, Reggie sat beside Adam in the surrey, a picnic hamper at their feet. The Peavys and Jack sat behind them, and Buck trotted alongside.

She hoped her smile looked more genuine than it felt, because their party was getting a lot of notice as they drove through town.

Her neighbors were still abuzz with the news of her engagement. Though no one said it to her face, she'd heard enough talk to know folks were surprised that an eccentric woman like herself, well on the way to spinsterhood, had snared such a prize catch.

But her neighbors' opinions were the least of her concerns. In fact, she was getting downright desperate. Nothing she'd tried had worked. Though Mitchell, Everett and Chance had put an end to their evening visits, Adam had continued to join them for supper. After all, even though neither of them was happy with the situation, they had to maintain appearances.

She'd used the after-supper discussions with Adam to try to change his mind. Her broad hints that she wouldn't be opposed to his returning to Philadelphia after the wedding had met with an outright refusal.

Then she mentioned perhaps her grandfather would wish to rethink his plan since she'd found a loophole in the contract. Adam responded by showing her a telegram he received from the judge welcoming him to the family.

All her other stratagems had met with similar fates. Only one option remained. But could she pull it off without turning into a stuttering puddle of red-faced embarrassment?

Reggie squared her shoulders. They would soon find out.

This picnic had been Adam's idea. To give him credit, he was trying to make this as easy as possible on Jack. He'd come by every day, like a true beau, and had included time with Jack during his visits.

It both warmed and broke Reggie's heart to see how well they were getting on. Adam would make a fine father.

Too bad she had to try to make sure he never assumed that role with Jack. The boy's future, as well as her own, was at stake.

At the moment, Ira was doing a good job keeping Jack distracted in the backseat. The conversation between her and Adam, however, was restricted to polite comments about their surroundings and the directions to Split Oak Meadow.

She'd chosen the picnic spot with care. The meadow was beautiful, with a shallow brook, lots of open space for Jack and Buck to romp, and wooded trails that offered secluded spots for private conversation.

Two hours later, Reggie stared at Adam's back as he watched Jack and Buck play fetch.

She took a deep breath. Time to get this over with.

"Mr. Barr," she called softly.

"Don't you think you should call me Adam?" he said without turning. His voice was even, his tone offhand. Had he decided to call a truce then?

"Adam." She tried matching his tone. "Would you mind joining me for a stroll?"

He did turn to look at her then, his brow quirked up in question. After a moment he nodded and extended his arm. "Of course. Lead the way."

Reggie cast a quick glance at Ira, tilting her head toward Jack and her old friend nodded a reassurance.

Then Reggie directed their steps toward the tree line. They walked in silence. She turned before they actually entered the woods, following the edge as it curved to accommodate the brook.

Before long, they were out of sight of the others, but still Reggie kept walking. Adam kept pace, obviously waiting for her to break the silence.

At last she stopped and turned to him.

"So," he asked, "what new plan have you hatched to prevent the wedding?"

She grimaced. "I'm afraid I've given up on that for now."

"Don't tell me that imagination of yours has finally run dry?"

She smiled in spite of herself. "Let's just say I'm ready to pursue a new course."

"So, you didn't bring me here to discuss wedding plans?"

"Not exactly." Reggie moved slightly away from him,

tearing a strip of gauzy bark from a cottonwood. "I want to discuss what happens afterward."

"Afterward?"

Reggie met his gaze with some difficulty. "We both agree that this marriage is not one either of us would go through with if we had any real choice." She looked down, pretending to study the bit of cottonwood bark. "Well, we might not have any choice over whether or not to get married, but we do have a choice in how we conduct ourselves after the ceremony."

"I'm afraid you're going to have to spell things out a little plainer than that."

Heat suffused Reggie's face. This was even harder than she'd imagined. "What I'm saying is, we don't have to actually..." She floundered for the right words. *Just say it.*

She swallowed the sudden obstruction in her throat and tried again. "We don't have to actually consummate our vows."

There. That should be plain enough.

The silence drew out for what seemed an eternity. Reggie shredded the bark, feeling her emotions fray along with it. If he didn't say something soon—

"I see." His tone had a self-mocking edge. "And here I was thinking what a fine catch I made."

Reggie jerked her head up. She'd expected sarcasm, perhaps even anger, but not this bitterness. She hadn't stopped to think that he might view it as a rejection of him personally.

"I... I thought you would... I mean surely you agree it would be best, at least for now..."

Her words trailed off as he stepped closer. "Is that *fear* I see in your eyes? I wonder—what is it you're afraid of?" His irises darkened from blue to storm cloud gray as his gaze captured hers. Even though she heard the mocking tone underlying his words, the intensity in his expression sent a shiver through her, trapped the breath in her throat.

She should move away, put some distance between them so she could think. But her feet refused to respond.

"Is it me that you fear?" He raised a finger to stroke her chin.

His touch was so soft, so gentle.

His finger moved to trace the line of her jaw. "Or is it your reaction to me that has you so on edge?"

Reggie couldn't speak, couldn't move. She was very, very afraid he'd just hit the nail on the head.

Adam saw emotion in Regina's eyes, saw the softening in her expressive face, and suddenly he was no longer mocking.

He placed his hands on her shoulder, all the while holding her gaze captive with his. When she didn't pull away, he slowly lowered his head, ready to draw back at the slightest indication she didn't want this.

But instead of pushing him away, she leaned forward, as if impatient with his dallying.

Adam didn't require further encouragement. He touched his lips to hers, lightly at first, then more fully as she responded in kind.

Truth be told, he'd wanted to kiss her since she'd stepped out onto the road that day, disguised as a sassy country miss. She'd stood up under their disdain with a mix of confidence and self-directed humor that had intrigued him and made him want to protect her.

Suddenly, she stiffened, shattering the mood.

"No!" she protested sharply. "We can't do this."

He loosened his hold, allowing her to pull back. "It's okay. We've done nothing improper," he said, trying to reassure her. "Engaged couples are allowed an occasional kiss."

She took a step back. "You don't understand. We *can't* do this. I won't have it."

"You won't have it?" He dropped his hands to his sides, stung by her vehement rejection. "Seems to me you were of a different mind a moment ago."

"You caught me by surprise. I wasn't expecting you to take such liberties." The fear was back in her eyes, along with an almost haunted desperation.

"Do you find the thought of my touching you so repugnant?"

Her eyes widened in shock. "No! I mean, it's not that. I just..." Her chin came up in stubborn defiance. "We just can't, is all."

He'd never seen her so rattled before. Was it an embarrassed reaction to her own response to their kiss? Or did thinking about the kind of intimacy a man and woman shared after marriage frighten her? "It's all right if you want to take it slow."

Her lips compressed in a stubborn line. "You don't understand."

That was an understatement. "Then *help* me understand."

"I don't want any of this." She waved her hands, as if trying to encompass the world. "I don't know what Grandfather told you, but I'm unwed because I choose to be, not because I haven't had offers." Her face hardened. "Surely you're not the sort of man to take an unwilling woman to his bed."

Adam's back stiffened. If a man had dared say that to him, he'd be eating those words right now. "I wouldn't force myself on any woman," he bit out. "But I also don't see myself remaining celibate the rest of my life. And since I also don't intend to break my wedding vows, we have a problem."

He folded his arms. He didn't for one minute believe Regina was truly content with her spinster-aunt status. She was too spirited, to vibrant a woman for that. "You can either tell me what's really bothering you, or I'll consider you've broken faith with our contract. And that means I take Jack to Philadelphia."

The stricken, trapped look in Regina's eyes was almost his undoing. But Adam held firm. He had to get to the bottom of whatever was causing her to take this irrational stand.

She rallied quickly, squaring her shoulders. "The contract only states that I have to select a groom and then marry him within the allotted time. I intend to fulfill that obligation, so far as it goes." She tossed her head. "If you don't like my terms, there's still time for you to walk away."

Adam shook his head. "I've already explained I can't do that. And from where I'm standing, honoring your marriage vows appears an implicit part of the contract."

He raised a brow. "I'm just a lawyer, though. If you insist on sticking by your interpretation, we can ask Judge Madison to decide which of us is correct."

Regina's hands fisted. Her face reflected so much tightly leashed desperation he expected her to use those fists to pound against him.

She stood locked in that stance for an eternity of seconds. Dark emotions stirred her features, an outer sign of the inner war she must be fighting.

What was it that had such a strong hold over her?

Adam recognized the exact moment she realized she had no choices left, that she had lost the struggle between them. Despair, so deep and poignant it was tangible, flashed across her face. Then her expression closed off.

Without another word, she spun around and walked away.

He let her go, disappointed she hadn't chosen to tell him what was really bothering her.

Regina was no coward or simpering miss, so what was she so afraid of? Had some man taken advantage of her, hurt her in some way?

A rush of fury flooded through him at the very thought.

That would explain so much—why she had never married, why she'd contented herself with raising someone else's child, with living in someone else's home.

He had to convince her to trust him enough to tell him the full story. Once everything was out in the open between them, he could reassure her, could give her the time she needed to overcome her trepidations, to learn what a beautiful thing the God-ordained institution of marriage could bring a loving couple.

Could avenge her honor if that was called for.

But without honesty, any relationship between them was doomed to failure.

Reggie's mind skittered in all directions, trying to find a solution to the problem.

There had to be another way out of this mess.

She couldn't tell Adam the truth, couldn't take the chance. The stakes were too high.

But, oh, if things were different…

Her lips tingled from the memory of that kiss. There was something so achingly sweet, so affirming, so right about it.

Buck's barking startled her back to the here and now. She looked up to find Ira watching her with a worried frown. She tried to return a reassuring smile, but could tell he wasn't fooled.

She turned to watch Jack. He'd stooped down, studying something in the tall grass. Buck was by his side, tail wagging in excitement. Which probably meant they were looking at a bug or frog, definitely nothing dangerous.

Jack glanced up and gave her a little-boy grin, then returned to whatever he'd been studying.

She heard Adam's footsteps and tensed. She couldn't face him, not with her emotions so raw. If that made her a coward, so be it.

She quickly closed the gap between her and Mrs. Peavy. "I think it's time we headed back to town."

Mrs. Peavy nodded. "The hamper is already packed."

A few moments later, as they prepared to climb back in the carriage, Reggie had the cowardly urge to ask Ira to take her place in front while she slipped into the back. Her gaze met Adam's briefly, and the knowing glint she spied there stiffened her spine.

With a smile that felt as brittle as cracked glass, she allowed him to hand her up into the front seat.

That evening, Reggie wasn't certain if Adam would show up for supper, but sure enough, he arrived right on schedule.

She didn't understand. How could he act as if nothing had changed?

They'd barely settled around the table, when Jack turned to Adam. "Mr. Barr?"

Adam paused in the act of passing a platter to Reggie. "Yes?"

"Aunt Reggie says, if it's all right with you, I could call you Uncle Adam after y'all get married."

Reggie's gaze flew to Adam's. A startled expression flashed across his features, there and gone in a heartbeat. *Please say the right thing.*

Adam gave the boy a wide smile. "Uncle Adam. That has a nice ring to it." He nodded. "I'd be honored."

Equal parts relief and gratitude curled through Reggie.

"Do I have to wait until the wedding?" Jack asked.

Adam winked. "It wouldn't bother me if you started right away. After all," his gaze cut to Reggie, "it's not as if there's anything that's going to stop the wedding now."

Reggie reached for her glass with suddenly icy fingers. She could not become Adam's wife. To do so would render all her prior sacrifices meaningless.

But how would she ever explain things to Jack when this was over?

The rest of the meal passed by in a nightmarish parody of normalcy. They talked and ate as if everything was as it should be. But afterward, Reggie couldn't remember what had been said or what she'd eaten.

As Adam pulled her chair back for her after the meal, she thought about pleading a headache. And it wouldn't be stretching the truth by much.

But before she could say anything, Adam turned to Jack.

"If you don't mind, your Aunt Regina and I have some things to discuss about the wedding."

Mrs. Peavy waved a hand toward the boy. "Why don't you come along to the kitchen with me? I have a few cookies left over from our picnic, and Ira was just saying he wished he had someone to play checkers with."

Reggie allowed Adam to escort her into the parlor. The touch of his hand at her elbow evoked memories of the kiss they'd shared. She couldn't control the tiny, telltale quiver that sidled up her arm.

Did he intend to pick up the conversation where they'd left it this afternoon? Could he possibly be ready to see reason and actually help her find an acceptable compromise?

He led her to the sofa, then took a seat opposite.

"Was there something in particular you wished to discuss?" Reggie asked. The words sounded stilted even to her own ears, but she couldn't shake the edgy, jittery feeling. She clasped her hands in her lap just to keep them from trembling.

"There was." He leaned forward, his expression almost sympathetic. "I've been thinking about what you said earlier, about wanting a platonic marriage."

Hope and something poignantly remorseful stirred in her. He *was* ready to compromise.

His gaze probed hers. "Answer me truthfully. Are you committed to making this marriage work?"

Her hands tightened painfully as her hope fizzled. What did he expect from her? "I will do whatever I must to keep Jack."

Adam grimaced. "Not the most flattering response, but an honest one."

He leaned back and offered a reassuring smile. "That being said, I'll agree to take things slow, to give you time to adjust to the idea of being married. The best way to accomplish that would be for the two of us to spend the first few days after the wedding at your cabin."

Reggie felt the blood drain from her face. He couldn't mean it. The two of them, alone, hours from anyone.

"Don't worry—I won't force you to do anything you don't want to. But if we're going to try to work through your…reservations, then I think some time alone is a good way to start."

His smile took on a self-mocking edge. "Besides, I don't relish word getting out that I spent my wedding night in a separate bedroom from my new wife."

He raised a brow. "Any objections?"

Objections? Of course she had objections—dozens of them. How could he possibly see this as a solution? This problem couldn't be resolved in two *years*, let alone two days.

But if it would salve his pride to not make their arrangement known right away, she couldn't deny him that. Stunned by the ever deepening hole she was digging for herself, Reggie shook her head.

"Good." Adam stood. "Then, if you'll excuse me, I'll say good-night."

As she watched him leave, all Reggie could think about was spending two days isolated with Adam in her favorite place in the whole world.

Fear wasn't the only emotion she felt.

The next few days strained Reggie's control to the near-breaking point. It wasn't that Adam was unkind or demanding. In fact, it was just the opposite.

He treated her as if the conversation in the meadow had never taken place. He came by in the mornings, taking over the repair work Mitchell had started. Then he returned in the evening, joining them for supper.

Not even her studio offered a sanctuary. He would show up there occasionally while she worked. Not that he overtly intruded. He actually spent more time chatting with Ira than with her, which for some reason put her in even more of a snit.

But she was always conscious of his presence. Every time he touched her, be it a simple taking of her elbow to help her down the stairs, or an accidental brushing against her as they passed through a doorway, it set her on edge.

Nights were the worst. She lay awake for hours, trying to find answers on her shadowy ceiling. When she did fall asleep, her dreams were haunted by images of what could have been.

The day of her wedding, Reggie climbed out of bed with the grim realization that she'd run out of time. In six hours she would become Mrs. Adam Barr. She had to tell Adam the truth about her past.

With stiff, mechanical motions, she got dressed and plodded down the stairs. She ate her breakfast without tasting it.

Jack, excited about the upcoming wedding, carried most of the conversation.

When the meal was over, Reggie pulled Ira aside. "I'm going to my studio. Please find Adam and ask him to join me there as soon as is most convenient."

Ira gave her a searching look, then nodded and left. Feeling like a prisoner marching to the gallows, Reggie asked Mrs. Peavy to keep an eye on Jack, then headed out.

Myrtis Jenkins, her nearest neighbor, was working in her flower garden. "Good morning, Reggie. A lovely day for a wedding, isn't it?"

Reggie managed to smile through the queasiness in her stomach. "Yes, ma'am. A bride couldn't ask for a sunnier one." With a wave she hurried on. She had to endure two more such encounters before she was able to scurry safely inside her studio.

Then the waiting began. Unable to sit still, Reggie paced the length of the room and back, over and over.

Lately, she'd felt like she was in a slightly off focus dream. Adam never so much as mentioned their discussion in the meadow, nor had he tried to kiss her again. Yet every look they'd exchanged, every accidental contact they made had been fraught with meaning, to her at least.

The fact that he'd been so exactingly polite had only kept her off balance, unsure of what his feelings truly were.

It didn't matter though. What she was about to tell him would put an end to any hope she had of having a normal future as his wife. Not that she'd stood a chance before.

If only she could snatch Jack up and run someplace far away, someplace where they could never be found.

Her grandfather had given those three men a chance to start new—why couldn't she have the same opportunity?

A knock at the door stopped her in her tracks. She spun around and faced the door, feeling the contents of her stomach rebel. She couldn't do this.

A second knock, more insistent this time. "Regina, are you in there?"

Breathe.

"Coming."

Reggie smoothed her skirt, then stepped forward to open the door.

Adam stepped inside and took in the doomed expression on Regina's face before she turned away. He shut the door behind him and tossed his hat on the counter. "Ira said you wanted to speak to me."

She turned to face him and he sensed a desperate air of entreaty about her. "I want to ask you one more time to call this wedding off, or at least respect my wish to not push me to consummate it."

Adam swallowed an oath. He'd thought they were making progress on that front. He hadn't been oblivious to her awareness of him, to the signals her eyes sent, or to her reaction when he "accidentally" touched her.

Why was she so adamantly denying this attraction they both felt?

"As I told you before," he said firmly, "if anyone calls a halt to this wedding, it will be you, not me. And if you do, I will be forced to follow through with my obligations under that contract we all signed."

He approached her until only a hand span separated them. He could smell the fresh outdoor scent of her, could almost feel her breath on his skin, see the rapid pulse beat in her neck. "I'm not a monster, Regina. I'm willing to give you the time you need to adjust to the idea of being married. We can take it slow, get to really know each other along the way. But if we go through with the marriage, I want your word there will be a real effort on your part to make it work. I expect this to eventually become a true marriage, in *every* sense of the word."

He brushed a stray hair from her forehead and her eyes closed briefly at his touch. "Can you do that?"

Her eyes opened again and he saw a regret and pain there so deep he winced.

"I can."

Her unexpected capitulation set his pulse surging in a wild stirring of victory. "That's all I ask—"

She placed a finger to his lips. "No. Don't say anything just yet. I've tried to avoid this in every way I know how, but you've left me no choice."

What was wrong?

"Before we take this any further, before we make any vows or commitments to each other, there's something you should know."

"I'm listening." Anticipation stirred his blood. She was finally ready to tell him what had happened to make her so afraid of marriage. Whatever it was, he was confident he could help her work through it.

She squared her shoulders and looked him squarely in the eyes.

"Jack is not my nephew. He's my son."

Chapter Fourteen

Adam's gut clenched as if she'd delivered a blow. Several possibilities had swirled through his mind, but this had been nowhere on the list. Had some filthy bit of pond scum attacked her? "How?"

"The sordid details aren't important."

"They are to me." He reached for her hands, trying to comfort her.

But she pulled away. "Seven years ago, I let myself be seduced by a stranger who threw a bit of attention and flattery my way," she said bitterly. "Then, when he'd gotten what he wanted, he moved on."

Adam's whole perception of her shifted, turned upside down.

She glared a defiant challenge. "Is that enough detail for you, or do you want more?"

"Who knows about this?"

"Until a few minutes ago, Mr. and Mrs. Peavy were the only ones still alive who knew." She narrowed her eyes. "And I'd like to keep it that way."

"How did you manage to keep it secret?" These

weren't the questions he wanted to ask, but they were the only ones his mouth could form.

"Patricia lost two babies in the early years of her marriage. The doctor told her it would be dangerous to try again, so she and Lemuel resigned themselves to a childless marriage. When I realized I was carrying Daniel's child, once everyone got over the shock, we hatched a scheme where we would let everyone think she had disregarded the doctor's orders.

"She and I traveled to St. Louis, under the pretense that, because of her history, Patricia should be put in the care of a 'specialist' during her confinement. Changing places once we arrived was a simple matter. I became Mrs. Lemuel Willis, and she became Regina Nash. Once Jack was born and I had regained my strength, we came back to Turnabout with no one the wiser."

She made it sound so trivial, so ordinary.

"I hadn't realized what a clever little liar you were." He felt the fool. It hadn't been the intimacy she feared. It had been the discovery of her sordid secret.

Then the full import of her words hit him. "How could you just give your own son away to someone else to raise, like a garment that had become too constrictive? Was your reputation more important to you than your son?"

Her hands fisted and her eyes flashed lightning. "How *dare* you! You can judge me a fallen woman if you wish. I will freely admit my guilt. But don't you ever, *ever* suggest I don't love Jack or that I would do anything to cause him harm. Handing my son over to my stepsister was the hardest thing I have ever done in my entire life."

She took a deep breath, her eyes still flashing icy

fire. "I didn't do it for my reputation. If that was all that had been at stake, I would have braved the gossips and self-righteous finger-pointers."

She lifted her chin. "But I couldn't bear for my child to face that same ostracism. He shouldn't have to grow up with the stigma of being the illegitimate son of a man who seduced a sixteen-year-old girl and then abandoned her without looking back. Jack deserves a chance to live life unburdened by my sins."

Pretty words. Did they help her sleep easier at night? Is that how his own mother had justified abandoning him? "He deserves to know the truth."

"Maybe someday, when he's much older and able to understand such matters. But the 'when' and even 'if' is for me to decide, no one else."

"Judge Madison should be told."

"No." Panic flared in her eyes. "You can't tell him."

So much for her saintly motives. "Surely you're not saying you're worried about the judge's sensibilities as well?"

She flinched, then compressed her lips. "There may be no blood tie between Judge Madison and Jack, just like he's not my true grandfather, but there is more that binds a family together than mere blood. Jack *is* his great-grandson, for all intents and purposes. I wouldn't want to hurt Grandfather by informing him that he's the last of his line."

"Not to mention the inheritance Jack stands to lose."

The stinging slap resounded in the quiet room. Adam almost welcomed the sting.

"The other day you accused me of not knowing you." Her voice shook with passion. "You've just proved that you do not know me." She spun on her heel and stalked away.

Adam absently rubbed his cheek as he watched her retreat. She braced her hands against the counter and stood with her back to him. Her shoulders trembled slightly, whether from agitation or fear he couldn't tell.

His whole picture of her as a caring, honest woman was shattered.

She'd given away her son, turned him over to someone else to raise.

Just as his mother had with him.

Her reason might be different, might sound nobler, but it didn't change the facts. Abandoning a child was unforgivable, any way you looked at it.

Yet he couldn't tell Jack the truth about his parentage. Regina was right about that much at least. Putting the boy through that nightmare, forcing him to feel the wrenching pain of knowing that the person who should love you the most didn't feel you were worth fighting for, would be needlessly cruel.

But Judge Madison was another matter. Hearing the truth might be painful, but he deserved to know. In fact, Adam was certain, given the choice, he would *want* to know.

What was he supposed to do about the wedding now? The ceremony was only a few hours away. That confounded contract contained nothing to cover this situation.

How could he possibly marry a woman who'd acted so immorally, so heartlessly?

Amid the maelstrom of questions, an almost inconsequential one surfaced. What had happened to the stranger, this blackguard Daniel, who had seduced and abandoned her?

What sort of man could have so thoroughly turned the head of the fiercely independent Regina?

And did she still pine for him?

Reggie fought to control both her breathing and her churning emotions. This hadn't gone well at all. Her palm still stung from the blow she'd landed on his cheek.

The burning anger was gone now, replaced by sadness for what might have been and a panic that threatened to overwhelm her.

She had hoped for more sympathy, if not for herself, at least for the way she'd handled the subsequent situation. The depth of his rejection had taken her completely by surprise. What would he do now?

Would he cancel the wedding?

Would he tell Grandfather?

Would he expose her secrets to the town? To Jack?

Oh, please God, don't let him be that heartless.

Had she done the right thing in telling him? Or had this humiliation been for nothing? In her selfish desire to hold on to her son, had she given this prison-hardened man a weapon he could use to destroy her family?

It would be better to have Jack torn away from her and sent to boarding school than for him to be branded as the illegitimate son of a harlot.

She heard Adam approach and turned to face him. Trying to read any hint of his next action in his face was useless. The man's expression was closed as tight as a bank vault.

Adam stopped a few feet from her. What thoughts

were running through his mind? What decisions had he made?

The seconds ticked away as he stared at her. Seeing the icy contempt in his eyes while she waited for him to speak was agonizing.

Finally, Reggie couldn't stand it any longer. "If you're trying to torture me by your silence, you've succeeded. Can you just get on with telling me what you've decided?"

"Decided about what?"

The man was infuriating! "About the weather," she said sarcastically. Then she waved a hand. "About all of it—the wedding, Jack, my grandfather."

"The wedding will proceed as planned."

"It will?" She was surprised, not only by the answer but by his matter-of-fact tone.

"Of course. We are still bound by the terms of the contract."

Reggie wished the contract to perdition. How did he really feel about being married to her? More to the point, how did she feel about marrying him now that he could barely stand to look at her? Did he still intend to make a true marriage of it, or did the thought of touching her now repulse him?

She couldn't bring herself to ask the question.

"As for Jack, while I don't like being party to deception, you were right in saying he's an innocent in all this. It can only hurt him to learn the truth at this stage."

Relief surged through her, making her almost giddy. She could face even a cold, passionless marriage as long as Jack was protected.

Then she realized he hadn't answered her last question. "And Grandfather?"

"The situation with Judge Madison is a different matter."

Her heart tried to climb into her throat. *Don't do this to me. Please.*

"He deserves to hear the truth," Adam continued ruthlessly.

"The news will kill him." Reggie's voice was little more than a croak.

"Judge Madison is a strong man, both physically and emotionally. While this will be unpleasant, I'm certain he'll be able to weather it." A small tic appeared at the corner of his mouth. "However, it would be best if the news came from you rather than from me."

He couldn't know what he was asking of her. "What if I refuse?"

She hadn't thought it possible for his expression to harden further, but somehow it did. "You have one month to find a way to tell him. If you haven't done so in that time, I'll have no choice but to do it for you."

Why couldn't he understand how hurtful this would be, not just for her, but for Grandfather as well? "I can't tell him such news in a letter."

He waved impatiently. "Of course not. We'll plan a trip to Philadelphia soon after we return from the cabin."

Her heart stuttered. He still wanted to go to the cabin after the ceremony? The two of them, alone for two whole days?

"What could be more reasonable?" he continued. "We'll be getting your grandfather's belated blessing on the marriage, and it'll give me time to take care of unfinished business."

"That's right," she said. "You always see things in

terms of such absolute right and wrong. There's no room in your world for the shadowy lines between."

"As far as I'm concerned, shadows are where criminals and other miscreants hide." He straightened the cuff of his shirt. "Now, is there anything else you wanted to tell me?"

Reggie shook her head.

"Good. Then I believe we have a wedding to prepare for. If you'll excuse me?" With a mocking bow, he turned and left.

Reggie remained there long after the jingle from the bell above the door faded away. How could she go through with this? How could she marry a man who considered her little better than a harlot.

All the old feelings of humiliation and worthlessness from that long-ago morning when she'd had the last of her innocence stripped away came flooding back. The morning Daniel had stood there with that pitying smile and told her how nicely she'd helped him pass the time but he was ready to move on.

How could she smile convincingly as she repeated her vows when she felt so soiled and unworthy inside?

Would everyone in the church see that cold loathing in Adam's expression when he looked at her?

Slowly she locked the front door and moved to the side one. She wanted to get home as unobtrusively as possible. She couldn't face any of her neighbors right now, not when she felt as if she might shatter into a thousand pieces with just the slightest touch.

As she stepped outside, though, she took a deep breath and tried to regroup. After all, she'd managed to take this huge step, confessing the story no one had spoken aloud in over six years. And she'd revealed it to Adam no less, the man who held her future in the palm of his hand.

The man who had once held her heart there as well.

If she could survive that, surely she could survive whatever came next. She just had to do as she'd always done: square her shoulders, face her problems without flinching and do what she had to do to make certain those she loved were safe.

"I now pronounce you husband and wife."

Reggie looked into her new husband's eyes and saw a flatness there that sent icy fingers up her spine. When he bent to give her the traditional kiss, she had to force herself to hold still. The cold-as-a-tombstone brush of his lips was mercifully brief.

Somehow, she managed to smile as they turned and walked down the aisle, arm in arm. A reception awaited them outside and the church lawn was already crowded with friends and neighbors. It appeared the whole town had gathered to see them wed.

She moved among her friends with a smile pasted on her face, feeling as if this were a waking nightmare. How was it no one seemed to notice anything out of the ordinary? Couldn't they see the brittleness in her expression, the fragility of her control?

She paused at each cluster of guests only long enough to receive their well wishes. She must have made sensible responses, though she couldn't for the life of her remember just what she said.

For his part, Adam received claps on the back and good-natured jabs. The citizens of Turnabout seemed more than happy to welcome him into their midst.

But each time their glances met across the churchyard, she saw that same flatness that chilled her to her very core. She imagined that would be the same look he'd give to whoever had framed him and sent him to jail for six years.

At last the buggy was brought around. Their bags and a large hamper of food was already stowed inside.

Reggie noted Trib was tied to the back.

Amid more well wishes and knowing glances, the newlyweds were escorted to the buggy and Ira handed the reins to Adam.

Neither said a word as they rode away. When they turned onto the rutted trail that would eventually lead to Reggie's cabin, Adam slowed the vehicle to a stop.

"I assume you know how to handle a buggy?" His tone was excruciatingly polite.

She nodded.

"Good." He handed her the reins and stepped down. A moment later he'd untied Trib and mounted up. Riding around to the front, he met her gaze again. "If you feel the need to stop and rest, just call out." With that, he nudged Trib into a trot.

Reggie flicked the reins and set the buggy in motion. It was a relief not to have his stony, disapproving presence sitting beside her. But this lonely ride was giving her too much time to think about what might happen once they reached the cabin.

Did he intend to continue with this chilly politeness?

Adam stayed within easy hailing distance, but he never once looked back. Although Reggie would have enjoyed an opportunity to stand up and stretch for a few minutes, she held her peace. Better to endure a long ride without pause than to face the look of betrayal and distaste in his eyes again.

There would be time enough for that at the cabin.

An eternity later, Regina sat up straighter. They'd reached the spot where she'd first encountered the four men. Had it been only three weeks ago?

Something in the way Adam shifted in the saddle told her he recognized the spot, too. What was he thinking? Would he finally glance back at her?

Instead, he nudged Trib to a faster pace. By the time she reached the cabin, Adam had already dismounted.

He stepped forward to hand her down, but didn't maintain contact longer than absolutely necessary. "Just tether the horse to that branch," he said, already moving away. "I'll unload the bags and unhitch the buggy after I take care of Trib."

Reggie watched him disappear behind the cabin, then secured the horse as he'd directed. Ignoring his other instructions, she lifted the hamper and carried it inside. She wouldn't be able to eat anything tonight, but Adam might be hungry.

She dusted off the table and spread a cloth on it. She'd just laid out a simple meal when Adam walked in, carrying two buckets of water.

"I thought you might want to freshen up after that ride." He glanced at the table. "Don't bother setting out anything for me. What I ate at the reception will hold me until morning."

He moved back to the door and returned shortly with her bags. "You can take this bed," he said, depositing her things near the curtained alcove. "I'll take the loft."

Well, that answered one of her questions.

As she picked up the dishes she'd already laid out, Reggie noticed her hands trembled slightly.

It was just as well he wouldn't look at her.

"Don't bother waiting up for me," he added. "I plan to do some exploring. I may be a while."

"Be careful," she said as matter-of-factly as she could. "These woods can be tricky to find your way around in, especially after dark." She'd offer to guide him, but she knew her presence wouldn't be welcome.

"I'll manage." He gave her a ghost of his old smile. "If I get lost, I'll whistle." Then his expression shuttered again, as if he regretted even that small bit of thawing.

Without another word, he left.

That night, Reggie lay in bed, staring at the raftered ceiling and straining to hear some sign that he'd returned. Darkness had fallen an hour ago. Even though a full moon provided plenty of light, she was getting worried.

At last she heard his boots on the front porch and relief washed over her.

He didn't come inside, though. She imagined him leaning against the porch rail, staring off into the starry night sky.

What was he thinking? Was he railing against the fate that had tied him to her? Even without her sordid past, she wasn't at all like the woman he'd been engaged to before.

Emma Silverton.

She'd been the most sought-after debutante in Philadelphia and she'd set her sights on Adam.

The woman was classically beautiful, had skin like cream, the voice of a songbird and hair like spun gold. She moved with a feminine grace and her smile could reduce even the hardest-hearted person into a willing lackey.

She'd also had the greed of a spoiled two-year-old

and all the compassion of an adolescent bully. It hadn't surprised Reggie to learn the self-centered socialite had abandoned Adam the moment he was arrested.

But did Adam still have feelings for her?

Reggie had kept up with Emma through the years—a sort of macabre fascination on her part. She knew Emma had married someone else while Adam was in jail. Another lawyer in the firm Adam had worked for, the son of a senator no less.

Reggie rolled to her other side. Then stilled as the cabin door opened.

Adam stepped inside and her heart began an erratic thumping. She stared at the curtain as if she could see though it, following his progress by the sound of his footsteps.

He stopped halfway across the room. What was he doing? She was afraid to move, to even breathe for fear she would miss some sound he might make.

After what seemed an eternity he moved on and she heard him climb the ladder to the loft.

That was it then. He'd made his decision and obviously wanted nothing to do with her.

Reggie pulled the pillow tight against her chest, trying to smother the pain there.

Adam undressed in the cramped loft and stretched out on the pallet, staring up at the ceiling. Last night when he'd gone to bed, his mind had been full of ideas on how best to woo his marriage-shy bride. He'd vowed to be patient with her, to do his best to gain her trust.

Marriage-shy—hah! She would no doubt think it a grand joke that he'd been so concerned with her maidenly reluctance.

He had seen her bold, independent manner as another facet of honesty and an unwillingness to compromise her values. Her refusal to let what others think influence her actions had seemed a refreshing change from the attitude of the women he'd known before. But she'd taken that I'll-do-as-I-please attitude one step too far.

By her own admission, Regina was more sinner than saint. A woman who could freely give away both her innocence and her child was too cold-hearted and uncaring for him to develop any tender feelings for.

Even if she did look like a wounded innocent tonight.

So why did he still feel this strong attraction to her?

And what did he intend to do about it?

Chapter Fifteen

Adam woke to the tempting smell of freshly brewed coffee and frying ham. He was suddenly very aware of how long it had been since he'd last eaten.

Regina glanced up briefly when he joined her. "Good morning. Breakfast will be ready in a minute."

"Thanks." He sat at the table, determined to maintain the polite detachment he'd assumed yesterday.

Then he took a good look at her as she set a plate in front of him. Dark smudges underlined her eyes, as if she hadn't slept well. But gone was the vulnerable, cowed woman from yesterday. There was determination in the set of her shoulders, a glint of challenge in her eyes, purpose in her movements.

She'd apparently recovered from whatever crisis of conscience she'd been feeling.

Regina set her own plate on the table and looked him square in the eyes. "We have to talk," she said firmly.

He picked up his fork. "I'm listening."

"My confession yesterday outraged your personal moral code—I understand that. However, there's nothing I can do to change what is in the past. I need to know what I can expect from you going forward."

He detected no guilt in her demeanor, no sense that she felt shame or remorse. Only a determination to regain control over her situation.

"If you're referring to our time here," he said, "I think it would be best if we had as little interaction as possible. In fact, I suggest you proceed for the most part as if I'm not here and I'll do the same."

He noticed a tightening of her jaw, there and gone from one heartbeat to the next. "And when we return to Turnabout?"

"I believe we're both capable of maintaining an air of civility when we're around others. I will, of course, take a separate bedroom."

"And will your 'civility' extend to Jack also?"

"Don't worry. I plan to treat Jack as if he were my son." He'd try to make sure Jack never felt neglected or unwelcome.

Then he paused with his coffee cup halfway to his lips. "As a matter of fact, I suppose Jack's actually my stepson now."

She leaned forward. "I'd still like to formally adopt him."

He nodded cynically. "That way you can finally have him call you mother without revealing any embarrassing little secrets." He set his cup down and gave her a hard look. "I believe you gave up that right when you gave *him* up."

She flinched, the first sign of vulnerability he'd seen today. "Are you saying you're opposed to my adopting him?"

"*Our* adopting him, you mean. Of course I'm not opposed, but let's resolve some of the bigger issues first, like having that talk with your grandfather."

He pushed away from the table. "Thank you for breakfast. Now, I think I'll take Trib out for a bit of exercise."

Reggie didn't watch him leave. She pushed the food around on her plate with a fork until she heard him step off the porch.

Is this what she had to look forward to—chilly politeness and stilted conversation?

If so, she'd have to make it work. She couldn't let Jack see her misery. But was she that good an actress?

Reggie took her time cleaning up from breakfast. Once that was done, she stood in the middle of the cabin, at a loss for what to do next. She didn't have her camera equipment with her or even a book to read. She had to find something to keep herself occupied, something to keep her maudlin thoughts at bay.

Grabbing a rag and scrub brush, she set about cleaning the already neat cabin with a vengeance.

Adam came back from his ride about lunchtime. What little conversation they had consisted mainly of excruciatingly polite requests to pass one dish or another.

As soon as he'd finished, he once again pushed back from the table. "I noticed you're getting low on firewood. I assume there's an axe here somewhere I can use to cut a fresh stack."

She nodded. "There's one out in the feed crib. But this is the hottest part of the day. You should wait until later this evening when it cools down a bit."

"I'll be fine."

Was her company so distasteful that he'd rather work out in the midday heat than sit in the same room with her?

Fine. Let him go. He could work himself down into a little puddle of sweat for all she cared.

He moved toward the door. "When I'm done with the firewood I'll probably try my hand at some fishing."

Not trusting herself to say anything, Reggie merely stood and began clearing the table. She took her time with the housework, but there really wasn't much to do. As she put away the dish rag, she compressed her lips in a determined line. She was not going to just sit here and mope.

A vigorous walk was just what she needed.

It was late afternoon before she saw him again. His indifference was harder to take than anger would have been. If only she could force some emotion from him. Any emotion!

She had to find a way to get through to him, to make it difficult for him to continue to ignore her.

Hearing him outside, she stepped out on the porch to find him sitting on the steps, whittling on a stick.

She hesitated, then stepped forward and leaned her stomach against the porch rail. "No luck with the fishing?"

He didn't look up. "I don't seem to attract good luck in much of anything I do."

Reggie mentally winced. Not a promising start.

Just keep talking.

"I checked the food hamper. There's only a little of the ham left. But there's cheese and bread and some fruit preserves, too. It's not fancy vittles, but I should be able to fix us something filling for supper."

He shrugged. “Don’t go to any trouble on my account. I’m used to prison fare, remember?”

Reggie doggedly tried again. “Thank you for refilling the water barrel and for taking care of the firewood.”

His knife bit a deep gouge in the wood. “Don’t worry, I intend to carry my share of the load.”

Something inside Reggie snapped. Her feelings of guilt gave way to good old-fashioned anger.

She stomped down the stairs and whirled around to confront her stony-faced husband. “I’ve had enough of you trying to make me feel like I’m a no-account jezebel who’s less appealing than snail slime. Yes, I did something terrible and foolish seven years ago. But I was only sixteen, for mercy’s sake! And I’ve been paying for it ever since.”

She fisted her hands on her hips. “For good or ill, I’m your wife now, and I deserve at least a smidgeon of respect.”

He very deliberately folded the pocket knife and brushed the shavings from his pants leg. Then he stood, towering over her like someone about to pronounce sentence. Would he give her a blistering set-down? Argue with her? Stalk away?

But his expression remained maddeningly impassive. “I intend to afford you every respect you are due. If at any time you feel I’ve failed to do so, please don’t hesitate to say so.”

He stepped down. “Please don’t bother to wait supper for me, I’m going for a walk and—”

“I know,” she interrupted bitterly, “it may be quite late before you return.”

Without even a flicker of change in his expression, Adam nodded and stepped past her.

As quickly as it had come, her anger died.

It was no use. She couldn't even rile him to anger anymore.

Reggie trudged up the steps and sat down on the porch swing. With a listless push of her foot, she set it in motion. She wished she at least had Buck with her. He would have been better company than her so-called husband.

It was nearly dusk when Reggie finally went back inside. She lit a lantern then stood wondering what to do next. She was too restless to go to bed, but she didn't really have anything to do.

She hadn't packed so much as a book to read.

Book. That reminded her of something.

Reggie moved to the wooden chest that rested to one side of the loft ladder, and knelt beside it. She hesitated a moment, then lifted the lid. Pushing aside some linens and blankets, she unearthed Granddaddy Noah's Bible.

Plopping down cross-legged on the floor, Reggie set the heavy book in her lap. She brushed her hand lightly, almost reverently, on the leather-bound cover, then opened it up.

There, printed in different inks and hands, was her family history on her mother's side, all the way back to her great-great-grandfather, Hiram Forrester. It was all recorded here—births, marriages, deaths.

As a child, whenever she'd seen Granddaddy Noah with his Bible, she'd asked him about those people. He'd tell her wonderful stories about who they'd been, how they'd lived, how they'd died. And he'd always ended by pointing to her name and saying that someday her own husband and children would be listed there, and that she could pass the volume down to one of her children who would continue the tradition.

She'd look at the blank section and envisioned the unending march of names that would fill it. The thought of all that history, and her part in it, had fascinated her, had given her a sense of belonging as nothing else ever had.

Regina crossed the room and placed the Bible carefully on the table. Then she searched around until she found some writing materials. With painstaking care, she added Adam's name next to her own with yesterday's date. Then she sat back and looked at the entry, bittersweet sadness clogging her throat.

That would quite likely be the last entry ever made into this book. It all ended with her.

Jack's name should be recorded here, of course. But the thought of him stumbling upon the entry had been too daunting. As Adam had pointed out with such moral righteousness, she had given up the right to claim her son long ago.

And since her new husband had also made it abundantly clear he couldn't bear to spend even a few minutes alone with her, there would be no children from this union.

What an awful mess she'd made of not only her own life but Adam's as well.

She traced the names listed there with her finger, feeling as if she'd let every one of those people down. When she reached her grandfather's name, her finger started trembling. "Oh, Granddaddy, I'm so sorry."

Then, as if he'd been standing beside her, she heard the words he'd uttered so long ago.

"But this book contains more than our family history. It contains the glorious story of God's love for us and the key to true happiness, in this life and the next. Don't ever forget that."

But she had. Somewhere along the way, she'd let her shame push her away from that all-encompassing love. Was it too late?

And with that, she folded her arms on the table and lay her head on them, finally letting the pent-up sobs come.

Adam dropped the stub of his cigar and ground it with the heel of his boot. Night had fallen and he had only the moon and stars to light his way. Not that he really needed them. He'd walked this path so many times today he had every twist and turn, every dip and bump memorized.

The cabin finally came into view and all seemed quiet inside. The only light visible was a single lamp shining from the kitchen window.

Still, Adam hesitated. He wasn't ready to go inside yet, at least not until he was certain she was asleep. He couldn't face that bruised look in her eyes again, not tonight. Yes, she'd done something terrible. The same unforgivable thing his mother had done to him.

But that didn't mean he enjoyed seeing her spirit crushed.

He'd actually been relieved when she'd roused enough to give him what for earlier. Not that he'd ever admit that to her.

Was he being too unbending? She was right about one thing. They were married, and, for Jack's sake if nothing else, they had to find a way to live together in some semblance of harmony.

Perhaps before they headed out tomorrow they could sit down and talk about it.

Satisfied with that decision, and confident that she'd turned in for the night, Adam climbed the porch steps. He slipped his muddy boots off by the door and quietly stepped inside.

Then stopped. Regina was asleep all right, but she hadn't gone to bed. She was seated at the dining table with her head pillowed on her arms. A book lay open beside her.

Should he just slip quietly past her and go up to bed. Surely she'd wake on her own before morning and seek out her own bed. Especially if he made a bit of extra noise settling in upstairs.

But that didn't feel right.

With a sigh, Adam moved toward the table. As he approached, the book caught his eye. A Bible? Had she turned to the Good Book in penitence? Or was she searching for answers?

Then he realized it wasn't open to scripture, but to the front pages that listed family history. Curious, he peered over her shoulder, trying to read the names. Her elbow covered a portion of it, but it seemed to be a record of her maternal lineage.

His gaze fell on the last entry. When he saw his name listed beside hers, his breath caught. It was as if a whole clan had reached out and welcomed him into their midst.

Then he got his first good look at her face.

She'd been crying! And not just dainty, ladylike weeping. The tracks on her cheeks attested to a raging flood of tears.

His churlishness had brought her to this.

Her luminous eyes drifted open, and she gave him

a sleepy smile. “Are you ever going to kiss me again?” she asked wistfully.

A heartbeat later, the dreamy fog cleared from her eyes. She stiffened and her face suffused with color. “I’m sorry. I was still dreaming—”

“You were crying.” It came out harsher than he’d intended, like an accusation. She’d been dreaming about his kissing her?

Regina swiped guiltily at her cheeks. “It was nothing,” she said almost convincingly. “I was just feeling sorry for myself.”

She tried to turn away then, but he stopped her with a hand to her arm. “I suppose I owe you an apology.” He clenched his jaw. “I haven’t handled this whole business very well.”

She stiffened. “Don’t go feeling sorry for me. I told you, it was a momentary lapse. It won’t happen again.”

He raked a hand through his hair. It appeared they were going to have this conversation tonight after all.

He pulled out a chair and took a seat. “We need to talk.”

Reggie rubbed her upper arms, trying to tamp down her embarrassment. What she’d said to him—

Her cheeks warmed all over again at the memory.

She glanced his way and his serious expression raised a prickle of apprehension.

But mostly she felt relief. Whatever else resulted from this discussion, it signaled that he was through ignoring her.

“I won’t lie,” he began. “I don’t think I’ll ever be able to forget what you did.”

She thought she'd braced herself for censure, but his words still had the power to lash at her.

Adam leaned back. "However, I realize I've acted churlishly and for that I apologize."

Reggie kept very still, her hands clasped in her lap. He'd apologized—that was something.

"As you said," Adam continued, "what happened in the past can't be changed. It's the present and future we need to concentrate on, and how to make them livable for the both of us."

She knew those words hadn't come easily to him and that she should be grateful. He'd offered an olive branch of sorts, a sign of compromise from a man who thought compromise was a weakness. Expecting more from him would be unrealistic. The least she could do was meet him halfway. "How do you suggest we do that?"

Was that flicker in his expression a flash of relief?

Whatever it had been, he suppressed quickly. "We made vows to each other in front of God and your neighbors," he said. "It's important that we be true to those."

"I never planned to do otherwise."

He gave her a tight smile. "Then we're agreed. It might take some effort at first, but in time it will likely become second nature for us to get along amenably."

Now didn't that just sound like the most romantic way to start off a new marriage?

Reggie, stood, needing some activity, some distance from Adam. "You haven't eaten anything tonight. Let me at least get you some cheese and bread."

Adam stood as well. "I *could* use a bite of something."

She unwrapped the block of cheese and reached for

a knife while Adam took a clean cup from the drain board and uncorked the jug of cider.

He stood beside her, so close their shoulders nearly touched. It rattled her for some reason, made her breath uneven.

Did he feel anything at all?

Reggie sliced into the cheese with more vigor than care, then jerked her finger up to her lips, wincing at the metallic tang of blood.

Adam immediately set his cup down, concern furrowing his brow. "Let me see that."

She pulled her finger out of her mouth and shook her head. "It's nothing. The knife slipped. I—"

"Don't argue." He took her hand, examining the cut with a concerned frown.

Reggie stared down at her hand in his. A tiny rivulet of blood seeped from the shallow cut, curling around her finger and onto his, like a narrow ribbon binding them together.

Amazing that such large, work-callused hands could feel so warm and gentle without losing their sense of strength.

"I'm sure it's nothing serious," she said. "It doesn't even hurt." Not a lie since all she could feel at this moment was his touch, his nearness.

"Let's clean it and get a better look, just in case." Still holding her hand, he dipped a clean rag in the nearby bucket of water, then slowly squeezed it over her finger. Head bent, he gently dabbed at the remaining blood.

Reggie stared down at his head, so close she could smell the scent of soap and cigar smoke and night air. So close her breath stirred his hair. So close she could press her lips to his temple without moving much at all.

She pulled slightly back at that very inappropriate thought.

His head came up, his gaze seeking hers. “Did I hurt you?”

Not in any way I can explain. She shook her head, not trusting herself to speak.

“Well then, I think you’re right. It’s not serious. The bleeding’s already stopped.” He let go of her hand. “You’re obviously tired. Go on to bed. I can fix my own meal.”

“But—”

“Don’t worry. I’ll clean up when I’m done.”

Reggie nodded and turned away, realizing nothing much had changed. He was talking to her again, but he didn’t care to spend any more time in her company than he had to.

Adam stared up at the rafters, wishing for sleep that refused to come.

He’d done the right thing, hadn’t he?

Civility was the best, the only, approach.

A soft sound interrupted his thoughts. Footsteps pattered across the floor below and then the cabin door opened and closed.

She was making a late-night trip to the privy, no doubt.

He lay there, waiting for the sound of her return. As the minutes ticked by, he began to imagine all the things that might have gone wrong.

Had she stumbled in the dark and injured herself?

Encountered a snake, or something worse?

Had she somehow gotten turned around and wandered into the woods instead of back to the house?

After several more minutes, Adam couldn't stand it any longer. Pausing just long enough to dress, he climbed down the ladder and headed out the door.

Only to find her safe and sound, leaning against the porch rail, looking out into the night.

He knew she must have heard him. He certainly hadn't made any effort to move quietly. But she didn't bother to turn around.

He remained where he was, waffling about whether to leave her to her solitude or join her. He'd just about decided his company wouldn't be welcome, when she spoke up.

"I've always loved it out here." Her voice had a musing, reminiscent quality to it, as if she were talking to herself.

Taking that as an invitation, he moved next to her and rested his elbows on the rail. She wore a worn cotton robe, belted at the waist, covering whatever nightclothes she had on underneath. Her hair fell in soft waves down her back. It stirred slightly in the night breeze, like a living thing, inviting his touch.

She let out a sigh, drawing his attention back to her face. "It's so peaceful. Even the sounds—insects, animals, wind—have a soothing quality to them."

She didn't seem to expect an answer so he held his peace.

"Granddaddy Noah built this cabin with his own hands," she continued in that same dreamy tone. "He and Nana Ruth and my mother lived here until Mother married my father."

Regina pushed away from the rail. "Let me show you something." She moved to the door but instead of going inside as he'd expected, she paused at the threshold. "Give me your hand."

Without a word, he complied.

Regina guided his hand to the sill above the door. “Feel that?” she asked.

Something was carved into the wood. He carefully traced the design with an index finger.

A heart? And there was something inside the outline.

“It’s Granddaddy and Nana Ruth’s initials and wedding date. He carved it there the day he brought her here. He said their marriage finally made his house a home.”

Was that what had evoked her pensive mood? Thoughts of her grandparents’ marriage?

Regina moved back to the rail. “I remember when I was very little, Granddaddy used to tell me that story. Then he’d lift me up so I could trace the carving with my fingers, like you just did.”

She cut her gaze his way, and even in the dark he saw her expression had lost that dreamlike quality, saw her lips twist into a self-deprecating smile. “I’m sorry. You didn’t ask for a lesson in my family history.” She rubbed her upper arms. “It’s just that they’re all very much on my mind tonight.”

“I saw you added my name to your family Bible.”

She stiffened warily. He could tell from the flicker of surprise in her expression that she hadn’t intended for him to discover that entry.

“It seemed appropriate.” Her tone managed to sound matter-of-fact. “I hope you don’t mind.”

“Actually, I’m honored.” He shifted to face her more fully, resting a hip against the rail. “That makes the family history you were just recounting part of mine as well.”

She glanced away, bracing her hands on the rail again. “I see. However, you don’t understand what I was trying to say. My grandfather meant for this to be a home, a place full of love and laughter. I've not lived up to that. I'm afraid he'd be disappointed in me."

Adam felt his own thoughts shift and tangle. He still believed that in giving her son away she'd done the unforgivable. But that didn't mean he wanted her to castigate herself this way.

He covered one of her hands with his. "You're being too harsh on yourself.

She stared down at his hand resting on hers a moment. Then she jerked it away, looking at him with eyes that were suspiciously moist.

"Don't do this." Her voice was tight, almost desperate. "Don't be sweet to me if you don't really mean it. I couldn't bear it." She spun around and stepped away from him.

Why did she have to be so unflinchingly honest, so noble? It made hearing the pain in her voice that much harder to bear.

Adam placed his hands on her shoulder and gently turned her to face him. "Right now, here with you in the moonlight, it's difficult *not* to mean it."

He slid his hands down her arms, capturing her wrists. "Come along." He drew her toward the porch swing. "It seems neither of us is in the mood for sleep right now. Why don't we sit out here and talk?"

She nodded, and docilely followed him. But he sensed a wariness about her, as if she was braced for another set down.

He supposed he couldn't blame her.

"What should we talk about?" she asked as she settled into the swing.

"Tell me about Jack's father."

Chapter Sixteen

Adam kicked himself as he heard Reggie's indrawn breath. Her expression reflected shock and a sense of betrayal.

"I'm sorry." He raked a hand through his hair, trying to hide his chagrin. He'd intended to comfort her, not deepen her pain. "I don't know why I asked that. I—"

She placed a finger to his lips, silencing his apology. Her color was returning and she faced him squarely. "Of course you're curious. It's only natural."

She wrapped a cloak of dignity around her, as if for protection. "Perhaps it *will* help, if you know what happened."

"You don't have to—"

"Yes, I believe I do." Her smile was bittersweet.

She paused and he could almost see her mind casting back through the years to pull out the memories. "It happened the year I turned sixteen. My parents died six months earlier and I had moved in with Patricia and Lemuel. Patricia was recovering from her second miscarriage. And—"

She cut him a cryptic look. "Let's just say I'd reached a low point, both in morale and self-confidence."

What had happened to put that wounded look in her expression?

"A couple of months after our annual visit to Grandfather's," she continued, "a theater group came through Turnabout. They only intended to stay for three days, but then one of their wagons broke down, and by the time it was repaired their lead actress had injured her leg. All in all, they ended up staying four weeks."

Her hand fiddled with the collar of her robe. "I'd taken over Father's photography business by then, and convinced most of the performers to pose for me."

She smiled reminiscently. "Daniel wasn't like the other members of the troupe. He was quiet and unassuming and seemed genuinely interested in my work. He asked intelligent questions, and spent lots of time with me. He complimented my work, and picked flowers for me, and even wrote me a poem."

She waved a hand. "I guess I was flattered. Since I wasn't one of the pretty girls, or well-to-do girls, and was a mite unconventional to boot, I wasn't used to such attention."

Didn't the male population of Turnabout have eyes and minds?

"Anyway, for the first time a man noticed me, *really* noticed me, in a romantic sort of way. I let it go to my head. For a while I even thought I was in love."

Adam tried to ignore the stirring of jealousy her words prompted.

She grimaced. "Lemuel didn't like the attention I was getting. He said theater people were unreliable and loose-moralled. But I knew Daniel was different."

Hearing the self-condemnation in her voice, Adam felt sympathy for the girl she had been.

"The day before the troupe was to leave, he asked me to marry him."

Adam went very still.

"He offered to go to Lemuel and ask for my hand," she continued. "But he wanted to be sure I returned his feeling first. I was elated and nervous at the same time. I desperately wanted the life he offered me, but I knew Lemuel would never consent. Daniel argued with me, but I finally persuaded him it would be best if we eloped and then told my family after it was done.

"He finally consented to my plan. I let Patricia think I was coming here to visit my grandparents. I even took Cap, Buck's sire, with me, just like always. Daniel found a justice of the peace to tie the knot all proper like, and then he took me to a nice inn for our wedding night. I'd never felt so loved and pampered in my life."

She twisted her hands in her lap. "It wasn't until the next morning that I learned Daniel had hired that man to pretend to be a justice, and the whole marriage was a sham."

Adam stared at the pain and mortification on her face and would gladly have throttled the life out of the contemptible bit of snake spit who'd done that to her if he'd been within reach.

"I should have realized from the first that the whole courtship was just a way for him to pass the time while he was stuck in Turnabout. Why else would someone like that have paid so much attention to someone like me?"

"Don't think that. You are worth a hundred of him."

Her lips attempted a smile. "Thank you. But you

needn't try to make me feel better. I know my limitations." She gave a bitter laugh. "Daniel must have been quite amused by my vehement arguments against his going to Lemuel. I played my part in his little production perfectly without ever having read the script."

The blackguard had taken advantage of an innocent sixteen-year-old girl and then abandoned her without a qualm. She must have felt so betrayed.

Adam tamped down his anger at the man, determined to concentrate on comforting Regina. He placed his fingers under her chin and tilted her head up to meet his gaze. "You can't blame yourself for what happened. You thought you were married."

"But I wasn't, and there's no changing that."

"Perhaps not, but Daniel did wrong, not you."

Regina stared at him with a don't-lie-to-me expression. "Are you saying you no longer blame me?"

Her hair was disheveled, her wrapper patched and faded. She should have looked pitiful. Instead, she looked so lovely, so vulnerable. His thumb gently stroked the curve of her chin. He wanted to give her the answer that would put a smile on her face.

But he couldn't lie to her. "Not for that night."

There was a flicker of disappointment at his conditional response, and then acceptance. Her eyes closed. "Thank you for that at least."

His fingers still supported her chin but her eyes remained closed, as though she were too weary to open them.

He lifted his other hand and brushed the hair from her temple.

She leaned into his touch, and her gesture of trust was achingly sweet.

If he kissed her now, would she break it off again?

There was only one way to find out.

He lowered his head, capturing her lips with his. When she wrapped her arms around his neck, he tightened his hold on her. A part of him knew he should put some distance between them immediately, but for the life of him he couldn't remember why.

A heartbeat later reason returned, and this time it was he who broke it off.

Reggie opened her eyes, confused. What was the matter? All the old feelings of inadequacy came crashing back around her.

"Regina?" He gave her shoulders a squeeze then leaned back to stare into her eyes.

"Yes?" His expression was solemn, troubled. He stood and she thought he was going to walk away from her. Again.

But he only moved as far as the porch rail. "I'm not really certain what I feel right now."

Reggie's chest squeezed painfully. She wasn't sure she wanted to hear this.

He raked a hand through his hair, as if trying to gather his thoughts. "I like you, make no mistake about that." A ghost of his old grin appeared. "While you can be stubborn and bossy at times, there are many things I admire about you as well."

"But?"

"But the fact is, you willingly gave your son away. And right now, that's something I can't get past. I can't promise I ever will."

She almost laughed at the irony. The one act she

considered the single most selfless and noble of her lifetime, was the one that condemned her in his eyes.

But at least Adam was trying to be honest, letting her know what he could and couldn't give. Could she live with knowing he would always hold a large part of himself back from her?

What choice did she have?

"Just promise me you won't ever reveal any of these feelings to Jack."

"Of course not." He held her gaze. "We made vows that I intend to honor. I won't do anything, either publicly or privately, to embarrass you. But neither can I promise to ever get beyond this issue between us."

She rose, trying not to let him see into her heart. "You understand that the—" the heat rose in her cheeks but she forced herself to go on "—the *intimacies* of marriage, without love and respect…would be—"

He waved a hand abruptly. "If it's a platonic marriage you want, I will respect that."

She wasn't sure *what* she wanted at this point, but she nodded.

"Then we shall resolve to behave as a married couple should in public, and in private—" his jaw tightened "—we shall behave civilly to one another, and nothing more."

"Agreed." Eager to be alone with her thoughts, she moved to the door. "Now, if you'll excuse me, I believe I'll turn in."

"Regina, I—"

She raised a hand to stop his words. "I'm okay. After all, I'm the one who kept telling you I didn't see marriage in my future, so it's not as if you wrecked any dreams I held." Was she trying to convince him or herself?

She pushed that thought away. "Good night, Adam."

As she prepared for bed, her thoughts moved from her current misery to the family Bible and what it stood for. It had been so long since she'd felt worthy to go to God in prayer for her own needs, her own hurts. But tonight, fingering Granddaddy Noah's Bible, she'd remembered something very important that he'd taught her. It didn't matter what she'd done, how far she'd strayed, God loved her deeply and would never turn her away.

Heavenly Father, I come to You with a shattered heart and confused mind. I won't ask that You change Adam's heart. You gave everyone free will and, if it's to be, that's a choice he must make on his own. But please help me face the coming days with acceptance and dignity, to not wear my heart on my sleeve, to not make things harder for Adam.

She paused a moment, mulling over that last request.

It's my fault Adam's in this situation. Please show me, no matter how uncomfortable the task, how I can help him come to terms with our uneasy marriage and find some peace going forward. Oh, and shield Jack from any hurt that might result from my actions.

And in everything, let me give glory to You. Amen.

Feeling more at peace than she had since things had gone so wildly awry, Reggie climbed into bed and promptly fell asleep.

Adam stayed on the porch long after Regina had retired. His thoughts were a tangled mess. A part of him admired and respected Regina, wanted to cherish and protect her, wanted to slay all her dragons—those past and those to come. But whenever he remembered that she had given her son away, his reaction was gut-level and all the rest flew out the window.

Still, it would be quite sometime before he could rid his mind of the wounded look in her eyes just now as she made her exit.

Chapter Seventeen

They neared the edge of town near midafternoon the next day. To Reggie's relief the morning had passed pleasantly enough. By unspoken agreement they kept the conversation to neutral topics and Reggie had shown him some of her favorite spots near the cabin before they left. Adam had even decided to join her in the buggy for the ride back to Turnabout.

It gave her hope that they could make this platonic arrangement work after all.

When they arrived at her house—*their* house now, she realized—Jack came barreling through the front gate.

"Aunt Reggie! You're finally home."

Reggie stooped to catch him in a big hug. "I missed you, too." Then she leaned back and tousled his hair. "I think you must've grown a full inch while I was gone."

Jack stood a bit taller. Then he looked over her shoulder. "Hi, Uncle Adam."

"Hello, Jack. Have you been taking good care of things while we've been gone?"

"Yes, sir."

Reggie stood, taking quiet pleasure in the bond she could already see forming between these two.

She turned and smiled a greeting as Ira and Mrs. Peavy joined them. Before she could do more than exchange hellos, however, Jack tugged on her hand, reclaiming her attention. "Grandfather Madison sent you and Uncle Adam a wedding present. Wait 'til you see it."

"Careful," Ira cautioned. "You don't want to spoil the surprise."

Reggie cut a suspicious glance Ira's way. That amused tone meant there was mischief afoot. "And just where might we find this surprise?"

"It's at the depot," Jack answered. "Arrived on the morning train."

And they hadn't brought it to the house? Which meant this "surprise" was either very large, of questionable taste, or both.

Reggie swallowed a groan, then glanced at Adam who had a similar look of caution on his face. Of course, he, too, would remember her grandfather's notorious fondness for new-fangled gadgets.

"I'm almost afraid to find out," she said.

"Coward." Adam's lips twitched in a challenging smile.

"Well, I suppose, once we've unpacked and freshened up, we can—"

"I wouldn't wait that long," Ira warned. "It's already getting a fair amount of attention, and besides, Jack might just bust if you don't have a look."

"Please, Aunt Reggie, can we go now? It's really grand. Even better'n that mechanical rug beater he sent last year."

Reggie turned to Adam. "We just got in from a long ride. Are you up to one of Grandfather's surprises?"

Adam swept an arm back toward the buggy. "By all means. I admit to being a tad curious."

Reggie threw up her hands in surrender and allowed Adam to help her back into the buggy. Jack, Ira and Mrs. Peavy climbed in the backseat.

When they arrived at the depot, it seemed the whole town had gathered. Folks stood in clusters talking excitedly. Small children sat on their father's shoulders, staring openmouthed at something hidden from Reggie's view.

"Come on," Jack urged as he jumped down.

The crowd parted for them. Reggie noted various expressions, ranging from excitement to disapproval.

Her first glimpse proved to be rather anticlimatic.

A new carriage? Shiny and impressive, yes. But why all the excitement about a carriage?

Then she heard Adam's low whistle and took a closer look.

"It's a motor carriage, Aunt Reggie," Jack said excitedly. "Mr. Dawson says it'll run without any horse to pull it. Have you ever heard of such a thing?"

She met Adam's gaze over Jack's head and saw that same little-boy excitement under his tolerant grin.

"What in the world does Grandfather expect us to do with such a thing?"

"Ride in it," Adam responded.

"Can we, Aunt Reggie? Please?"

"We don't even know how to run the thing." Reggie's exasperation rose. As if she needed this gigantic child's toy to complicate her life right now.

"There's a packet under the seat," Chance volunteered. “I imagine it contains instructions on how to operate it.”

Chance had already looked it over, had he? She took in his eager expression and decided it had probably been a major trial for him to *just* look. Most of the men pressing around her wore similar expressions.

Adam reached in and pulled out the packet. After a moment he nodded thoughtfully. “Doesn’t seem too complicated.”

“So we *can* ride in it.” Jack was almost hopping in his excitement.

Over her dead body. “Now, Jack—”

“Not just yet,” Adam intervened. “I want to make certain I can operate it safely before taking on any passengers.”

“I’ll be glad to lend you a hand with that,” Chance offered. “Always wanted to get my hands on one of these.”

There were a number of onlookers who chimed in with similar offers. And others who echoed Jack’s eagerness to ride in it.

Even Reverend Harper stared at the carriage with more than passing interest.

Which gave her an idea.

She turned to Adam. “Do you really think you and Chance can figure out how to operate this thing?”

“Of course.” His frown was a vision of insulted male pride.

She rolled her eyes, then turned back to the crowd.

“Thank you for your offers of assistance,” she announced loudly. “I believe my husband and Mr. Dawson will be able to figure this out on their own. But, assuming they get it running safely, everyone will have an opportunity to ride in it.”

That promise earned her some cheers and applause.

She placed a hand on her hip and smiled. "We'll have a booth set up at the fair next week, a nickel a ride. All proceeds go to the church organ fund."

The cheers changed to groans, most of them good-natured.

Jack tugged at her skirt. "Can I stay and watch?"

Reggie hesitated a moment then nodded. "Of course. Just make sure you stay out of the way." Then she sent Ira a meaningful look. "Why don't you stay as well."

"Wild horses couldn't drag me away." Ira clapped Jack on the back with a grin. The slight nod he gave Reggie, though, let her know he would keep a close eye on her son.

"Well, then, I suppose Mrs. Peavy and I will leave you menfolk to it while we head home."

She turned back to the crowd. "I wouldn't stand too close if I were you. I saw some of these at an exhibition in Philadelphia a few years back and they tend to be noisy and unpredictable."

As she and Mrs. Peavy moved to the carriage, Mitchell stepped from the crowd to help them climb aboard.

"Thank you." Regina smiled, then she raised a questioning brow. "I don't see Everett about. Is this excitement not to his taste?"

Mitchell grinned. "I don't think the arrival of the motor carriage even registered with him. His printing press came in on the same train."

"Ah. So we can expect our first issue of the *Turnabout Gazette* soon?"

"I heard him mention something about having an issue ready in time to report on the fair."

A loud wheezing exploded through the depot area.

Mitchell grabbed the leads as Reggie's carriage horse, along with just about every other animal and person nearby, jerked in startled surprise.

Adam's gaze flew to hers, and she was gratified to see the flash of relief on his face when he realized she was all right.

Then he straightened and turned to the crowd. "My wife was correct," he announced. "It would be best if you all went about your business and gave us some room to work here."

Reggie felt a small thrill pass through her at the way he said "my wife" so naturally. It was a start.

She saw some of the women tug their husbands' arms and lead them away. Bit by bit most of the businessmen went back to their shops and offices. A small crowd remained, however, mostly boys and young men.

Reggie worried her lower lip, concerned they would ignore caution and get too close.

"Don't worry, Mrs. Barr," Mitchell said quietly. "I'll stick around and make certain those lads don't cause mischief."

Reggie smiled her thanks, then took the reins.

This little distraction for her menfolk would actually work out for the best. The morning of the wedding, she'd left instructions that Adam's things, and *only* Adam's things, be moved into Patricia and Lemuel's old room. Now she'd have time before Adam arrived to make certain Mrs. Peavy hadn't taken it in her head to alter those instructions.

Adam stared inside the carriage house one last time before he closed the large double doors. The photography wagon and the motor carriage sat side by side. An interesting combination.

He shook his head at the contrast as he secured the door with a shiny new, solid-as-granite padlock. He'd already gone around inside and secured all of the windows as best as he could.

He and Ira had decided this was the best place for the judge's gift—out of the weather and out of sight. He didn't want to tempt some adventurous youth to try the vehicle out on his own.

Adam rattled the door, satisfying himself the lock would hold. Then he stood there, rubbing the back of his neck as Ira's words echoed in his mind.

Just before the old codger had left to escort Jack home, he'd informed Adam that all of his things had already been transferred from the boardinghouse to his new home.

Home.

Adam rolled the word around in his mind, letting it conjure up images of cozy family gatherings, of putting down roots, of belonging somewhere. It was the same feeling seeing his name in Regina's family Bible had given him.

But, given his ambivalent feelings toward Regina, did he deserve that honor?

Still wrestling with that question, he turned and headed toward Regina's house—his house, too, now.

By the time he arrived, supper was ready. Jack chattered on through most of the meal about the motor carriage, then about what he'd been doing while they were away—most notably the merits of a turtle shell he'd found.

Adam noticed Regina pushed food around on her

plate but didn't eat much. She obviously had something on her mind.

After the meal was cleared away, Jack hopped up from the table. "You want to come see my turtle shell?"

"I'd love to," Regina answered, pushing away from the table.

"Of course," Adam said almost simultaneously. He'd never been beyond the first floor and was suddenly curious to see the rest of his new home.

Regina took Jack's hand and mother and son led the way out of the room and up the stairs. When they reached the top, Adam discovered the stairs opened onto a long gallery-like landing with a much shorter open hallway jutting from either end.

Jack tugged Regina to the left and led her to the far end of the corridor.

"So, you have the corner room, do you?" Adam asked.

Jack nodded and threw open the door. "I like it 'cause it has windows on two sides." He waved Adam over to one of the windows. "You can see a mocking bird's nest in that tree branch over there."

Adam made appropriate noises as he admired the view.

"And come see this."

Adam caught Regina's indulgent smile as Jack dragged him across the room. He then solemnly examined a rock collection, the rattle from a rattlesnake, a wooden whistle and the promised turtle shell. He felt a small stirring of pride when he spotted the bag of marbles he'd given the boy prominently displayed with the other treasures.

Then Jack picked up a photograph. "This is my

mother and me when I was a baby." He held it up for Adam to see. "She was real pretty."

Adam cut a quick glance Regina's way. "Yes, she was."

Jack placed it back on the chest, carefully aligning it to his satisfaction. "I wish I could have known her."

Adam heard the wistfulness in the boy's voice and remembered his own lonely childhood, felt again the awful hole left by the abandonment of his mother. Jack had been cheated of that special relationship as well, not because of his mother's untimely death, but because Regina had given him up.

This time when he met her gaze, neither of them were smiling.

But Jack seemed oblivious to the strain between the adults. "Your room is a corner one, too," he told Adam. "It used to be my pa's."

"You don't mind me moving into it, do you?"

"No sir." Jack's chest puffed out. "Me and Ira will be glad to have another man around here."

"Time to get you ready for bed, young man," Regina said firmly.

Adam took his cue. "I'll get my things unpacked and meet you downstairs later."

Regina nodded and led him to the door. She pointed across the landing to the room in the opposite corner. "That's your room," she said unnecessarily.

With a nod, he stepped past her and quickly covered the distance to the master bedroom, all the time feeling her eyes on him.

He stepped into the room and shut the door. He raked a hand through his hair, then looked around. It was a large chamber, furnished with good solid pieces. Everything was neatly arranged with no sign of clutter or personal belongings anywhere, other than his own. Had all of Lemuel's things been removed? Or had the man not surrounded himself with any of the little touches that would have hinted at his personality or taste?

By the time Adam had put away his things and stepped back into the corridor, he found Reggie at the head of the stairs.

"Oh." She paused. Her smile had an uncertain edge. "Did you find everything to your liking?"

"I did."

She tucked a stray tendril behind her ear. "Would you like a little tour of the house?"

He smiled. "Good idea." Why did she seem so nervous?

"There's not a whole lot more to see up here." She pointed to the set of double doors next to the one he'd just exited—the only other doors on this side of the landing. "That's a linen and storage closet. It backs to the small dressing room that opens off of your bedroom."

She quickly turned and swept her hand in a gesture that included the rest of the upstairs. "The rest are all bedrooms. Mine is next to Jack's."

He raised a brow. "This house was built either to hold a large family or a number of visitors."

"Lemuel and Patricia planned to have lots of children. They were heartbroken when they learned it was not to be." She pointed to the stairs leading up. "That takes you to the attic. You can explore it on your own later, if you'd like. Right now I'll show you the rest of the ground floor."

Once downstairs, she stepped into the dining room

and waved toward the far wall. "That door leads to the pantry and the kitchen. Ira and Mrs. Peavy's rooms are on that end of the house as well. Since you've already seen the kitchen, we won't risk disturbing them."

As she stepped back out, her arm brushed his. He immediately felt a connection. The color rose in her cheeks, a sure sign she felt something, too.

But she pushed on, passing the parlor and moving to the next door. "This is what we call the library." She opened the door and stepped aside so he could view it. He noticed she was careful this time not to touch him.

It didn't matter. The connection was still there, invisibly binding them together.

He glanced inside, taking in the large set of bookcases lining one wall and the small desk near the window.

"It's small compared to Grandfather's, but it suits our needs." Regina moved on to the end of the hall. "This was Lemuel's study. When he was home, this is where he spent most of his time. Feel free to use it however you wish."

He detected a note of censure in her tone. "You said 'when he was home.' Was he gone often?"

"Lemuel spent most of his time in here or at the bank. We rarely saw him, except for meals."

She ran a finger along one of the bookcases, then absently rubbed it with her thumb, as if checking for dust. "Lemuel's office at the bank will be at your disposal now, as well as this study. If at some point you wanted to start up your law practice again, it's the perfect place."

"I'll keep that in mind." Then he leaned back and

folded his arms. "Now, why don't you tell me what's really on your mind?"

She started guiltily. "What do you mean?"

"You've been more nervous than a kitten in a kennel since I walked in here this evening. So out with it."

She straightened. "If you must know, I've been wondering if you still intend for us to make that trip to Philadelphia we discussed."

So that was it. She was worried about having to make her confession to her grandfather. He felt a vague sense of disappointment. "I think we should get that bit of business taken care of as soon as possible. Why don't we plan to leave the day after the fair?"

She nodded dejectedly. "Very well."

He took her hands. "I know it won't be easy, but it needs to be done. Just explain the full story. He loves you—that won't change."

She nodded again but she didn't appear convinced.

He tamped down the stirring of sympathy—the sooner this was behind her, the sooner she could start to free herself of the shame she felt.

He gave her hands one more squeeze then let them go. "It's been a long day. Off to bed with you."

"What about you?"

"I'd like to glance through these papers your brother-in-law left here before I turn in."

She nodded. "Of course. I'll leave the upstairs lamp on."

Adam watched her leave, then sat behind the desk.

And suddenly the realization that he was truly the man of the house settled in him. For good or ill, he was responsible for the well-being of those under this roof. It was a sobering thought. But a not unpleasant one.

* * *

Reggie climbed the stairs, trying to decide how she felt about the turn of events. She knew he still felt strongly about the way she'd handled the situation with Jack. But it was just as obvious he was trying to make this arrangement work.

In all other ways he was solicitous and considerate toward her. Not to mention how wonderful he was with Jack.

There was a real chance that, even if theirs wasn't a true marriage, they could at least build a family atmosphere in this house, that they could provide some wonderful childhood memories for Jack.

Why couldn't she be happy with that?

She opened her bedroom door and tried to shake off her melancholy thoughts. Perhaps, in time, Adam would relent. Surely, once he had time to understand how much better this was for Jack than the alternative would have been, he'd see things her way.

She just had to be patient.

In the meantime, she would go on as if everything were all right. She had agreed to do her utmost to make this arrangement work, and that's what she intended to do.

Chapter Eighteen

Adam strolled along Main Street the next morning, looking at the town with fresh eyes. This was his town now, his neighbors he passed. And while Turnabout might not have been his first choice of a place to settle down, he was beginning to see some definite silver linings to life here.

He stepped inside the bank, ready to dig into his role as administrator of Jack's business interests. But before he could do more than look around, Thomas Pierce appeared at his elbow.

"Why, Mr. Barr, what an unexpected surprise." The banker pumped Adam's hand enthusiastically. "Let me again offer my felicitations on your wedding."

Adam bore the man's effusiveness with a smile. "Thank you."

Pierce leaned back on his heels. "I see Reggie's had better luck than I in convincing you to settle here." The banker waved him into a nearby office. "I must say I'm pleased you're going to be part of our growing community."

"I consider myself the lucky one."

"That motor carriage caused quite a stir yesterday." Pierce settled into the large leather chair behind his imposing desk. "Yes, sir, quite a stir. And her idea to sell rides at the fair—absolutely brilliant. I predict it will earn quite a bit of money."

Adam casually leaned against a bookcase. "My wife is an enterprising woman."

"That's our Reggie," Pierce agreed good-humoredly. He steepled his fingers. "So, what I can I do for you today? Do you wish to open an account?"

"I'll need to do that, of course. But that's not why I'm here this morning. I know we've been putting it off because of other priorities, but now that I'm married to Regina, she's asked me to formally take over the management of Jack's affairs."

The banker frowned. "I hope she's not concerned with how I've handled matters so far. I assure you—"

"Nothing of the sort. In fact Regina was singing your praises to me just this morning."

The jovial smile returned. "Well, that's a relief. And I'm happy to do what I can for Jack. Lemuel and I were partners for fifteen years. I almost feel like the boy's uncle."

"Regina and Jack certainly appreciate all you've done, but it's my duty to assume those burdens now." He flashed a man-to-man smile. "Since I'm new at this family man business, I want to prove I'm up to the task."

"A commendable attitude. But I'm certain you've nothing to prove to Reggie."

Adam wished he was as confident of that as Pierce. "Regina mentioned something about an office here?"

"Ah, Lemuel's old office. Of course, you must consider it yours."

"Thank you, I will." Adam hadn't really been asking the man's permission.

"Oh, yes, well, let me show you where it is."

The personal escort was unnecessary since it turned out the office was right next to Pierce's. The room was a mirror image of the other in size and layout, but there the similarity ended. Pierce's office had a pretentious opulence about it, much like the man himself. This office reflected more of the dark, somber heaviness Lemuel's study had.

Pierce seemed to read his mind. "Lemuel was a good friend and a solid businessman," he said solemnly, "but these last few years he didn't seem to have interest in, or time for, much else."

Then the man shook off his uncharacteristic gloom. "I'm sure you'll want to put your own stamp on this place. Take your time. You're a newlywed after all. I can keep an eye on Jack's investments a bit longer."

Adam nodded, then managed to maneuver Pierce out the door without being rude. He rolled up his sleeves and began familiarizing himself with the ledgers and books in his new office.

Lemuel had been well organized, but it took Adam a while to accustom himself to the man's filing system, and deciphering his personal shorthand was proving a challenge.

After three hours hunched over the books, Adam decided he needed a break. He stood and grabbed his coat. A walk seemed just the thing.

A few minutes later, without conscious thought, Adam found himself outside Regina's studio.

As usual, the jingling bell announced his presence

when he opened the door. A moment later Ira bustled out from the back room.

"Is Regina around?" Why did he feel like a callow youth talking to his sweetheart's father?

Ira pointed his thumb toward the stairs. "She's in her office."

Adam hesitated. She'd seemed very protective of her privacy last time he'd indicated an interest in her third-floor office.

"You're married to her now," Ira said with a knowing smile. "She might get her back up, but I don't think she'll throw you out."

With a nod, Adam headed for the stairs. The closer he got to the top floor, however, the more of an intruder he felt. After all, everyone was entitled to a bit of space they could claim as entirely their own.

"Ira, is that you?"

"It's Adam. Mind if I come up?" At least now the choice was hers.

There was a long pause. "No, of course not."

Not quite an open-armed invitation, but he'd take it. When Adam stepped onto the landing, the first thing he spotted was Regina at her desk, an open ledger at her elbow.

He groaned. "Don't tell me you're working on your books. I've seen more than enough columns of figures for one day."

She grinned. "That bad?"

"I'm just out of practice. I'll have it figured out soon." He looked around. "So, this is your inner sanctum."

She grimaced. "More like my junk room."

The walls were covered with pictures, but these were

quite different from those on the first floor. "Your personal collection?"

She nodded.

He moved closer. These were mostly of her family. He recognized her father, stepsister and stepmother in several poses. One photograph captured Patricia with a baby on her lap and a man at her shoulder—Lemuel? Another depicted an elderly couple. Her grandparents perhaps?

And everywhere he looked were photographs of Jack, at every stage of his life.

She had spoken once about helping people preserve their history through photographs. She obviously took her own advice.

Something was missing though. "I thought you kept some of your botany pictures up here."

"I ran out of wall space." She waved to a table across the room. "Most of them are in those albums if you want to have a look."

Adam moved to the table and discovered a number of albums stacked here, some of them seeming to date back several years. He pulled out an older one first and studied the images with interest. These weren't as polished and sharp as the photographs he'd seen in her workroom that first day, but he could see the beginnings of the professional she became.

In the third album that he opened, he spotted the photograph of a young man. It wasn't anyone Adam had seen around town, but there *was* something familiar about him.

"That's Daniel."

Adam started and glanced up. She still sat in her

chair, but had pushed back from the desk and watched him with a guarded expression.

"You kept his picture?" He didn't understand. Why was she still holding on to a likeness of him after all the pain he caused her? Could she possibly still have some tender feelings for him?

Regina crossed the room and her jaw clenched as she stared at the picture. Then she moved to the window and rubbed her upper arms. "I thought someday, if Jack learned the truth, he'd wonder about his real father." Her words were soft, muted. "I wanted to be able to show him what Daniel looked like."

Adam moved beside her. "Is that all it is?"

She faced him, a look of guilt and something fierce in her eyes. "I hate what he did to me, how he made me feel. But despite all of that, he gave me Jack."

Her eyes blazed a challenge. "And as awful as it may sound, I will be forever grateful to him for that. If that makes me a terrible person, I'm sorry."

Adam pulled her into his arms and kissed the top of her head. "On the contrary, it makes you a very honest, very brave person."

Reggie strolled across the field, greeting other workers as she passed the booths and attractions.

She'd left Jack and Mrs. Peavy at the food booth, unloading a small hand cart full of some of the housekeeper's finest pies and breads.

The morning was beautiful—perfect fair weather. Puffy white clouds floated in a bluebird sky. She could tell it was going to be another scorcher, but a light breeze wafted through that promised to keep the humidity down.

Reggie inhaled deeply, enjoying the smells—food, sawdust and freshly trampled grass being the dominant ones. The dew was still on the ground and soaking the hem of her dress, but she didn't care. It would dry soon enough, and today was too gorgeous for such petty worries.

Not even thoughts about their planned departure tomorrow for Philadelphia could dampen her mood. She'd come to terms with telling her grandfather the truth about what happened seven years ago. Difficult as it would be, she owed it to both him and herself. She would just have to trust that God would give her the right words.

"There you are," Ira hailed. "I've got everything set up for you."

"Don't go preaching at me about being late," she said with a mock pout. "The fair won't officially open for another thirty minutes. Besides," she added, "you moved. I thought we were going to set up in the competition area so we could talk the winners into getting their photographs taken."

"Moving here was my idea." Adam strolled up from her left. "I thought there might be more folks who'll want to get their photograph taken sitting inside a genuine motor carriage."

She glanced toward the vehicle in question. It sat proudly under a nearby oak, waiting to sputter to life again. Although it already gleamed like a beacon, Chance was lovingly polishing it with a rag.

She nodded, coming back to his question. "Good idea." Besides, this new location would give her more opportunities to spend time with Adam.

"Well, ready or not," Ira warned, "it looks like some folk decided not to wait for the official opening time."

The rest of the morning was a blur of activity.

It seemed everyone wanted to ride in the motor carriage. Young men cajoled their less daring sweethearts to ride with them, children pleaded with their parents for a turn. And Adam's instincts had been correct—almost everyone wanted their picture taken as they sat inside the new-fangled vehicle.

Chance and Adam took shifts driving, and there was rarely a time when there wasn't a line waiting.

Reggie caught an occasional glimpse of Everett, pencil and pad in hand, strolling the area. She smiled as she wondered what he'd consider newsworthy. This had to be a far cry from the events he'd covered for the paper in Philadelphia.

Around eleven o'clock, Adam wandered over to where she'd set up her camera. "It's Chance's turn to drive the motor carriage," he announced. "Why don't find Jack and take some time to enjoy the fair ourselves."

"Go ahead," Ira encouraged. "Mabel's bringing my lunch here in a little while. We'll keep an eye on things."

Reggie didn't need any additional arm twisting. After shedding her smock, she placed a hand on Adam's arm and prepared to be entertained.

They found Jack excitedly cheering on his favorite entry in the frog jumping contest under Mrs. Peavy's watchful eye.

As soon as he spied them he ran over. "Look what I won." He proudly held out a small wood carving of a horse.

Reggie made suitably impressed noises. "How did you win it?"

"At the ring toss." He grabbed Reggie's hand. "The three legged race is gonna start in a few minutes. Petey and his dad are entered and I want to watch."

"I have a better idea," Adam said. "Why don't you and I enter and give them a little competition?"

Jack's eyes grew round with excitement. "Jumpin' jackrabbits, can we?"

Reggie's heart melted there on the spot. Even though she'd forced Adam into this marriage, he treated Jack as a son rather than a burden. Already she could see Jack blooming under the attention.

It *shouldn't* matter that she'd never have all of Adam's heart, she told herself fiercely. What he *was* willing to give was so much better than living without him.

The problem was, it *did* matter. Because a little piece of her died each time some reminder of that unforgiving hardness in him surfaced.

Would he ever forgive her, ever understand that she'd done the absolute best thing she could have for Jack?

It was nearly two hours later before Adam escorted Regina and Jack back to where the Peavys waited. He'd enjoyed escorting them to all the attractions, cheering Jack on, entering some of the competitions himself to show off a bit for his new family. This sense of protecting and belonging was a whole new experience for him and he rather liked it.

"Land sakes, now don't they just look like the perfect family." Mrs. Peavy beamed at them with grandmotherly affection.

Regina glanced sideways at him then ducked her

head. But not before he saw the shy smile tug at her lips. Something warm settled in chest.

He reached for her hand, but paused when an outraged hail snagged his attention.

"Hey, come back with that!"

That was Chance's voice.

Adam turned sharply to discover the motor carriage puttering onto the track. But rather than Chance, Wade Sanders was gleefully manning the tiller, his friends cheering him on. Chance sprinted after him, but the mayor's son had enough of a lead to guarantee him a nice ride before he was caught. And Wade's friends were deliberately slowing Chance down.

Confounded show-off! He could get himself or someone else hurt. Adam pushed Jack toward Reggie. "Get over by that tree and stay put." Adam sprinted toward the motor carriage. Between him and Chance, they should be able to head the kid off before he did too much damage. But, mayor's son or no, Wade Sanders was in for an earful when Adam caught up to him.

Suddenly the motor carriage hit a large rock, jarring the whole vehicle. It picked up speed then, and began weaving wildly. Adam adjusted his own direction, pushing himself to an even faster sprint.

Wade's grin turned to openmouthed alarm as he tried to get the vehicle back under control.

In a panic, the boy leapt from the still-moving vehicle. Adam didn't give him more than a passing glance—he had to stop the runaway vehicle which was now headed for a busier area of the field. People began scrambling to get out of the way.

All except one.

Constance Harper, holding a bright red candy apple

in one hand, turned to see what the fuss was about, then froze.

Adam yelled at her to move—he'd caught up with the vehicle, but knew he wouldn't reach the controls in time to turn it, if in fact it could still be steered at all.

Then, out of nowhere, Chance dived at the girl, tackling her and rolling her to safety.

Adam pulled himself into the carriage and yanked on the tiller.

It didn't budge.

He tried again, and this time it moved just enough to steer away from the milling crowd. But before he could draw a relieved breath, Adam found himself facing more trouble.

The vehicle was now pointed directly toward Regina's photography wagon.

Chapter Nineteen

Regina's heart jerked painfully. Her mind rebelled, refusing to believe her eyes. "Jump!" she screamed. "Get out of there." But it was no use.

The scene unfolded with tortuous slowness. Each detail etched itself in her mind with gruesome vividness—the grim determination on Adam's face, the bulging muscles in his arm as he strained to turn the tiller, the bone-jarring jolts his body absorbed as the runaway motor carriage careened toward the wagon.

Then the motor carriage slammed into the wagon and time whooshed forward again.

Only when Ira's hand released her did Reggie realize she'd been struggling to race forward. Now she picked up her skirts and dashed toward the splintered mess.

Please God, let him be all right.

She repeated that prayer a dozen times before finally reaching the wreckage. Her knees crumpled in relief when Adam climbed shakily out of the crazily tilted motor carriage.

Then she saw blood trickling down his forehead and she scrambled back to her feet. "You're hurt!"

Reggie yanked a handkerchief from her pocket. "Find Doc Pratt!" she yelled. Then she gently dabbed at Adam's cut.

"How do you feel? Are you hurt anywhere else? You should be sitting down." She knew she was babbling, but she couldn't stop.

Chance raced up. "Is he okay?" he asked, struggling to catch his breath.

Reggie rounded on him, finding a target for her roiling emotions. "How could you let this happen? Adam could have been killed."

Chance looked abashed. "I'm sorry. I don't know how it happened. I only turned my back for a few seconds—"

"A few seconds! It—"

Adam grabbed her wrists. "I'm all right, Regina. Truly. Just a little sore."

She met his gaze and tears welled in her eyes. "Are you sure? When I saw the crash, I was so afraid—"

He tugged her closer. "I'm sorry. I tried my best to avoid hitting the wagon, but the tiller was stuck."

Reggie jerked away. "You *what?*" Suddenly she was furious.

A puzzled pucker appeared between Adam's brows. "I said I'm sorry I wrecked both vehicles. I did my best but—"

Reggie shook a trembling finger in his face. "Of all the inconsiderate, fool stunts. How *dare* you do such a thing, Mr. Adam Must-Play-the-Hero Barr. Don't you ever, *ever,* put me through that again."

He grabbed her wrist again, but this time more firmly. "Whoa, there. I said I was sorry about the wagon. I—"

"The wagon! I don't care a fig about the wagon. It's just a *thing*. Ira and I built it and we can build another one. I'm angry because you didn't jump. You put me through sixty seconds of absolute torment just to save that stupid collection of paint and timber. Must have taken ten years off my life."

She crossed her arms and tilted her chin up with a watery sniff. "Not that I give a plug nickel about your sorry hide right now."

Adam's expression twisted into a tender smile and he pulled her back into his arms. She offered only token resistance—just enough so he wouldn't think she was ready to forgive him.

"Mrs. Barr," he whispered, "I'm very much afraid you're as terrible a liar as you are a singer." And with that he kissed the top of her head.

"What's this all about?"

At the question, Reggie guiltily freed herself from Adam's embrace to find Doc Pratt studying them.

"My husband was riding in that motor carriage when it crashed into the wagon." Reggie patted her hair self-consciously.

Doc Pratt glanced at the wreckage with a raised brow. "Doesn't seem to have been doing too good a job of it." Then he turned to Adam. "Let's have a look at you, son."

"That's not necessary. I—"

Reggie gave him her fiercest frown. "Do as the doctor said."

Adam responded with a long, hard look, then rolled his eyes and allowed the doctor lead him to a spot where he could sit comfortably.

Reggie watched them a moment, then turned to survey the damage. Before she could do more than grimace, however, Mayor Sanders approached, hauling a red-faced, profusely sweating Wade by the shirt collar. With some not-so-gentle prompting, he forced a stammering apology from his son.

Reggie listened silently until Wade's words came to a stuttering halt. "What you did was both foolhardy and dangerous." She fought to keep her voice steady. "It's only thanks to my husband and Mr. Dawson that no one was seriously hurt."

The mayor's wife came huffing up. Eula Fay stayed in the background but commented loudly to no one in particular that Reggie and Adam had brought this on themselves by introducing such a dangerous contraption into their midst.

Reggie ignored the woman and instead turned on her heel and marched off to see what Doc Pratt had to say about Adam's condition.

"Your husband here is a very lucky man," the doctor said as soon as she arrived. "He's a bit battered and bruised, but there shouldn't be any lasting effects."

Adam rolled down his sleeves. "I told you it was nothing to worry about."

Doc Pratt frowned as he snapped his satchel closed. "I said it won't have any lasting effects, but, to make certain of that, I strongly suggest you don't exert yourself unduly over the next few days."

Before Adam could protest, Reggie spoke up. "Thank you, Doc. I'll make sure he follows your instructions."

Ignoring Adam's glower, she continued to address the physician. "We were planning to board a train for Philadelphia tomorrow. Should we postpone?"

"If he's feeling back to normal tomorrow, then travel

shouldn't be a problem. Just make certain he takes it easy."

"You can count on me." She turned to Adam. "You heard the doctor. You may give orders to your heart's content, but if I see you so much as lift a finger to help clear out that wreckage I'll recruit Mitchell to sit on you."

Jack was once more consigned into Mrs. Peavy's capable hands while the cleanup effort got underway.

The mayor offered to furnish some wagons to haul whatever salvageable items they recovered back to her carriage house, or wherever else Reggie wanted to take them.

The motor carriage seemed basically intact, but no amount of effort or cajoling would coax the engine back to life.

"If you don't mind," Chance offered, "I'd be glad to tinker with it and see if I can get it running again."

"Help yourself." Reggie gave a dismissive wave. "I don't care if I never see the ornery thing again."

Taking a deep breath, she turned to survey the wreckage of what had been her photography wagon. Luckily, much of her equipment had been set up where she was taking photographs. But the wagon itself seemed unsalvageable.

There were plenty of helping hands initially, but gradually the crowd dwindled to just a handful. Her three former suitors, however, stayed the whole time. Surprisingly, somewhere along the way, they had all become good friends.

Despite Reggie's best efforts, Adam managed to slip in and help a bit. After a few hours though, she saw signs that he was tiring. When she saw him sway slightly, she decided he'd had enough. Signaling Mitchell to follow, she marched up to her stubborn husband.

"Mr. Fulton, I believe my husband has had enough for one day. I'd be obliged if you'd escort him home. And please see that he stays put, even if you have to sit on him."

"Now, Regina—"

"Don't you know better than to argue with a lady?" The corners of Mitchell's eyes crinkled. "Especially when she's so obviously right."

It was late when Reggie and Ira returned to the house and Mrs. Peavy met them at the door. "Look at you two," she fussed. "Practically asleep on your feet. Ira Peavy, don't you know better than to let Reggie work so hard?"

Ira held up his hands. "Have you ever succeeded in getting her to quit when she's made her mind up?"

The housekeeper tsked. "Hardheaded, the both of you."

Reggie smiled as she rolled her shoulders. "I'm fine. How's Adam?"

"Been upstairs most of the evening. I didn't even bother him for supper. Thought it best to let him rest."

Reggie nodded. "Good. I'll look in on Jack and then turn in myself."

As she trudged up the stairs, Reggie sighed, sparing a moment to mourn the loss of her beautiful wagon. Tomorrow the remains would be consigned to a bonfire with the rest of the discarded trash and materials from the fair.

Ah, well, as she'd told Adam, she could always replace a wagon. People were another matter.

Reggie eased open the door to Jack's room and

leaned against the jamb. She heard his even breathing, smiled at his abandoned sprawl.

Her gaze moved to the bedpost where the third place ribbon he and Adam had earned for their showing in the three-legged race hung. Jack had been as proud of that ribbon as if it had been a gold crown.

She quietly eased the door closed and crossed to Adam's room. She peeked inside to find him asleep as well.

Reggie stood there a moment, reflecting. She'd discovered something this afternoon when she watched him crash into her wagon.

She loved him.

It was as simple and as complex as that.

Realizing how she felt didn't make living with their half marriage easier. On the contrary, it made it a thousand times harder.

But there it was.

For good or ill, she was in love with her husband.

She just didn't know if she could pretend to be content with half his heart much longer.

"Are you sure you're up to starting that long trip to Philadelphia this afternoon?"

Adam, who'd just stepped onto the first floor, raised a brow. "And good morning to you, too."

Reggie waved impatiently. "Good morning. And before you say anything else, no, I'm not trying to delay my talk with Grandfather. I just think it might be best if you rested another day or two."

"I'm fine. Now stop trying to mollycoddle me. I spent all of yesterday afternoon and last night in bed just to humor you. But I refuse to do it again today."

Her expression turned prim. "Well, if bad humor is a sign of healing, you *must* be on the mend."

Adam smiled in spite of himself. Reggie certainly wasn't shy about speaking her mind.

"The rest of us have already eaten," she said moving to the door. "Mrs. Peavy is keeping your breakfast warm in the kitchen. I'll be at my studio packing up the equipment I want to take with me."

"Hold on." He placed a hand on her arm. "Give me a minute to grab a quick bite and a cup of coffee, and I'll join you." He folded his arms. "Or would you prefer to not be seen with the infamous man who wrecked not one but two of your carriages?"

She raised a brow. "Think about those two vehicles. Do you really think I shrink from 'infamous'?"

He laughed. "I see your point."

"Besides," she said, softening, "as far as I'm concerned you're a hero. There's no telling what might have happened if you hadn't risked your neck the way you did."

Then she fingered her collar. "I suppose I *could* check on Jack and see how his packing is coming while I wait for you."

"Excellent idea. I'll be quick."

Her expression turned prim again. "Rushing through your meal is not good for your digestion."

"Yes, ma'am." And with a smile he headed into the dining room.

Fifteen minutes later they were stepping onto the sidewalk.

Myrtis Jenkins, pruning shears in hand, stood by her own front gate. "Mr. Barr. I'm so glad to see you looking well today."

Adam bowed. "Thank you. I feel right as rain this morning." He ignored Regina's disbelieving sniff.

Myrtis, however, apparently had something else on her mind. "Did you hear what happened?"

"What was that?" Regina asked politely.

The woman dramatically placed a hand to her throat. "Thomas Pierce was attacked on his way to the bank last night. Someone stole all the fair money."

Adam frowned. A robbery? Here in Turnabout?

"Is he all right?" Regina's voice echoed his own shock.

"According to Doc Pratt, he'll be sporting a lump the size of a lemon for a few days, but otherwise he'll be fine."

"Do they have any idea who did it?" Adam gave Regina's hand a comforting squeeze.

Myrtis shook her head. "He said the thief came up from behind and it was dark. Some think it might be one of the peddlers who set up at the festival yesterday." She drew herself up, the picture of moral indignation. "Wouldn't surprise me none. Sheriff Gleason is checking the wagons of the ones who haven't left town yet, but the thief's likely long gone by now."

"Thanks for the news." Adam tipped his hat and drew Regina forward.

Regina fingered her collar as they resumed their walk. "Everyone worked so hard to raise that money, and now it's gone. It's like stealing from the church itself. Who would do such a terrible thing?"

"Someone either very greedy, or very desperate." Adam tightened his jaw. "Tell me about Sheriff Gleason."

"What do you want to know?"

"What kind of sheriff is he?"

"He's been sheriff here for as long as I can remember," she said carefully. "I've always thought of him as fair-minded." She shrugged. "Of course, the most he normally has to deal with are the occasional Saturday night brawls or mischief makers trying to steal melons from Carl Mason's garden. Why?"

"I just wondered if he'd be likely to detain any of these 'peddlers' without solid proof." He felt an obligation to make certain that didn't happen.

She gave his arm a squeeze. "If he does, I know a good lawyer who'll call his hand on it."

Adam returned her smile, pleased by her show of faith. "That obvious, am I?" They had reached the studio by this time. "I think I'll stop by the sheriff's office and see what I can find out. I'll be back to help you in an hour or so."

"Take your time." She waved him on. "Ira'll be here soon and he can help me pack up what I need."

As he passed the general store, a breathless youth rushed out, nearly running him over. "Sorry," he said. Then quickly followed with "Did you hear? Sheriff Gleason caught the thief! He caught him!"

"Did he now?"

"Yes, sir. It's one of them peddlers. The sheriff found the money hidden under a floorboard in his wagon."

"Is the man in custody?" Adam asked.

"Yes, sir. And his daughter is there, too, complaining something fierce that her father ain't guilty."

Adam moved on, deciding he really ought to have a talk with this peddler. The sheriff may have gotten the right man, but it wouldn't hurt to hear the other side of the story.

A few minutes later, Adam stood outside the sheriff's office. He could hear a belligerent female voice before he stepped through the open door.

"I tell you, my pa ain't never stole no money in his life. Why, he didn't even know that money was there."

The sheriff glanced up when he entered, looking as if he'd been thrown a lifeline. "Mr. Barr. You're looking none the worse for wear after your accident. It was downright neighborly of you not to press charges against Mayor Sanders's son."

"That was my wife's decision, not mine." Adam kept his eyes on the girl as he spoke. In turn she sized him up and dismissed him in the space of a few seconds.

The sheriff leaned back. "Was there something you were needing from me?"

The girl planted her hands firmly on the sheriff's desk and glared. "I was here first."

Sheriff Gleason let out an exasperated huff. "Look, miss, I don't like being disrespectful to a lady, but we've been through this a dozen times. Your pa was caught with the stolen money. He's staying right there in that cell until the circuit judge comes through next week."

"And I'm telling you that money is *mine*. I've been saving it up for near on five years. If Pa'd 'a known that money was there, he'd 'a gambled it all away by now."

Adam stepped in. "Pardon me, miss. Do you mind if I ask your name?"

She glared at him suspiciously. "Daisy Johnson."

"Miss Johnson." Adam executed a short bow. "If your father *is* innocent, perhaps we can clear this up quickly."

She still had a wary look about her, but some of the belligerence dimmed. "How we gonna do that?"

Adam turned to Sheriff Gleason. "Where's the money you found in their wagon?"

Sheriff Gleason seemed as suspicious as the girl, but he pulled a sack out of his desk drawer. "I was planning to take this over to the bank for safe keeping."

"That's my money, I tell you."

Adam held out a hand. "May I?"

At the sheriff's nod, Adam opened the sack and counted it out. "Over ninety dollars. Is that the amount that was taken?"

The lawman spread his hands. "No way to tell. They planned to count it this morning."

"I see." Adam raised a brow. "I did notice something interesting about this money."

"What's that?" the girl asked peering over his shoulder.

"It's almost all in large bills."

"Makes it easier to hide from Pa," she said defensively.

"I'm certain it does." He turned back to the sheriff. "It also means this is not the money from yesterday's fair. That would have all been in coins and smaller bills."

Miss Johnson brightened and turned to the sheriff with a smug smile. "There, I told you it weren't stole."

Sheriff Gleason appeared unconvinced. "I don't know—"

Adam interrupted his protest. "What time was Thomas Pierce robbed last night?

"Around nine-thirty."

"Miss Johnson, do you know where your father was at nine-thirty last night?"

She gave a confident nod. "Sure do. He was playing poker at the livery. I had to haul him out before he lost all the money we earned yesterday."

"And do you know who else was in this game?"

The girl rattled off a few names, then shrugged. "There were four or five others, but those are the only names I caught."

Adam nodded. "Sheriff, you should be able to check her story without much trouble. If the men verify what she's saying, I believe you'll have to admit you have the wrong man."

The sheriff glowered at Adam a moment, then turned to his deputy. "Go fetch Lester and Belcher for me."

Adam turned to the girl. "I think this will be straightened out fairly soon. You can find me at the photography studio on the edge of town for the next hour or so, however, if you need further assistance."

She gave him a curious look. "Why you doing this for me and my pa, mister?"

"Let's just say I hate to see an injustice done." With a tip of his hat, Adam excused himself and left the sheriff's office.

Chapter Twenty

Reggie approached her grandfather's study with her stomach in knots. But she couldn't put this off.

They'd arrived at her grandfather's house in Philedelphia three hours ago, and she needed to get this out of the way as soon as possible. She only hoped it didn't result in cutting their visit short. Saying a silent prayer for the right words, she knocked on the door and entered.

She inhaled the familiar scents of cigars and port and musty books with a smile. She would know where she was even if she'd been blindfolded.

"Adam took Jack out to the stables to look at the horses," she said as she took a seat. "I thought it would be good for you and I to talk alone."

"I agree, my dear. It's been far too long since we were able to chat face-to-face." He wagged a finger. "So, is this where you give me a severe dressing-down for forcing you to the altar?"

Her lips twitched. "No, though I plan to do quite a bit of that later." She straightened and took a deep breath. "I have a confession to make first."

"Oh." The judge leaned back and steepled his fingers. "I'm listening."

Reggie braced herself for his reaction. "Jack is not Patricia's son. He's mine."

Her grandfather's expression remained impassive as he watched her. "I see."

Reggie blinked in confusion. She'd just revealed her deepest, darkest secret, and he sat there looking as if she'd just mentioned it might rain tomorrow.

Why wasn't he outraged, or at least shocked? "Do you understand? I lied to you, made you believe Jack was your blood kin, made you believe I was some sort of paragon looking out for my stepsister's child."

That brought an amused chuckle from him. "Much as I appreciate your many qualities, Reggie, I have never, ever thought of you as a paragon."

Something was wrong here. He should be—

She straightened. "You already knew, didn't you? Did Adam—"

"Adam didn't breathe a word, though I'm glad to hear he knows. And I only suspected. I wasn't certain until just now."

"But how—"

"On your last visit it struck me how much Jack resembles you—your nose, your smile, your father's eyes. I couldn't see any similarity to Patricia or even Lemuel in the boy." He shrugged. "Of course, there could have been other explanations. But once the idea of your being his mother presented itself, it explained so much about your stubborn refusal to find a husband."

He'd known. And he didn't seem to love her less. "Why didn't you say something?" she whispered.

Her grandfather stood and came around to her side of the desk. "I wanted telling me to be your choice."

Reggie clasped her hands tightly in her lap. "So, you don't hate me?"

The judge leaned forward and took her hands. "Reggie, my dear, I could never hate you, no matter what. You and Jack are my family and always will be."

"Oh, Grandfather." She threw her arms around his neck, her eyes watering. She related the whole sordid story then, and when she was done, her grandfather gave her a hug then leaned back against his desk.

"I'm sorry you had to go through such heartbreak alone," he said. "But it pleases me tremendously that you finally trusted me with your secret."

She sniffed. "You can thank Adam for tweaking my conscience."

"As well he should." He handed her his handkerchief. "That's much too heavy a burden for you to carry alone. Which is why I set up this whole matchmaking scheme in the first place. I figured you would either turn to me with the truth, or to Adam when you selected him for your husband."

Her head jerked up at that. "But how'd you know I'd select Adam? He wasn't even in the running."

The judge smiled smugly. "Who else would you select? I've thought you and Adam would make a fine match for some time. But he would never have seen it on his own, thus the unorthodox but brilliantly conceived nudge."

Proud of himself, was he? Well, she supposed he had reason.

Then he leaned back. "You are both happy with the

match, I trust. I'd hate to discover my actions resulted otherwise."

Happy? "I couldn't ask for a better father for Jack," she answered carefully. "The two have grown close over the past weeks—I think the relationship has been as good for Adam as it has for Jack."

His keen gaze didn't relent. "That's good to hear, of course, but it's not what I asked. Are you happy in this marriage?"

"I truly love him, Grandfather."

"And how does he feel?"

"He's been very kind and respectful, and he wants to make this work."

"But?"

She wanted no more lies between them. "But he can't forgive me for what I did."

Her grandfather stiffened. "He blames you for what that villain did to you?"

"No. For my giving Jack to Patricia and Lemuel."

"I see." He rubbed his jaw. "Because of his mother—I should have realized." Then he patted her hand. "I'm sorry, my dear. Perhaps, in time—"

Reggie stood and moved to the window. "Don't worry, he's really been quite the gentleman. And we're both determined to make life as pleasant for Jack as possible. It's not his fault that he can't give his heart to me, too." The instances when Adam looked at her with that hard edge in his gaze were getting fewer but they were still there.

She turned back to her grandfather, a bittersweet smile on her lips. "I've been spending more time with my Bible these past few weeks. You know the passage in the book of Philippians about the peace that passeth all understanding? I've been clinging to that verse and it has helped me find that promised peace in my situation."

She moved back to her grandfather and took both his hands in hers. "Be happy for me. In a lot of ways, I'm so much better off than I was before. After all, it's much more of a family life than I ever dreamed I'd have."

Before he could respond, Reggie heard some familiar voices in the hallway. "That sounds like Jack and Adam now." She linked her arm through his. "What do you say we join them?"

When they stepped out of the study, Judge Madison disengaged his arm and moved to Jack. "Have I ever showed you my stereopticon?"

"No, sir."

"Well, come along then, I have some slides of the great pyramids that I think you will enjoy."

As they walked away, Adam led her into the parlor and sat next to her on the settee. "How did your talk go?"

Better than the one I had with you. "Quite well, really. It turns out Grandfather already suspected much of what I told him."

Adam smiled and nodded. "Not much gets by him."

"Thank you for helping me see this needed to be done. I feel as if an enormous burden has been lifted from my shoulders."

He gave her arm a gentle squeeze. "I'm glad."

His hand remained on her arm and there was warmth in his smile that she longed to respond to. But she knew she was reading emotions there that didn't exist.

She withdrew her arm on the pretext of smoothing her skirt, then changed the subject. "Do you mind if I ask you something?"

* * *

Adam eyed Regina cautiously. Was that tightness about her due to the conversation she'd just had with her grandfather? Or was something else causing it? "What would you like to know?"

"Now that you're back in Philadelphia, do you have a plan for how you're going to go about clearing your name?"

Her question caught him off guard and he stood, moving to stand near the fireplace.

"If you'd rather not talk about it, I'll understand."

"It's not that. I just don't want to say anything yet, not until I'm certain."

"Certain?"

"I had a lot of time to think about this while I was in prison. And every time I went through it in my mind, who stood to gain, who knew my habits, who had access and opportunity—it all kept coming back to one name."

"You mean it was someone you *know?*"

He'd been such a blind fool back then, too trusting by far. "Like I said, I'm not saying anything until I'm certain."

"Is there anything I can do to help?"

"No." From the expression on her face, he realized that had come out more harshly than he'd intended. "This is something I need to do myself," he said in a milder tone.

"Of course." She rose and moved to stand in front of him. "And what is it you want to accomplish?"

What kind of question was that? "Clear my name, of course."

"I guess I'm asking if it's justice you want, or vengeance?"

Her question felt like a slap. "In this case they're the same thing."

"Are they? Will you take pleasure in seeing your nemesis be punished?"

"It's what he deserves." Why did he suddenly feel so defensive?

"Just search your heart, and make sure, whatever you do, it's for the right reasons. Remember, God reserves vengeance as *His* province. And besides, revenge never tastes as sweet as you think it will. In fact, sometimes it can be pure poison."

Then she smiled self-consciously. "I'm sorry. That was awfully melodramatic and I certainly didn't mean to read you a lecture. Come on, let's find Grandfather and Jack and see if they'd like to go for a ride in the park."

Adam mulled over her words as he followed her out of the room. She was wrong. He was after justice, clearing his name, nothing more. But if getting justice resulted in a bit of vengeance at the same time, there was nothing wrong with that. He'd waited to long for this to stop now.

The ride to the park never materialized. Adam and Regina had just joined Judge Madison and Jack in the library when the housekeeper handed Regina a telegram.

Adam watched her expressive face as she read the missive and closed the distance between them when he saw her dismay. "What is it?"

"The Peavys were in a carriage accident. Doc Pratt thinks they're going to be okay, but neither one should be up and about for the next few weeks. Myrtis has been looking after them, but she's due to go out of town in a few days." She turned to her grandfather. "I'm so sorry to cut my visit short, but I really should be there for them."

"Of course. Go see about your friends. You can come back and finish your visit when they're better."

Adam took her hand, trying to comfort her with a squeeze while he addressed the judge. "Do you know the train schedule?"

"The next one headed that direction is early tomorrow morning. I'll have Hodgkins take care of the tickets."

"Just two tickets," Regina said.

Adam frowned. "I'm going with you."

She shook her head. "No, you're not. You need to stay here and finish your investigation. Jack and I will be fine for the next few weeks."

He couldn't do that. "I'm not—"

She pressed a finger to his lips. "I've quite made up my mind. Take care of this business so you can come back to Turnabout with your spirit free."

Chapter Twenty-One

Judge Madison insisted Adam stay at his home, and Adam was happy to oblige. He missed Jack and Regina more than he'd have thought and it was good to be around someone else who knew them.

Just before she'd gotten on the train, Regina had pulled him aside.

"I can't leave without telling you two very important things," she'd said. "I want you to listen carefully, and I don't want you to try to respond."

She definitely had his attention. "Very well."

"First, I need you to know that no matter how this quest of yours works out, it won't change how I feel. I *know* you are innocent, and whether or not you prove it to the rest of the world, you don't need to try to prove it to me."

Something warm settled in his chest at those words. Did she know what a gift she'd given him?

"And secondly..." Regina fiddled with her collar a moment, then straightened and looked him right in the eye "...I love you."

Adam went very still inside, not certain what he felt.

He couldn't remember anyone ever saying those words to him before. "I—"

She placed a finger to his lips. "No, don't say anything. I didn't say that to make you uncomfortable or to try to force a similar declaration from you. And I don't expect it to change anything between us. I just said it because it's how I feel and I wanted you to know." She stepped back with an overly bright smile. "Now hurry and get this investigation over with and come home to us." With that she'd turned and walked away.

He still wasn't sure how he felt about her declaration, wasn't certain anymore what his own feeling were. So instead of thinking too much about it, he threw himself into his investigation. At the end of two weeks he had the proof he needed—at least proof enough to convince himself that he finally knew the truth. Lawrence Hadley—a man he'd called friend, who'd moved in the same circles, worked at the same law office, visited in his residence—was the real culprit. Not only had he stolen that money, but two months after Adam was sentenced to jail, he'd married Emma, Adam's former fiancée. He'd not only stolen the money, he'd stolen Adam's life.

With a keen sense of anticipation, Adam climbed up Hadley's front steps that afternoon and knocked on his door. As he waited for someone to answer, he cynically admired the impressive facade in the expensive neighborhood. It seemed Hadley had done well for himself since Adam had last seen him. Had he only committed extortion the one time, or had there been other cases?

A servant opened the door and took Adam's name, asking him to wait in the entryway. Would Hadley refuse to see him? No matter, Adam would not be turned away.

But when the servant returned, he indicated Adam was to follow down the hallway. Within moments, Adam and Lawrence Hadley were alone in the man's study.

Hadley remained seated at his desk, a cautious look on his face. "Hello, Adam. You're looking well."

"As are you." But not for long.

"I must admit to being surprised to see you here. If you are looking to get your old job back—"

"I know."

Hadley tried to cover his wince with a cough. "You know what?"

"I know it was you who stole that money and framed me six years ago."

"You're wrong."

"Oh, no. I have someone who saw you make those false entries in the books, and who'll swear to it in court."

This time Hadley's face paled. "Even if that were possible, no one will believe him after all this time."

"Perhaps, but why don't we let the courts decide?"

"Listen, Adam, I—"

The door burst open and a little girl who looked to be slightly younger than Jack ran into the room. "Poppa, Poppa, we saw a hot air balloon at the park."

Hadley scooped up the child, but before he could say anything, a little boy with an irritated expression on his face entered as well. "Alice, you were supposed to let me tell him."

"You can both tell me all about it later," Hadley said, casting a pleading look Adam's way. "But right now I have company and we're discussing business."

The two children studied Adam with curious expressions, but before they could say anything, Adam heard someone else enter the room behind him.

"I'm sorry, Lawrence, they got away from me. And I didn't know you had company."

Adam was quite familiar with that voice. He stood and as soon as he turned, she gasped and her hand went to her throat.

"Adam!"

"Hello, Emma. You're looking as beautiful as ever." And she did. But somehow, her beauty didn't affect him as it once had. He found himself comparing her elegant features and blond coloring to a more down-to-earth lady with dark hair, blue-green eyes and a smile that could light his world.

Her gaze flew to her husband's and then back to him. "How…how nice to see you. What—"

"Emma," her husband said firmly, "Adam and I have business to discuss. Would you and the children excuse us for the moment?"

"Of course."

Adam saw the worry furrow her brow, saw the unspoken messages pass between them, the body language that expressed concern, and realized with surprise that these two seemed to genuinely love each other.

Then the little boy stopped in front of him on the way out. "If you've come to my poppa for help, don't you worry. He's the best lawyer in all of Philadelphia."

As the door closed behind the three of them, Adam wondered what this little boy and his sister would feel when their father was unveiled as a criminal.

He turned back to his former friend. "Does Emma know?"

Hadley, who now looked years older than he had when Adam walked in, shook his head. "No one does."

"Why did you do it?" Not that it mattered. The man had committed a crime and had to pay.

"I was madly in love with Emma, but she only had eyes for you. I thought, perhaps if I had money to buy her nice gifts that perhaps I could win her away." He leaned forward earnestly. "I never intended to frame you. I thought I could pay it back before anyone discovered the money was missing. Then, when the theft *was* discovered, everything just sort of spiraled out of control."

He raked a hand through his hair. "I know I was a coward to let you take the blame, and I've hated myself for it ever since." He leaned back, an air of hopelessness surrounding him. "So what do we do now?"

Adam couldn't get the image of those two little children out of his mind. "Have you stolen any more?"

"No, absolutely not. I learned my lesson."

Vengeance belongs to God. "Can you pay back what you stole?"

"Why, yes, but—"

"No buts. You need to pay back every penny. You can do it anonymously, if you wish, but it has to go back."

At the word anonymously, a small light of hope slid into Hadley's expression. "Does this mean you're not going to accuse me publicly?"

Adam stood. "As long as you pay back what you stole—and rest assured, I'll know. I'm also going to have my eye on you in the future. If I so much as get a hint that you've committed any such crime again, then our deal is off."

"Don't worry, you'll never have reason to be sorry. I don't know how to thank—"

"Don't thank me. I'm not doing this for you, I'm doing it for your children." And for myself. "No child should have to grow up in the shadow of their father's sins."

Adam left Hadley's home feeling oddly off kilter. He'd waited so long to clear his name, and now, when it was within reach, he'd thrown the chance away. Had he done the right thing?

All his life he'd tried to prove that his mother had been wrong. That he was worth caring about.

He'd studied harder, worked harder, tried harder than everyone around him. By doing so he'd not only graduated at the top of his class, but had become junior partner in a prestigious law firm in record time.

He'd taken on impossible cases against tough opponents and had come out the winner.

He'd pursued the most sought-after woman in Philadelphia and won her favor.

But as soon as the first whisper of scandal attached itself to his name, all those accomplishments counted for naught. Like his mother, nearly everyone he cared about had turned their back on him.

Yet Regina had said she loved him. And he'd let her go without responding, because deep inside, he knew he hadn't done anything to earn that love. And he knew, he *absolutely* knew, that you only received approval and acceptance if you proved yourself worthy of it in some fashion.

Regina *loved* him.

Something inside him, some weight that had been there so long he'd ceased to feel it, began to crumble, then evaporate entirely. His world shifted from one heartbeat to the next, leaving him with a lost, almost dizzy feeling.

Then he straightened.

It was time he headed back to Turnabout.

Reggie strolled down the quiet street, a decided bounce to her step. Adam was due back tomorrow and she couldn't wait to see him again. There hadn't been any hint in his telegram as to whether or not he'd cleared his name, but they could discuss that when he arrived.

She'd have a lot to tell him, too. Things had been happening in Turnabout while he was away. The most startling bit of news was dark and sad. The person who stole the fair money turned out to be Pierce himself, who'd ended up committing suicide rather than facing the music. It turned out he'd been skimming funds from the bank to help support his wife's expensive tastes and Adam's talk of looking at the ledgers had made him desperate.

On the brighter side, Ira and Mrs. Peavy were doing better now. Both had gotten up for a little while yesterday and this morning, and according to Doc Pratt they were well on their way to a full recovery. And Ira had the irritable disposition to prove it.

And her three suitors were settling into the community quite nicely. Everett had already begun printing the paper weekly, Chance had become enamored with the motor carriage and had decided he wanted to work with mechanical conraptions and Mitchell was preparing for the first day of school which would start in just a little over a week.

Her thoughts circled back around to Adam, as they

frequently did, and she wondered what he'd thought of her train-side declaration. Had he accepted it as the no-strings-attached gift she'd meant it to be, or had it merely made him uncomfortable? Would it change anything about their relationship, and if so, what?

Gradually she became aware of a racket coming from somewhere nearby. It sounded like a man singing, though he definitely had more fervor than talent. In fact, he wasn't much better than she was, though she admired his enthusiasm.

Reggie turned, trying to identify where it was coming from. Her eyes widened and she stopped in her tracks.

Adam was riding down the road atop the strangest wagon she'd ever seen, singing at the top of his voice.

People were coming out of their houses to see what was going on. As soon as they caught sight of Adam, most of them stood grinning and watching the show.

When Adam drew up beside her he set the brake, grabbed a bouquet of flowers from the seat beside him and jumped to the ground.

Reggie's heart stuttered, then beat faster. But she was afraid to believe this meant what it seemed to. "I thought you weren't getting in until tomorrow."

"I managed to get away sooner that I'd thought. And I couldn't wait to see you again."

Her pulse kicked up a notch. "You couldn't?"

He took her hand. "I've finally come to my senses. I've been every kind of fool, Regina. You offered me your love and instead of seizing it like the precious gift it was, I let you walk away."

The look in his eyes revived that stubborn spark of hope. "But what about—"

He moved his hand to her lips. "I *said* I've been a fool. You did what you did with Jack as an act of love, not of selfishness, I understand that now. You've given him your love, unselfishly, and I will never forgive myself for calling that an ugly thing."

Did he truly forgive her? "Oh, Adam—"

"Let me finish. You are a caring, brave and generous woman, and I don't deserve you. But your spirit is embedded deep within my heart and soul, and if you took it away from me I would shrivel up into the half-man I was before."

His words entranced her, touched her deeply. No one had ever said such things to her, spoken to her with such vulnerable honesty. "I would never take back that which is so fully yours."

To the delight of the growing number of onlookers, Adam got down on one knee.

Reggie felt her cheeks warm. "What are you doing? Stand up this instant."

Adam only smiled. "When you learned about your grandfather's scheme, you said you wanted it all—flowers, gifts, love songs, pretty words. Well, you didn't get any of that and I think it's time you did."

With a flourish, he offered her the bouquet. "Here are your flowers, the first of many more to come if you'll accept them. And this wagon is your gift. You can decide how you want it decorated and I'll follow your instructions to the letter." He gave a self-deprecating smile. "The love song you already heard, which gives you some indication why you haven't heard it before."

He squeezed her hands. "As for the pretty words, I'm no poet, but here goes. Regina Nash Barr, I want to love and cherish and care for you with every breath in my body and every moment of my life. If you will accept me, I want to marry you again."

Reggie's vision blurred slightly, hindered no doubt by the moisture in her eyes. "Adam Barr, I'll marry you whenever and however many times you want. Just don't ever dare leave me again."

He sprang up and pulled her to him, giving her a kiss designed to take her breath away. The cheers and catcalls from the onlookers, however, cut it short.

"Come on." Adam wrapped an arm around her waist with a can't-wait grin. "Let's find us a more private spot to finish this discussion."

Epilogue

Reggie sat beside Adam in her new photography wagon as they rode toward the cabin, contentment washing over her like a warm, scented bath. Jack and the Peavys would follow tomorrow, but for today they'd have the place to themselves.

It had been nearly a month since they'd had that second wedding ceremony Adam had promised her, and it had been everything she could have hoped for. This time they'd gotten it right, sealing their vows with love and laughter and a genuine commitment to each other.

And the belated wedding present he'd given her was perfect.

"You did a wonderful job on the wagon," she said. "I do believe it's better than my other one."

Adam grinned. "Who would've thought orange, pink and green would go together so well."

"My favorite part is the weather vane." She glanced over her shoulder at the bright blue rooster perched on a gold arrow on top of the wagon.

How would he feel about the gift she had for him? A smile teased her lips in anticipation.

Cutting him a challenging look, Reggie let her emotions spill out into exuberant song. With a grin, Adam joined in. Their raucous, totally unmelodic efforts echoed through the woods.

When they reached the end of the chorus, Reggie drew herself up. "Did I see the birds scatter?"

Adam swallowed a grin at Reggie's mock outrage. "They just don't appreciate our unique talents," he said with a mournful shake of the head.

But he couldn't hold that expression for long. In truth, his life was pretty near perfect. As long as his independent-minded, spirited, wonderful wife was here beside him, he didn't think a man could be happier than he was.

Reggie sighed. "I'm afraid our children won't stand a chance, musically speaking."

Adam had a sudden image of her, flushed and round with their child. It was an image that pleased him tremendously.

She linked an arm through his. "And speaking of children, there's something I need to tell you."

Adam's gaze jerked to hers, and his heart nearly stopped when he saw the soft message in her eyes. He yanked on the reins and set the brake, then placed his hands on her shoulders. "Are you saying… I mean, are you…"

She nodded. "You're going to be a father."

Unable to speak, Adam drew her to him and stroked her hair.

He'd been wrong earlier. A man always had capacity for more happiness.

* * * * *

THE BRIDE NEXT DOOR

Do not store up for yourselves treasures on earth,
where moths and vermin destroy,
and where thieves break in and steal.
But store up for yourselves treasures in heaven,
where moths and vermin do not destroy, and
where thieves do not break in and steal. For where
your treasure is, there your heart will be also.

—*Matthew* 6:19–21

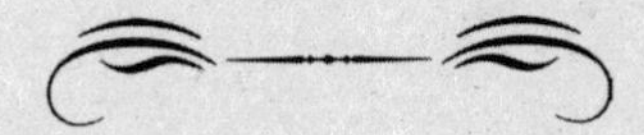

To my accountability partner, Sherrie,
who helped me stay on track as I was writing this book. And to my sister Tammy, who took the time from her busy schedule to read the finished product and give me her honest feedback.

Chapter One

Turnabout, Texas, April 1895

The ornery, splinter-ridden door refused to budge, no matter how hard she shoved. Or how hard she glared.

Daisy Johnson stood on the darkened sidewalk, glowering at the weathered barricade that stood between herself and her new home. She absently scratched a splinter from her thumb as she glanced down at the black-and-white dog sitting patiently at her heels. "Don't worry, Kip. I'm going to get us inside, one way or the other."

Kip gave her a supportive yip, then began scratching his side.

A noise from over to her left caught Daisy's attention. Down the street, a shadowy figure exited the livery and headed unsteadily down the sidewalk toward the hotel. Probably coming from one of the poker games the locals held there—an activity she was unfortunately all too familiar with.

Other than that, things were quiet. Which was fine by her. Kip was the only company she needed tonight.

Daisy spared a quick glance at the adjoining building, which housed the newspaper office, and thought briefly about knocking on the door to see if she could borrow something to use as a pry bar. But she discarded the thought almost before it had fully formed. Not only was the hour late, but from what she recalled about the man who owned the place, he was an uppity gent with a highfalutin accent of some sort. His attitude reminded her too much of her grandmother. Not the sort who would take kindly to being roused from sleep. Or someone she'd want to owe any favors.

Turning back to the stubbornly closed door, she jutted her chin out and tilted her hat back. No warped slab of lumber was going to get the better of her, not when she was so close to her goal.

Using her foot to shove aside one of the rotten boards she'd pried from across the door frame, Daisy jiggled the key and turned the knob again. There was just enough light coming from the glow of the nearby streetlamp to confirm the door wasn't locked. Which meant it was just stuck.

"If you think you can out-ornery me," she muttered at the door as she rolled up her sleeves, "then you better think again." With that, she took firmer hold of the knob, twisted it as far as it would go, and led with her shoulder as she rammed against the door. Kip stopped scratching and gave her a you-can-do-it bark.

The door held a moment longer, then scraped noisily open a few inches. Progress. But not enough. Kip might be able to squeeze through that opening, but not her.

Steeling herself, Daisy threw her shoulder into it one more time, grunting at the impact. With a last creak of protest, the door gave up its fight and opened wide enough to allow her to pass.

With a triumphant grin and a prickling of anticipation, Daisy retrieved her pack, tossed her bedroll up on her shoulder and met Kip's curious glance. "This is it, boy. We're home."

With a deep breath, Daisy took her first step inside the building, Kip at her heels. The room was mostly cloaked in shadows, illuminated only by what light filtered in from the streetlamp, and it took a few moments for her eyes to adjust.

As she surveyed what little she could see of the room, her grin disappeared. "Jehoshaphat!" She'd spent the night in abandoned barns that were cleaner and neater than this place.

Striding farther into the room, Daisy muttered a few unladylike epithets under her breath as she batted at cobwebs and felt things crunch beneath her boots that she wasn't ready to examine more closely.

She spied a lamp sitting on the counter and was relieved to find a bit of oil still in the base. It took several attempts, but she finally managed to get it lit and then took a closer look around.

She could hear Kip sniffling around, picking up goodness only knew what kind of scents. A couple of loud doggy sneezes confirmed that it was as dusty at his level as it was at hers.

She hadn't expected a servant-scrubbed palace, but hang it all, she'd hoped to find something in a little better condition than *this.* No wonder the previous owner had been so quick to gamble it away.

She started to close the outer door, then changed her

mind. It wouldn't hurt to leave it open for a little while to help air out the place.

Daisy tromped across the room, ignoring the skittery scrambling sounds coming from just outside the circle of lamplight. Hopefully, whatever critters had taken up residence in here were on their way out. Still, she was glad for Kip's company.

The back room wasn't much better than the front. In the yellowish light of the lamp, she could see dust, debris and a smattering of rickety furniture scattered higgledy-piggledy across the space. Daisy kicked at an old sack lying in her path, then let out an explosive sneeze as a cloud of dust billowed up in her face.

Great! This was just pointy-fanged-rattlesnake perfect.

She fanned the air in front of her between sneezes. Why should the day end even a gnat-speck better than it had started?

Then she caught herself up short. *Not that I'm complaining, mind You, Lord. I know You answered my prayers in a powerful way when You took Pa's weakness for gambling and turned it to good by providing me with the deed to this building. And I truly am mighty grateful. Besides, I do know there's nothing wrong with this place that a bit of honest sweat and elbow grease won't fix up just fine and dandy. You've done Your part, and now I aim to do mine.*

Daisy looked around again. *Make that* a lot *of elbow grease.*

But that didn't scare her none. No, sir. The place was more than roomy enough for what she had in mind. She could already picture how it would look all cleaned up and put to rights. It would be so wonderful to have a place of her own, a place to set down roots and build a proper life. And to finally make some genuine friends of her very own.

And maybe, if she was very, very good, she could have a family of her very own one day, as well.

I know, Lord, baby steps. I asked for a family of my own, and instead, You gave me the seeds of one by providing a means for me to settle down in one place. I'm going to do my best to make myself an acceptable helpmeet in the eyes of some God-fearing man. I promise to look past appearance, manner and finances to see the heart of whoever You send my way.

Feeling focused and enthusiastic once more, Daisy went back to work. First order of business was to clear herself out a place to sleep. There was no way she could lie down in the midst of this gritty, grimy, cluttered mess, so if she was going to get a good night's rest, she'd best start cleaning.

She tested the soundness of a crate near the doorway, then set the lamp and bedroll down. Plopping her hat and pack beside them, she rolled up her sleeves. No time like the present to get started.

Everett Fulton forced his heavy eyelids open, peering blearily around his darkened room. The faint memory of his dream lingered a moment—childhood images of his home in England. Already it was fading, leaving him to wonder if the muffled clatter that had awakened him had been real or only part of his dream.

A moment later, another series of thuds answered the question.

Jerked to full awareness, he tossed off the covers and swiveled so that his feet hit the floor.

It sounded as if someone was rummaging around

downstairs. If the not-so-stealthy intruder did any harm to his printing press…

Swiftly crossing the room, Everett paused only long enough to pull on a pair of pants and retrieve the iron poker that rested against the cold fireplace.

Just because he didn't own a gun didn't mean he couldn't defend himself.

Without bothering with a lamp, Everett stole down the stairs, carefully avoiding the fourth tread that had an annoying tendency to creak. His ears strained for some sign of just where his trespasser might be lurking.

He moved to the larger front room first, the room that housed his printing press and served as his office. A faint light filtered in from the large window that faced the street. His gaze went immediately to the bulky shadow that was his printing press. Most of the type was already laboriously set for this week's paper. He would have no compunction whatsoever in trouncing anyone who dared tamper with his work.

Everett's brow furrowed. All was quiet now, but he'd been certain the noise had come from down here. And everything seemed as he'd left it when he locked the doors and headed upstairs earlier.

Tightening his grip on the poker, he eased farther into the room. Taking a deep breath, he sprang around the corner of the press, his makeshift weapon raised. "Ha!"

But no thug crouched behind the machine's shadowy bulk.

Feeling foolish, he lowered his arm. Had he misjudged the direction the disturbance had come from? Everett turned to his desk, a sour smile tugging at his lips. If the intruder was after a cash box, he would be sadly disappointed.

Nothing.

He moved into the back room where he stored his blank paper and other supplies, but again, nothing.

Everett rubbed his neck, slowly exiting the room. Maybe he'd imagined the whole thing, after all.

Scriiittch.

He swung back around. It sounded as if something heavy were being dragged across the floor. He approached the far wall cautiously, then heard it again.

The noise was coming from the other side. Someone was in the adjoining building.

He frowned. The supposedly *vacant* adjoining building.

He'd never been inside, but understood the building didn't house anything more valuable than cobwebs and a jumble of rubbish and cast-off furnishings. What possible reason could someone have for rattling around in there in the middle of the night?

Everett shrugged and moved back toward the stairs. Other than the annoyance of having his sleep disturbed, it wasn't any of his concern.

Then he stilled. Except that there might be a story in it. Something more newsworthy than births, deaths and barn raisings for a change. Since he was already awake, it couldn't hurt to check things out. His pulse accelerated at the idea of a *real* story, a chance to resume his role as reporter rather than mere transcriber and typesetter. It had been quite a while…

Everett hurried upstairs, donned a shirt and shoes, then padded lightly down again.

He still carried the poker. Not that he intended to use it unless he had need to defend himself.

He was a reporter, after all, not a confounded hero.

Stepping onto the plank sidewalk, Everett paused a moment to listen. Somewhere in the distance, a dog barked and was answered by a second mutt. Four blocks away he could see light seeping from the windows of the livery. An ash-colored moth lazily circled the nearby streetlamp.

Other than that, everything was quiet. Enough light filtered down from the streetlamps and gauze-covered half moon that he could see the building next door easily.

He moved forward, studying the front of the run-down establishment. The boards that had barred the door were now lying on the sidewalk against the building, and the door itself gaped open.

He peered in, but it was too shadowy to make out anything but irregular shapes. However, he did notice a yellowish light emanating from the back room—the area where the sounds had come from.

Was it a squatter? Or a misguided thief?

Everett hesitated, listening to the scrapes and muffled grunts, torn between his reporter's instinct to find out the truth of the matter and the niggling voice that told him he'd be wise to arm himself with more than a poker before proceeding.

Besides, what if it was Gus Ferguson, the building's owner? Gus was a crotchety old hermit who kept to himself, except for the occasional trip to town to get supplies and indulge in a bit of drinking and poker playing. In the nine months Everett had resided in Turnabout, he'd never seen Gus look twice at the place, much less go inside. Why would the man choose this unlikely time to come here? Unless he'd decided to stop in after tonight's poker game.

Perhaps it would be best if he just quietly slipped away and forgot the whole thing.

Everett winced at the sound of falling crates. The

sound of a woman crying out, however, had him through the door as if shot from a pistol. And was that a dog yapping?

He swallowed a yelp as he bumped his knee against the edge of a sagging counter. He kept going, though, albeit with somewhat impaired agility.

Charging into the back room, the first thing he spied was the rubble of storage shelves that had given way, dumping splintered lumber and unidentifiable contents in a dusty heap.

A grumbled *humph* drew his attention to a woman sitting on the floor, trying to pull her foot free of the mess.

"I'm okay, Kip. But as for this worm-ridden, rickety pile of junk, the only thing it's good for is kindling."

Everett recognized the voice before he got a good look at her face—it had a distinctive lilt to it and boasted a slight accent that he couldn't quite place, but was unmistakable.

Daisy Johnson. What in the world was the peddler's daughter doing here? She and her father had left town two weeks ago.

Miss Johnson looked up and recognized him at the same time. "Mr. Fulton. What're you doing in here?"

"Apparently rescuing a damsel in distress." Still concerned about her predicament, Everett crossed to her in long strides.

The dog seemed to take exception to his approach and assumed a stiff-legged, curled-lip stance in front of Miss Johnson.

"It's okay, Kip," she said, giving the dog a reassuring pat. Then she turned a frown on him. "I'm not a damsel. And I'm not in distress. My ankle just got caught under this mess, is all."

Did she even know what distress meant? "Let me give you a hand with that." Not bothering to wait for an answer, he heaved up on the piece her foot was trapped beneath, allowing her to free herself, all the while keeping a wary eye on the dog. And the dog returned his look, stare for stare.

Once she'd shifted her leg away from danger, he set the offending shelving back down. Then he knelt beside her, doing his best to ignore the dust and grime that surrounded him. "Allow me," he said, taking over the job of unlacing her boot.

"There's really no need," she protested, trying to push away his hands. "I can do that—"

He gave her his best don't-argue-with-me stare. "Be still, please. You're stirring up more dust, and I'd rather not succumb to a fit of sneezing."

She paused, an abashed look on her face.

Good. He'd gotten through to her for the moment. Time to drive his point home. "It's important to make certain you're not badly injured before you try to stand. Or would you prefer I ask Dr. Pratt to take a look at you?"

His words had the opposite effect of what he'd expected. She glared at him. "There's no need to be so snippy. And no, I do *not* prefer to have you bother the doc at this late hour over a few bruises."

Snippy? Didn't the girl recognize authority when she heard it? Clenching his jaw to contain his irritation, he gently slid the worn, dirty bit of footwear, including her stocking, off her foot. He studied her ankle, unhappy with what he saw. "It's already starting to swell and darken. It might be wise to have Dr. Pratt take a look at you, after all."

"Glory be!" She brushed his hands away and smoothed down her skirts. "It's nothing more than a bad bruise." She flexed her ankle to prove her point, but he noticed the wince she couldn't quite hide. "It'll be fine by morning," she insisted.

Everett leaned back on his heels. He wasn't going to force the issue. After all, he wasn't her keeper—nor did he want to be. "Mind if I ask what you're doing in here?"

"I was trying to clear the way to the back door so I could open it up and air out the place."

Was she being deliberately obtuse? "I mean, why are you in here in the first place?"

She tilted her chin up. "Not that it's any of your business, but I'm cleaning the place up so Kip and I don't have to sleep in the middle of this rubbish and dirt."

He resisted the urge to roll his eyes. Daisy Johnson's lack of ladylike sensibilities went beyond the unrefined rustic "charm" that he'd grown to expect from the women of this backwater that circumstances had forced him to call home for the present. She was outspoken, obviously uneducated and her manner was rough and belligerent.

"It *is* my business if you wake me up from a sound sleep in the middle of the night," he countered.

At least she had the grace to blush at that. "Oh. Sorry. I wasn't thinking about the racket reaching over to you."

He stood and offered a hand to help her up. "Apology accepted. As long as you cease and desist until a more civilized hour."

"Fair enough."

He noticed another quickly suppressed wince as she put weight on the injured foot, but she didn't utter a sound.

"If you won't see the doctor," he said, keeping a hand at her elbow, "at least tell me where your father is so I can fetch him to tend to you." The sooner he could turn her over to someone else and return to the comfort of his bed, the better.

She tugged her arm out of his grasp and hobbled over to a nearby crate to sit down. He grimaced at the little cloud of dust that rose as she settled.

"I reckon he's halfway to the Louisiana border by now," she answered, reaching down to scratch her scruffy-looking dog.

Had her father abandoned her? Despite himself, Everett felt a stirring of sympathy. He spied the bedroll next to the lamp. "So you broke in here looking for a place to spend the night."

She shifted as if to find a more comfortable position for her foot, and he saw a snatch of cobweb caught in her tawny hair. He had an unexpected urge to brush it away, but quickly shook off the impulse.

"I aim to spend more than the night here," she said with a smile.

Did she intend to claim squatter's rights? Well, it was her bad luck that the building already had an owner. "Despite the way this place looks," he said, trying to let her down gently, "it's not abandoned. And I'm afraid the owner might not look favorably on your plans to take up residence."

"That's where you'd be wrong." There was a decidedly smug look to her smile. "*I'm* the owner, and I don't have a problem with it at all."

Chapter Two

Everett stared at her, feeling his momentary sympathy fade. Had he heard correctly? But there she sat, like a queen on her dusty throne. How could that be? "Last I heard, Gus Ferguson owned this place." He managed to keep his tone neutral.

"He *did.*" She gave a self-satisfied smile. "Until he lost it to my father in a poker game."

A poker game? That shouldn't surprise him as much as it did. "And your father, in turn, gave it to you, I suppose."

She brushed at her skirt, not quite meeting his gaze. "Let's just say he owed it to me."

A cryptic turn of phrase, but he brushed aside his curiosity for now. There were more important matters to get to the bottom of. "If you don't mind my asking, what are your plans for the place?" If she was going to be his neighbor, he wanted some idea as to what he was going to be in for.

"I'm going to set up my business here."

Not the answer he'd expected. "What kind of business?"

From the look she gave him, he surmised some of his displeasure had come through in his tone.

"Well," she replied, eyeing him carefully, "I eventually want to open a restaurant."

She was just full of surprises. "You know how to cook?"

Her brown eyes narrowed, and her smudged chin tilted up. "You don't have to say it like that. I happen to be a great cook—everybody says so."

Just who did *everybody* include—her father and dog, perhaps? Then he took a very pointed look around him. "A restaurant—in *here?*"

"Of course I won't be able to open it right away." Her voice was less confident now. "I'll need to earn some money first so I can fix this place up and furnish it proper. And of course I'll need to buy a good stove."

She didn't seem particularly daunted by the task ahead of her. "And how do you intend to do that? Earn the money, I mean."

She shrugged. "I'm not my father's daughter for nothing. I'll figure something out."

Her father's daughter—did that mean she planned to try her luck in the poker game over at the livery?

She rotated her neck, and Everett saw signs of fatigue beneath her bravado. For the first time, he wondered about the particulars of her arrival. "If your father didn't come back to Turnabout with you, how did you get here?"

"I walked, mostly." Then she grinned proudly. "Made it in three days."

Her father had allowed her to take a three-day journey alone and on foot? Everett felt incensed on her behalf. Had the peddler given any thought at all to what might have happened? The man should be thoroughly trounced.

A suspicious rumbling from the vicinity of her stomach brought up another question. When had she last eaten?

The faint pinkening of her cheeks was the only acknowledgment she made of the unladylike noise. "Right now, though," she said quickly, "I'm just going to clean up a spot where I can spread my bedroll and get some sleep while I wait for the sun to come up."

He looked around at the layers of dust and the lack of useable furnishings. "You plan to sleep on the floor?"

"I don't see any fancy beds in here. Do you?" Her cheerful tone lacked any hint of self-pity. "Besides, I've bedded down on worse." Her pleased-with-herself grin returned. "And being as it'll be my very first night in my very own place, I expect I'll sleep very well."

She placed her hands on her skirt and levered herself up. "I'm sorry I disturbed your sleep, and I thank you for checking in on me, but you can go on back to your place now. I promise Kip and I won't be disturbing you anymore tonight."

Apparently feeling she'd dismissed him, she turned and started picking her way across the room.

Everett contemplated her words while he watched her limp toward a relatively uncluttered spot near the wall that adjoined his place. Her state of affairs wasn't really any of his concern, and she'd just made it abundantly clear she felt the same. She seemed content with her circumstances, and he had a busy day planned for tomorrow, so he should return to his bed and try to get what sleep he could before sunup.

But for some reason, he stood there a moment longer, watching her. His thoughts turned unaccountably to Abigail, his fifteen-year-old sister. What if she were in this situation? Which was a ridiculous thought, of course. Abigail was safely ensconced in a nice boarding school in Boston and would *never* find herself in a situation like this.

Still…

Daisy frowned as she heard her visitor—or was it intruder?—leave. For all his fine airs, he could be mighty rude. He'd all but said he didn't believe her claim to being a good cook, and it was obvious he didn't think she'd be able to open her own restaurant. And if that wasn't bad enough, she'd seen the way he looked down his nose at her.

Reminded her of Grandmère Longpre—one was *always* aware when she was displeased. Of course her grandmother would never dream of being impolite. The niceties of civilized society were too important to her.

Ah, well, Mr. Fulton didn't really know her yet, and she'd just roused him from his sleep. She couldn't really blame him for being in a bad mood. And she shouldn't forget that he *had* helped her out from under that shelving, so she should be grateful and more forgiving. As her father would say, never moon over *should bes* when your *have nows* are enough to get you by.

She'd just have to prove to Mr. Fulton and the rest of the townsfolk that she aimed to be a good, neighborly citizen of this community. Starting with making this place clean and inviting. Too bad she didn't have a broom and mop yet. She'd need to take care of that first thing in the morning. For now, she'd just make do as best she could.

She maneuvered an empty crate next to the space where she planned to place her bedroll, wincing at the bit of noise she made. Hopefully it hadn't been loud enough to disturb her neighbor. Again.

Once she had the crate in place, she eyed it critically, then nodded in satisfaction. "This'll make a fine table for now—just right for setting my lamp and Mother's Bible."

Kip answered her with a couple thumps of his tail.

She decided her change of clothing and the rest of the meager belongings she'd brought along with her could stay in her pack until she found an appropriate and *clean* place to store them.

She arched her back, trying to stretch out some of the kinks. Tomorrow she'd give this place a good scrubbing, and maybe pick some wildflowers to add a bit of color. It would take a while to fix it up the way she wanted, but the cleaning and scrubbing part didn't cost anything except time and effort.

Already, she could picture it the way she would eventually fix it up—with bright curtains on freshly washed windows and a new coat of paint on the walls. She'd have a roomy pantry and sturdy shelves built in here for all her cooking supplies, and a big, shiny, new stove over on that far wall.

She grabbed her bedroll, still thinking about the red-checkered tablecloths and the ruffled curtains she'd purchase. But before she could get the makeshift bed unrolled properly, her neighbor returned, a scowl on his face. What now?

"Mr. Fulton, I'm so sorry if I'm making too much noise again. I promise—"

He shook his head impatiently, interrupting her apology. At the same time she noticed he was carrying a broom and a cloth-wrapped bundle.

He set the broom against the wall, nodding toward it. "I thought you might be able to make use of this," he said. Then he thrust the parcel her way. "I also brought this for you."

His tone was short, gruff, as if he wasn't happy. Was it with her or with himself? His accent had deepened, as well.

And more important—just what in the world had he brought her?

She gingerly unwrapped the parcel and was pleasantly surprised to find an apple, a slab of cheese and a thick slice of bread inside. "Why, thank you. This is so kind of you."

He waved aside her thanks. "It's just a few bits left over from my dinner." He nodded toward the broom. "And that's just a loan."

That might be true, but the food seemed a veritable feast to her, and the broom would cut her work tonight in half. "Still, it's very neighborly." Just saying that word cheered her up.

But he still wore that impatient scowl. "Yes, well, I'll leave you to get settled in." He glanced at the sleeping area she'd set up and then back at her. "See that you keep the noise down."

She smothered a sigh, wondering why he had to spoil his nice gesture with a grumpy attitude. "Of course. Good night."

"Good night."

As she watched him leave this time, her smile returned. Regardless of his sour expression, Mr. Fulton had been quite kind. Perhaps she'd already made her first friend.

Bowing her head, she said a quick prayer of thanks for the unexpected meal, and for the man who'd given it to her.

Then she looked down at Kip as she broke off a bit of cheese to feed him. "Look here, boy. We have a nice meal to help us really celebrate our first night in our new home. Isn't God good?"

And, much as he tried to hide it, she was beginning to believe Mr. Fulton had some good in him, as well.

The next morning, as Everett prepared his breakfast, he could hear the sounds of his new neighbor's renewed efforts at cleaning out her building. He certainly hoped she didn't keep that racket up all day. Besides, did she really think she could single-handedly turn that musty, junk-cluttered place into a working restaurant?

Glancing out his window, he saw a pile of rubbish in their shared back lot that hadn't been there yesterday. He rubbed his jaw, impressed in spite of himself at the amount of effort she'd already expended this morning. Apparently, she planned to try to make her ambitious but improbable dream a reality.

As he stuck a fork in his slightly overcooked egg, he wondered how she'd fared after he left her last night. Had she gotten any sleep at all given her less-than-ideal accommodations?

He took a sip of coffee. Perhaps he should go over and check on her this morning. Not that her welfare was his concern, but she didn't seem to have anyone else to look out for her. And, even if it was confoundedly inconvenient, someone should make certain her ankle wasn't any worse this morning and that she had something to eat.

When he carried his dishes to the counter he spied her through the window, dragging another load of debris to toss on her trash pile. That unfortunate-looking mutt she'd had with her last night was racing from her heels to the far end of the lot and back again.

At least she didn't seem to be favoring her left foot. As for food, he waffled a few moments over whether to involve himself further in her business. He supposed, as long as he made it clear he expected her to fend for herself going forward, it wouldn't hurt to offer sustenance one more time.

He'd do the gentlemanly thing and invite her up for something to eat, or at least a cup of coffee. And maybe see if she was as optimistic about her enterprise this morning as she'd been last night.

But before he could act on his decision, he saw her reappear carrying a sack and head toward the edge of town, the dog trotting beside her.

What in the world was she up to now?

Feeling slightly deflated, Everett washed his dishes and headed down to his office. Enough of this unproductive preoccupation with his neighbor. He had work to get to.

But over the next few hours he had trouble focusing on his work. He found his thoughts drifting to speculation as to where she'd gone off to and, to his irritation, caught himself listening for her return.

He supposed it was only natural to worry about any unprotected female heading out on her own in unfamiliar surroundings. No matter how far she'd walked to get here.

Everett was finally rewarded a couple of hours after her departure by the sound of her return. Minutes later, he could hear items being moved around and other evidence of her renewed efforts. Did she plan to work the entire day? He even thought he heard snatches of some cheerful but slightly off-key humming a time or two. It appeared that, no matter what other qualities Miss Johnson might have, she wasn't afraid of hard work.

And apparently, word of the new arrival had spread through town. There was a steady parade of folks strolling past his glass-fronted office, and stopping by his neighbor's place. With all the interest Miss Johnson was garnering, he wondered just how much work she was actually managing to get done.

He resisted the urge to walk over and see for himself. The impulse had been born of his desire to check on how she was faring after last night's rough start, but she apparently had plenty of drop-in visitors to assist her now.

Near noon, Everett was on his knees in front of his type cabinet, picking up the bits of type that had scattered when he dropped a tray. He blamed the incident on Miss Johnson, or rather the bothersome distraction she'd become. That and his interrupted sleep last night—also her fault—were the most likely culprits for his lack of focus today.

All he needed was an uninterrupted night's sleep tonight; then he'd be as efficient as ever tomorrow.

He was just putting the last piece back in place when his office door opened. He glanced up to see Adam Barr, one of the three men who'd traveled with him from Philadelphia to Turnabout last summer.

Everett pushed to his feet, at the same time pushing away his faint disappointment. He took a moment to slide the tray back into place and then greeted his visitor.

"You're early today," he said as he grabbed a rag to wipe his hands. Most days, Adam stopped by on his way back to the bank after having lunch at home with his wife, Reggie. He and Adam had an ongoing chess game that they both enjoyed and took quite seriously.

"Reggie has my afternoon planned out for me," Adam responded. "Jack's seventh birthday is tomorrow, and she wants my help planning a small surprise for him."

Jack was Reggie's nephew, and she and Adam had adopted him after their marriage last fall.

Adam headed toward the chessboard that was set up on the far end of the room with their game. "If I remember correctly, it was my move."

Everett followed him. "It was. And I'm looking forward to seeing how you'll answer my last move."

Adam sat down, studying the board. "I hear you have a new neighbor," he said as he fingered one of the pawns he'd captured.

"Word gets around fast. If you haven't heard a name yet, it's Daisy Johnson. You remember her—the daughter of the peddler who was arrested for stealing the money from the fair last year." Adam had been instrumental in getting the man cleared of the charges.

"*Falsely* arrested," Adam corrected. "Yes, I remember her. Spirited young lady, if I recall."

Everett agreed with that assessment but decided to change the subject. "So how is Reggie faring?"

"As stubborn as ever. She refuses to accept that she

needs to curtail her more vigorous activities until the baby comes."

Adam set down the captured pawn and slid his bishop across the board. "There," he said as he stood. "That should keep you busy for a while."

Before Everett could study the move, the door opened and in came his new neighbor, carrying the broom he'd loaned her last night, and a small parcel.

While she still wore a dress that had seen better days, there was a pleased-with-the-world smile on her face that overshadowed her dearth of fashion sense. From the bounce in her step it appeared she'd managed to sleep just fine last night. There was no hint of cobwebs in her hair this morning; rather, it was well combed and neatly pulled back in a loose bun.

And, like a shadow, her dog was once more right beside her. In the daylight, the animal looked only marginally more presentable than he had last night. Black and white with a shaggy coat, the mutt had obviously led a less-than-pampered life. One ear was torn, and there was an old scar on one hind leg. And if Everett wasn't mistaken, the dog had one blue and one brown eye. Very disconcerting.

He took all that in within the few seconds following her entrance. It was the reporter in him, trained to notice even the smallest of details.

That quickening of his pulse—that was due to nothing more than curiosity as to what had brought her to his office.

Chapter Three

Daisy paused when she saw that Mr. Fulton wasn't alone. "I'm sorry. I didn't realize you were busy."

Mr. Fulton's visitor turned, and she smiled in recognition. "Mr. Barr! How nice to see you again."

Adam executed a short bow. "The pleasure is mine. I understand you've decided to take up residence in our fair town. Let me add my welcome to the others I'm sure you've already received."

Now *this* welcome seemed genuine. "Thank you. I'm looking forward to setting down roots here." The idea of finally having a permanent home was more than enough to carry her through all the work ahead of her.

"I'm sure I speak for my wife as well as myself when I say we'd be pleased to have you join us for supper one evening when you're available."

Her cheeks warmed in pleasure. "Why, thank you. I'd like that."

"Be sure to let me know if you need help getting settled in." Then Adam turned back to Everett. "It's time I headed home. I'll be back tomorrow, same time as usual, to see if you've figured out your next move."

He tipped his hat her way. "Enjoyed seeing you, Miss Johnson. Good day."

Once he'd departed, Daisy felt her smile grow a bit more forced.

Which was totally unfair. After all, Mr. Fulton had been more than kind to her last night—in his own way, of course. But it was hard to remember that kindness when his disapproving demeanor reminded her so much of her grandmother.

"I don't allow animals in my office," he said stiffly.

He certainly wasn't making it easy for her to remember his kindness. "I gave him a bath out by the stream this morning." She did her best to keep her tone light. "And I assure you he's very well-behaved. So he won't leave tracks on your floor or bother any of your things."

"Nice to know, but I still don't allow animals in here."

She sighed, then looked down at Kip. "You heard the man, boy. You'll have to wait outside." She opened the door and, meeting the animal's gaze, tried to smile reassuringly as she pointed to the sidewalk. Kip, tail drooping, slowly exited. "I won't be long."

She turned back to Mr. Fulton and had to rein in the urge to glare outright.

But he apparently had no idea what she was feeling because he wore that infuriatingly condescending look on his face.

"You talk to that animal as if he understands you," he said.

"Because he does." She lifted her chin. "If not the words, then at least the feelings behind them. Dogs are smarter than most folks give them credit for."

Mr. Fulton strode forward. "I trust your foot is better this morning?"

The thoughtful question put her more at ease. "Yes, thank you, good as new." Then, remembering her reason for coming over, she thrust out the broom. "I wanted to bring this back in case you were needing it. I sure appreciate you loaning it to me. There was a wagonload of dirt that needed sweeping out of that place."

He accepted the cleaning implement and set it against the wall. Then he waved her to a chair in front of his desk. "So you're finished cleaning."

If only that were true. "Afraid not. It's going to take more than one day to take care of all that needs doing. But I made a good start." She took the seat he'd indicated.

"I saw you heading out for a walk this morning," he said as he took his own seat. "Checking out what our town has to offer?"

Had he been *spying* on her? "Actually, I went out and gathered up the materials to make my own broom. There's still a lot of cleaning to do, and I didn't want to wear yours down to a nub." She smiled. "Besides, me and Kip needed to get out in the fresh air and sunshine for a bit after stirring up all that dust and dirt this morning."

He raised a brow. "You're *making* a broom."

Why did he sound so surprised? "It's not difficult. The hardest part is finding a stick that's straight enough and sturdy enough to serve as the handle." She'd learned to be resourceful, not to mention frugal, in the time she'd spent traveling with her father.

Then she remembered the other reason she was here. "I spotted some dewberry vines out behind the schoolyard when Father and I were here before." She smiled, pleased with herself. "'Course, most of them won't ripen for another week or so, but there were some that were ready to pick. I gathered up a bunch and they made for a right tasty breakfast."

Something flickered in his expression, but she couldn't quite read what it was. Not that it mattered. She handed him the cloth-wrapped bundle. "And I brought you some, as well."

He didn't seem particularly eager as he accepted her gift.

"I assure you that wasn't necessary," he said. "All I did was loan you a broom."

"*And* brought me supper last night." Daisy watched him unwrap the cloth. "Anyway, it's not much. But they *are* quite tasty." She didn't believe in not returning favors. "Thank the good Lord there's a plentiful crop of them this year."

He stared at her offering for a moment without saying anything. Was something wrong?

"It's quite kind of you," he said, finally looking back up. "But shouldn't you keep them for yourself?"

Was he feeling sorry for her? That wouldn't do at all—she wanted friendship and respect, not pity. "Don't you like dewberries?" She couldn't quite keep the starch out of her tone.

"I don't believe I've ever tasted them. It's just—"

"Then it's settled," she said firmly. "I can pick more when they ripen—the vines are thick with them."

Looking for a way to change the subject, she blurted out the first thing that came to mind. "Do you have any idea what sort of business used to be in my place?"

"I haven't a clue. Someone who's been in Turnabout a lot longer than I have could probably tell you."

That confirmed something she'd already guessed. "So you're not from around here?"

He spread his hands. "I've only settled here recently. I lived in Philadelphia before that."

"Philadelphia. That's over on the east coast, isn't it?"

He nodded. "It is."

She'd seen a map of the entire country once, and the east coast seemed a far piece from Texas. "So how'd you end up way out here?"

His expression closed off again. "Just looking for a change of scenery." He straightened a few papers on his desk. "So what do you have left to do?"

Had she gotten too nosy? Curiosity *was* a weakness of hers. "I've sorted through most of the furnishings downstairs, but I'm sorry to say most of what was in there wasn't fit for anything but firewood. There were a few pieces worth salvaging, though. And I found an old bed frame upstairs that'll be good as new once I get some new rope to string it with and some ticking. I figure I can collect some straw and then stuff me a fresh mattress. Before you know it, I'll have a proper bed to sleep on."

He shifted in his chair when she mentioned her bed. Her grandmother would chide her for being so indelicate.

She'd best change the subject again. "Do you know of anyone looking for help? I need to find a way to earn some money."

He leaned back in his chair. "What kind of work are you qualified to do?"

Something about the way he asked the question got

her back up. "I can cook, clean, do laundry—I'll take just about any honest labor I can find. I'm not afraid of hard work or of getting my hands dirty."

"I haven't heard of anything, but you might want to check with Doug Blakely over at the mercantile. His store seems to be a gathering place for most of the townsfolk, so if anyone's looking, Doug's probably heard about it. In the meantime, how do you plan to get by?"

Now who was being nosy? "Don't you worry about me. I have a roof over my head, and I know how to live off the land when I need to. Besides those berries, there are plenty of edible roots and plants around here if you know what you're looking for."

"You can hardly live entirely on berries and roots for very long."

A gent like him probably didn't have any idea what it meant to go hungry for days at a time. "You'd be surprised what a body can live on when one has to. I also plan to set me up a little kitchen garden out behind my place. I'm especially eager to plant some herbs. Not only will they add flavor to my meals, but I use some in my concoctions."

"Concoctions?"

"Yes. I make balms and potions to keep on hand for cuts and burns and such. Father calls them my concoctions."

"And is that something you sell?"

"Oh, no. It's mostly for personal use, though I've given some away when I saw a need." She lifted her head proudly. "Some of those folks *have* asked to buy more from me, though." She shrugged self-consciously.

"But I don't really feel right taking money for healing potions."

"It appears you are a woman of many talents." The sarcasm in his tone killed any chance that she would think he was paying her a compliment.

But she chose to ignore his lack of manners. Instead, she gave him her sunniest smile. "That's kind of you to say. And you'll see the proof of that when I open my restaurant."

Everett realized he'd been harsher with his new neighbor than the situation warranted. But she'd apparently misread his tone. He glanced down at her offering of berries, and his conscience tweaked at him again. "Speaking of a job," he said impulsively, "I can't offer you anything full-time, but I do have a proposal for you."

This time she leaned forward eagerly, apparently ready to forgive his earlier rudeness. "What did you have in mind?"

He was beginning to rethink his impulse, but it was too late to back out now. "Since you say you're a good cook, what do you think about cooking for me?

"Really?"

Her hopeful expression brushed away the last of his hesitation. Besides, what could it hurt? "I'm the first to admit I'm not much of a cook myself, and I'm getting tired of the few dishes I've learned to prepare. I can't pay you much, say two bits a day, but if you did the marketing and cooking for me, you could also share in the meal." At least this way he wouldn't have the distraction of worrying about her not having enough to eat.

She smiled at him as if he'd just handed her the keys

to the town. Did that mean she'd forgotten his earlier rudeness?

"That's more than generous," she said. "And you won't be sorry—cooking is something I'm good at. You'll see."

She folded her hands in her lap and struck what he supposed she thought of as a businesslike pose. "Just to make certain I understand what you're wanting, are you looking for me to provide three meals a day, seven days a week?"

He waved a hand. "I believe I can get by with something a little less all-encompassing. I was thinking six days a week, with Sundays off. I'll manage my own breakfast. And I'm not averse to eating the same thing twice, so if you prepare a large enough meal at noon, I can dine on leftovers for the evening meal."

"That's agreeable. When would you like me to start?"

"Is tomorrow too soon?"

"Not at all." Then she fingered her collar. "Do you have much of a larder?"

"It would probably be best if you start from scratch and pick up anything you think you'll need. I'll leave the menus up to you. And I'll let the shopkeepers know to put your orders on my tab."

"Good. And don't worry, I know how to be frugal with my purchases."

A good quality, but he should make certain they were both working under the same definition of acceptable spending. "I will develop what I consider a reasonable budget for your weekly purchases. If there should arise a situation where you require more, we can always revisit the matter."

"Agreed." Apparently, she was finished with the

businesswoman persona, because her face split into another of those delighted smiles. "Mr. Fulton, I'm beginning to think of you as my guardian angel."

Now there was something he'd never been called before. And it was definitely *not* something he aspired to be.

"Not only is this job going to give me some security," she continued, "but since you'll only need me for part of the day, I'll have time to find other odd jobs, as well."

Other jobs? Did she even realize what she was saying? "That's an admirably industrious attitude, but I imagine just getting your place in shape will take up most of your free time, at least for a while."

She waved a hand as if that was of no consequence. "I'll have to just fit that in when I can. Like I said, I need to earn some money, not just for staples, but to get my place furnished properly. Because the sooner I can open my restaurant, the better."

She was back to that again. Oh, well, far be it from him to harp on a point once he'd made it. "If you're serious about finding another job, as I said before, check down at Blakely's Mercantile."

"Thanks. I'll do that." She stood. "Now I'll get out of your way. I know you're busy, and I have some more work to do over at my place. Besides, I've made Kip wait on me long enough."

Would the rest of her meals today consist of nothing more than a handful of berries? "I was thinking, Miss Johnson, that I might do an interview with you for the paper."

"With me?" She seemed genuinely startled at the idea.

"It's not every day someone new moves to town and

sets up shop." Although that's exactly what he and his companions from Philadelphia had done less than a year ago.

He saw her hesitation and pressed further. "It would be doing me a favor. I'm always looking for something fresh to print in the paper."

Her face puckered as she contemplated his words. Then she gave him a doubtful look. "If you really think it will help you…"

He jumped in, not giving her time to change her mind. "Wonderful. Let's discuss this over supper tonight. The hotel has a small restaurant where we can go. And eating there has the added bonus of giving you an opportunity to check out your future competition." Not that he truly expected her to ever open her own restaurant.

"All right, I'll do it."

"And of course it will be my treat, since I am imposing on you for this interview."

She fingered her collar. "That's not necessary. I—"

He schooled his features in his haughtiest expression. "I assure you, for a business meal such as this, it's customary for the reporter to pay."

She studied him as if not quite believing him. But he didn't relax his expression, and she finally nodded.

"Good. I'll stop by your place at six o'clock, and we can walk to the hotel together if that's agreeable." Even though he'd concocted the idea on the spur of the moment to see that she had a meal this evening, he was fully prepared to take advantage of the opportunity to practice his reporting skills. This wouldn't be a very challenging interview subject, but at least it would give him something interesting to write about.

Then he gave her a severe look. "And please, leave your dog at home."

Chapter Four

"So let's start with where you're from. Originally, I mean."

Daisy shifted, uncomfortable with Mr. Fulton's scrutiny and with having to talk about her background. She sat across from him in the hotel dining room, trying to decide if there was some polite way for her to get out of this. After all, she'd come to Turnabout to make a fresh start, not dredge up the past.

Still, he'd been kind to her, and this was the first thing he'd actually asked from her in return. Determined to focus on his kindness, she sat up straighter and smiled. "If you're asking where I was born, it was in a little community called Bluewillow, Texas. I didn't live there long, though."

He scribbled a few strokes, then glanced up again. "Well, then, where did you grow up?"

"We traveled around a lot—Father was a peddler, even then. Most of the time, our wagon was our home. Then, when I was about four, my mother's health began to go downhill, and traveling became difficult for her.

So the two of us went to live with her mother while she tried to recuperate."

"And where was that?"

"New Orleans." Daisy brushed at the tablecloth, smoothing away a wrinkle. That wasn't a part of her life she wanted to elaborate on. "Do you think the folks around here are really going to want to read about this stuff?"

His smile had a cynical twist to it. "I find that people everywhere have an infinite curiosity about the lives of others." He poised his pencil over his pad again. "How much time did you spend in New Orleans?"

"Eight years." Eight of the most smothering, uncomfortable years of her life. "Then I went back to traveling with my father."

"Only you? What about your mother?"

Daisy nudged the lamp on the table about a quarter inch, not quite meeting his gaze. "She passed on when I was eight."

"I'm sorry."

There seemed to be genuine sympathy in his voice.

"Thank you," she said. "Mother was a good person, you know, the kind who always tries to see the best in everyone. She was real pretty, too. Want to see?" Without waiting for his answer, she lifted the locket from beneath her bodice, then slipped the chain over her head. Opening the catch, she smiled at the picture, then handed it to Everett.

He studied the picture for a moment, his expression unreadable, then handed it back to her. "You're right. She was quite lovely."

Daisy carefully slipped the locket back over her head, feeling slightly disappointed at his lack of reaction. "What about you? I mean, I know you don't have a locket, but do you have any kind of pictures or likenesses of your family?"

"No. Now let's get back to the interview."

She smothered a groan. If only the meal would come so they could end his string of uncomfortable questions.

"If I'm doing the calculations properly," he continued, "it sounds as if you spent another four years with your grandmother after your mother passed on."

"That's right. Father thought it best to wait until I was older to resume traveling with him." She tried not to dwell on that.

"Understandable."

That pronouncement stung. It *hadn't* been understandable to the grieving child she'd been. To her, it had felt like a second abandonment.

But Everett was already moving on to his next question. "Once you resumed traveling with your father, did you enjoy it?"

Daisy relaxed. This was a topic she was happy to talk about. "Very much. It gave me a chance to meet lots of wonderful people and to see places I'd never have seen otherwise. There are so many interesting folk out there, and they all have their own story to tell."

"Stories? Now you sound like a reporter."

She grinned. "Not at all. I'd be too fascinated listening to what they had to say, I'd forget to write anything down."

His smile warmed for just a moment, then he seemed to come to himself, and he resumed his cynically amused expression. "If you enjoyed all that traveling, why did you decide to settle down?"

"Because I'm not twelve anymore." She leaned forward. "Because I want friends and a family of my own and to be part of a close-knit community."

"So why here?"

"Simple—because this is where there was a place that I owned the deed to." She realized how flippant that sounded. "But I'm glad that was the case," she added quickly. "Turnabout seems like a nice town with lots of friendly folk. A good place to put down roots."

"You speak as if you plan to make Turnabout your permanent home."

Hadn't he heard anything she'd told him the past twenty-four hours? "I sincerely hope so."

"You don't think you'll miss the traveling life?"

She understood why he'd ask that, but he'd learn eventually that she wasn't that girl any longer. "Not at all. I've discovered I'm more of a homebody than I thought." Assuming she found the right home. "The idea of setting down roots, creating a cozy homeplace, someday starting a family of my own—well, that kind of life has a whole lot of appeal to me."

"Does that mean that after you went back on the road with your father, you found yourself missing the life you had with your grandmother?"

She gave a snort of disagreement before she could stop herself. He was so far off the mark, it was laughable. But his raised brow indicated she might have revealed a little more than she'd intended. "My grandmother's home wasn't exactly the warm, loving household that I'm hoping to build for myself."

"Would you care to elaborate?"

She met his gaze without blinking. "No."

"I see." He stared at her a moment longer, as if trying to read answers in her face. Then he moved on.

"Would you like to talk about the restaurant you hope to open someday? Or would you rather wait until you're closer to making it a reality before spreading the news of your intentions?"

Daisy was surprised but pleased that he hadn't pressed her. "Oh, I don't mind. I want folks to know what they have to look forward to." She leaned forward again, trying her best to communicate her vision. "I don't intend to make it all fancy and highfalutin. I want folks to feel comfortable and happy when they walk in. I'm going to serve hearty, homey food that fills the belly and warms the soul, because that's what I do best. And I'm going to paint the place in bright cheery colors and have flowers on all the tables."

"That's fine for this time of year, but it might be hard to do during the winter."

That was just like him to look for gray clouds in a sunny sky. To her relief, the food arrived just then, saving her from further inquisition.

At least for the moment.

Everett set his pencil and pad aside as the waitress fussed with serving their food.

The interview so far had raised as many questions about her as it had answered. The way she'd described her planned restaurant was indicative of how little business sense she had. She'd focused on feelings and cosmetics instead of a sound plan to achieve her goals.

She'd said she was looking for, among other things, a family of her own. So that indicated she was looking for a husband. Which probably meant the restaurant idea was only something to get her by until she had a man to provide for her.

She hadn't wanted to discuss her time at her grandmother's, yet she hadn't been happy traveling with her father, either. What was she really looking for? Did she even know herself? And would she be able to find it in Turnabout? Or would she only face disappointment and find herself moving on once again?

As soon as their waitress departed, and before he could resume his questions, Daisy beat him to the punch.

"So is it my turn for questions?" she asked with a teasing smile.

He raised a brow, not at all certain that would be a good idea. Better to treat her question lightly. "Are you planning to write an article for the paper, too? I thought you said you weren't good at writing things down."

"Don't worry. I'm not looking to give you competition, just trying to satisfy my curiosity." Her smile broadened. "You're not afraid to get a taste of your own medicine, are you?"

He couldn't let that veiled challenge pass. "What do you want to know?"

"How did a particular gent like you end up here in Turnabout?"

A *particular gent?* He wasn't sure what that meant. And more important, had she intended it as a compliment or criticism?

Better not to ask. "Before I came here, I was a reporter for a newspaper in Philadelphia. Unfortunately, the editor and I had a falling out. When I learned of an opportunity to actually own my own newspaper business here, I jumped at it." Mainly because that was the only option open to him at the time. There was nothing to be gained by mentioning the scandal he'd been involved in, the scandal that had cost him nearly everything. And deservedly so.

"So how'd you hear about this great opportunity? I mean, I wouldn't think most folks in Philadelphia have even heard of Turnabout."

Everett decided being on this end of an interview wasn't nearly the same as being on the other. "A friend of mine has some connections here—a granddaughter, as a matter of fact. He knew I was looking for something different, and he told me about it." He raised a brow. "Anything else?" he asked in his chilliest tone.

"Do all the folks in Philadelphia talk like you do?"

Was she being deliberately impertinent or merely trying to make conversation? "My accent, you mean?" She'd probably never heard a British accent before. "Actually, I lived in England until I was twelve."

Her hands stilled, and her eyes widened. "Oh, my goodness. You crossed the ocean when you were twelve?"

That part of his life seemed a dream now. Or should he say a nightmare? He wondered if his father had ever given him another thought once he'd sent him and his mother away.

He smiled at her reaction. "I didn't do it alone." Then he locked his gaze with hers. "And no, I'm not going to discuss my life before arriving in America with you, so you may as well move on."

She gave him an arch smile, or at least her version of one. "Keeping secrets of your own, are you? I guess we all have them." She didn't seem unduly bothered by his words. "So, moving on to another topic, what about family?"

Best to stick to the living. "I have a sister."

Her expression softened. "I always wished I had a sister or brother. Is she older or younger than you?"

"Much younger. And before you ask, she's attending a boarding school in Boston." He pointedly stabbed a chunk of potato with his fork. He'd had enough. "Now, why don't we put aside the interrogation and eat our meal before it gets cold."

She held his gaze for a few moments, and he could almost see her trying to decide whether or not to push forward. She finally nodded, and they both turned their focus on their food without another word.

After several minutes Everett relented, but there was no more talk of a personal nature. "Have you had that dog of yours very long?" he asked.

Her stiffness eased, and her smile returned. Apparently he'd found a question she didn't mind answering.

"No. As a matter of fact, we're brand-new friends. I'd only been on the road to Turnabout for a couple of hours when Kip showed up and took to following me. I checked with folks at a couple of the farms I passed, and no one laid claim to him. Which was okay with me. He was friendly, and I was happy for the company."

He imagined a woman traveling alone would be—especially at night. He still couldn't believe her father hadn't taken the time to escort her back here. The man should be horse whipped.

"He's barely left my side since," she added as she reached for her glass.

"And you plan to keep him?"

She seemed surprised by the question. "Of course. Like I said, we're friends now. As long as Kip wants to stick around, he's welcome to do so."

Everett resisted the urge to shake his head. He could

understand her wanting the animal's companionship and protection while she was on the road. But now that she was settled in and trying to establish herself, couldn't she see he would only be a drain on her limited resources?

But he'd said his piece. If she was an overly sentimental sort, then that was her problem.

The rest of the meal passed pleasantly enough. He was even forced to grudgingly admit, at least to himself, that Daisy could be a pleasant companion when she tried to be.

Later that evening, after he'd seen Daisy to her door and she'd promised to show up about nine o'clock the following morning since it was her first day, Everett returned to his own office.

He settled at his desk where he went to work transcribing his interview notes into an article. Tomorrow was Friday, one of the two days a week the paper went out. Tuesday was the other. That meant he had a long night ahead of him. Luckily, he'd already set aside space on the second page for his interview with Miss Johnson. He just had to craft his article so that it fit the allotted space.

As he wrote the article, he thought about what he'd learned from the sketchy details she'd given him. She was an optimist and a dreamer, that much was clear. And she wasn't afraid of hard work. She had a certain amount of courage, too, as evidenced by her striking out on her own, on foot, with nothing but what she could carry to start her new life with. But did she really have it in her to stick with a project like this and see it all the way through?

He was certain there was more to the story of the time she'd spent with her grandmother than she'd been willing to tell him. That hint of a story to uncover intrigued him.

Then there was her idea of opening a restaurant. That was reaching a bit high, especially for a female with no experience running a business. To make a go of it, she would need more than optimism and elbow grease. She would need financial reserves and business acumen, neither of which he saw much evidence of in her.

No, it would be much more practical if Miss Johnson took on a permanent job as cook for some family in town who needed her more than he did. And once he was satisfied he could vouch for her expertise, he would be willing to give her a recommendation to help her find such a position.

That should fulfill his obligation to see her settled properly.

Perhaps then he could get back to life as usual.

Daisy settled onto her makeshift bed, tired but pleased with the recent turn of events. It had been a long day, but she'd gotten a lot accomplished. This storeroom that still served as her bedchamber was now clean as a rain-washed wildflower. She'd crafted a broom of her own and rigged up some of the broken crates and furnishings to serve as temporary tables and chairs. She'd traded the telling of her tale for a satisfying meal, and she'd landed herself a job without having to look too hard.

All in all, a good day.

Daisy rolled over on her side. She was still having trouble figuring out Mr. Fulton. He could be so nice at times, and at others…

Even when he was being nice, he had that snippy, amused air about him that was just downright irritating.

The snooty tone he'd used when he asked if she intended to keep Kip still irked her. What she should have told him was that if given the choice between Kip's company and his, she'd likely pick Kip's.

I know that's not a very charitable thought, Lord, especially since I have him to thank for my meal and my job, but something about that man just riles me up. I can't abide a person who's constantly looking for warts rather than dimples.

She thought about that for a moment, then winced at her ungrateful attitude.

That was a poor excuse for an excuse, wasn't it, Lord? You tell us to judge not, and here I go judging again. And we both know I've got a wagonload of faults myself, so I've got no call to go throwing stones. I promise to try to do better in that regard. Just be patient with me if I slip again. And I'll add him to my prayers. He obviously has some kind of bee in his bonnet, and he could use some help to learn how to look for the good things around him. Maybe he just needs someone to show him the way.

Feeling better, she settled down more snugly on her bedroll. Starting tomorrow, Mr. Fulton was going to be a part of her daily life and she a part of his. If this was her purpose for being here, then she aimed to tackle it with all the enthusiasm at her disposal.

Mr. Fulton was going to learn how to shed some of that stiff-necked, snobbish air of his, or her name wasn't Daisy Eglantine Johnson.

Chapter Five

"Good morning, Mr. Fulton. You got those papers ready for me?" Jack Barr, Adam and Reggie's adopted son, stood in the doorway of Everett's office. Ira Peavy, the Barrs' live-in handyman and sometimes photography assistant to Reggie, stood behind him.

Everett smiled a greeting at the pair. "That, I do. Your stack is the one closest to the door."

Jack pulled a red wooden wagon into the building and started loading papers into the bed.

When he'd first opened the newspaper office, Everett had hired Jack to take care of making household deliveries to his regular subscribers. Of course, Ira Peavy usually went along, too, ostensibly to provide Jack with some company.

Everett exchanged greetings with Ira, then looked past the man to see the faint hint of the approaching dawn. He prided himself on having the paper available when his patrons started their day.

"You'll find one extra paper in your stack," he told Jack. "Mr. Cummings over on Second Street started subscribing this week."

"Yes, sir, I'll add him to the list."

As they loaded the last of the papers, Everett reached into his pocket and pulled out a coin. "Here's this week's pay."

Jack's eyes lit up. "Thanks!"

Ira placed his hand on the boy's shoulder. "We'd best be on our way if you want to get these deliveries done before school starts."

As soon as they departed, Everett grabbed the other three bundles of papers waiting by the door. In addition to the copies he printed for his subscribers, he always printed a number of extras. Those who chose not to subscribe often purchased copies when they were out running errands.

He kept some of those copies here at his office, of course, but he'd also made arrangements with the proprietors at the mercantile, hotel and railroad depot to sell copies in exchange for a small portion of the purchase price.

He stepped out on the sidewalk and exchanged greetings with Tim Hill, the town's lamplighter. Tim was in the process of turning off the streetlight outside the newspaper office, which meant Everett was right on schedule. Punctuality was a virtue he considered an indication of character.

As he walked through town delivering the bundles of papers to the appropriate locations, he took time to visit the merchants where Daisy would need to make purchases for her role as his cook. As he'd promised her, he instructed them to bill her purchases to him.

That request raised questions, naturally, but he offered up only the bare information that he had hired her to cook for him. Anything else they wanted to know about her, they'd have to ask her.

By the time he returned to his office, a light was shining in Daisy's downstairs window. So she was already up and about. Was she looking forward to her first day working for him? Or dreading it?

At precisely ten minutes after nine, Daisy walked into his office. He supposed that was as close to punctual as he should expect from her.

"Good morning, Mr. Fulton," she said by way of greeting.

Everett stood and moved around the desk as he returned her greeting. She carried a heavily laden basket on her arm, but didn't seem unduly burdened by it.

"I enjoyed doing the marketing today. There are some fine shops here, and most of the shopkeepers seem willing to negotiate a bit. And don't worry, I was very frugal with your money, but I think you'll be pleased with the results."

The woman did like to chatter. "As long as you stay within the budget we discussed, I won't have any complaints on that score."

She patted the basket. "I got a good deal on a couple of rabbits at the butcher shop. I hope you like rabbit stew. It's one of my specialties."

Was she looking for some kind of approval or praise? That wasn't really his way of doing business. "As I said, the meal planning is in your hands. I'm sure whatever you cook will be an improvement over what I've been preparing for myself."

She grinned. "Not the most enthusiastic response, but I hope to win you over with my cooking."

Surely no one could be this cheerful all the time? "I look forward to your attempts."

She spotted the small stack of newspapers near the door. "Are those your papers?"

"Of course." What else would they be? "It's this morning's edition of the *Turnabout Gazette*."

She eyed them as if not sure she wanted to get any closer. "Is that interview of me in there?"

Was she worried about how he'd portrayed her? "Yes, it is." He crossed over and picked one up. "Would you like to have one so you can read it?"

Her cheeks reddened slightly. "I'm afraid I don't have any extra money to—"

"Consider a copy of the paper part of your pay." He always had a few copies left over at the end of the day.

"Why, thank you."

This talk of extra funds brought something else to mind. He cleared his throat. "I daresay there are other things you might need to get settled in properly, so when you are done for the day I will give you your first week's pay in advance."

Her cheeks reddened. "Oh, that's not necessary. I—"

He held up a hand. "No argument. I won't have my cook distracted by thoughts of how she'll make it through the week. And use this money wisely, because I'll do this only for the first week."

She smiled. "Thank you for your thoughtfulness."

He brushed that aside. "Now, let me show you to the kitchen." Everett took the basket from her, then waved her ahead of him up the stairs.

She stepped aside when she topped the stairs, pausing to look around. The stairway emptied into an open space that served multiple functions. To the left was the kitchen and dining area, and to the right was what passed for a sitting room or visitor area. Not that he ever had visitors up here. Beyond the sitting room were the two bedchambers, one of which currently served as more of a storage room. It did have a small bed—more of a cot, really—but he didn't expect to be hosting overnight guests anytime soon.

Everett placed her basket on the table and she moved past him, her gaze sweeping the room.

"This kitchen is nice," she said. "A bit spare but clean and neat. It gives me hope for what my place might look like once I get it fixed up."

How bad was it over there? If what he'd seen of the ground floor was any indication, she really had her work cut out for her.

Daisy ran a hand lightly over the edge of the stove. "Yes, sir, a fine kitchen, indeed. This is a good stove. And you already have the fire stoked. Thanks!"

Everett waved his hand in an inclusive gesture. "The dishes are in the top cupboard, the pots and pans are over there, and the cooking implements are in that drawer. This door opens to the pantry. Feel free to use anything you find there."

She nodded as she peered inside.

He straightened. "I should warn you, the stove is a bit temperamental." Something he knew from his own less-than-successful attempts at making biscuits.

She closed the pantry door and smiled. "Most stoves take some getting used to. I'm just happy to have a real stove to cook on instead of a campfire."

That statement gave him pause. "But you *do* have experience with a household stove, don't you?"

"Of course. When I lived with my grandmother I

spent a lot of my time in the kitchen, and I pestered the cook until she gave in and taught me all about cooking."

"So you haven't used one since you were twelve years old?"

"Not so. During the worst of winter each year, my father would find a town where we could rent rooms for about six weeks, rather than live in the wagon. To help pay for our lodging, and replenish our wares, he would find odd jobs and I'd find work in a kitchen somewhere."

That admission caught him by surprise. "So this isn't your first time to hire on as a cook?"

"Goodness, no. I told you, I know what I'm doing."

That remained to be seen. But he'd had enough of idle talk—time to return to his work. "I'll leave you to it, then. There's extra kindling and firewood for the stove in that corner. If you need anything else, you know where to find me."

He descended the stairs, accompanied by the sound of her cheerful humming. Was he going to have to put up with that all morning?

He supposed there were worse distractions he could be presented with.

Still, it didn't seem quite normal for someone to be so relentlessly cheerful all the time, especially someone with her less-than-ideal circumstances.

Before he'd made it back to his desk, his door opened and Alma Franklin walked in, looking for a paper. She glanced toward the stairway at the sound of Daisy's humming, and mentioned that she'd heard he'd hired a cook and asked how that was working out for him. Right on her heels, Stanley Landers came in, also looking for a paper, and he also commented on his new cook.

It was that way for the next hour—a steady stream of people either wanting to buy a paper or checking on notices that were already scheduled or purchasing advertisements. And all of them found a way to work Daisy's presence into the conversation. At least the townsfolk's curiosity had generated a few new sales. At this rate, he'd be sold out by noon.

Around ten-thirty, he caught the whiff of a mouthwatering aroma drifting down from his kitchen. Thirty minutes later, the aromas began to tease and tantalize his senses in earnest. Perhaps she really *was* as good a cook as she claimed to be.

When Everett finally got a break, just before noon, he considered heading upstairs to check on Daisy. She hadn't left the kitchen all morning, and he wanted to assure himself she was handling things appropriately.

But his door opened once more and Hazel Andrews, the very prim woman who owned the dress shop, marched in with her usual brisk, no-nonsense air. "Good morning, Mr. Fulton."

"Miss Andrews." He waved her into a seat, then took his own. "What can I do for you?"

She sat poker straight in her chair, but her smile, while small, seemed genuine enough. "I was at the train station dropping off a package to ship to my sister," she said, "when Lionel told me he had a letter for you. I offered to deliver it since I had business with you, anyway."

Everett accepted the letter and placed it on his desk with barely a glance. "What kind of business?"

The seamstress looked pointedly at the letter. "I don't mind waiting if you'd like to read your letter first."

"I'll read it later." He could tell it was from his sister, and he'd prefer to save it for a time when he could read it alone to savor it.

Miss Andrews nodded. "On to business, then. I'm planning to run a sale on my dressmaking services next week. I'd like to buy an advertisement in the paper to announce it."

Everett opened his notebook and reached for a pencil. He was always happy to sell advertisements. "I can certainly accommodate you. What size were you thinking of?"

Once they'd discussed the particulars of the advertisement, Miss Andrews sat back, apparently ready for some casual conversation. "I hear you've hired your new neighbor to cook for you."

So even the straightlaced seamstress was interested in the town's newest citizen. Everett closed his notebook and nodded. "That's right. She needed the work, and I was tired of eating my own cooking."

His visitor nodded approval. "Sounds like a practical arrangement." Then she changed the subject. "It'll be good to see that place next door all fixed up again. Any idea what Miss Johnson plans to do with the place?"

Everett repeated the same answer he'd given to everyone else this morning. "She mentioned plans to open a restaurant in the interview you'll find in today's newspaper. Other than that, you'll have to ask her."

She lifted her head and sniffed delicately. "I must say, if that aroma is from whatever Miss Johnson is preparing for you, she would likely do quite well as a restaurant cook."

The pesky creak that signaled someone was on the stairs sounded, and they both turned toward it.

"Mr. Fulton, I—" Daisy looked toward his visitor and paused. "Oh, sorry. I didn't mean to interrupt."

Everett and Miss Andrews both stood.

"Miss Johnson." The dressmaker stepped forward. "Allow me to introduce myself. I'm Hazel Andrews, owner of the dress shop down the street."

"Pleased to meet you, ma'am. I've walked by your place a few times. From what I can see through your shop window, you do beautiful work."

"Why, thank you." The seamstress studied Daisy with a critical eye. "If you'd like to come in for a fitting, I'd be glad to set up an appointment for you."

"Thank you for the offer," Daisy said with an apologetic smile. "As tempting as it sounds, I'm afraid purchasing new clothes is going to have to wait until I've taken care of other, more pressing matters."

The dressmaker tightened the strings to her handbag and nodded. "I understand." She gave Daisy a head-to-toe look. "Just keep in mind that appearances set the tone for a business relationship as well as a personal one."

Everett stiffened. Her tone had been friendly enough, but the words carried a barb. Had Daisy felt it?

Then Miss Andrews turned back to him. "I assume I can look for the advertisement to run in the next issue of the *Gazette*."

"Of course." Everett still had his mind on how her words might have affected Daisy as he gave her a short bow of dismissal. "And thank you for delivering the letter."

Once the door closed behind the dressmaker, Everett turned to Daisy. He still didn't detect any hint of distress or affront in her expression. Perhaps he'd overreacted. "Was there something you needed?"

She blinked, as if just remembering her errand. "Yes, of course. I wanted to tell you your meal is ready to be served. But there's no need to rush upstairs if you're busy. I'll just keep it warm until you're ready for it."

"Thank you. I'll join you there in a moment."

He waited until she had started up the stairs to open his letter, smiling in anticipation. Abigail's letters reflected her personality—they were chatty, exuberant and overly dramatic. He unfolded the missive and leaned back in his chair, prepared to be entertained.

Daisy set the table for the two of them and then ladled the stew into a serving bowl.

Had Miss Andrews offered to make her an appointment just to drum up business? Or did she think Daisy's clothing was really that awful? Daisy hadn't wasted time worrying about her wardrobe since she'd left her grandmother's. Function was what mattered, and the pieces she had—this skirt, two shirtwaists and her Sunday dress—had that going for them.

In fact, one of the things she'd disliked about living in her grandmother's home was the emphasis everyone placed on appearances. Daisy had vowed to leave all that behind her when she left there. Nowadays, as long as her clothing was serviceable and modest, she didn't give it much deeper consideration.

But Miss Andrews's words had given her pause. She *was* planning to be a businesswoman now. Perhaps it was time she gave such things a little more consideration.

Her musings were interrupted by the sound of Everett on the stairs.

"It smells good," he said as he entered the kitchen.

Her mood lightened at his praise. "Thanks." Then she felt the need to give a disclaimer. "I'm afraid the bread is a bit scorched, though. It may take me a couple of tries to get a feel for your oven."

"I daresay you're right. But I'm sure the rest of the meal will be fine."

Coming from him, she supposed that was praise of a sort. Daisy placed the stew and bread platter on the table. "I have apple pie for dessert. And I'm pleased to say it hardly got scorched at all."

He took his seat without comment, and she sat across from him.

When he reached for the bread platter, however, she cleared her throat. "Would you like to say the blessing before we start?"

Everett slowly drew his hand back and gave her an unreadable look. "Why don't you perform that service for us?"

Was he the sort who didn't like to pray in public? She hadn't thought of him as the reticent sort. But she nodded and bowed her head. "Heavenly Father, we thank You for this food and for all the other blessings of this day. Help us to remain mindful of where our bounty comes from and to whom our praises belong. And keep us ever aware of the needs of others. In Your name we pray. Amen."

She smiled up at him as he echoed her *Amen.* "Eat up."

The silence drew out for several long minutes as they concentrated on their food. Finally, she gave in to the urge to break the silence. "I read that newspaper of yours."

"Oh?"

"Yes, and I want to thank you for the job you did on that interview. You took my uninteresting life and made it sound, well, plumb interesting."

He seemed more amused than flattered by her comment. "That's the job of a good reporter—to find the hidden gem in any story."

"Hidden gem. I like that." She pointed her spoon at him, then quickly lowered it. "I didn't read just the interview, though—I read the entire thing. You did a fine job with all of it."

"Thank you. I suppose it *is* fine, for what it is."

"What it is?" His tone puzzled her.

"Yes—a small town, nothing-ever-happens, two-days-a-week newspaper."

"So you're not happy with it."

"As I said, it's fine for what it is." He gave her a pointed look. "Do you mind if we change the subject?"

Why was this such a touchy subject for him? But she obediently reached for another subject and said the first thing that came to mind. "I heard you mention something about a letter. It wasn't bad news, I hope." Maybe that's why he seemed so out of sorts.

He studied her as if searching for some ulterior motive behind her question. She thought for a moment that he would change the subject again.

But then he reached for his glass as he shook his head. "Not at all. It's a letter from my sister, Abigail."

Why wasn't he happier about it? "How nice. The two of you must be close."

He didn't return her smile. "She wants to come here for a visit."

His grim tone puzzled her. "Isn't that a good thing? I mean, wouldn't you like to see her?"

"Of course I would." He took a drink from his glass, then set it back down. "But, as I've told her any number of times, it's better if I go to Boston than if she comes here. Unfortunately, she doesn't see it that way."

"But if it's that important to her, perhaps you could allow her to come here just one time. You know, to satisfy her curiosity."

His exasperated look told her she'd overstepped her bounds. "For her to come here," he said, "there are significant arrangements that would need to be made—things such as finding a traveling companion and making certain she doesn't fall behind in any of her classes. Besides, Turnabout is no place for a girl like Abigail. And there aren't an abundance of activities to entertain and enlighten her here."

He broke off a piece of bread with more vigor than was absolutely necessary. "No, it's much better if I visit her."

A girl like Abigail? What did that mean? Was his sister one of those spoiled, pampered debutantes like the ones who'd graced her grandmother's parlor? Girls who never got their hands dirty or even knew what a callus looked like? But that wasn't a question she'd ask out loud. "Do you plan to do that? Go visit her, I mean."

"Of course. I traveled to Boston to see her over the Christmas holidays and will make another visit sometime this summer. She and I spend our time going to the theater, visiting museums, attending the opera and whatever else she cares to do."

Those were the kind of things they enjoyed doing together? "Don't you two ever go on picnics or take buggy rides through the countryside or just take long walks together?"

"Since my time with Abigail is limited, I always strive to make it count for something." His demeanor had stiffened, and his accent was more pronounced. "My sister is being raised as a proper lady, not a hoyden. Those activities add to both her education and her social polish. Their entertainment value is merely an added bonus."

Daisy straightened. She supposed she'd been put in her place. And she'd also gotten the distinct impression that Miss Abigail Fulton might be every bit as stuffy as her brother.

Ah, well, there wasn't much danger that they would cross paths anytime soon—not if big brother had his way.

Everett was glad when Daisy finally let the silence settle between them. He didn't care for all this prying into his personal life. Didn't she understand there were lines one just did not cross? Someone should sit her down and explain the rules of polite society. Not that he thought it would do any good.

Perhaps she would learn from their interaction.

His thoughts drifted to that prayer she'd voiced earlier. It had surprised him, in both its simplicity and sincerity. He hadn't heard anyone pray like that outside of church before. It seemed that her faith was a deeply personal one. But then again, he was beginning to see that she approached nearly everything in her life with everything she had.

If she was going to make it on her own, and try to establish a business, she'd have to learn to be more objective and circumspect in her approach.

Perhaps that was something else he could teach her.

Chapter Six

Daisy blew the hair off her forehead as she dried the last of the dishes. There was plenty of stew left over, and it would keep fine on the stove's warming plate until Mr. Fulton was ready for his evening meal.

She hung the dishrag over the basin, then looked around to check if anything else needed her attention before she headed home. Kip would be ready to go for a walk, and she was eager to get back to work fixing up her new home. But she wouldn't leave until she'd made certain she met her obligations here.

Mr. Fulton was fastidiously neat, and she was determined to leave the place as orderly as it had been when she arrived, if not more so. And she'd start by arranging his cupboards in a more logical manner. Logical from a cook's perspective, at any rate.

A freestanding cupboard on the far wall seemed to be the ideal place to store items that were seldom used. She crossed over to it and opened the doors, then smiled when she found it held only a few mismatched cups. She could certainly put it to better use than that. Satisfied, she closed the doors, then paused.

Was that a crack in the wall behind the cupboard? It was mostly in shadow, but as she looked closer, she noticed the crack was perfectly straight.

Then her eyes widened. It was a door, painted over to match the surrounding wall. What with that and the fact that it was mostly hidden by the cupboard, it was easy to overlook.

Why had the door been so cunningly hidden? And what was behind it? It didn't appear to have been opened in quite some time. Did Everett even know it was here?

The doorknob was behind the cupboard, making it impossible for her to even try to open it. She studied it, hands on her hips, her curiosity growing. After all, who could resist the allure of a hidden door?

Removing her apron, Daisy headed downstairs.

Everett finished cleaning his printing equipment and arched his back, trying to ease the kink in his muscles. After ten months of trial and error, he finally considered himself proficient with the various aspects of the printing process, though there were some tasks he still didn't particularly enjoy. Back in Philadelphia, he'd been a respected reporter with a major paper. His job had been to write the stories—getting those stories to print had been someone else's job, and he'd rarely given it a second thought. But here he was responsible for every aspect of getting the paper out.

Which was another reason he was doing everything in his power to find another position as a reporter for a large newspaper once more.

He wiped his hands on a cloth as that squeaky stair announced Daisy was on her way down. "All done?" he asked, moving toward his desk to get her payment.

"I am." She glanced at one of his trays of print type. "How come all your letters look backward?"

"That's the way type is set for printing." He saw her puzzled look and explained further. "Think of it as looking at a reflection. The type is the mirror image of what the printed page will be."

Her expression cleared. "Imagine that. So you have to set all those letters into backward words so the print comes out frontward on the paper."

"Not the most eloquent way of explaining it, but yes."

She shook her head. "That sounds like it would be difficult to keep straight in your head. I know it would make me go all cross-eyed."

She did have a colorful way of speaking. "It *is* a tedious job. I will admit, even after several months at it, I find myself having to focus totally on what I'm doing or I'll get it wrong." It had given him a whole new appreciation for professional typesetters. He just hoped he didn't have to *be* one much longer.

But enough of this chitchat—he had work to do. "Here are your wages," he said, handing them over.

She accepted them with a thank-you, but didn't head for the door as he'd expected.

"Was there anything else?"

"I was wondering if you knew about the door in the wall behind your cupboard?"

What was she talking about? "A door? Are you certain?"

That got her back up. "I know a door when I see one."

Everett moved toward the stairs. "Show me."

She marched up ahead of him, then wordlessly waved him toward the far wall.

Everett drew closer to the cupboard, studying the

wall behind it. Sure enough, there was the obvious outline of a door. How had he missed spotting it in all the time he'd lived here?

"I take it from your reaction you hadn't noticed it before." Daisy was right at his shoulder. "What do you suppose is in there?"

He glanced at her, and she had the grace to blush.

But Everett was curious now, too. "Let me just shift this over so we can find out."

Everett put his shoulder to the cupboard, waving off her offer of assistance. That done, he grabbed the doorknob and twisted. It was locked. "This cupboard was here when I moved in. I wonder..." He felt along the top of the cupboard, and sure enough, he found a key.

Daisy's eyes sparkled with excitement. "Must be something mighty important in there to keep it locked up."

Was she expecting a treasure of some sort? It was more likely to be nothing but a shallow closet. He quickly unlocked and opened the door, but instead of finding the storage space he'd expected, he faced the backside of another door.

"How strange," Daisy said, her disappointment evident. "It's not even deep enough to store a sack of flour. Maybe it's where they kept their brooms."

"It's not for storage at all." He moved aside so she'd have a clearer view. "This back wall is another door. I believe this is an upstairs access between our buildings, with a lock on both sides for privacy."

"You mean that other door opens from my side?" She studied it closer. "I haven't reached this far in my cleaning yet, but I can picture just where it might be."

She straightened. "How about that. The original owners must have been good friends to set this up."

Everett nodded, still mulling over the implications. "I believe I heard somewhere they were brothers."

"That makes sense." Daisy nodded in satisfaction. "Their families probably did a lot of visiting back and forth."

He dusted his hands. "Either they had a falling out or the new owners valued their privacy when the buildings changed hands."

"That's a shame. Neighbors should be, well, neighborly." She tilted her head thoughtfully. "But there's no reason we can't make use of this."

What in the world was she thinking now? "Miss Johnson, I—"

"How would you feel about leaving the doors open whenever I'm over here cooking?"

Before he could respond, she quickly continued.

"With such easy access, I can work on a few things at my place while the food simmers. And I can even check in on Kip occasionally while I'm at it."

Somehow that arrangement didn't seem quite respectable. "I don't—"

But she wasn't finished. "Oh, and don't you worry, I won't skimp on the work I'm doing for you. I'll only go over to my place when I'm not needed here."

He shook his head irritably. "I don't mind you splitting your time, as long as the meals are prepared properly. But there are proprieties to be observed."

Her brow furrowed, and then she waved a dismissive hand. "I really can't see how that would be an issue. After all, I'll be over here cooking for you just about every day, and we haven't made a secret of that. What difference can it make if that door is open when I'm at work here?"

It went against the grain with him to give even the appearance of bending the rules of polite society. Still, she was making sense in a roundabout kind of way. "If I agree to this, and I haven't said I will, then I need your word that that animal of yours stays on your side of the wall."

"That won't be a problem." Her eagerness was palpable. "This would be such a big help to me in getting my place livable more quickly."

"I suppose there wouldn't be any harm in it." Though he still wasn't fond of the idea. "But only during your working hours. And it would probably be best if we don't spread the word about this easy access between our apartments. Some individuals might take it amiss." Did she understand what he was saying?

"Thank you. I promise I'll handle it just as you say. And don't worry, I'll keep my side securely locked when I'm done here for the day, just as propriety dictates."

Maybe she'd gotten the message, after all.

She straightened. "Now, I'm going right over to my place to see if I can find my door and the key that goes with it. It seems the previous residents *really* wanted to shut each other out."

"Family disputes can be among the bitterest." Everett pushed away the memory of his own father.

She was still studying the door. "If I'm recollecting the layout right, I think there's a rickety bookcase in front of the door on my end."

He knew a hint when he heard one. "I suppose you'd like me to help move it."

But she shook her head. "Oh, no, I was thinking out loud, not asking for help."

She might say that, but it would be ungentlemanly not to lend a hand after her comment. "Of course. But I'll accompany you all the same." Besides, he was curious to see what progress she'd made since the night she'd arrived.

As soon as she opened the door to her place, her dog raced up, tail wagging. He jumped up, planting his front paws on her skirts, and she gave his head an affectionate rub. "Hey, Kip, did you miss me, boy? I promise we'll go for a walk just as soon as I check something out upstairs."

The animal was every bit as foolishly cheerful as his mistress.

The front room was mostly bare but surprisingly clean. Daisy had apparently scrubbed the floors and walls until there wasn't a speck of dirt to be seen. Interesting that she'd worked on the downstairs before the living quarters upstairs.

She caught him looking around, and smiled proudly. "There's still a lot to be done, but I'm making progress. Right now I'm trying to decide if I want to buy yellow paint or blue paint for the walls. Yellow would be brighter and cheerier, but blue would be more relaxing and remind folks of the blue skies of springtime. What do you think?"

He had a feeling she wasn't talking about muted shades of those particular colors. "I favor more sophisticated colors, such as white or gray."

Daisy wrinkled her nose. "Where's the joy in that?"

Joy? What an odd thing to say about a color choice. But apparently, the question had been moot.

She moved to the stairs and her dog stayed right on her heels, seemingly determined to make up for the time they'd been apart. "I warn you," she said over her shoulder, "I haven't done much to fix up the second floor. You're liable to get a bit of dust and grime on you."

"I feel sufficiently warned," he said dryly. Just because he liked to maintain a neat appearance didn't mean he was averse to a little dirt when there was no help for it.

The upstairs wasn't as cluttered as the downstairs had been that first night, but it was every bit as dusty and unkempt. Gus had really let the place go. It made him wonder if there were soundness issues with the structure itself. Everett studied the walls and ceilings more closely. But there were no visible water marks or signs of crumbling woodwork.

He followed Daisy to the wall that adjoined his, and sure enough, once you knew where to look, the door was evident. He helped her shift the clutter away from the wall and they discovered the key still in the lock, so finding it wasn't an issue. When they opened the door they found themselves looking into his apartment.

Her smile widened to a broad grin. "This is wonderful—I'll be able to get twice as much work done now."

"Just remember, the dog stays on your side of the wall."

"Don't worry, he knows his place."

Everett very deliberately turned and headed down Daisy's stairs to make his exit. Regardless of how "neighborly" the prior tenants had been, there would be no use of that adjoining door as a shortcut access other than during her working hours.

He would not do anything to set the local tongues

wagging. Regardless of how innocent a person was, perception and reputation were everything.

After Everett left, Daisy took Kip for a walk. As usual, she grabbed a cloth bag so she'd have something to hold anything edible or useable she found along the way. At the last minute, she remembered she needed to gather the stuffing for her mattress ticking, so she grabbed a larger gunnysack as well.

Once on the edge of town, she let Kip have his head and followed wherever the animal led, only redirecting him when he seemed headed for mischief.

This was only her second day here, if you didn't count the night she arrived, and already it felt familiar, comfortable. Everything was falling into place just as she'd hoped, even better than she'd thought possible.

She could build a good life here. She'd already made a few acquaintances that, in time, she hoped could bloom into true friendships.

The discovery of that door between her and Mr. Fulton's places had been exciting, something unexpected and fun. Sharing a secret with him made her feel closer to him somehow, even if he didn't feel any of that excitement himself.

Too bad her employer-neighbor seemed unable to appreciate a bit of adventure. Did he realize how much he was missing by being so guarded? He seemed to like reporting on what was happening around him much more than experiencing it.

Was that because he'd never felt swept up in the joy of letting his imagination run free, of focusing on the fun in whatever situation you were in? That was probably hard for him to do, what with his inflexible, cynical outlook on things. Instead of looking at that doorway as something fun and exciting, he'd seemed more concerned with how it might look if word got out about it. Looking for warts instead of dimples again.

Then she caught herself up on that thought.

She had no right to judge him. She had no idea what had made him the way he was. Maybe he'd never been taught how to have fun. Or maybe something had happened that made it hard for him to see the silver lining in things.

Well, if that was the case, it was up to her to show him how to relax and not hold on to his need for control so tightly.

Now, if she could just figure out how to accomplish that…

Chapter Seven

Saturday morning, Daisy arrived at Everett's office a few minutes after nine o'clock. It was a beautiful day and one that promised to be highly productive.

"Good morning," she said cheerily. "Fine day, isn't it?"

Her boss glanced up, then went back to looking at his ledger. "I suppose."

Not a very cheery response. "The butcher had some fine-dressed venison this morning," she continued. "I hope venison is something you like." She was already planning the way she would cook it up with a thick, rich onion gravy and some beets and dandelion greens seasoned with bacon on the side.

"Venison is fine."

He still seemed to be paying little attention to what she was saying. She hefted the basket and tried one more time to get something other than a distracted response. "By the way, I opened the door on my side of the wall when I left this morning. But don't you worry. I made sure Kip understands he can't cross the threshold."

This time he did look up and actually met her gaze. "You made sure..." He gave her a look that seemed to call her sanity into question. "And do you honestly think he understood?"

Maybe drawing him out hadn't been such a good idea. "He's actually pretty smart."

"There's nothing pretty about him," he said dryly.

"Mr. Fulton!"

"Sorry." His tone sounded anything but. "Just see that you reinforce that little talk you two had with some firm discipline if he doesn't appear willing to follow directions."

What would he do if she stuck her tongue out at him?

Cheered by the image that evoked, Daisy turned and headed up the stairs. As soon as she set her market basket down, Daisy opened the adjoining door. Kip was sitting there waiting on her, his tail wagging furiously. Daisy stooped down and ruffled the fur on his neck. "Hey, boy. What do you say we prove Mr. High-and-Mighty Fulton wrong? I'll pop over and visit you occasionally, but I have a job to do so you'll have to stay over here."

Kip gave a bark, which she took as agreement, so with one last pat, she stood and returned to her work. Today she was determined to conquer the eccentricities of the stove, and turn out bread rolls that were perfectly golden-brown.

Yes, sir, there would be nothing for her employer to fuss about today.

All morning, Everett heard the sounds of Daisy bustling around in his kitchen, more often than not humming or singing some cheery song. He could also hear her talking to her mutt, carrying on one-sided conversations as if the raggedy animal could actually understand her words.

He gave in to the urge to go upstairs and check on her at about ten-thirty. It only made sense, he told himself, to make certain things were going as they should with this new arrangement of theirs.

The angle of the adjoining door was such that, once his shoulders topped the second floor, he was able to see through it to her place. Her dog sat at the threshold but, as she'd promised, no part of him was across it. How had she managed to make her pet obey—especially when the food smells were so tempting?

Beyond the animal, he could see enough to tell him that she'd made quite a bit of progress since he'd been up there yesterday. Despite himself, he was impressed with how much she was getting accomplished.

The dog barked. Everett wasn't sure if it was a greeting or a warning, but it caught Daisy's attention and she turned, smiling when she spied him.

"Hello. If you've come to check on the meal, I'm afraid it'll be another hour or so until it's ready."

Feeling as if he'd been caught doing something he shouldn't—which was ridiculous—he tugged at his cuff. "Not at all. I just need to fetch something from my room."

He strode purposefully to his bedchamber, grabbed the notebook he kept by his bedside, then headed back out.

"I want to thank you again for letting me prop these doors open," she said as he neared the stairs. "I've already been able to get quite a bit of work done in my place this morning." She nodded toward the door. "As you can see, Kip is behaving himself just like I told you he would."

Everett made a noncommittal sound and, with a nod, headed back downstairs.

When she called him upstairs for the noonday meal, Everett deliberately took his time. No point appearing overeager.

"Your oven and I are getting along much better today," she said as they took their seats at the table. "You won't find nary a scorch mark on these rolls."

Again she asked if he'd like to say grace, and again he passed the task to her. He noticed the speculative look she gave him, but he kept his expression bland. There was no reason for him to explain himself.

He didn't pray aloud, or pray much at all if you got right down to it. The clergyman who held the living on his father's estate in England had made certain he was familiar with the Bible and that he attended church services regularly. And for most of his childhood, Everett had been quite faithful to those teachings.

That had changed when he'd realized that his illegitimate status made him and his mother lesser people in the eyes of those oh-so-pious folks who surrounded him. And then he'd been summarily exiled from his home to America.

Now he knew that religion was for children and women, those who needed something spiritual to cling to as an emotional crutch.

He considered himself more of a social Christian—one who went to church service because it was expected. And to set the proper example for his younger sister.

But there was no point going into all of that with Daisy. She obviously felt quite differently.

As she passed him the platter of meat, she smiled. “I hope you like venison cooked this way. It was my father’s favorite meal. I do believe he would’ve eaten it every day if it had been available.”

Everett met her gaze as he served himself. “I find it strange that you speak of him with such affection.”

“Strange how?”

“You ran off to get away from him. And worse, he didn’t come after you, but rather let you travel alone and by foot, though he had to know where you were going.” Such actions were unforgivable.

“My relationship with my father is complicated, but regardless of how we parted, I do still love him very much.”

Was she just being tactful? “Admirable of you, it seems.”

She shook her head. “You sound like you don’t believe me, but it’s true. It’s just that, even though I love him, there are times when I don’t like him very much.”

She wasn’t making a whole lot of sense.

Apparently, she saw the doubt in his expression. “My father always said it was my mother who kept him on the straight and narrow,” she explained. “When she was around, there was no temptation strong enough to lure him away. That’s what kept him sober and happy when I was little.”

She pushed her food around her plate with a fork. “I tried to be a good daughter when I started traveling with him again, to take care of him and give him as much love as Mother did. But I guess I wasn’t enough. He’d be okay for a while, but the yearning for drink and cards would get hold of him, and the next thing I know he'd have gambled away most of our earnings."

And she still claimed to love him? Had her affection made her so blind?

"When I learned he'd won the deed to the building next door, I tried to convince him to come with me, but he kept saying he was too set in his ways to change."

"That doesn't excuse his letting you set out on your own instead of giving you a proper escort."

She dredged her fork through her gravy. "That's not exactly how it happened."

"What do you mean?"

She still didn't quite meet his eyes. "I never gave him the chance to bring me here." She finally looked up. "We were over in Thornridge and had another of our arguments."

She looked so lost, so regretful that Everett almost reached out to touch her arm in support. But he'd never been comfortable with such emotional gestures.

"It was a small thing," she continued wistfully, "but it felt big at the time. So I told him to leave me in town to do some shopping and 'cool off' while he visited a few farms to try to make some sales. As soon as he was out of sight, I left a note with the owner of the mercantile and headed out on my own."

She traced a line on her glass with one finger. "It was cowardly of me, but I knew if I had to look him in the eye and tell him my intentions, I wouldn't be able to go."

Everett wasn't convinced. There's no way he would have let Abigail go like that, no matter how much they disagreed on matters. "He still should have headed out after you when he realized you'd gone."

"Well, first off, he may not have realized I was gone

until the next day. Because if things followed their normal course, he would take whatever money he made on sales and find a card game. Which meant he'd have stayed out until the wee hours."

Is that the kind of existence she was accustomed to? How had she held on to her optimism all this time?

"When he did realize I was gone," she continued, "and got the note I left for him, he would have read my plea for him not to follow me."

Everett frowned. She'd said her relationship with her father was complicated—it seemed she hadn't been exaggerating. "So you deliberately severed ties with him."

"Not permanently. He'll come back through Turnabout in a few months. By then the break will have healed, and I'll be settled and we'll be able to meet on more comfortable terms."

There was that seemingly unquenchable optimism again.

She smiled wistfully. "Someday, I hope Father will be ready to settle down, too, and when that time comes, I'm hoping he'll move in with me."

She shifted in her chair, and her smile brightened. "Now, why don't we talk about something else. And since you asked me a personal question, I think a question for you is in order."

He wasn't sure he liked that challenging glint in her eye. "Such as?"

"Such as, why don't you like dogs?"

Everett immediately felt his guard go up. But there were worse things she could have asked. "It's not that I don't like dogs. I just have no use for them. They are overly exuberant, serve no useful purpose and are always trying to claim your attention. They are fine as hunters or herders, but why would one want a beast like that in one's home?"

"They also love you without question, provide warm companionship and never judge you, but instead reward every kind gesture with joy."

It almost sounded as if she were describing herself. "I suppose we shall agree to disagree on this."

"Have you ever let yourself just play with a dog?"

He was *not* going down that conversational path with her. "Not since I was a child." He pushed those foolish memories aside and changed the subject. "I can see why your father considered this his favorite meal. It's quite good."

To his relief, she followed his lead and the conversation stayed on safe, nonpersonal topics for the rest of the meal.

Once they stood up from the table, Everett waved toward the adjoining door. "Please don't forget to close and lock that door before you leave."

At her nod, he turned and headed downstairs. She probably thought he was being too much a stickler, but he was a firm believer that you couldn't go wrong if you followed the rules of propriety to the letter. That was what separated polite society from barbarians.

After Daisy returned to her own place, she locked the door on her side of the wall, just as she'd promised Everett she would. The man was just so rigid in his thinking, so very conscious of appearances. But it wouldn't hurt to follow his rules.

Then she turned to Kip. "Ready for our walk, boy?"

The dog's tail started wagging furiously, and he gave an excited bark.

Daisy laughed as she led the way. "How can anyone say they have no use for dogs? Especially a smart, friendly dog like you." Another example of how stuffy her boss could be.

Then again, Mr. Fulton *had* admitted to playing with a dog when he was a child. So at one time he'd known what it was to have fun. What had happened to him?

As soon as she stepped outside, Daisy pushed those gloomy thoughts aside and lifted her face to the sky, enjoying the feel of the warm sunshine, inhaling deeply of the fresh air. Did Mr. Fulton ever do this, just take a moment to enjoy what the day had to offer?

She doubted it.

As they headed toward the outskirts of town, Daisy began her usual one-sided conversation with Kip. "Remember all those berries I picked yesterday? Well, I traded them to Mr. Blakely over at the mercantile for some rope. Tonight I'm going to string it on the bed frame and make it good as new. Now if I can just gather up enough grass to finish stuffing my mattress, I can have me a proper bed. I'll sure be glad when I don't have to sleep on the floor anymore."

Kip answered with a bark.

She smiled down at him. "Don't worry. There's a new bed in the works for you, as well."

Kip gave another bark, then took off after a squirrel he spotted across the road.

Daisy watched him tree the bushy-tailed sprinter with a smile. Kip was such a good companion. Mr. Fulton would see that if he could look past his stuffy notions.

Maybe that was something she could teach him, unobtrusively of course, to repay him for all the nice things he'd done for her. Surely she could find ways to teach him to smile—genuinely smile, not flash that amused-at-the-world, snobby twist of his lips that passed for a smile.

He might appear stiff and cold, but he'd done so much to help her, whether he cared to admit it or not. She had to believe that there really was a kind heart under that don't-need-anybody exterior of his.

And she aimed to make him believe it, as well.

On Sunday, Daisy stepped out onto the sidewalk at almost the same moment as Everett left his building. "Good morning, Mr. Fulton. Are you on your way to church service, too?"

"I am."

So he *was* a churchgoer. She was relieved. Perhaps his reluctance to say grace at their meals was no more than a dislike of praying aloud.

He gave her an approving glance as he fell into step beside her, and she stood a little straighter, feeling a tiny touch of pride. The dress she wore was one that had belonged to her mother. It wasn't as fine as some of the other dresses that would no doubt grace the women filling the pews this morning, but it was one she could hold her head up proudly while wearing.

As they strolled down the sidewalk, Daisy felt a little self-conscious walking beside him. But she considered him her friend, not just her boss. Did he feel the same? "It sure is a beautiful day," she said, breaking the silence.

"So it is."

So much for starting a conversation. But he seemed

perfectly at ease, and within a few moments she began to relax.

They received several greetings from the townsfolk they encountered, with Everett taking the time to introduce her to those she hadn't yet met, and Daisy suddenly caught another glimmer of what it would feel like to be an accepted part of this community. It felt every bit as good as she'd imagined it would.

"Good morning to you, Miss Johnson, Mr. Fulton." Hazel Andrews, the seamstress, had stepped out of her home to join them.

Everett tipped his hat, and the three exchanged pleasantries. Then Miss Andrews smiled Daisy's way. "That's a very fine dress you're wearing. A bit dated perhaps, but I can tell the workmanship is exceptional, and the fabric and detailing are quite lovely."

"Thank you. It belonged to my mother."

They arrived in the churchyard, and Miss Andrews excused herself to join a group of friends. Before Daisy could do more than look around, the bell began to peal, indicating it was time for the service to start.

Everett took her elbow and looked at her with a raised brow. "Shall we?"

The feel of his hand on her elbow startled her. He likely only meant to offer support as they climbed the stairs.

Once inside the church, he released her and moved toward a pew halfway down the aisle. She thought for a moment he was planning to join Adam and what was undoubtedly the rest of the Barr household, but he stopped one pew shy of them.

Daisy was uncertain whether to join him or if that would be considered presumptuous. But before she could even complete that thought, Everett was stepping aside to let her precede him into the pew.

There were already two men seated there, and they slid down to accommodate her and Everett. The gentleman to her left, an intimidatingly large man, gave her a friendly smile. "Good day, ma'am. I'm Mitchell Parker. And this—" he indicated the boyish looking gentleman to his left "—is Chance Dawson."

"So good to meet you. My name is Daisy Johnson."

There was no time for further pleasantries, since Reverend Harper was already stepping up to the pulpit.

When the choir led the congregation in an opening hymn a few moments later, Daisy was surprised by Everett's strong, deep voice. It seemed to set off echoing vibrations deep inside her, vibrations synchronized to the rhythms of her heartbeat and breathing.

She shook off the fanciful notion when Reverend Harper stepped up to the podium. His sermon dealt with finding joy in whatever your circumstances. Daisy almost felt as if God Himself were blessing her self-appointed mission to help Everett with this very thing. She wondered how well Everett was listening.

After the service, Adam and his obviously expecting wife stood and turned to greet them. Mrs. Barr focused her attention on Daisy first. "You must be Miss Johnson."

Daisy was immediately put at ease by the woman's warm and genuine smile. "Please, call me Daisy."

"And I'm Reggie." She waved a hand to include the three other men in Daisy's pew. "These gents have a standing invitation to have Sunday luncheon with us. I hope you'll join us, as well."

Daisy was caught off guard by the invitation. "I don't..."

Reggie patted her hand. "Please, you can't say no. The invitation is entirely selfish on my part. It would be so wonderful to have another female at my table." Then she tilted her head apologetically. "Unless you already have other plans."

"No. I mean, of course I'd be happy to accept your invitation."

"Good. It'll be great to have some female company to help me hold my own against all of these men."

Adam tucked his wife's arm on his elbow. "I have never known you to have problems holding your own, my dear," he said affectionately.

Daisy felt a little stab of jealousy at the obvious love between these two. Was that something she'd ever find for herself?

She pushed that thought away. "Before I join you, I need to check on Kip—he's my dog."

"Of course. In fact, bring him along if you like." Reggie placed a hand on her son's shoulder. "We have a dog of our own, and Jack will be glad to keep an eye on him for you. Won't you, Jack?"

The boy nodded vigorously.

Reggie turned to Everett. "You'll show her where we live." It didn't sound like a question.

But Daisy was aghast at the suggestion that Mr. Fulton should act as her escort. "Oh, no, that's not necessary. If you'll just tell me where your home is, I'm sure I can find my way on my own."

Reggie waved her objection aside. "Nonsense. If Everett doesn't want to—"

"I will be happy to provide Miss Johnson with an

escort." Everett's dry tone indicated he was humoring the ladies.

But it would be churlish to refuse now, so she simply nodded, and thanked him.

As they walked down the sidewalk together, she clasped her hands in front of her. "I apologize for taking you away from your friends."

"Where Reggie is concerned, it's best just to go along."

So he was on a first-name basis with Adam's wife. "Still, I feel as if you were put on the spot, and it was very kind of you to be such a good sport about it."

He gave her an odd look. Had she said too much again? When would she learn to think before she spoke?

When they arrived at her building, he didn't go in. Instead, he indicated he would be just inside his office and for her to knock on the door when she was ready.

As always, Kip greeted her as if she'd been gone for days rather than a few hours.

When she stepped back outside a few minutes later, Mr. Fulton joined her before she could so much as move toward his door. He gave Kip an annoyed look but refrained from saying anything. In return, Daisy was careful to keep her dog to her far side.

When they arrived at the Barr home, Jack and his own pet were waiting for them. Kip and the large, muddy-colored dog the boy called Buck sniffed each other, then started a friendly tussle that ended when Jack threw a stick and called out a fetch command.

"They like each other," the boy said with a broad smile.

"So it seems." Mr. Fulton's tone was noncommittal.

Reggie joined them. "I thought I heard you arrive. Please come in."

Jack gave his mother a pleading look. "Can I stay out here and play?"

"For a few minutes, but Mrs. Peavy will have the food on the table soon."

With a quick nod, he ran to the backyard, both dogs on his heels.

Reggie shook her head with a smile. "It'll be like lassoing the rain to get him inside for lunch." Then she turned back to her guests and escorted them inside.

Reggie led them to a cozy parlor where Adam and the two other gentlemen were already seated. They all rose as the ladies entered, but Reggie quickly waved them back down.

Daisy learned that Mr. Parker was one of the town's two schoolteachers, and that Mr. Dawson did some sort of mechanical work. She also learned that these were the other two men who had traveled here from Philadelphia at the same time Everett and Mr. Barr had. That must account for the bond they seemed to share.

The conversation was lively, and it wasn't long before Daisy felt at ease with these people. She was content to sit back and listen for the most part, but her hostess would have none of that.

"I read the article Everett wrote about you for the paper," Reggie said. "You seem to have led a fascinating life."

"I'm afraid most of that is due to Mr. Fulton's writing skill rather than my own accomplishments. To my way of thinking, my life has been rather ordinary."

Reggie laughed. "I suppose everyone thinks that

about their own lives. I imagine it's been every bit as ordinary as that of everyone else in this room."

Daisy pondered that statement. Did that mean there were some tales to be told here? "Did Mr. Fulton interview each of you as well?" She'd sure be interested in reading those stories.

"I'm afraid none of us were as obliging as you were," Mr. Parker said dryly.

Before Daisy could dig further, Mrs. Peavy announced the meal was ready.

Meals at the Barr household were anything but formal. Jack was allowed to eat with the adults, and Ira and Mabel Peavy also joined them at the table.

Adam said a simple but heartfelt prayer before the meal, and once everyone was served, the conversation started up again. The food was delicious, and Daisy complimented Mrs. Peavy on her cooking.

"Why, thank you, dear. But I understand you're quite a cook in your own right. Planning to open a restaurant, even."

"Yes, as soon as I can get my place fixed up and acquire the equipment I need. Maybe you and I can swap recipes some time."

Mrs. Peavy gave her a broad grin. "I'd like that."

"Opening a restaurant." Chance Dawson was seated to her left, and he gave her a boyish grin. "That's something this town needs. You let me know if there's anything I can do to help you along." The young man, with his ready smiles and teasing attitude, was as different from Everett as a songbird was from a hawk.

"Thank you. I may take you up on that someday soon."

Everett sat across from her, and she noticed he was frowning at Chance. Was his stand against her opening a restaurant such that he didn't want anyone else to offer her a show of support? He glanced her way, and his expression immediately switched back to the aloof indifference she was so familiar with.

The conversation continued in a lively give-and-take that Daisy thoroughly enjoyed. Mr. Parker was the quiet sort, but he could suddenly pipe in with a touch of dry wit that one had to be paying close attention to catch. Mr. Dawson was cocky, but his manner was charming rather than off-putting. And Reggie presided over the gathering with relaxed charm and humor. Despite what she'd said earlier, Daisy could see that Reggie needed no help in holding her own with this group.

When at last the meal was over, Reggie invited them to join her out in the garden for dessert.

But Daisy shook her head. "Thank you so much for a wonderful meal, but it's time for me to take my leave."

"You can't leave without tasting Mrs. Peavy's peach cobbler," Reggie protested. "It's her specialty."

Daisy smiled regretfully. "I'm sure it's wonderful, but I have something at home that requires my attention this afternoon."

"Well, if you must go, then I won't pout. But I've enjoyed having you here, and I insist you consider yourself part of our Sunday gatherings."

"Thank you. I would like that very much."

As she headed back toward her home, with Kip at her heels and a carefully packaged piece of cobbler in her hands that Reggie had insisted she take, she sent up a silent prayer of thanksgiving. She'd made a new group of friends and had spent the past hour feeling like a genuinely welcome part of that group. It was almost like having a family. Or rather, what she imagined a loving family would be like.

Everett watched Daisy make her exit, and was surprised to find her departure left a hole in their gathering. Did the rest of them feel that way, or just him? It was strange how smoothly she'd fit into their Sunday afternoon gathering—as if she'd always been part of it.

He'd kept an eye on her, unobtrusively, of course. After all, he felt some responsibility for introducing her into their midst.

Chance had sat next to her at lunch, and the would-be lothario had actually flirted with her. Which was ridiculous. Despite her lack of polish, Daisy was much too mature for him. Not that it was really any of his concern. It's just that it was unseemly. Not only was Chance younger than Daisy—at least he seemed to be—but he was entirely the wrong sort of man for her. Daisy needed a man who could lend a bit of pragmatism and worldly wisdom to temper her foolishly optimistic outlook on life. Chance was basically a good person, but he was also brash and reckless and counted on his charm a little too much at times.

Everett pulled his thoughts back to the present and saw Reggie eyeing him speculatively. What was that look for? He tugged his cuff sharply and turned to ask Mitchell about doing an article on the students who would be graduating soon.

As for that gleam in Reggie's eyes, she obviously suffered from an overactive imagination.

Chapter Eight

Later that afternoon, as Daisy stitched up the side of the ticking she'd finally finished stuffing, her mind kept wandering to the gathering at the Barrs' home. She'd really had a wonderful time.

A sound from the other side of the wall told her Mr. Fulton had made it home.

How had he felt about her intrusion into their gathering today? After all, Reggie had invited her in a way that hadn't allowed anyone else in the group to object without seeming rude. She'd felt his gaze on her often during the meal, but more often than not, whenever she'd glance his way he was looking elsewhere. Perhaps that had just been her imagination.

Daisy pushed those thoughts away as she placed the last stitch in her ticking and tied off her thread. She knotted it three times, just to make sure it would hold. Yesterday she'd laced the bed frame nice and tight, so it was ready and waiting for the mattress. Would it hold? She maneuvered the bulky mattress onto the frame, then gingerly sat on it. Nothing crashed to the floor—so far, so good.

She flopped back to really get a feel for it. Again, it held. It was a bit lumpy, but she could live with that. And spreading her bedroll on top ought to help smooth it a little. It sure would beat sleeping on the floor.

She popped back up and smiled at Kip. “Guess who’s going to be sleeping in a real bed tonight?” Catching her mood, the dog gave a playful bark. “That’s right, me. And look at this.”

She stood and quickly crossed the room where she scooped up a colorful oval of cloth. “I’ve made a rag rug that’ll be perfect for you to sleep on. See, I’ll spread it right next to my bed, and we’ll both have comfortable places to sleep tonight. What do you think?”

Kip’s wagging tail marked his approval.

“I think this calls for a celebration.”

She’d been hoarding a small tin of cocoa powder for just such an occasion. A cup of hot cocoa would be perfect to celebrate this little step to furnishing her new home. And she’d set aside a bone from the butcher to give Kip tomorrow, but he deserved to celebrate, as well.

She dug the cocoa tin out of her pack, then paused. A celebration was so much nicer when there was someone else to share it with. And while Kip was always great company, it would be nice to have another *person* to share this with.

Did Mr. Fulton like cocoa?

She chewed on her lip for a moment, then nodded to herself and opened the pass-through door on her side of the wall. She knocked firmly on the one that opened into his place.

After a moment of silence, there was the sound of

movement and he opened the door. His face wore a cautious expression. Had she been too bold, after all?

"Is something wrong?" he asked.

"Not at all." She offered him her broadest smile. "I was in the mood for a celebration and thought I'd fix myself some hot cocoa as a treat." Daisy held up her battered tin. "I wondered if you'd like to have a cup with me?"

He frowned, almost as if upset she *hadn't* had a problem. "I thought we agreed not to use these doors for casual visits."

That was what had him glowering at her. She refused to let his mood dampen her spirits. "My apologies. Shall I close the door and go downstairs and knock on your office door?"

He held his pose a moment longer, then relaxed. "Now that the doors are open, I suppose that would be foolish. And thank you for the invitation." He opened his door wider and stepped back, signaling her to enter. "Why don't we use my stove to heat the milk?"

"I was going to use the fire pit outside, but your way sounds better." Then she looked down at her dog. "But only if you allow Kip to join us. He deserves to be part of the celebration, too."

Everett frowned. Before he could refuse, though, she jumped in with, "It's Sunday afternoon. Can't we call a truce on this day of rest? I promise if Kip does the least little thing to bother you, he and I will both go home."

He grimaced, but then nodded. "Oh, very well."

Relieved, Daisy stepped across the threshold, signaling Kip to follow her. Maybe she was already chipping away at his stuffy exterior. And winning this concession, small as it was, from the normally unbending stickler, gave her something extra to celebrate.

While Everett added additional wood to the stove, Daisy crossed the room and fetched a boiler. She added enough water to fill their two cups, then set it on the stove. "I don't have milk, but I'll add a little extra cocoa to make up for it." It would finish up the last of her stores, but she felt the occasion warranted it.

"I have some cream you're welcome to use."

She smiled, glad to see he was finally getting into the spirit of things. "That'll be lovely. I'll add it when I pour our cups."

He leaned negligently against the counter a few feet from her, and crossed his arms. She felt his eyes on her, silently studying her. Suddenly she felt nervous, self-conscious.

"So what are we celebrating?" he asked, finally breaking the silence.

It seemed a little indelicate to speak of her bed with him. But she couldn't *not* give him an answer, or worse yet, lie. So she chose her words carefully. "The fact that I won't have to spend another night sleeping on the floor."

The water in the pot started bubbling, and she slowly added in the cocoa and then the sugar, stirring to make sure it dissolved without leaving lumps.

She inhaled the rich aroma and looked over her shoulder with a smile. "Doesn't it smell wonderful?"

"It does smell good."

With one last stir, she lifted the pot and carefully poured the dark, aromatic liquid into the two cups. By the time she set the cups on the table, he was there with the cream.

"We probably ought to let that cool a minute," she said. Then she remembered Kip. "I'll be right back." She hurried back to her apartment and fetched the bones she'd set aside.

She caught Everett rolling his eyes when she placed the treat down in front of Kip, but thankfully he refrained from saying anything. Another sign that he was learning to unbend? Daisy quickly took her seat at the table.

"It should have cooled enough to drink by now. Shall we?"

They both sipped on their cocoa, and then Everett lifted his cup toward her in a salute. "Very nice."

"Thank you. Cocoa is one of my favorite tastes in the whole world, so I save it for special occasions."

He raised a brow. "That's quite a pronouncement."

"Oh, but it's true." She gave him a cheeky smile. "And I did say 'one of.'"

"Ah, so now you're qualifying it."

She grinned in response. "What about you?"

He eyed her cautiously. "What do you mean?"

"What's your favorite taste?"

He shrugged. "I haven't really given that much thought."

"Well, think about it now." Could she get him to be frivolous or whimsical for once? "Surely there's one thing you enjoy tasting above all others. A taste that's not just good in itself, but one that brings back pleasant memories."

He looked at her as if she were a child in need of humoring, then his expression changed and she could almost see a memory sneaking up on him. "Once, when I was a boy of about five or six," he said slowly, "my father and mother were both at Hellingsly—that's the estate where I grew up—and we were sitting down to a meal together. That in and of itself was a rare occurrence. Cook had fixed a special dinner, and the dessert consisted of a raspberry tart. I don't think I've tasted anything quite as delicious since."

If he'd been five or six at the time, that would have happened before he came to America. With an estate and a cook, had he come from a well-to-do background? That would account for his highfalutin manner.

But that memory he'd just shared, that had been a simple moment, a time of family and togetherness. Obviously those things had been important to him once upon a time. Perhaps, somewhere inside him, they still were.

He straightened and, as if realizing he'd revealed more than he intended, changed the subject. "I think Jack took a liking to your dog today."

Daisy smiled. "He seems like a sweet boy. It was very kind of Reggie to include me in your gathering today. I like your friends."

"I believe you can count them among your friends now, as well."

Daisy wasn't certain how to respond to that, so she countered with an observation of her own. "So you and Mr. Barr, Mr. Dawson and Mr. Parker traveled here together from Philadelphia last summer."

"We did."

"It's hard to credit it. You're all so different."

Something flickered in his expression—irritation, perhaps, there and gone in an instant. The next second he looked merely amused.

* * *

Everett took himself firmly in hand. First he'd talked about a childhood memory that had been all but forgotten until this very moment, and now he was imagining she was comparing him to Chance. Which, even if she were, was something of little consequence.

But she was waiting for a response from him, so he pulled his thoughts back to the conversation. "Not everyone who comes from the same place is the same. Philadelphia is a big city, undoubtedly larger than any place you've experienced. But even in a small town like Turnabout, there are marked differences in people. Look at Reggie, Hazel Andrews and Eunice Ortolon over at the boardinghouse. All born and raised here in Turnabout. But you'd be hard-pressed to find three more different women."

She nodded. "You're right, of course. I guess I just expected a group of friends who decided to undertake such an adventure together would be more alike in temperament. But I can see how being so different would actually work in your favor."

Everett didn't respond. Their concurrent trip here hadn't happened quite as she assumed, but he didn't feel the need to correct her assumptions. He'd already revealed too much personal information, and he didn't intend to give her more.

But he would do well to keep his guard up. For some unfathomable reason, she seemed able to get him to talk about himself more than he cared to. And he'd worked too hard putting his past behind him to have this curious woman pry it out of him, no matter how innocently. He was accustomed to being the one doing the digging and prying—he did *not* like being on the other end of an interrogation.

When Everett sat down to his noonday meal on Monday, he could tell something was up with Daisy. He'd learned to read her moods, and today she seemed more fidgety than usual. He was curious as to what put that distracted look on her face, but decided to hold his peace for the moment. Questioning her only resulted in her prying into his own private affairs.

It was almost a relief when, after they had served their plates, she cleared her throat. "I need to ask you something."

He carefully reached for his glass. "And what might that be?"

She took a deep breath, then spoke all in a rush. "I was hoping you'd be willing to let me off one day a week."

Was that all? Then he frowned. Was she feeling overworked already? Were his strictures too much for her? Or did she just want to spend more time fixing up her own place? "Might I ask why?"

"Just like you suggested, I asked Mr. Blakely to let me know if he heard about anyone looking to hire somebody."

She was going to work for someone else? "But you have a job now."

"Of course, but I have some free hours in the afternoons and thought I'd find a way to use them to earn a bit of extra money. And this morning, Mr. Blakely mentioned that Mr. Dawson is looking for someone to take in his laundry for the next few weeks. Seems his regular laundry lady, a Miss Winters, is going away somewhere for a while." She leaned forward, her eyes sparkling with excitement.

Was that gleam for the job or for Chance?

"He also said there are other folks Miss Winters does laundry for," she continued, "and that I might be able to get several customers if I want them."

"Doing laundry is a tough job." He'd seen washer-women at work before, and he knew it was hot, menial, enervating work.

But she waved his concerns away. "I know what I'd be getting into. It's not my favorite job by any means, but I've done it before and it's only for three weeks. And I could definitely use the extra money."

Again he reminded himself that he was not her keeper. And he was actually one of Selma Winters's customers, as well. He'd intended to ask around for someone to fill in for her, but it had slipped his mind until now. "In that case, I suppose I should hire you to do mine, too."

Daisy's hopeful expression immediately changed to a sunny smile. "Does this mean you're okay with me taking a day off to do this?"

Everett shrugged. "Far be it from me to stand in the way of your ambitions."

"Thanks." She stabbed a vegetable enthusiastically. "I was thinking I'd set aside Thursdays for the job. And I could make certain whatever I cooked on Wednesdays could carry over into a cold meal on Thursday."

It seemed she'd already put a lot of thought into this. But did she really know what she was getting into? "Are you certain you're not taking on more than you can handle?" He expanded on that so she wouldn't mistakenly believe he was taking a personal interest. "I wouldn't want you to be too worn out to cook come Friday."

"Don't you worry about me. I'm used to hard work."

He didn't doubt that for one minute. "That's all well and good, but are you set up to handle such a volume of laundry? Miss Winters has set a high standard."

"I already spoke to her. She's so relieved to have someone to fill in for her while she's away that she's offered to let me use her equipment and to give me some pointers."

Had she been that certain of his approval?

As if reading his mind, she elaborated. "Of course I told her it was all based on you letting me have that day off. Now that that's settled, I'll go see her this afternoon. She has some notes she wants to give me to make sure her customers are well taken care of."

Knowing Daisy, Miss Winters's customers had nothing to worry about. And he'd never seen anyone appear so gleeful at the prospect of tackling a mountain of laundry. It remained to be seen if she'd feel the same way once she'd finished a week's worth of laundry.

This was going to be a good test as to just how well that sunny disposition could survive real adversity.

Wednesday afternoon, Everett heard an unusual racket out behind his building and went to the window to check it out.

What in the world? Daisy was driving a horse-drawn wagon into the yard, a wagon loaded with washtubs and other laundry equipment. Had she loaded all that up on her own? Didn't she know how to ask for help?

He set his coffee down and headed for the stairs. By

the time he stepped outside, she had jumped down from the seat and was moving toward the back of the wagon.

She paused a moment when she spotted him. "Oh, Mr. Fulton, I hope I didn't disturb you."

"Not at all. I'm just curious as to what you think you're doing."

Daisy continued on her way around the wagon. "I'm getting set up for laundry day tomorrow. Miss Winters is loaning me her equipment."

"Forgive my curiosity, but why didn't you just arrange to do the laundry at her place? Surely she would have let you have the use of her washhouse."

Daisy let down the tailgate of the wagon. "She offered. But I figure in order to make this work, I'm going to have to do some work the night before and the night after. That'll be much easier to do if I'm working from my own place."

So she realized it would take more than a day's work to get it all done. "How many of her customers did you agree to take care of?"

"Three other gentlemen besides you and Mr. Dawson. I also agreed to take in the wash for the mayor's family, since Mrs. Sanders hurt her foot yesterday."

Five individuals and a family of four? "It sounds as if you're going to have your hands full."

She nodded. "I've got all the work I can handle—and since it's only one day a week for three weeks, I can manage it without wearing myself down to a nub."

He joined her at the back of the wagon and helped her up into the bed. She began pushing items toward him, and he lifted them out and set them on the ground. It felt as if they'd been working as a team for some time.

"Is this one of Fred Humphries's wagons?" Fred

owned the livery stable and had several wagons and carriages that he rented out.

"It is. I traded him a dewberry cobbler and the promise of two more in exchange for the use of this rig and horse."

Everett happened to know that Fred's new wife had a reputation as an excellent cook, so Fred was no doubt just being obliging. Foolishly sentimental of him, but the livery operator had revealed a softer side of himself since his marriage.

Once the wagon was unloaded, he turned to help her down. Rather than simply giving her his hand, however, he impulsively grasped her waist and swung her to the ground. Her eyes widened in surprise, and she instinctively placed her hands on his shoulder. He liked the feel of them there, the warmth and the implied trust.

Their gazes locked. Her feet touched the ground, but for several heartbeats neither of them pulled away. The look in her eyes, the sound of her breathing, the faint scent that was so uniquely her were like silken ropes holding him in place. Was surprise the only thing she was feeling? Or was it threaded through with something stronger?

His own pulse quickened, and he felt a vein in his neck jump.

Then her dog ran up, barking, and the spell was broken. Both of them dropped their hands and took a step back.

"Thanks for your help." Daisy had stooped down to rub her dog's head, effectively hiding her expression from him. But her friendly tone sounded forced. She stood and moved to the front of the wagon, still not meeting his gaze. "I should get this rig back to the livery. I told Mr. Humphries I wouldn't keep it long."

He followed and handed her up. Their contact this time was brief and entirely businesslike. With a short nod and a stiff smile, she set the horse in motion. He watched as she expertly turned the wagon and headed off with her dog trotting alongside.

Everett didn't move. What had just happened? He'd come very close to crossing a line he had no business crossing. Not only was Miss Johnson his employee, but she'd made it very clear she planned to set down roots in Turnabout. And he planned to move on at his first opportunity.

Even if that wasn't the case, they were totally wrong for each other. And he needed to make that perfectly clear to her.

And to himself.

Daisy walked slowly back to her place. She wasn't sure exactly what had happened when he helped her down. For the merest heartbeat of time, she'd thought he might try to kiss her. What a ridiculous notion.

But what *would* have happened if Kip hadn't interrupted them? What would she have done if he *had* tried to kiss her?

Mr. Fulton wasn't at all the kind of man she'd been praying to find. She wanted to spend her life with a man who valued family and affection, who knew how to laugh and who wasn't afraid to show emotion.

Someone who liked dogs and kittens, for goodness' sake.

Best she stay focused on those things and not on how very nice it had felt to be in his arms.

Because only disappointment lay that way.

Chapter Nine

When Daisy turned the corner of the building, she was surprised to see Everett still there. How were they supposed to act toward each other now?

Kip's bark drew his attention, and she noted his cynically amused smile was back. It appeared he wasn't having any bothersome thoughts about their encounter. So why wasn't she more relieved?

She also noticed he'd been busy in her absence. "You set up my washtubs. Thanks so much, but you didn't have to do that."

As usual, he ignored her thanks. "I placed them here so they would be near the clotheslines but would drain away from them." He waved a hand. "But if you prefer to have them somewhere else, they're easy enough to move." His tone indicated he didn't think that would be particularly wise.

"No, no, this is perfect." Apparently, they were supposed to pretend that moment of awareness had never happened. Then again, perhaps for him it hadn't. Had she read more into it than had been there?

Of course she had. Why would a stuffy, undemonstrative man like Mr. Fulton want to embrace her?

He brushed his hands together, no doubt getting rid of some speck of dirt. "Is there anything else I can help you with?"

"Actually, I *could* use your help with one more thing."

He raised a brow as if he hadn't expected her to take him up on the offer. "And that is?"

She pointed toward the clotheslines he'd referred to earlier. "I checked those yesterday and they seem sturdy enough. But I'll need more line for all the clothes I'll have to hang. Miss Winters gave me some extra cord she had lying around, and I'd like to string it from that pole to the pecan tree, assuming it's long enough."

"Let's have a look."

She fetched the cord, and they determined by the simple expedient of stretching it between the two anchor points that it was indeed long enough. Everett retrieved a hammer and some nails from his place, and in a matter of minutes the task was accomplished.

Daisy stepped back and reviewed their work. It was easier than focusing on him. "Thank you for all your help. I hope it didn't put you out too much."

He merely shrugged. Didn't the man know how to accept a simple thank-you with grace?

Keep this businesslike, she reminded herself. "Would you mind bringing me whatever articles you want laundered? I've asked the others to do the same. I'm going to get everything marked and sorted tonight so I can start bright and early tomorrow."

"Marked?"

"That's one of the tips Miss Winters shared with

me. It's how she keeps everything identified to a particular customer. She sews a couple of small identifying stitches on each piece—different colors or different patterns for each person. Once the clothes are ready for pick up, she removes the stitches."

He nodded approvingly. "Clever."

Of course he would appreciate such an efficient system.

Mr. Dawson came around the corner just then, toting a large sack. "Ah, here you are. No one answered my knock, and I thought I heard voices back here."

"Hello. Sorry—I should have been keeping an eye out."

"No need to apologize." He nodded a greeting to Everett. "Hope I'm not interrupting anything."

"Not at all," Daisy hastened to reassure him. "Mr. Fulton was just helping to get everything prepared for tomorrow."

"Was he, now?" Mr. Dawson gave his friend a speculative look.

But Everett's expression didn't change, and he didn't speak.

With a grin, the cheeky young man turned back to Daisy and lifted the sack. "Where would you like me to put this?"

"If that's your laundry, just set it there on the porch. I should have everything ready for you by Friday afternoon."

"That's fine. I can't tell you how glad I am to have someone fill in during Miss Winters's absence."

Everett interrupted them. "It appears you have no further need of my assistance, so if you'll excuse me, I have some things of my own to tend to."

"Of course. Thanks again for your help."

Later that evening, as Daisy sorted through and marked the mountain of laundry piled in her storeroom, she thought again about that moment when Everett, however unintentionally, had held her in his arms. Even if it hadn't meant anything to him, she *had* felt something. Was she developing feelings for Mr. Fulton, feelings beyond those of a neighbor and friend?

She wanted to find a good man to marry, of course, but that didn't mean she should fall for the first gentleman who showed her a bit of kindness. Besides, he obviously didn't have any feelings toward her other than those of an employer. It had been his own brand of neighborliness that she'd mistaken for something more.

Because, of course, he'd associated with debutantes and sophisticated ladies during his prior life in Philadelphia. She knew how poorly she compared to such women—her grandmother had always made that very clear.

She wouldn't apologize for who she was. She just aimed to find herself a man who would appreciate what qualities she did have.

And that obviously wasn't Mr. Fulton.

If that left her feeling disappointed, so be it. She'd get over it.

Everett rose bright and early the next morning. Truth to tell, he hadn't gotten a lot of sleep last night. He'd felt a restlessness, an edgy kind of disquiet that kept him from settling down. But today was a new day, and he intended to take control of his life again.

He looked out from his kitchen window and wasn't surprised to see Daisy already heating water over a fire.

Two of her tubs were half-filled with water, and she was currently pouring the contents of a steaming kettle into the third. The sun was barely up. When had she found time to get so much done?

In that, at least, he intended to emulate her. Without her incessant humming and singing to distract him, he'd be able to focus and be much more productive than he'd been these past few days. Which was a good thing, because the paper was scheduled to go out tomorrow and he hadn't even started laying out the type. It wasn't like him to be this far behind schedule. Of course, that schedule was carefully structured to include time for unexpected delays, so he still had time to get the job done if nothing else interfered with his work.

But first he would bring Daisy a cup of coffee. That would keep him from being distracted by thoughts of her missing breakfast.

She greeted him cheerfully, apparently undaunted by the mountain of work before her. She thanked him profusely for the coffee, but as soon as she'd gulped it down, she turned right back to her work.

So, no idle chitchat today. Which was fine by him. He had work of his own to tackle.

Throughout the rest of the morning, Everett found himself missing the sound of Daisy's voice and her cheerful clattering about. Had her presence insinuated itself into his routine to the extent that he felt its absence?

He checked on her through the window a few times to see her variously working with the scrub board, stirring the clothes in steaming water or cranking it through the wringer.

At noon, he stepped outside and insisted she pause

long enough to eat. They ate together on her porch in companionable silence. She shared bits of her sandwich with her mutt, but he didn't call her on it. And as soon as she finished eating, she thanked him and went back to work.

If he'd worried about there being any awkwardness between them after that little incident yesterday, his fears were put to rest. She was the same sunny, smiling Daisy as ever.

Daisy wiped her brow as she set the basket of wet laundry on the ground below the last bit of unoccupied clothesline. Not only was the day hot, but using kettles of boiling water had sapped a lot of her energy.

But the washing was done, and once she had this final load hung she'd be finished with this part of her job. Of course, it would soon be time to take down the earlier loads and begin ironing and folding.

It was going to be a long evening. Not that she was complaining. She'd prayed for other earning opportunities, and that's exactly what this was. With the money she earned from this job she'd be able to purchase some additional paint and lumber.

Mr. Fulton had done his part to make things easier on her. Not only had he helped her get everything set up yesterday, but he'd checked on her several times today—bringing her coffee this morning and a meal at noon. He'd even stepped out here a couple of times just to make certain she was okay. Not that he'd admitted such, but she knew.

Kip's bark alerted her that she was no longer alone. When she turned, sure enough, Everett was back.

"I see you're still at it," he said by way of greeting.

Dredging up enough energy to smile, she glanced at him over her shoulder. "Just finishing hanging up the last load." She placed the final pin on the final garment, then turned. "What time is it?"

"Just past four-thirty." He shook his head. "I still say it seems a hard way to earn a little extra money."

Why did he keep saying that? Was he trying to discourage her? "Nothing I can't manage for a few weeks."

"So now that you're done with the hanging, do you plan to take a break?"

"A very short one. The first load will be ready for me to take down in a little while. And that means I'll need to start sorting and folding." She tried not to let her tiredness show. "I can start on the ironing tonight, but I probably won't have time to finish." She gave him a hopeful look. "I can finish it while I'm cooking tomorrow, if that's okay with you."

"As long as you get your cooking done, whatever extra time you have is yours to use as you please."

"Do you mind if I set up my ironing board in your kitchen tomorrow, or would you prefer I keep all my business on my side of the wall?"

"As long as it's not in my way, do what works best for you."

"Thanks. Now, you might want to step back. When I pull the plugs on these tubs, the water will likely slosh over on anything in the vicinity."

She pulled the plug on the first tub, then moved to the second and did the same. Water came gushing out of both of them, flowing in wide, crooked rivulets toward the back of the lot.

The third tub, unlike the other two, sat flush on the ground. When she pulled the plug, not much happened.

"Looks like you'll need to bail the water out of that one," Everett observed.

"That'll take an awful long time." Not to mention more effort than she felt she could give at the moment. She could just kick herself for not thinking to elevate it a few inches off the ground before she'd filled it. Then she had an idea.

She looked to Everett hopefully. "Do you think, if I can lift the edge of this a few inches, you could shove a piece from the woodpile under it?"

Everett was affronted by her request. Did she think so little of him as to assume he'd stand by and let her lift that thing? He stepped forward, rolling up his sleeves. "I'll do the lifting, and you slide the wood underneath."

"Oh, but I don't want to—"

"Miss Johnson, I don't have all afternoon to argue this with you. Now, let's find some suitable pieces of wood, shall we?"

Once they found the appropriate pieces of wood, Everett moved to the large washtub and got his hands under the bottom edge to tilt it forward. Some of the water sloshed over the lip and, since he'd had the bad judgment to stand on the downhill side of the washtub, the already damp ground he stood on became soupy as the water flowed back his way. He winced as he thought about the damage to his shoes.

Daisy quickly shoved the first scrap of wood under the washtub. Grabbing the second piece, she quickly moved around him to slide it under the other side.

In her rush, however, she lost her footing and landed with a plop right on her backside. Her mutt ran up and managed to sideswipe Everett. Like a row of dominoes tumbling, Everett also lost his balance and pitched forward. Unfortunately, his left hand ended up partially under the tub, and to add insult to injury—literally—his body weight added more pressure to the already crushing weight.

The pain was immediate and excruciating. It was all he could do not to blister the air with his imprecations.

Through the haze of pain, he was aware of Daisy scrambling to her feet. "Oh, I'm so sorry. Your suit is—" Then she caught sight of his predicament and immediately grabbed hold of the tub and lifted it enough for him to pull his hand out.

The throbbing agony tripled. He gingerly tried to flex his fingers and was relieved when he was able to do so, albeit not without exacerbating the pain.

"That looks awful!" She stared at his hand, stopping just short of touching him. "Oh, this is all my fault."

It *felt* awful, too. But he refrained from saying so. "Please, just let me sit here a minute and catch my breath."

"Of course. You stay right where you are, and I'll go fetch Doc Pratt."

"Nonsense." He took another long breath, attempting to think clearly. He gingerly moved his hand again and tried to smother his groan. "I can tell it's not broken, so there's nothing the doctor can do for it that time won't accomplish, as well."

"Shouldn't we at least get him to look at it?" She pushed a damp wisp of hair from her forehead. "Please—it would make me feel better."

Why did she think that plea would convince him?

But somehow it did. "Very well. But you're not going to ask him to come here. It's my hand that's affected, not my feet." He stood. "I'm perfectly capable of walking to his office."

"Then I'm going with you."

Did she think he'd renege if she wasn't with him? But it wasn't worth arguing over.

"Give me a minute to change into something dry. And if you'd care to do the same—"

"Don't be such a fusspot." She sounded almost angry. "A little water and mud won't hurt anything, but not getting your hand looked at right away might."

Did she just call him a *fusspot?* And did she really expect the two of them to walk through town with mud-plastered backsides? He wasn't sure which offense he found the more egregious.

She swept out an arm with her finger pointed, like a general ordering his troops forward.

And without a word, he headed in the direction she'd pointed.

They walked the five blocks to Dr. Pratt's office in silence. Everett was acutely conscious of his undignified appearance, and of the curious looks they were getting, but Daisy seemed oblivious. He hadn't felt like such a spectacle since he'd been the subject of one of Reggie's unorthodox trials last summer.

Trying to block that out, and prove he was not a fusspot, but rather a confident and fastidious gentleman, Everett focused on keeping a steady pace and not jostling his hand.

When they finally reached the doctor's home, Daisy scurried ahead to knock on the door.

Dr. Pratt's wife let them in and immediately escorted them to the wing that served as the doctor's clinic. A moment later, Dr. Pratt was examining Everett's now painfully swollen hand.

In the end, he confirmed Everett's earlier prediction. "Nothing's broken, but it's going to hurt something terrible for the next few days. And I'm afraid you may lose the nail on your index finger." He rolled down his sleeves. "But I don't see any reason why those fingers won't heal cleanly, assuming you take good care of yourself."

"Thank you." Everett gave Daisy an I-told-you-so look, but refrained from saying it aloud.

"Is there anything Mr. Fulton can do to ease the pain in the meantime?"

The physician studied her a moment, then nodded. "I could provide him with laudanum if the pain gets to be more than he can bear, but—"

"That won't be necessary." Everett stood, ready to be done with this.

"In that case, I recommend some of this medicinal tea to help you sleep tonight." He pulled a small packet from a glass-fronted cabinet. "And it would be a good idea to wear a sling to keep that hand shielded from accidental bumps until it's less tender."

As they walked back toward their offices, Daisy patted his arm as if comforting a child. "I'll feed Kip, and then I'm going to fix you a nice dinner."

"There's no need for you to trouble yourself. I plan to eat some of the food left from earlier and then get back to work."

She eyed him uncertainly. "Do you really think you're up to that?"

Her concern was beginning to sound suspiciously like mollycoddling. That fusspot comment still rankled.

Did she think he was some milksop who couldn't deal with a bit of pain? "Please don't concern yourself," he said stiffly. "Yes, I smashed some fingers on my left hand, but that's more of an inconvenience than a problem."

He saw the determination in her expression, but it was mixed with exhaustion. He wasn't about to let her add to her own workload over some misguided sense of guilt. "Don't you have some laundry-related chores to take care of?"

She nodded, but her expression remained mulish. "A little delay won't hurt anything."

By this time they'd reached her door, and he decided a firm tone was in order. "I appreciate your concern, but you take care of your business and let me take care of mine." With a short bow, he turned and entered his own office.

An hour later, Everett wasn't quite so sure of his ability to manage things, after all. His hand still throbbed painfully, and it seemed to have infected him with an unaccustomed clumsiness. It turned out typesetting was considerably more difficult to do one-handed than he'd imagined it would be.

He bumped his injured hand, and his reaction resulted in type scattered across the floor. The echoes of his frustrated growl still hung in the air when his door opened. Daisy stood there, hesitating on his threshold, a small basket on her arm. What did she want now? "Can I do something for you?"

She stepped farther into the room, leaving the door open behind her. "I've done all I plan to do with the laundry tonight. I thought I'd check in to see how you were faring."

"I'm fine."

Her quickly suppressed wince let him know his frustration had come through in his voice. A low growl from the doorway drew his gaze. Her dog sat there, watching him balefully. Just what he needed right now—an edgy dog and an oversolicitous woman.

He turned back to Daisy and moderated his tone. "I'm doing all right, but I *am* busy right now."

She raised the basket. "I brought some willow-bark tea—it's my own special recipe. And I have an ointment that'll help deaden some of the pain." Her smile and tone had an uncertain quality to them, as if she expected to be turned away. "I know you don't like to be fussed over, but there's no point suffering any more than necessary."

Everett heaved a mental sigh. "I suppose a spot of tea would be nice about now."

He was rewarded with a generous smile as she hurried over and unpacked her basket at his desk.

He joined her there and watched as she quickly unscrewed the lid on a mason jar and poured its contents into a cup. "Here you go," she said, offering it to him. "One cup of my special medicinal tea."

He took a tentative sip and was surprised by the flavor. It had a slightly metallic tang to it, but there were notes of vanilla and some spice that was almost pleasant.

As she reached for the other item in her basket, she frowned at him. "I thought the doc told you to wear a sling."

"I think it was more a suggestion than a directive."

He could tell she wasn't pleased with his response, but to his surprise, she let it go and pulled out a small pot. "If you'll allow me, I'd like to massage this on your injured hand."

He looked at her skeptically, not sure he wanted anyone touching his still-tender digits.

"I promise I'll take it easy," she said. "But this really will help ease the pain." She dipped a flat wooden stick into the pot and scooped up the waxy-looking concoction. Then she extended her left hand expectantly, palm up.

He gingerly placed his swollen, painfully bruised hand in her palm.

She ever so gently began to spread the ointment onto his bruised skin. Her motions were deft, gentle, butterfly soft. The palm under his hand was warm and supportive.

In a matter of seconds, he began to feel a cooling sensation wherever the ointment touched, and then a blessed numbness.

She finally looked up, meeting his gaze. "How's that?"

He found himself captured by the way the soft light brought out the bronze glints in her coffee-colored eyes. "Much better, thank you."

With a pleased nod, she turned to replace the lid on her ointment pot.

He swallowed, then tried to hide his momentary discomfiture with a lighter tone. "You should go into the apothecary business rather than opening a restaurant."

She smiled but shook her head. "I enjoy cooking much more. Besides, Turnabout already has an apothecary."

She frowned as she took in the sight of the scattered

type. "You're working on getting the paper ready to print."

"Of course. Tomorrow *is* Friday."

"But your hand is injured. Can't you delay the newspaper a day or so? I'm sure folks will understand when they hear what happened."

That just showed how little she understood him. "That's not necessary. I might be slower and clumsier than normal, but I'll manage. I haven't missed a deadline since I printed the first *Turnabout Gazette,* and I see no reason to start now." It was a point of pride with him to get his paper out on time, every time.

Then he grimaced. "This is no more than what I deserve for getting off schedule. I should have had most of this set by noon instead of leaving it until this evening." He wouldn't look too closely at why that had happened.

She crossed her arms in front of her chest. "If you're so set on this, then I'm going to assist you."

Everett noticed the dark circles under her eyes and the hint of weariness in the set of her shoulders. She'd had an exhausting day—she probably hadn't rested at all since they'd returned from Dr. Pratt's office. She needed to get some sleep, not help him with his work.

Besides, just how much help could an untrained female be? "I told you, I don't hold you responsible for what happened."

"But *I* do." She firmly tucked a tendril behind her ear. "I know I can't do the job as well as you, but I can be your hands. You stand next to me and tell me what needs doing, and I'll get it done."

Everett thought about all he had left to accomplish before morning and was sorely tempted. But he didn't want to take advantage of her. "I'll be working quite late."

That didn't appear to weaken her resolve. "All the more reason I should help—maybe together we can shave a few hours off that time. Besides, I've stayed up through the night before and probably will again."

Stubborn female. But all this arguing was wasting time. He gave a short nod. "Very well. Let's see if we can make this work." He moved to one of the wall sconces. "But first we should brighten this room up." Dusk had fallen, and shadows were creeping into the room. He also opened the outer door wider and made certain the shades on the storefront windows were up. She could call him a fusspot if she liked, but he planned to take every precaution that no hint of impropriety was attached to Daisy's presence here.

Daisy moved to the other wall and lit the sconces there.

Once the room was suitably illuminated and all hint of privacy removed, Everett showed her the articles that needed to be prepped and then walked her through the process. Then he painstakingly, letter by letter, instructed her on where to place the type and which type to use.

Daisy was surprisingly dexterous and took direction well. It was equally surprising that it didn't take much longer than it usually did when he worked alone. But by the time they were done, the day's events had taken their toll on both of them. Exhaustion had turned Daisy's natural cheery outlook into a mild case of giddiness.

And he was tired enough to find it amusing.

When the last page was finally printed and placed on the drying rack, Daisy turned and stretched.

"We did it," she said, as if it had been a monumental accomplishment. Then she giggled and did a triumphant little dance step. Unfortunately, she bumped into a nearby file cabinet as she did so.

She continued giggling as Everett reached out to steady her, and suddenly she was in his embrace again. Her giggling abruptly stopped as her eyes widened in surprise, and something else. Was his reaction equally telling? Because she felt every bit as good in his arms today as she had yesterday.

Everett closed his eyes to steady himself, but that was a mistake. His senses were immediately flooded with an awareness of her scent, her breathing, her warmth—of *her*.

After what seemed ages, but was probably only a heartbeat or two of time, they separated. There was no sign left of her giddiness, and bright spots of red stained her cheeks.

"I'm so sorry." She didn't quite meet his gaze. "I don't know what—"

"No need to apologize. We've both had a long day." Everett was glad his tone held steady. He cast a quick look at the open doorway and was relieved to see that, except for her dog, the sidewalk was deserted. It had been an accidental and totally innocent embrace, but others might not view it that way.

He put more distance between them, moving to the type cabinet. "Thank you for your help tonight, but I think I can finish the rest on my own."

"Yes, of course." She took a deep breath and looked around, as if seeking an answer from his furnishings. Then she straightened and turned an over-bright smile on him. "I'll take my leave, then."

"Of course. Good evening, and it'll be okay if you're a little late tomorrow."

She crossed to the door, her shoes beating a rapid tattoo across the floor. Out on the sidewalk, she gave her dog a quick rub. "Come on, Kip. Time to go home."

Everett followed slowly, watching to see she made it safely inside her place.

She never so much as glanced back.

Everett closed his door and then lowered the shades and turned out the lights. What was wrong with him? He wasn't interested in her in that way, yet this was the second time in as many days that he'd found himself holding her in his arms. And enjoying every minute of it.

They'd both been exhausted tonight, he'd still been in some pain and neither was thinking clearly. It had been nothing more than that.

Still, the memory of how right she'd felt in his arms lingered with him long after he'd climbed the stairs.

Daisy stared at the ceiling as she lay in bed. What had come over her? If she was being honest with herself, that embrace hadn't been totally accidental, at least not on her part. She'd never hugged a man before—well, except for her father and that didn't count. Yet now she'd found herself in Everett's arms twice in as many days. And she was certain, just for a minute, that stuffy ole Everett had hugged her right back.

How was she going to face him tomorrow? She rolled over on her side. The trouble was, she couldn't find it in her heart to regret either incident. There had been a curious mix of strength and gentleness in his embrace, as if he wanted to both cherish and protect her. It had been a foreign and altogether wonderful feeling.

But she knew it was wrong.

Dear Lord, I'm not sure what's come over me, and I need Your help to be strong. I know You have a man in mind for me, and it can't be Everett because we're so different. I'm truly willing to wait for the right man, and I know it will happen in Your timing. I never thought of myself as fickle before, but maybe I am and that's what You're trying to show me—that it's something in me I need to work on.

She rolled over once again, and Kip let out a small whine from his spot beside her bed.

"Sorry, boy, I'll try to settle down." Kip was right. There weren't many hours left before sunup—she needed to stop this fretting and get some sleep.

She had a feeling she'd need all her wits about her tomorrow.

Chapter Ten

As usual, on paper delivery day, Everett rose before dawn. Not that he'd have gotten much sleep, anyway. This morning, however, with his hand still throbbing, he had to figure out an alternative to making the deliveries to the local merchants. He solved that problem by paying Jack and Ira a little extra to make those deliveries for him in addition to the household deliveries they normally made.

When Daisy breezed into his office, he braced himself for a bit of awkwardness, but it turned out to be an unnecessary precaution. She gave him a quick "good morning," then set a small jar on his desk. "Here's more of that ointment I used last night," she said. Then she headed upstairs without stopping for her usual chitchat.

Had her smile been a bit more forced than normal? Or was that only his imagination? He was relieved, naturally, that she'd chosen to act as if nothing had happened—wasn't he?

As he applied the ointment, he remembered how good it had felt when Daisy did that for him. Then he grimaced—he was turning into a blasted mooncalf.

He'd better focus on his work before he lost all sense of self-respect.

But by midmorning he was so off his game that he actually welcomed the distraction when Chance walked in. The greeting died on his lips, however, when he recognized the young girl accompanying him.

"Abigail!" What was his sister doing here? More important, how in the world had she gotten here?

"Hello, Everett. I've come to visit," she said unnecessarily.

That was all she had to say for herself? "Abigail Blythe Fulton! What—how—" He was having trouble deciding whether to start with questions or a severe scolding.

"I came in on the train, and your friend Mr. Dawson offered to show me to your office." She gave Chance a dazzling smile.

Chance's smile had an I'm-really-enjoying-this edge to it. "I met the train this morning because I was expecting some parts I'd ordered. They didn't arrive, but I found this young lady there, asking Zeke where your place was. When I found out she was your sister, I thought I should escort her here myself."

Did that mean she'd traveled completely unaccompanied? Everett's blood froze at the thought of what could have happened to her. He tore his eyes away from his sister long enough to nod Chance's way. "Thank you."

"You're welcome. Now, I'll leave you two to your visit." Chance tipped his hat toward Abigail. "Nice meeting you, Miss Abigail."

Abigail gave him a bright smile. "And you, as well, Mr. Dawson. You've been most kind, just like a real cowboy."

"Oh, for goodness' sake, Abigail, surely you're not still infatuated with those silly romantic notions. Not every man in Texas is a cowboy. In fact, Chance here came west with me from Philadelphia."

Abigail's lips formed a pout. "Aren't you glad to see me, even a little bit?"

Everett huffed in exasperation. "*Of course* I'm happy to see you, but that's entirely beside the point. How did you get here?"

Abigail finally had the grace to look abashed, but she rallied quickly. "By train, of course."

"Don't be impertinent."

She crossed the room to stand directly before him, hands clasped together in front of her. "Please don't be cross. After all, I made it here safe and sound, and it was *such* a grand adventure. I could almost imagine I was an adventuress, like Nellie Bly."

"That imagination of yours is going to get you into serious trouble someday, young lady." Then he pulled her to him in a hug, a fierce longing to protect her from all the ugliness in the world overtaking him. A moment later he set her away, keeping his uninjured hand on her shoulder. "Miss Haversham will be hearing from me. I don't understand how she could have let you travel all this way on your own. I pay her dearly to make certain you're well looked after." Had it been just a few days ago that he'd congratulated himself that Abigail would never be faced with a solo journey the way Daisy had?

"Don't blame Miss Haversham." Abigail's smile faltered, and she dropped her gaze. "I'm afraid I misled her."

Not surprising. "What did you do?"

She removed her bonnet, still not quite meeting his

gaze. "I led her to believe you sent for me and that I needed to leave immediately."

His exasperation once more overtook his concern. "And she believed you?"

Abigail nibbled at her lower lip a moment. "The official-looking telegram I sent her was quite convincing," she finally said in a small voice.

This was too much, even for his impulsive little sister. He dropped his hand. "Abigail! Such actions are not only dishonest, they're rash and unthinking."

"I know." Abigail's expression turned to something very like a childish pout. "It was wrong, and I'm truly sorry. But it's the only way I could get away." She met his gaze full-on. "And I *had* to get away from that stifling place."

"Thinking that the ends justify the means is a slippery slope you don't want to start down, Abigail." He ran his right hand through his hair. "Regardless of whatever tales you spun for her, however, it's still unconscionable that Miss Haversham let you travel alone."

"Actually, I wasn't alone when I departed. Miss Haversham hired a very stern woman, one even you would approve of, to accompany me. But partway into our journey, the poor woman took ill. She got off the train at one of the stops in Illinois, and I decided to continue on without her."

"You decided—" Everett's blood ran cold at the idea of his overly trusting little sister traveling such a distance on a train full of who knows what kind of people, entirely alone and unprotected. "That was quite reckless. Do you have *any* idea what could have happened to you, a young girl traveling alone?"

"But my escort *couldn't* travel, and it wouldn't have

been any better for me to travel back to Boston alone than to go forward. And nothing *did* happen, so all is well." She clasped her hands, her eyes pleading with him to understand. "Oh, Everett, I know lying to Miss Haversham was wrong and I promise to write her a very pretty and penitent letter of apology, and if you want to put me on a strict diet of bread and water for a month I won't complain. But truly, I could not stand to be in that place any longer. And you made Turnabout sound so wonderful in your letters. You know I've always dreamed of one day traveling to Texas."

Turnabout—wonderful? How had she possibly gotten that from his letters? "Yes, you will most assuredly write that letter of apology, a letter that you will hand deliver when you return to the school on tomorrow's train."

Abigail's whole expression crumpled. "You *can't* send me back so soon. I've only just arrived."

He refused to let himself be moved by her plea. "You are mistaken. I can, and I will."

"You don't understand. The telegram I gave Miss Haversham said I wouldn't be returning—at all. She's having all of my things packed and sent here."

Where had his sister learned such devious behavior? "That's quickly remedied. I'll send her a telegram today informing her that there's been a mistake."

Her expression turned mutinous. "If you send me back, I'll run away again."

Everett clenched his jaw in frustration. The idea of his sister pulling this dangerous stunt yet again was enough to turn his hair gray. He had to find a way to convince her to see reason. "Abigail, you only have another year and a half of school left." By that time, he would have moved someplace with more polish and refinement than Turnabout. "Once you're through with your schooling, of course you can live with me."

"A year and a half is *forever.*" She moaned. "Please, don't make me go back, not right away. I promise I won't get in your way. I'll even be a help. You'll see. I can keep your place neat and clean, and do your laundry and cooking. I can even help here in the office if you like. I—"

"I didn't send you to boarding school all these years so you could turn into a household drudge."

"Then why *did* you send me to that place? It certainly wasn't to make me happy."

That gave him pause. Had she truly been so unhappy at Miss Haversham's? He quickly dismissed that thought—she was just being melodramatic. "I sent you there to make certain you received a good education and that you were surrounded by persons of breeding and good character." He absently rubbed his chin, then winced as his injured digits protested.

"What's wrong?" She saw his injury, and her demeanor immediately changed to one of concern. "Oh, my goodness, what did you do to your hand?"

He waved aside her concerns. "I smashed it yesterday. It'll be fine."

"Well, it doesn't look fine." She stepped closer and gingerly touched the back of his hand. "In fact, it looks awful. Did you have a doctor look at it?"

"I did. And he agreed with me that it'll be good as new given time." Sensing her distress, he moderated his tone. "It looks worse than it is."

"But it must be terribly painful." She straightened.

"I'm more pleased than ever that I'm here. I can take care of you."

"I've been managing fine, thank you."

She tilted up her chin. "You *do* need someone to look after you."

"I don't—"

She held up a hand and cocked her head toward the stairs. "What's that?"

It took him a moment to realize she was talking about Daisy's singing.

Before he could explain, she gave him a wide-eyed look. "Everett, do you have a *woman* upstairs?"

Why did he suddenly feel self-conscious? "That's Miss Johnson, my cook. And don't go changing the subject. We were discussing your return to Boston."

Abigail ignored the last part of his statement. "A cook. Why didn't you mention this Miss Johnson in your letters?"

"Because it's a recent development. Now, as I was saying—"

But Abigail was no longer paying attention.

"I want to meet her." Without waiting for permission, she headed for the stairs. "Besides, I want to see what the rest of your place looks like. You can continue your scolding later."

With a growl of frustration, Everett followed his too-impulsive-for-her-own-good sister upstairs. As he did so, it occurred to him to worry about what the meeting of these two impulsive and sometimes reckless females would result in.

Daisy, working at the ironing board, tensed as she heard that telltale squeak of the stairs. She took a deep breath and steeled herself to face Everett for the first time since she'd headed upstairs this morning. But the person who appeared wasn't Everett, but a slender, well-dressed young lady with ginger-brown hair and sparkling eyes.

"Hello," the young lady called out. "I'm Abigail, Everett's sister. And you must be Miss Johnson."

Everett's *sister?* When had she arrived? And why hadn't she been told the girl was coming? Surely this wasn't something that would have just slipped his mind.

She spied Everett just behind his sister, and he looked none too happy. What was going on?

Remembering her manners, Daisy set down the iron and wiped her hands on her apron. "Glad to meet you, Abigail." She closed the distance between them. "And yes, I'm Daisy Johnson, your brother's cook and next-door neighbor."

"I'm so pleased to meet you." The girl's smile was infectious. "And also very glad to know Everett no longer has to subsist on his own cooking."

Daisy grinned. "Your brother didn't tell me you were expected, or I would have cooked something special." She cut Everett an accusing look, then wondered if he'd intended to tell her before their little encounter last night. "But don't you worry," she said, shaking off those uncomfortable thoughts. "The food might not be special but it'll be plentiful enough."

Abigail brushed at her skirt. "Don't blame Everett. My visit was a surprise."

"A surprise." Daisy cast another glance Everett's way and realized why he looked so grim. "I see. Well, I'm sure it was a lovely surprise."

Kip, lying in the doorway, let out a couple of attention-getting yips.

Abigail immediately spun toward the sound.

"That's just Kip," Daisy said. "He's probably wanting an introduction." Did Everett's sister share his dislike for dogs? "Don't worry, though," she added quickly. "Kip stays over on my side of the wall, just like your brother asked."

Abigail glanced up at her brother. "You banished this sweet animal from your home?" She shook her head sadly. "I shouldn't be surprised." Then she turned to Daisy. "Unlike Everett, I love dogs. I always wanted one of my own, but they aren't allowed at Miss Haversham's. Do you mind if I pet him?"

"Not at all. And he loves it when you scratch him behind the ears."

Abigail stooped down in front of Kip and ruffled his fur. "Aren't you just the handsomest animal?" Then she glanced back, her expression one of childish delight. "Look, Everett, he has one blue eye and one brown eye."

"I'm aware."

The fact that he'd noticed surprised Daisy. But his dry tone, indicating he didn't find it particularly endearing, did not.

"Oh, that must be your place." Abigail was looking past Kip into the room beyond.

"It is." What did the girl think about the sparse, makeshift furnishings?

But Abigail went back to cooing over Kip, and Daisy cut a questioning glance Everett's way.

His expression had a long-suffering look. "I'm sorry if having an extra person to cook for complicates things for you. As Abigail stated, I wasn't aware she was coming until she showed up on my doorstep."

She could tell he wasn't pleased by that occurrence. "But now that she's here, surely you can look on it as a nice surprise."

"Nice is not the word I'd use. Abigail ran away from school and is refusing to go back."

Ouch. That couldn't be easy to swallow for a man who liked to be in control of everything. "Don't worry about it putting me out. It's just as easy to cook for three as two. You just enjoy your visit together, for however long it lasts. If you two want to eat alone, I can take my portion to my place and eat there." In fact, it might be better all the way around if she did.

"That won't be necessary." He cast an exasperated look his sister's way. "Besides, if I'm alone with Abigail any time soon I might end up changing my mind about letting her stay for now."

As if suddenly aware he'd said more than he intended, Everett's expression closed off. He cleared his throat and turned to his sister. "Come on, Abigail. Let me show you where you can sleep while you're here."

The girl immediately popped up. "Whatever accommodations are available will be fine."

"That's a good thing," he said as they crossed the sitting room, "because I use the spare bedchamber for storing odds and ends. You're lucky the place came with a small bed in there."

Daisy knew him well enough now to read the affection beneath his dry tone. Regardless of how he felt about *how* his sister had traveled, he was undeniably glad to see her.

Daisy moved to the stove to check on the stew. She

didn't have a good read on Abigail yet. At first glance, she could very well be the spoiled little socialite Daisy had expected. But there was a spark of something—innocence, playfulness, vulnerability—that told her Abigail might have more to her.

Had she really run off and traveled here on her own? Daisy could understand Everett's concern. So many things might have gone terribly wrong.

A moment later, Everett returned to the kitchen, alone. "Abigail is settling in," he explained. Then he cleared his throat. "I apologize again for my sister's unexpected arrival. She's always tended to act impulsively, but this is the first time she's acted with such blatant disregard for her safety."

Was he actually worried how she was taking this? "There's no need to apologize to me for your sister."

"Abigail is bright, good-hearted and generous. She's also overly trusting, impulsive and more of a child than she will admit."

Understanding dawned. He wanted to make certain she didn't take too dim a view of his sister. "There are worse faults to have," she said with a smile.

He didn't return her smile. "If her welfare was your responsibility, you might not think so."

"I can see how her escapade would shake you up. But she's safely here now, so you should make the most of the chance to visit with her."

His irritation seemed to deepen. "It did not *shake me up.* I'm merely concerned for her safety. Undertaking such a journey, without letting anyone know what she was about, was foolhardy and reckless. It only proves how much of a child she still is."

Before Daisy could respond, the downstairs bell

sounded, indicating someone had stopped by the office. Everett tugged at his cuff. "Don't let Abigail get in your way. If she becomes a bother, send her down to me."

Daisy returned to her ironing, pondering the pointed look Everett had given her before he left the room. She supposed, on the surface, her trip here bore some similarities to Abigail's. She'd slipped away, traveling on her own to a destination where she wasn't expected.

But there were important differences. She was much older than Abigail. Her trip had been shorter. And she'd covered familiar ground, so she knew what she'd be facing. So there'd been nothing foolhardy or reckless about her journey.

"Is he gone yet?"

Daisy looked up to see Abigail peeking out of her room.

"If you're speaking of your brother," she answered dryly, "he's downstairs."

"Good." Abigail strode into the kitchen with a let's-be-friends smile. "It's probably best if I give him a little time to get used to my being here before we encounter each other again."

Daisy held her gaze. "He's only looking out for you, you know."

"Oh, I know." Abigail waved a hand. "But I'm fifteen now, and he still treats me like I'm six."

"You could be sixty, and you'd still be his little sister."

The girl traced a pattern on the table. "I thought he'd be just a little glad to see me."

Daisy took pity on the forlorn-looking girl. "He is. Just give him time to get over the fright you gave him."

Then she tried for a cheerier subject. "Did you really travel all the way here from Boston by yourself?"

Abigail preened a bit. "I did. And it was the grandest adventure. I know Everett won't ever look at it that way, but I've never done anything so frightening and so exhilarating in my life."

Daisy didn't know whether to consider Everett's sister brave or henwitted—perhaps she was a little of both.

Abigail sat at the table and studied Daisy. "Tell me about yourself. How long have you been working for my brother?"

What was Abigail thinking? "I moved to town about ten days ago. Your brother has been kind enough to help me get settled and find work."

"Kind—Everett?"

Daisy nodded. "I think of your brother as a very kind man, don't you?"

"Oh, yes, Everett has a very big heart. But he usually hides it well. I'm just surprised you saw it."

Daisy focused on her ironing. "Like I said, he's been good to me."

"Do you know what happened to his hand? It looks really bad."

Daisy's stomach clenched. "That was my fault."

Abigail's brow furrowed. "What happened?"

Would Everett's sister look at her differently when she heard her confession? "He was helping me empty a heavy laundry tub yesterday when Kip tripped him up, and he ended up falling in the mud and dropping the thing on his hand."

The girl's eyes rounded. "Oh, my. I'm sure that was a sight to see."

Daisy blinked. That wasn't at all the reaction she'd expected. "It wasn't funny—he was seriously injured."

"You're right, nothing funny about it at all." But the twinkle in Abigail's eyes told a different story. "He landed in the mud, you say?"

Daisy tried to keep a straight face. "Yes. And I marched him through town to the doc's office without letting him change."

Skepticism mixed with the amusement in Abigail's expression. "My *very* fastidious brother did that without a fuss?"

This time she didn't attempt to hide the grin. "I never said he didn't fuss."

"Oh, I wish I'd been here to see that." She gave Daisy an appreciative smile. "My brother may have finally met his match."

Daisy's treacherous mind went immediately to thoughts of the two embraces they'd shared, and she barely managed to make a noncommittal response.

Luckily, Abigail changed the subject. "If you just moved here, where were you before?"

It seemed Abigail had her brother's reporter instincts. "I traveled around a lot with my father. He's a peddler."

"A peddler—how exciting. So my little jaunt here would have been nothing to you."

Another unexpected reaction. "Oh, I wouldn't say that. We traveled a lot, but didn't cover nearly the territory you did on your trip. And I usually didn't do it alone." No point mentioning her little three-day walk to get here.

"Still, you must have seen some interesting sights in your travels. Up until now, I haven't spent much time outside of Boston."

"Well, you've certainly made up for it now."

"I have, haven't I? Now if I can just convince Everett to let me stay."

Daisy silently wished the girl good luck with that. She had a feeling having Abigail here would be good for Everett, and for Abigail, as well.

She also had a selfish reason to be glad Abigail was here. Because if it accomplished nothing else, Abigail's presence would give her and Everett something to focus on besides the awkward aftermath of last night's encounter.

Chapter Eleven

Saturday morning, Abigail's belongings arrived from Boston. It took the delivery boy over a dozen trips up and down the stairs to get all of her trunks and crates transported to the sitting room.

After he'd paid the boy and sent him on his way, Everett headed upstairs to see how his sister was faring with sorting and stowing her things. He could hear her and Daisy before he ever topped the stairs.

"That sure is a mighty fine collection of books," Daisy said.

"Oh, that's nothing," Abigail replied. "Everett's collection is even more impressive."

"In both quantity *and* quality," he said dryly as he topped the stairs. Daisy was in the kitchen peeling carrots while Abigail sat on the floor of the sitting room, surrounded by her newly arrived belongings. He winced when he saw her belongings cluttering every piece of furniture and most of the available floor space.

Abigail gave him a smile. "There you are. And speaking of books, where *are* yours? Don't tell me you left them behind when you moved here."

That was something he and his sister had in common: their love of books. "Of course not. Some are in my room and the rest are in crates down in the storeroom. I just haven't gotten around to unpacking them."

"Why ever not? You've been here almost a year now."

Everett raised a brow. "Contrary to what you may think, little sister, setting up a newspaper from scratch is a lot of work, regardless of how small the town or the paper."

He moderated his tone. "Besides, I'm hoping to have a new job somewhere else soon, so I didn't see the point in unpacking more than what I needed to live."

Abigail frowned up at him. "Why would you want to do that? Move, I mean. Don't you like it here?"

He tried to strike a diplomatic tone. "It's fine for what it is—a small country town. But the big city is where we belong." He was aware of Daisy listening, and wondered what she made of that. Then he became irritated with himself for caring.

Abigail gave his arm a mock punch, bringing his thoughts back to the conversation at hand. "Don't be such a snob. Besides, if that's the way you feel, why did you come here in the first place?"

Again he had to choose his words carefully. "As I said at the time, my former editor and I had a parting of the ways, and I was ready to move on to something new. When I heard about the opportunity to open a newspaper here, that seemed like the perfect *temporary* solution."

All of which was true. Hopefully, she'd never learn the rest of the story. "It's been a good experience—it's allowed me to learn all the inner workings of the newspaper business. But I never intended for this to be a permanent stop. I'm first and foremost a reporter, and I need to be in a big city where things are happening to report on and where there is a staff of more than one person to get the paper out."

"I'm sure there are lots of things happening here."

"You know what I mean, Abigail." He glanced toward Daisy and cleared his throat. "Now, I've made up my mind about this and it's not up for discussion. So let's change the subject, shall we?"

Abigail shrugged and went back to digging through her trunks.

Luckily, Daisy spoke up. "I still say that's a wealth of books. Between the two of you, you could open your own library. The only time I've seen that many books in one place was at my grandmother's house."

Everett heard that strange note in her voice that crept in whenever she mentioned her grandmother. He'd be very interested in learning the story behind that. Strictly from a reporter's perspective, of course.

"That was one thing I *did* enjoy about my time in New Orleans," Daisy said wistfully. "Access to all those books. I haven't had many chances since then to do much reading."

She was well-read? Everett wasn't sure why that surprised him. Some of his assumptions about her shifted, realigned. He'd seen glimpses of intelligence in her, of course—intelligence she downplayed with her rustic, straightforward way of speaking.

"You're more than welcome to look through my books," Abigail offered. "You can borrow any that strike your fancy."

Daisy's face lit up, making Everett regret he hadn't been the one to make the offer.

"Why, thank you," she said. "I don't have much free time right now, but as soon as I get my place set to rights I may take you up on that offer."

Everett stared pointedly at his sister. "That's another thing you'll not find in Turnabout. There are none of the civilized entertainments you're accustomed to—no libraries or bookstores, no theater or opera, not even a manicured park or conservatory."

His sister's smile wavered a moment, then she rallied. "There are several books I've been intending to reread. And I'm certain I can treat myself occasionally by ordering new titles from a catalog. As for the rest, there must be other amusements the locals indulge in, and I'm willing to experience new things."

"I understand they have town dances every few months," Daisy said, "and sometimes picnics on the ground after church services."

Abigail perked up immediately. "Oh, that sounds like fun! I do love picnics."

Everett shot Daisy a warning look. He was trying to give Abigail reasons to leave, not stay. "At the moment, you need to decide where you're going to store your things. It all needs to fit in your room or in the storeroom—and I warn you, I won't have you overcluttering my storeroom. What doesn't fit will need to be gotten rid of." He gave her a pointed look. "Unless, of course, we ship most of it back to Miss Haversham's to await your return."

Abigail lifted her chin. "That won't be necessary. In fact, I'm certain there are several of these items that I'll no longer require in my new life here."

How could he make his sister see that returning to school was the right thing to do? She obviously wasn't going to give any of his arguments serious consideration.

Could he recruit Daisy's help? Better question—should he?

Daisy placed the rolls on the table, then joined Everett and his sister. Yesterday, with Abigail sitting down to lunch with them, she had thought Everett would want to offer the blessing, but he had again deferred to her. So today, with only a quick glance his way for confirmation, she bowed her head and said, "Let us pray."

Once the amens were said and the bowls started around, Abigail cleared her throat and glanced at Everett. "I've been thinking about what you said earlier—about there being no source for books here. I'd imagine there are a number of people who would make use of a library if one were available."

Everett shrugged. "Perhaps. But the point is moot. I don't see that happening in the foreseeable future. So there's no point getting your hopes up."

She gave him a sideways look. "Maybe we can do something to change that."

Everett eyed her suspiciously. "What do you mean?"

"What if I opened a circulating library myself?"

Daisy got caught up in Abigail's proposal. "What a wonderful idea. It perfectly complements your brother's newspaper business. And you're right—I can't imagine folks not wanting to take advantage of such a wonderful opportunity."

"Nonsense." If one didn't notice the sternness in Everett's tone, his expression left no room for doubt. "You don't know the first thing about managing such an operation."

"Oh, but I do." Abigail didn't seem intimidated by her brother's lack of enthusiasm. "I used part of the allowance you sent me to join a circulating library near school, and I became good friends with Miss Teel, the librarian." She leaned forward. "I also spent a lot of time in the school library. Miss Abernathy, the teacher who managed the library, allowed me to help her in exchange for my getting first look at any new books that came in. So you see, I do have experience."

Daisy could tell Everett wasn't convinced, but she found the idea of having access to all those books downright exciting.

"Assuming you could manage such an undertaking," Everett said, "where do you propose to set up this library? There's not much room downstairs, and I refuse to have folks trooping up and down the stairs to our living quarters."

Abigail gave him a breezy smile. "It wouldn't take up much room. I could start with just a couple of bookshelves along one wall, and a drawer in one of your file cabinets to keep all the records."

He shook his head. "I don't think—"

Daisy couldn't hold her tongue any longer. "That doesn't sound like much space at all. If your brother doesn't have room for it, you can use my place. After all, I plan to be one of your first customers."

Abigail rewarded her with a dazzling smile. "Do you mean it? I promise I won't take up too much space, and you can take a portion of my earnings for rent payment."

Daisy waved that offer aside. "Don't worry about that. In fact, the more I think on it, the more it seems good business sense on my part. It'll get folks used to coming in and out of my place so that when I'm ready to open my restaurant, they'll already be familiar with it."

She became aware that Everett was glowering at her, but couldn't find it in herself to be sorry. She liked Abigail's idea, as well as her enthusiasm for it, and could see no harm in it. She gave him a sideways glance, then focused back on Abigail. "Once your brother gets that sour look off his face, you might even be able to charm him into giving you an advertisement in his newspaper."

Abigail laughed delightedly, then turned to her brother. "You need to make certain you hold on to her."

Daisy's cheeks warmed as Abigail's words reminded her of those two embraces earlier in the week.

She risked a quick glance Everett's way. His expression didn't reflect anything but irritation with his sister.

That was a good thing. Wasn't it?

As Everett went downstairs, the lunchtime conversation played back in his head. He had to admit, Abigail's idea of a lending library had merit. It was resourceful, ingenious and enterprising all at the same time. He almost hated not to give her the approving go-ahead she so obviously wanted. But it wasn't a good idea to allow her to set down any sort of roots or strong ties here in Turnabout—not if he ever hoped to convince her to return to Miss Haversham's school. Which he fully intended to do.

He'd have to have a word with Daisy. She'd obviously meant well when she offered Abigail the use of her place, but she needed to learn to stay out of anything involving his sister. She wasn't the best example of biddable and ladylike behavior for his sister to follow.

And what was this about his "sour look?" Is that how Daisy and Abigail saw him? He took exception to that. They should understand his strictures were motivated by a keen sense of purpose and responsibility. He was every bit as capable of enjoying life as the next man. He was just more circumspect in how he handled it.

Unbidden, Abigail's artless comment about making certain he held on to Daisy popped into his thoughts. It conjured up images of him literally holding on to her. He and Daisy hadn't spoken of it, of course. That would have given it more importance than it merited. But that didn't mean he hadn't thought about it, thought about it much more than he should have. And thought about how it would have felt to follow through and kiss her.

What about Daisy? Did she think about it at all? If so, in what light?

"So what's put that perplexed expression on your face?"

Everett looked up to see Adam staring at him, an amused smile playing on his lips.

How long had he been standing there?

Everett assumed his most dignified demeanor. "I wasn't expecting you to come by since it's Saturday. Are you so eager to answer my last move?"

Adam's expression indicated he knew Everett had avoided answering his question. "I just wanted to let you know that we won't be having our usual luncheon gathering after services tomorrow. Reggie's got it in her head to take a quick trip out to the cabin while she's still up to the trip. We're heading out in an hour or so."

Everett didn't understand what Reggie found so appealing about that rustic cabin of hers way out in the back of beyond. He and the others who'd traveled here from Philadelphia had spent their first night there upon their arrival in Turnabout. It was not an experience he cared to repeat.

More to the point, Reggie was less than two months from her confinement date. "Is that wise?"

"I'm not keen on it, but you know how Reggie can be when she sets her mind on something. I spoke to Dr. Pratt, and he's given the go-ahead. And of course, we'll have Mrs. Peavy with us."

Everett certainly intended to be firmer with his own wife when the time came. But this matter was really none of his business. "I wish you a good journey. I'll let Miss Johnson know."

"Thanks. Like I said, this is going to be a quick trip. We'll be back Monday afternoon, so Jack and Ira will be here to deliver the papers on Tuesday."

As Everett headed upstairs to deliver the news to Daisy, he figured he'd take Abigail to the hotel dining room for Sunday lunch. And it would only be polite to include Daisy in the invitation, as well.

Daisy, however, had a different idea.

"Why don't we plan a picnic?"

Everett frowned. He wasn't much for eating on a blanket spread on the ground. But before he could say anything, Abigail took up the idea.

"Oh, what fun. And it'll give me the opportunity to see more of this area. I've been cooped up inside since I arrived here."

"That was only yesterday," Everett said dryly. "And I thought we'd go down to the hotel diner—"

"Oh, Everett, please," Abigail pleaded. "A picnic

sounds ever so much more fun. For once, forget about being so stuffy and proper and just enjoy yourself."

Everett's mouth snapped shut, and he felt his jaw tighten. He looked from Abigail to Daisy, then tugged on his cuffs, one after the other. "Very well, if that's what the two of you prefer, then a picnic it is."

Abigail popped up from her seat and gave him an enthusiastic hug.

But it was Daisy's gaze he sought. And the warm approval he saw there made him glad he'd given in.

Sunday morning dawned sunny and warm—perfect picnic weather. Daisy had been in good spirits ever since yesterday when Everett made his unexpected capitulation about the picnic. Perhaps there was hope for him, after all.

She joined Everett and Abigail as they walked to church. Almost immediately they encountered Chance, and Abigail greeted him like an old friend. "Mr. Dawson, how wonderful to see you again."

Chance tipped his hat. "Good morning, Miss Abigail, Miss Johnson. Don't you ladies look lovely."

Abigail held out one side of her skirt and swished it, giving him a saucy smile. "Why, thank you."

Daisy noticed Everett had a very big brotherly frown on his face.

"How do you like your stay thus far?" Chance asked as he smiled Abigail's way.

"Very much, thank you."

"And will you be here long?"

"I'd like to stay indefinitely, if I can convince my brother not to exile me back to Boston."

"Abigail." There was a warning note in Everett's tone.

"Ah, big brothers," Chance said sympathetically. "I have three of them. They seem to always think they know best—whether they do or not."

Abigail gave him a broad smile. "Exactly!"

Everett didn't appear amused. "Please don't let us keep you, Chance," he said stiffly. "I'm sure our sedate pace is a bit tame for you."

While Everett's tone was polite, Daisy could hear the gritted-teeth undertones in his voice.

But Chance merely smiled. "Not at all. I'm enjoying the company of the two prettiest ladies in town."

Daisy decided it was time to give Everett something else to focus on before his expression locked in a perpetual glower. "Mr. Dawson," she said, "I understand you have a motorized carriage."

"Please call me Chance. And yes, I do. Let me know if either of you ladies would like to take a ride in it sometime." He glanced Everett's way. "And naturally, you could come along, too."

Daisy gave a mental wince. Seemed she'd made matters worse instead of better. Trying to avoid any additional opportunity for Chance to flirt with Abigail, Daisy maneuvered things so that she and Chance walked ahead, leaving Everett to escort his sister.

Chance gave Daisy an amused, knowing look, but he went along with the plan, and the rest of the stroll passed pleasantly enough.

Later, as they exited church after the service, Everett introduced Abigail to Reverend Harper.

"I'm pleased to meet you, Abigail. Your brother has become a valued member of our community. I hope you're here for a nice long visit."

Daisy wondered if the reverend would one day be able to say the same about her.

"Yes, sir," Abigail answered. "In fact, I'm hoping to make this my home."

Home. The word resonated inside Daisy with that same longing that had brought her here in the first place. Did it mean the same thing to Abigail? Right then and there, she determined to do everything she could to support Abigail's stand.

Everett suppressed a sigh. Why did Abigail insist on pressing the matter so publicly? "We haven't decided the length of her stay."

Reverend Harper looked from one to the other, then smiled indulgently. "Well, at any rate, I look forward to seeing you here again next Sunday."

"Yes, sir, I look forward to it, as well."

"Wonderful." The reverend looked up and waved someone over. "Here's my daughter, Constance. Let me introduce you."

As Abigail and the Harper girl latched on to each other like long-lost sisters, Everett found himself looking for Daisy. Was she still with that pup, Chance?

He spied her standing alone a few feet away, eyeing him with an exasperated look. What had gotten into her now?

It didn't take him long to find out.

"You have to quit glowering at your sister. Folks will think you don't like her. And so will she."

Had he been glowering? "I'm more frustrated than angry." He took a deep breath and schooled his expression. "It's important that she return to school as soon as possible. The longer she's here, the more ties she'll make."

"Would it really be so terrible if she didn't go back?"

"She needs to complete her education."

Daisy gave him an even look. "There are many important lessons to be learned outside the schoolroom. Perhaps it's time she focused on those."

"There will be time enough for that later." He could see Daisy still wasn't convinced. "And she needs to learn some discipline. What sort of lesson will she learn if she gets rewarded for her reckless actions?"

"I'm not talking about rewarding her—simply listening to her and giving her what she needs, not what she wants."

"And you think you know what she needs better than I do?"

"She needs the same thing we all do. She needs to know she is loved and wanted, that she belongs."

Abigail came rushing up just then, cutting off any response he might have made. Which was just as well, because for once he had no words.

Chapter Twelve

Daisy spread the blanket under a large oak while Everett took care of the horse and buggy. Abigail had run off with Kip to explore the meadow and nearby stream almost before the buggy had come to a complete stop.

As Daisy unpacked the basket of food, she smiled at the sound of Abigail's exclamations of delight and Kip's playful barking. These were the kind of outings a girl Abigail's age needed, not more museums and operas. Would Everett be able to see that?

He came over and stood stiffly at the edge of the blanket.

"Have a seat," she said conversationally. "I'll have the food set out in a minute."

Everett sat, but didn't seem any more at ease. He shaded his eyes as he glanced his sister's way. "What's Abigail doing?"

She paused and gave him a pointed look. "Exploring. Playing. It's what children do."

Everett frowned, still keeping his eyes on Abigail. "She's fifteen, not eight."

"She's still a child. And I'm not certain just how much playtime she's had in her life."

This time his gaze swung around to meet hers. "You know nothing about Abigail's childhood."

"And how much of it do you know?" Daisy wished the words back as soon as they left her lips. Everett's expression didn't change, but there had been the briefest flicker in his gaze that told her her words had hit their mark. "I'm sorry. I had no right—"

"Forget it. What are we having for lunch?"

It seemed the subject was closed. "Nothing fancy. Cold ham, cheese, bread, apples and lemonade. I also brought the leftover pecan pie from yesterday."

"Sounds good. I'll go let Abigail know we're ready to eat."

Daisy sighed as she watched him walk away. It was obvious Everett truly loved his sister. But it was equally obvious he had a blind spot when it came to what she needed.

A few moments later, Abigail and Kip came racing over, with Everett following behind at a sedate walk. "This is the most marvelous place," the girl said as she plopped down on the blanket. "I actually saw some turtles by the stream, and Kip chased a rabbit into the brush."

Daisy smiled. "That's what's so great about picnics—you never know what the day will bring." She started passing plates as Everett walked up. "Now, why don't we eat and then we can see what other entertainments we can find?"

Most of the conversation during lunch was led by Abigail, who kept up a constant stream of chatter about what she'd seen during her short exploration.

Daisy noticed Everett watching his sister speculatively. What was he thinking?

During a lull in the conversation, Daisy looked up at the sky and pointed. “Look, a rabbit.”

Abigail immediately started looking around. “Where?”

“Up there. See that cloud? If you turn your head just a little bit, it looks like the head and ears of a rabbit.” Then she grinned at the girl. “It’s a game I played with my mother when I was younger. We’d see who could find the best image in the clouds. Why don’t you give it a try?”

“Okay.” Abigail leaned back, bracing herself on her arms, and studied the sky. Then she pointed. “There. That one looks like a lady’s hat with a feather.”

“Oh, I can see it. Very nice.”

Abigail gave her brother a nudge. “You try, Everett. It’s fun.”

But Everett shook his head. “You ladies have your fun. I’ll watch.”

“Oh, come on, try it.”

Daisy gave in to an impish impulse. “Don’t bother your brother, Abigail. I don’t think he understands whimsy.”

Everett straightened and gave her an affronted look. She raised a brow in challenge, and their gazes locked for several heartbeats. Finally, he gave in.

“Very well. Let’s see…”

Daisy didn’t miss the pleased expression on Abigail’s face. Did Everett notice?

A moment later, he pointed. “That one looks like a rather plump maple leaf.”

"Oh, it does," Abigail exclaimed. "See, you're good at this."

Daisy smiled as she slipped a morsel of ham to Kip. The smile on Everett's face as he accepted Abigail's praise was a fine sight, indeed.

"If everyone's had enough to eat, I'll put the leftovers back in the basket so the bugs don't get at it."

Abigail immediately straightened. "Let me help."

But Daisy waved her off. "I can handle this. Why don't you show your brother that turtle you saw earlier?"

"Okay." She stood and tugged on her brother's arm. "Wait until you see it, Everett. It was the most amazing thing. But it's kind of small so you'll have to look real close."

Everett glanced Daisy's way. There was something unreadable in his eyes. Then with a nod, he turned back to his sister and allowed her to lead him toward the stream.

Daisy watched them, pleased with the way Everett was thawing, at least in regard to his sister. If nothing else, the girl would have some very pleasant memories to take back to Boston with her.

As she repacked the basket, her treacherous mind began to wonder if this thawing would seep over into other areas of his life, as well....

Monday dawned as a gray, drizzly day. The kind of day, Daisy decided, that cried out for a hearty soup. She hummed as she chopped the vegetables to add to the chicken and broth already simmering on the stove.

She glanced over her shoulder as Abigail returned upstairs and plopped down in one of the kitchen chairs.

"Is something wrong?" she asked the unhappy-looking girl.

"Everett is in one of his more grumpy moods. He's having trouble with the layout for the front page, and apparently my presence is a distraction."

Daisy hid a grin. The girl was definitely not the shy, retiring type.

"Is there something I can help *you* with?" Abigail asked hopefully.

Daisy didn't think Everett would appreciate her putting his sister to work doing things he paid her to do. "Thank you, but I have it under control."

"That's the same thing Everett tells me when I try to help him." The girl sighed dramatically. "I feel so useless."

If it wasn't raining, she'd let Abigail take Kip for a walk. "You could always pull out one of those books of yours and read for a while."

"I suppose." Abigail's tone carried a decided lack of enthusiasm. And she didn't stir from her seat.

Daisy reached for another topic. "How are you coming with your circulating library idea?"

That drew out a bit more energy. "I mentioned it to Constance yesterday, and she was very excited. She said she'd be happy to help me set everything up."

"So you two are getting along well?"

"Oh, yes." Abigail sat up straighter, her expression growing more animated. "We only talked for a few minutes after church, but I can tell already that we're going to be great friends. She invited me to join the choir so she'd have someone else her age there." Abigail's expression turned mischievous. "I told her I would, but she might regret the invitation. My music teacher absolutely despaired of ever teaching me to carry a tune."

"Surely you're exaggerating."

"Only a little. But I like to sing, and I think it'll be nice to have a new friend here."

The girl was quickly going about setting down roots, just as Everett had feared. And speaking of Everett…

"Have you convinced your brother to let you go through with your plans yet?"

Abigail's expression returned to its former gloomy state. "He still thinks I'm not up to the task."

Daisy wasn't sure she agreed with him, but she was reluctant to interfere. "That's too bad. I'm sure he's trying to do what he thinks is best for you."

"Good intentions don't necessarily equate to right thinking."

Daisy agreed, but refrained from comment.

Abigail sat up straighter. "Maybe, if I got everything all set up, he'd realize how serious I am."

Daisy kept her expression neutral. "You know your brother better than I do." Seeing Abigail's hopeful expression, she relented slightly. "Why don't you take a look at the space I offered you and decide how you want to set it up? I'm sure Kip would be glad to keep you company."

Abigail hopped up and moved to the doorway. "What do you say, Kip?" She stooped to scratch his ears. "Want to help me check things out?"

Kip stood, tail wagging enthusiastically.

Daisy smiled at the suddenly energetic pair. "I figure you can set up your library on the wall that backs up to your brother's office. There are a few pieces of makeshift furniture in my storeroom, along with some crates that were sound enough to save from the scrap heap. The layout over there is similar to the one on this side. Help yourself to anything you think you can use." Surely Everett wouldn't find anything to scold either of them about if Abigail just looked around.

"Thanks." Abigail was already moving away. "I'm sure it'll all be perfect."

Daisy added more vegetables and seasoning to the pot, then smiled as she heard Abigail rattle down the stairs. Everett's sister was so excited about her venture—almost as much as she herself was about someday opening her restaurant. Come to think of it, Everett was treating his sister's idea as dismissively as he had hers.

She frowned. Despite Everett's best efforts, Abigail was already building ties here. And if he was going to continue to leave his sister to her own devices, then surely she had a right to find a way to occupy her time. And if that resulted in her establishing her library, then surely there could be no harm in it.

Just like there'd be nothing wrong with her opening a restaurant.

Perhaps she did have reason to interfere, after all.

Chapter Thirteen

An hour later, Abigail returned with a decided spring to her step.

"What do you think?" Daisy asked. "Will the place serve your needs?"

"It'll be perfect." Abigail sat at the table, her eyes sparkling. "I'll need some actual bookcases eventually, but I can probably stack my books on trunks and crates to start with. Hopefully the mercantile will have card-stock that I can use to make my individual book and patron records. And I can find a bandbox or some such to keep my files in."

It sounded as if Abigail had given this a lot of thought. "As I said, you're welcome to use anything you find in my storeroom until you can acquire better."

"Thanks. Once I've earned a little money, I can hire someone to build shelves."

Daisy found herself admiring the girl's spirit. "So what do you see as your next step?"

"I'll need to catalog my books. Then I'll set up my system for tracking who has what. Fortunately, I already have notebooks that I should be able to make do with."

"That sounds like quite an undertaking." It was also something Abigail could occupy herself with before setting up the physical library.

"Yes, but only to set it all up. Once I have it in place, it will be done." She leaned her elbows on the table. "Miss Abernathy and Miss Teel used different systems, but I think I prefer Miss Abernathy's. She arranged the nonfiction books by subject and the fiction books by author."

"That's similar to the way my grandmother had her books arranged."

Abigail gave her a speculative look. "I don't mean to pry, but you get this strange tone in your voice when you mention your grandmother."

The girl was perceptive. "I was never very comfortable in my grandmother's home. Everything there was very formal, very elegant and fancy. And I was anything but."

"You have something much better than all that," the girl said earnestly. "You have a natural warmth and grace about you that puts everyone at ease."

Daisy blinked at the unexpected compliment. "What a nice thing to say."

"Oh, it's true." Then Abigail grimaced. "But I know what you mean. It sounds like Miss Haversham's school. I felt as if I didn't have room to breathe, to be myself."

Daisy felt that surge of sympathetic kinship again. If only Everett could hear what his sister was saying, both the words and the tone, maybe he wouldn't be so quick to send her back.

Everett had paused halfway up the stairs, unabashedly eavesdropping when he heard Daisy talking about her grandmother. But her words, rather than satisfying his curiosity, only stirred it further.

Abigail's words, on the other hand, gave him something else to think about. Had she truly felt so stifled? Or was it merely adolescent theatrics?

He resumed his climb. "What are you two up to?"

Daisy smiled brightly. "Just girl-talk. You're right on time—I'll have the meal on the table in a moment." She moved to the cupboard to fetch a large serving bowl.

Abigail popped up. "I'll set the table while you dish everything up."

Everett watched the easy camaraderie between his sister and Daisy with mixed emotions. He'd become less judgmental of Daisy, but he still didn't want the peddler's daughter's rough edges to rub off on his sister. He'd worked too hard to see that she turned into a young lady who would be welcome in any society drawing room.

This was yet another reason why the sooner he could move out of Turnabout and into more civilized surroundings, the better. It was time he started putting a few more feelers out to larger newspapers.

Once they were seated and Daisy had said grace with her usual down-to-earth eloquence, they dug into the meal.

Abigail passed the basket of rolls to Daisy. "I saw the pretty embroidery work hanging in your place," she said with a smile. "Did you do that yourself?"

Daisy shook her head. "Thank you, but no. That's some of my mother's work."

Everett frowned at his sister. "What were you doing at Daisy's place?"

Abigail flushed guiltily. "I was looking for something to do earlier, so I went over there to look around."

"That was presumptuous, don't you think?"

"Oh, I didn't mind," Daisy said quickly. "In fact, I think I may have suggested it."

A look passed between the two of them that gave Everett the feeling they were up to something.

"Besides," Daisy added quickly, "Kip was glad of the company."

"About that, Everett." Abigail straightened. "Why won't you let Kip over here? He seems such a well-behaved animal."

"We've had this conversation before. Animals belong outdoors, not in one's home." This was one point he intended to hold firm on. "If Daisy chooses to keep her pet in her home, that's her business, but that doesn't mean I should make an exception for my home."

"But you're being so unreasonable." Abigail gave him a mutinous look.

"Don't argue on my account, Abigail," Daisy said quickly. "It's truly no hardship for Kip to stay on my side of the wall."

Abigail huffed and then dipped her spoon in her bowl. "I still think it's unnecessarily restrictive."

Everett didn't respond, but neither did he relent. Getting attached to that dog would just be one more tie she'd mourn when she had to leave. And he knew from experience just how quickly one could grow fond of a pet. No, he would not put his sister through that.

Once the meal was over and Everett returned to his office, Daisy began clearing the table. She still had so much work to do at her own place, and she was eager to get back to it.

Abigail wandered over to one of her trunks of books. “It’s kind of difficult to decide where to start.”

Daisy was feeling guilty about hiding their activities from Everett. “When are you going to discuss your plans with your brother again?”

Abigail grimaced. “I’m not sure. You saw how he was with Kip. Once he makes his mind up about something, it’s hard to change it.” She gave Daisy a just-between-us look. “I need to pick my moment carefully.”

Daisy understood the sentiment, but firmly believed there needed to be more honest communication between the siblings. “Well, you might want to give it a shot before you put too much more effort into it.”

“I don’t know. Maybe if he could see it first…”

“What do you mean?”

Abigail lifted a couple of books from her trunk. “Maybe I should set the stage—you know, arrange some books on the table and set up a few entries in my catalog. If Everett could actually see how well I’ve thought this through, and how serious I am, rather than just having him imagine it, he might be more inclined to approve the idea.”

“I see.” And she did. Because, behind all of Abigail’s scheming, she saw a girl who was trying to earn the approval of her brother.

“So it’s all right with you if I bring some of my books downstairs and set the stage for him?”

“Of course.” Everett would probably think she was interfering again, but Daisy thought Abigail deserved a shot at convincing him. And, assuming Everett didn’t dismiss it out of hand, perhaps it would get them talking to each other the way they had at the picnic yesterday. "Once I get done with these dishes, I'll be happy to help you."

Abigail shook her head with a smile. "Thank you, but I know you have your own projects to get to. I can take care of this."

The girl disappeared into her room, then reappeared with an armload of books. She smiled at Daisy as she headed for the adjoining door, giving Kip a friendly pat as she passed.

Daisy rubbed her cheek thoughtfully. How was Everett going to react when he saw how far his sister had taken her idea?

Daisy froze as she heard a loud cry and a clatter. A heartbeat later she was dashing through the doorway, a prayer racing through her head. "Abigail! Abigail, are you okay?"

No answer.

When she reached the top of the stairs, Daisy found out why. Abigail lay crumpled at the foot of the stairs amid a scattering of books. Kip was at her side, whimpering and nudging her gently with his nose.

Yelling over her shoulder for Everett, Daisy raced down the stairs, her pulse thudding loudly in her ears. *Dear God, please let her be all right. Please, please, please.*

Just as Daisy reached the foot of the stairs, Abigail stirred and groaned. "Abigail, sweetheart, are you okay?"

The girl's eyes fluttered open. "I… I think so." She winced and groaned again. "What happened?"

"You must have fallen." How far had she tumbled? How badly was she injured?

"What happened?" The staccato question came from Everett as he clattered down the stairs.

Everett aged ten years in the time it took him to get to the bottom of the stairs. He knelt beside Abigail, searching her much-too-pale face for signs of pain or disorientation. If she was seriously hurt, he'd never forgive himself. "Don't try to move." He heard the gruffness in his voice but was powerless to alter it. "Daisy," he said without taking his eyes from his sister, "please get Dr. Pratt. Make sure he understands he needs to come immediately."

With a nod and a last squeeze of Abigail's hand, Daisy sprinted off.

Everett gently moved the hair from Abigail's forehead. "Tell me where you hurt."

She grimaced, and one hand fluttered. "I feel sore all over, but I think I'll be all right if you just give me a minute to sit up and take stock."

He held her down as she tried to sit up. "Lie still until Dr. Pratt has had a chance to look you over."

"Please, I'd like to sit up. Lying here is undignified, and I promise to let you know if something seems amiss."

Everett hesitated a moment, but couldn't hold firm against the tears welling in her eyes. Keeping his hand square on her back, he held ready to lend additional support if she gave him the least cause to suspect she needed it as she awkwardly maneuvered herself into a sitting position.

"Ow!"

He searched her face. "What is it? Where does it hurt?"

She cupped her left wrist in her right hand. "I think I may have injured my wrist." She smiled, but he could see the pain in her expression. "It looks like we may have matching injuries."

Before Everett could question her further, Daisy and Dr. Pratt rushed in.

The doctor set his bag down and knelt beside Abigail, across from Everett. "Hello, young lady. I understand you took a tumble."

Abigail gave him a wavery smile. "Yes, sir. Not very graceful of me, was it?"

"Don't be embarrassed. You're not the first of my patients to take such a tumble, and I dare say you won't be the last. Now, let's have a look, shall we?"

"Her left wrist is bothering her." Everett's gut was still churning. *Please God, let that be the extent of it.*

"Well, then, let's have a look at that first."

Eunice Ortolon, the woman who ran the boardinghouse, bustled in from the sidewalk. "Hello. I don't mean to intrude, but I saw Doc come by all in a rush. I hope no one's hurt."

Everett gritted his teeth as the town busybody studied them with avidly curious eyes. He really didn't have the patience to deal with that kind of distraction right now. But good manners won out. "My sister fell down the stairs," he said.

The woman placed her hand to her heart. "Oh, my goodness. The poor dear. Is there anything I can do to help?"

He shook his head. "Thank you for the kind offer, but now that the doctor is here I think we have all the help we need." He nodded dismissively and deliberately turned from her to the doctor.

Dr. Pratt stood. "At first glance she seems to have nothing worse than a sprained wrist and some bumps and bruises, but I'd like to conduct a more thorough examination." He gave Everett a pointed look. "Perhaps we can find a place where she'll be more comfortable while I do so."

Everett nodded, eager to get his sister to a place with more privacy. "Of course. We can take her to her bedchamber—no, make that mine—the bed is larger." He scooped his sister up and stood.

Abigail protested. "Really, Everett, I'm perfectly capable of walking."

"Not until Dr. Pratt has completed his examination."

"But your hand—"

"Is healing nicely. Now hush and be still."

Daisy headed for the staircase. "I'll make sure the room is ready. Doctor, if you'll just come this way."

Everett followed the two of them more slowly, careful not to jar his sister. The whole time he held her, he wanted to squeeze her tight, to protect her against other dangers. This was the second time in a matter of days that she'd given him a fright. He was her brother and her guardian—he was supposed to protect her, but it didn't appear he was doing a very good job of it. Why did his well-ordered world seem to be crumbling around him lately?

By the time he reached his bedchamber, Daisy had the covers turned down and the pillows plumped up. Once Abigail was settled in, Dr. Pratt turned to him and Daisy. "Why don't you leave me and Miss Abigail? I'll call you when I've finished."

Everett wanted to protest. He wasn't ready to let Abigail out of his sight.

But Daisy touched his arm lightly and gave him a reassuring nod. "Let's let the doc do his job."

Everett gave a short nod. "Of course."

As he and Daisy stepped out of the room, however, he received yet another jolt of surprise. Mrs. Ortolon stood in his kitchen, eyeing the place speculatively. Apparently, rather than leave when he'd dismissed her, she had followed them upstairs.

"Is there anything I can do to help?" she asked with a bright smile.

Everett struggled to maintain his composure. "That's very thoughtful, but as I said, I think we have it under control now."

"Of course." Her gaze shifted from one to the other of them in a way that set the hair on the nape of his neck vibrating. What did that look mean? What was she thinking?

Then, with a mental groan, it suddenly hit him how compromising this must look to her. The doors between Daisy's and his living quarters were propped wide open. Daisy had entered his place from hers without hesitation, had entered *his bedchamber* without hesitation. He knew it had all been perfectly innocent, that Daisy's only thought had been for Abigail, but one could see any number of scenarios in this, and not all of them were entirely innocent.

Perhaps he was reading too much into the situation, but he didn't think so. But there was no way to go back and unring this bell now.

Mrs. Ortolon patted her hair. "I suppose I'll get out of your way. I do hope, Mr. Fulton, that you'll let me know if I can help in any way, won't you?"

"Of course." He had no doubt whatsoever that when

she spread word of Abigail's accident, there would be something more to the story than the bare facts.

There was nothing he could do about that now, however, and there was still Abigail to worry about. He stared at his bedchamber door and raked a hand through his hair. How badly was she hurt? This would never have happened if she'd stayed put in Boston where she belonged.

Needing a target for his pent-up worries, he rounded on Daisy. "How did this happen?" he asked stiffly.

Daisy touched her collar. "I didn't see the actual fall, but she was carrying an armload of books and apparently tripped on the stairs."

He made a sharp, dismissive movement with his hands. "That much I already figured out. What I'm asking is, what was she doing carrying those books on your stairs in the first place?"

"She was at loose ends and decided to work toward setting up her circulating library—"

That confounded library again! "I knew you two were up to something when I saw you earlier. She's been working on this behind my back, and you knew about it." He saw the flicker of guilt in her expression. "How could you have encouraged this?"

"Actually, it's more that I didn't *discourage* it."

Did she honestly want to nitpick with him?

She waved helplessly. "I didn't think it would hurt—"

"No, you *didn't* think." He saw her wince and tried to moderate his tone. But she needed to understand that Abigail was *his* responsibility, and she shouldn't encourage her to find ways around his strictures. "Didn't it occur to you that I was deliberately negative about her little project to encourage her to return to school?"

Daisy's expression lost some of its defensiveness, and she stiffened. "Return to school? Have you heard anything at all of what your sister's told you on that subject?"

"Abigail is a child trying to get out of school. I'm thinking about what's best for her. She belongs in a more refined environment than what Turnabout can provide."

Her face colored—was it embarrassment or anger? "Do you know anything at all about what it is your sister wants out of life? Or are you only concerned with what *you* want out of her life?"

The woman was definitely out of line. "I suppose, based on your entire three days of knowing Abigail, you know better than I what's best for her."

"Apparently so."

Such unmitigated conceit. "I disagree. And I'll thank you to remember that I am her brother and guardian."

"As if you'd let either her or me forget that."

"And another thing. She shouldn't have been carting heavy books down those stairs. I wouldn't be surprised to learn that that fool dog of yours tripped her up."

"You leave Kip out of this."

"Only if you keep him out of our way."

Before she could respond, the bedchamber door opened. They dropped the argument to turn their attention to Dr. Pratt.

Everett reached him in a few quick strides. "How is she?"

The doctor closed the door behind him and waved Everett back toward the sitting room. "Her wrist is sprained and she's got a number of painful bruises and scrapes, so she'll be quite sore for the next few days.

You'll want to watch her closely for signs of a concussion, but otherwise I think she'll be just fine."

Some of the tension eased from Everett's body. "Do you have any special instructions for how I should care for her?"

"I've splinted her wrist, and she should take care when using that hand for a while." He gave them a reassuring smile. "As I said, keep a close eye on her the next day or two. Fetch me immediately if she has dizzy spells or nausea or seems at all disoriented. Other than that, bring her by my office in a week so I can check her wrist."

Everett shook the physician's hand. "Thank you, Doctor. Let me show you out."

Dr. Pratt held up his hand. "No need. I know my way. I'm sure your sister is anxious to see you." He gave Everett a knowing look. "And vice versa." With a wave, Dr. Pratt moved to the stairs.

Daisy met Everett's gaze. "You go on. I have dishes to wash."

With a nod, Everett strode quickly to his bedchamber. He was already regretting the tone, if not the words, he'd used with Daisy. Should he apologize? But he was already at the bedroom door, and his need to see his sister drove everything else from his mind.

"How are you feeling?" he asked. She sat up in bed and he studied her closely, relieved to see more color in her face than the last time he'd seen her.

Abigail turned and set her feet on the floor. "Foolish and clumsy. I'm sorry I gave everyone such a scare."

He sat beside her and put an arm around her shoulder. "I'm just glad it didn't have more serious consequences." Then he gave her a squeeze. "What in the world were you thinking?"

"I just thought, if I could show you how the library would look when it was all set up, and demonstrate my ideas for the whole process, that maybe you'd change your mind."

Had it really meant that much to her? "Abigail, I know you're perfectly capable of handling such an endeavor—that wasn't the point."

"It wasn't?"

"Of course not. I just didn't want you to put all that effort into something you won't be here long enough to enjoy."

He pulled slightly away so he could study her expression. "And was this all your idea, or did it come from Miss Johnson?"

Abigail shook her head. "Don't blame Daisy for this. It's something I wanted to do, and it wasn't her place to stop me."

He noted she hadn't really answered his question, but he let it pass. "No, that's my place. And what in the world were you thinking, carrying an armload of books down those stairs?"

Abigail's frown turned inward. "I just tripped is all. I know I was lucky it didn't turn out worse than it did, but truly, Everett, it could just as easily have happened when I was carrying something down to you on our side of the wall."

"There's no dog to get underfoot on our side of the wall."

She gave him an indignant poke. "Don't blame Kip, either. He was behind me, not in front of me. As I told you, it was just a misstep on my part."

She made as if to stand, but Everett held her shoulders down. "Where do you think you're going?"

"Dr. Pratt said that if I take things slow and easy, it's not necessary for me to stay in bed."

"He also said you'd be quite sore for the next few days. Don't you think you'll be more comfortable resting here for now?"

She gave him an exasperated look. "Don't go fussing over me. I'd be bored silly if I had to stay cooped up in here for any length of time. I'd rather be where I can have some company. Besides, this is your bed, not mine."

"I'll allow you out of this room if you promise me you won't do anything more strenuous than reading a book or writing a letter."

Abigail rolled her eyes. "You're acting like a mother hen with an injured chick."

Which wasn't too far off the mark for how he was feeling. And he certainly didn't intend to let her cajole him. "I mean it, Abigail. I want your word." He still hadn't quite recovered from the sight of her crumpled in a heap at the foot of the stairs.

"Oh, very well. But you have to promise not to smother me."

Everett stayed by her side as she made her way to the sofa. At her request, he moved one of her trunks of books close at hand so she could go through them and select some reading material.

Once he had her properly settled, he stood back, unsure what to do next. Daisy apparently had no such worries. He watched as she bustled past him and fussed over his sister. He also noticed that she studiously avoided making eye contact with him. Was she still smarting over their earlier discussion? But he'd been in the right.

Hadn't he?

Then she turned to him, her expression subdued. "I know you need to get back to your office. Don't worry about your sister. I promise to keep a close eye on her until you're done for the day."

Was that guilt speaking, or concern? Maybe a bit of both. "Thank you. Make sure you call me if you see the least sign that all is not well with her."

"Go on, Everett," Abigail said with a shooing motion. "I'll be perfectly fine."

He slowly descended the stairs, feeling uncharacteristically confused. Had he handled that wrong? Should he have given both Abigail and Daisy more encouragement and support?

It wasn't like him to be so indecisive. It must be Daisy's influence. His well-ordered life had been turned upside down, and it had all started when she arrived on the scene.

He didn't like it, not one bit.

The question was, what was he going to do about it?

Chapter Fourteen

Before Everett reached the bottom tread, his office door opened. Had some other busybody come to pry into his household's personal business?

But it was Adam.

"Hello. Back from the cabin, I see."

"Just got back an hour ago." He sobered. "We heard your sister had an accident, and Reggie sent me by to see how she was doing."

By mutual accord they moved to the chessboard. "It could have been worse. She ended up with a sprained wrist and some bumps and bruises, but Dr. Pratt thinks she'll be okay."

"Glad to hear it."

The two men took seats and stared at the board. It was Everett's move and he studied the pieces silently, but he wasn't really seeing them. He fingered a captured pawn, struggling with whether or not to ask the question foremost in his mind. Finally, keeping his gaze on the board, he cleared his throat. "What else have you heard about our bit of excitement?" Had he kept his tone as casual as he'd attempted to?

Adam grimaced sympathetically. "I suppose you're referring to Eunice's gossip about the open doors between your and Miss Johnson's living quarters."

There it was. Everett clenched his jaw. It sounded quite unsavory when expressed that way. "That door is only open when Miss Johnson is working here, and only as a convenience to her. There's nothing untoward going on."

"I didn't think there was."

Everett frowned. "But it doesn't really matter, does it?"

Adam's expression remained carefully neutral. "There are always those who will read more into a situation than is there."

Is that what this was—a *situation?* "I was afraid of that." Everett gave a crooked smile. "What do you think the chances are that it'll blow over if we just ignore it?"

Adam raised a brow. "You're the man of the world here—what do *you* think?"

The walls closed in on Everett as he tried to think of some way out of this mess. Daisy was *not* the type of woman he'd pictured himself marrying—not even close. It was hard to picture her on his arm in a society drawing room or trip to the opera.

But that was beside the point now. He had to be man enough to shield her from the wagging tongues that could shred her reputation to pieces. He was not his father.

Besides, he'd already been responsible for ruining one life through the inadvertent but reckless spread of lies. He couldn't stand by and let unfounded rumors and innuendo ruin another life, not when he could do something to prevent it.

After a long moment of silence, Adam spoke up again. "I guess the real question at this point is, what are you going to do about it?"

Everett met his gaze head-on, and the weight of his responsibility settled squarely and with great finality on his shoulders. There was only one answer he could give. "What I have to."

Later that afternoon, Daisy heard a knock on her back door and opened it to find Everett standing there, his expression solemn—even more so than usual.

"Miss Johnson, if you have a moment, there's something I need to discuss with you."

Her imagination immediately kicked in. "Is it Abigail? Is something wrong? I checked on her just twenty minutes ago—"

He held up a reassuring hand. "Abigail's fine, or at least no worse than when the doctor left earlier. Constance Harper came by for a visit and the two have their heads together, thick as thieves."

She breathed a mental sigh of relief, then another possible reason popped into her head. "If this is about what happened, I'll admit I shouldn't have encouraged her, but—"

He shook his head. "I know you're not entirely to blame. My sister can be quite headstrong when she puts her mind to something. As her presence in Turnabout demonstrates."

His seeming change of attitude had her thoroughly confused. "Then what is it?"

He swept an arm out. "If you don't mind, I'd prefer to take a short stroll while we talk."

She stepped outside, still trying to figure out why he

was here. “Do you mind if Kip joins us?” She wouldn’t press him if he refused, but to her surprise, he merely nodded.

That really started her worrying as to what might be on his mind. “If it’s not about Abigail, or my part in her accident, then what has put that serious look on your face?”

Rather than answering her question, he asked one of his own. “What do you know about Eunice Ortolon?”

Was that really what he wanted to talk to her about—one of their neighbors? But she obediently answered his question. “She runs the boardinghouse, doesn’t she?”

“She does. She’s also got a wagging tongue the likes of which would be hard to match.”

Daisy gave him a mock-stern look. “A body could argue that you’re indulging in a bit of gossip yourself just by saying that.”

His half smile acknowledged her point. “True. But that still doesn’t negate my prior statement.”

Enough of this shilly-shallying. “And why should Mrs. Ortolon’s chattiness interest me? Surely you’re not worried over what she might say about your sister’s fall? There’s nothing about the accident that would reflect badly on her.”

“I agree. There’s nothing the woman can say that would reflect badly on *Abigail.* At least, not directly.”

She could tell he was trying to make a point, but for the life of her, she couldn’t figure it out. “Then what?”

“I realize things were unsettling in the first minutes after Abigail’s fall and that neither of us were thinking clearly. But now that things are back to normal, try to remember all that happened in the time after the doctor and Mrs. Ortolon arrived.”

She frowned as she did as he asked. There was obviously something specific he was concerned about—concerned enough to seek her out. "Well, Doc Pratt did a quick check of Abigail when he arrived. There was some discussion going on, but I was focused on your sister so I wasn't paying much attention." She met his gaze. "Is that it? Was something said that has you worried?"

Everett shook his head. "What happened next?"

She concentrated on trying to picture it all in her mind. "Then we all went upstairs so Doc Pratt could examine her in private." This was silly. Why didn't he just tell her straight out what was on his mind?

"Yes, we all went up *your* stairs and into *my* quarters through the adjoining door."

"Yes, of course. It was the quickest way to get her to bed. And it was—" Daisy put her hand over her mouth as the full implication hit her. "Oh."

"Yes. *Oh.*"

Her cheeks heated. "But, surely… I mean." She met his gaze and was suddenly glad he had directed their steps to the less populated areas of town. "Oh, bother! It's all perfectly innocent."

"So it was. And is. But that no longer matters. You were in my bedchamber, remember, which only compounded things." His tone dripped with exaggerated patience, as if he were talking to a child. "If it were only Dr. Pratt, we could count on his discretion, but I'm afraid with Mrs. Ortolon in the mix, there will be no containing talk of this. In fact, there is some talk already circulating around town."

Daisy rubbed her cheek, trying to take in what this meant. "Be honest with me. How bad is it?"

"To speak bluntly, our reputations will be tarnished, and it may very well splash over onto Abigail, as well."

Her spirits sank. Was her dream of being a welcomed member of the community over so soon? She wouldn't accept that. "But surely, if we just go on about our business, in time the rumors will die down."

He shook his head. "I wish that were true. But this sort of thing can take on a life of its own, and folks have long memories. Believe me, I know."

"Then what do you suggest we do?"

"There's only one thing we *can* do—you and I must immediately announce our engagement."

Daisy halted in her tracks and stared at him, not sure she'd heard correctly. Was he serious? The only hint of emotion she could see in his face, however, was that irritating hint of cynical amusement he wore like armor. Did he think of this situation as a joke? "Surely there's something else we can do."

He spread his hands. "I'm open to suggestions."

She'd come to Turnabout fully intending to find herself a husband—in fact, that was something central to her desire to have a family. But this—this was as far from normal as one could get.

The last thing anyone would call Everett Fulton was the settling-down type. And to have a man—*any* man—feel forced to offer for her, well, that was a terrible thing to base a marriage on. "I'm sure, if I had time to think, I could come up with something."

"I'm afraid time is something we don't have." He held her gaze. "The gossip is already spreading. I want to put it to rest before Abigail hears anything…unsavory."

Daisy's cheeks heated all over again. "We can't let that happen."

"Then you agree to our engagement?"

Daisy stared at him, unable to give in just yet, still mentally scrambling for another option.

His expression softened into something approaching sympathy. "I know this isn't the ideal pairing for either of us, but the choice has been taken out of our hands. And I give you my word that I'll do my best to make this as painless for you as possible."

Somehow that only made her feel worse. "Not the most romantic of declarations."

He frowned. "I'm sorry I can't offer you love poems and other romantic nonsense. You need to understand that this is a matter of necessity."

Well, that made his feelings perfectly clear. "Of course." Then she grimaced. "I feel like this is all my fault, like I should be apologizing for putting you in this position."

He shrugged. "What's done is done. Placing blame serves no purpose now."

She noticed he didn't try to contradict her claim to be at fault. Did that mean he *did* blame her?

"The newspaper goes out tomorrow," he continued. "I'd like to insert a notice of our engagement. Hopefully, that will stem some of the censure. Do I have your permission?"

She took a deep breath. It seemed there was no getting out of this. "It sounds like I don't have a choice."

He gave a small smile. "Good. It'll be just a small notice. We can visit Reverend Harper tomorrow and set a date."

This was all happening too fast. Better to focus on something less frightening. "How do you think Abigail will feel about this sudden engagement?" Surely Everett's sister had higher expectations for the woman her brother would marry than a peddler's daughter.

"She'll probably be surprised, but she seems to like you well enough. All in all, I don't think she'll have any objections."

Again, not an enthusiastic endorsement.

"Rather than standing here wondering, though," he continued, "why don't we go over and tell her the news?"

By this time they had returned to her back door. "Now?"

He led the way to his own door. "Of course. If I'm going to place an announcement in the paper tomorrow, don't you think we should tell her now?"

"Yes, of course." The thought of saying it out loud to anyone, even Abigail, made it seem more real, somehow. "If you don't mind, I'd like to avoid telling her that we're doing this because we were backed into a corner."

His brow lowered at that, and she rushed to explain. "It's not just to spare my feelings." She tucked a strand of hair behind her ear. "Though I'll admit that's part of it. But I want to spare *her* feelings, as well. I don't want her to suffer any pangs of guilt over this because of her accident. That wouldn't be fair to her."

He hesitated, then nodded. "I hadn't thought of that, but you're correct—Abigail has a keen sense of responsibility. I won't lie to her, but I don't see any reason to elaborate, either." He nodded toward the door. "Now, if you're ready, shall we?"

She nodded and preceded him inside. Were they really doing this? Or would she wake up soon and find this was all some kind of dream?

Please Lord Jesus, help me find a way through this.

I'm so confused right now. I know You led me to this place for a reason, and even though it looks like I've really messed things up good this time, surely You can make it all come out right. I don't know if I'm doing the proper thing or not, but I'm counting on You to show me a way out if that be Your will.

They entered Everett's sitting room to find Abigail lounging on the sofa with a book in her lap.

"Oh, there you are." Abigail gave them a mock frown. "I'd begun to wonder where you'd gotten off to."

Everett looked around. "Where's Constance?"

"She had to go." Abigail looked from one to the other of them, and a small frown puckered her brow. "Is something wrong? You both seem so solemn."

Daisy couldn't stop the guilty flush warming her cheeks.

Everett, on the other hand, seemed as coolheaded as ever. "We have something to tell you," he said.

Abigail sat up straighter. "Bad news?"

"Actually, no." Everett took Daisy's hand. "In fact, we hope you'll think it's happy news."

Daisy stood silently beside Everett as he delivered the news to his sister. A silent prayer was running through her head. *Please, please don't let Abigail be upset by the announcement.*

But almost before Everett finished speaking, Abigail launched herself at him with a squeal of delight, leaving no doubt as to her feelings.

"Oh, Everett, I'm so happy for you. This is so unexpectedly spontaneous and romantic of you."

Everett appeared momentarily startled, but he patted his sister's back and then set her away with a smile. "I'm not certain whether to be flattered or insulted by that statement, but thank you. Now, stop flailing about—you need to be careful of your wrist."

Abigail dismissed his concerns with a wave. "Oh pish-posh, my wrist can withstand a hug or two." She turned to Daisy and gave her an equally enthusiastic embrace. "I'm so happy. I've always wished for a sister, and now I'll have one. And such a wonderful one at that."

Daisy, unused to such easy and exuberant displays of affection, found herself squeezing the girl back.

Abigail gave Daisy's cheek a quick kiss then stood back, bathing them equally in the brilliance of her smile. "Isn't it marvelous that things worked out so I could be here for this? So much more exciting to hear the news firsthand than to read it in a dry letter."

Daisy mentally winced. How would the girl feel if she knew there would never have been a proposal without her being here? Not that Daisy blamed Abigail. Everett had warned her more than once to be circumspect in the use of that door, that perceptions were important. She should have paid better attention.

Everett gave his sister a pointed look. "If you think I'm going to say that this was worth you pulling that foolish running-away stunt of yours, you are very mistaken, young lady."

"Well, be that as it may, I think this was meant to be." She flounced back to the sofa and plopped down. "The three of us, living here together as a family—it will be absolutely wonderful."

Would it? Daisy sincerely hoped so, but right now she wasn't so sure.

Once Daisy had returned to her own apartment, Everett gave Abigail strict instructions to get some rest, and then he headed back downstairs. He needed to rearrange the type he'd already set in order to insert the engagement notice. He also wanted to make certain it was prominently displayed so there would be no possibility that it would be overlooked.

He rolled up his sleeves as he approached the press. The sooner he got the paper out, the sooner the worst of the rumors would die. And the better the chances that Abigail wouldn't be touched by them.

It would be a long evening, but the paper would be printed and ready to send out by dawn—even if he had to work all night to make that happen. At least his hand had healed enough that he could get the paper out on his own tonight.

But as he worked, his mind went back to the last time he'd worked on getting the paper out. The way he and Daisy had worked so well together. And how she'd ended up in his arms.

As her husband, he'd have the right to hold her like that again. It wasn't an unpleasant thought.

But then he remembered the discussion he'd just had with her. He'd expected that, once she understood the situation, she'd be eager to rescue her reputation. So her strong negative reaction to his marriage proposal had surprised him. As had his own reaction. It was only a matter of injured pride, he assured himself.

What else could it be?

That evening, as Daisy sat on her bed, brushing out her hair, she tried to make her peace with the day's events. Engaged to be married. And to Everett Fulton, no less.

What an unexpected turn her life had taken.

I know I've been praying for a husband, Lord Jesus. And I know the Bible says Your ways are not our ways and that Your plans are for our good, but I can't for the life of me figure out why You would play matchmaker this way. Surely this isn't Your plan. Everett Fulton doesn't even like me. So there has to be a way out—just show it to me and I promise to take it, no matter what.

Daisy bent down to absently ruffle Kip's fur. "I don't know what's what anymore, boy. Perhaps God is sending me a test of some sort. But if so, I can't seem to find the answer. How can Everett be the right man for me—I'm not sure if he even likes me. And it's clear he doesn't care for you. How can I marry a man who doesn't like dogs? No, he can't be the man God intends for me to marry. Which means He'll show me the way out if I'm patient."

Kip barked, but she wasn't sure if he was agreeing with her or just trying to encourage her.

She turned down the lamp and slipped under the covers. Thirty minutes later, she was still wide awake. Her conscience was prickling at her, telling her that faith required more than she had been giving lately. What if obedience in this situation meant going through with the marriage? Who was she to second-guess the hand she'd been dealt?

Oh, this was all just too confusing.

Forgive me, Lord. I said I'd look past all the outer trappings and accept whatever man You had in store for me. But then I go and get all stubborn and prideful when You put me to the test. If this is truly Your will, then so be it. I still don't understand it, but that's not a necessary part of Your plan, is it? My role is to hear and obey.

There. She'd done all she knew to do. It was in God's hands now.

Chapter Fifteen

The next morning, as Daisy walked beside Everett through town, she did her best to ignore the stares from the shop windows and passersby. The two of them were on their way to Reverend Harper's home, and she felt uncomfortably exposed.

The newspaper had gone out bright and early this morning—she wondered just how late Everett had stayed up last night working on it. She should have offered to help him get it ready. After all, much as he tried to downplay it, she knew his hand wasn't completely healed. But she'd needed time to herself last night.

So now the word should have spread that she and Everett were to be married. Had it been timely enough to offset any gossip that had begun to circulate yesterday?

"Chin up," Everett whispered. "You're doing fine."

Grateful for his unexpected we're-in-this-together tone, she straightened and pasted on a smile. She was a bride-to-be, after all. This was not the time for melancholy moods, at least, not in public.

Anna Harper, the reverend's wife, answered the door. "Good day, Mr. Fulton, Miss Johnson. Please come in."

She stepped back to allow them entry. "I understand congratulations are in order."

Everett gave a short bow. "Thank you, ma'am. And that's why we're here. We'd like to speak to the reverend about setting a date for the ceremony."

"Of course. He's in his study. Let me just let him know you're here."

Daisy tried not to fidget as she stood beside Everett in the Harpers' cozy parlor. The silence seemed to draw out forever. Finally, Mrs. Harper signaled for them to enter her husband's study.

Reverend Harper stood as they walked in. "Please have a seat. I thought I might be receiving a visit from you today."

Everett seated Daisy, then took the chair next to her. "As you've no doubt heard," he said, "Miss Johnson and I plan to be married. We'd like to make the appropriate arrangements with you for scheduling the ceremony."

"Of course. But I hope you won't mind if I ask a few questions first."

Daisy shifted nervously. What sort of questions?

But Everett seemed perfectly at ease. "Not at all."

Reverend Harper leaned forward, his hands clasped on his desk. "First, given the circumstances, I understand that the two of you may feel as if you have no choice in the matter. And I agree that this is the proper response to the situation. However, marriage is not an institution to enter into lightly or blindly. It is meant to last a lifetime, and to be a source of joy and comfort to the husband and wife."

Daisy nodded. That was exactly the kind of marriage she'd longed for. But was it what she'd be getting?

"So," Reverend Harper continued, "while it is admirable that you two want to do what is proper, I feel it incumbent on me to ask if you think this is a marriage you can sustain?"

Everett spoke up before she could even formulate a response. "Rest assured, Reverend, I fully intend to dutifully carry out my role as a husband, and to do what I can to make the partnership work."

"And you, Miss Johnson?"

Daisy lifted her chin, less than cheered by the tone of Everett's response. "I consider marriage a sacred institution, put in place and blessed by God Himself. If I utter my vows, then I will remain faithful to them."

Reverend Harper seemed satisfied. "Very well. I have one additional question for you, and this is something I ask all couples when they come to me, regardless of the circumstances. Have you taken the time to pray about this decision?"

This time, Daisy didn't hesitate. "Yes, sir. I've done lots and lots of praying since yesterday afternoon, and I truly feel this is where the Good Lord is leading me."

"Excellent." He turned to Everett. "And you?"

Everett's expression was closed, unreadable. "I have no doubt at all that this is the right thing to do, and that it is what a caring God would want."

The reverend gave him a long, searching look, obviously aware that Everett hadn't really answered his question. Then he nodded. "Have you given any thought to when you would like to hold the ceremony?"

They had discussed the time frame on the way over here. Daisy had wanted to draw out the engagement for at least a month to give herself time to grow accustomed to the idea. Everett had wanted to make it a matter of days in order to silence the gossips as quickly as possible. They'd reached a compromise of two and a half weeks.

"We would like to hold it two weeks from Saturday."

"That would be May twenty-fifth. Is that correct?"

"It is."

Reverend Harper opened a journal and made a notation, then looked back up. "I think that's everything I need for now. But before you go, would you allow me to pray with you?"

Daisy answered for them, not certain what Everett would say. "Of course, Reverend."

"Then, if you will join hands and bow your heads."

Daisy hesitated, but Everett's hand closed over hers in a warm, protective grip. She felt something tangible flash between them in that touch, something that gave her hope that they really could make this work.

"Lord God Almighty, watch over this couple as they move toward building a new life together. Show them that the seeds of this marriage, which were planted out of necessity, if watered in love and faith and with its roots planted firmly in Your Word, may produce the fruits of joy. Remind them daily to honor You and each other, to keep Your laws and to respect one another. Let them be ever mindful that in You, all things are possible. Amen."

"Amen," Daisy repeated.

Everett's echoing response was a few seconds behind hers. He gave her hand a little squeeze and then released it.

She found herself missing the warmth of his touch.

Everett was glad to get out into the sunshine as they exited the Harper home. He hadn't expected to be affected by this meeting—it had just been one more item to check off his list. But when he'd felt the slight tremble of Daisy's hand beneath his, he'd felt an unexpected surge of protectiveness, an overwhelming need to reassure her that all would be well. That hand, so small and fragile, reminded him that despite her fierce streak of independence, she was a woman in search of a place to belong. He had just begun to try to absorb that when the words of the reverend's prayer washed over him, reminding him of the lifelong commitment he was making, and of God's place in it.

Was he really ready to surrender to that?

Once they were back out on the sidewalk, they strolled quietly for a while. It wasn't until they passed in front of Reggie's photography studio that they broke the silence.

Reggie was there, unlocking the door, and she greeted them with a broad smile. "Everett, Daisy, I heard your good news. Congratulations!"

Everett gave a short bow. "Thank you."

Daisy merely nodded. Had Reggie heard the gossip? What was she thinking?

"Did you set a date yet?" Reggie asked.

Again, Daisy held her tongue, leaving Everett to respond. "The ceremony will be two weeks from Saturday."

Reggie nodded. "No point wasting time once the decision's made."

Daisy finally found her tongue. "You're invited, of course."

"Thank you, but I'd like to come as more than a guest. I'm hoping you'll let me be your photographer." She gave them a serious look. "A milestone such as a wedding should be captured in a photograph, not just for yourself, but for future generations."

"I've never been photographed before." Daisy's voice held a note of awe.

Reggie squeezed her hand. "Then that settles it. I must take your photograph. And it'll be my wedding gift to you."

Everett started to protest, but Reggie held up a hand to stop him. "I insist." Her grin turned mischievous. "Not only will it be my wedding gift to you, but I almost feel like I owe it to you."

Daisy's brow furrowed. "Owe it to us?"

The look in Reggie's eye gave Everett a hint as to where this was going.

"When Everett first came to Turnabout," she explained, "he was kind enough to assist me with some of my outdoor photography."

Everett made an inelegant sound. Kindness had had nothing to do with it.

Reggie's grin widened as she cut him a sideways look. "I'm afraid I took advantage of him by getting him to help me pose a pig." She shook her head. "By the time we were done, your beau here was wearing more mud than the pig."

Daisy couldn't contain a laugh. "Oh, my, that must have been a sight to see."

"Yes, well," Everett said, "it was not my finest hour. And now that you put it that way, we will most definitely take you up on your offer."

"Consider it settled." Reggie placed a hand to her heart. "And I promise you'll like this picture much more than the one with Mr. Keeter's pig."

When they resumed their walk, he expected some

teasing from Daisy about the pig. But instead, she had a solemn, troubled expression on her face. Was she having second thoughts about their engagement?

Finally, she turned to him. "I need to ask you something of a personal nature. I hope that's okay, seeing as we're to be wed."

He eyed her warily. "What is it?"

"Are you a God-fearing, Christian believer?"

Chapter Sixteen

Daisy's question took Everett by surprise, and he didn't answer immediately. He knew it was important that he not only be honest with her, but that he also choose his words carefully.

"If you mean, do I believe in Almighty God," he said slowly, "of course I do."

"But?" She appeared braced for a blow.

"But if you mean, do I believe that the almighty, all-knowing God concerns Himself with the everyday affairs of individuals, then I'm not so sure."

He saw the concern in her expression. "How can you believe in the God of the Bible and not believe He cares for all of us?"

"I didn't say He doesn't care. I said he doesn't concern Himself with minor affairs. Look, I go to church on Sundays, I tithe, I do my best not to lie and cheat—all in all, I feel like I'm an upstanding member of the congregation."

"Being a Christian doesn't have anything to do with what church you go to, or even if you go to church service at all." Her expression was so earnest, her eyes so expressive he couldn't look away.

"Father and I traveled around a lot," she continued. "That meant we weren't always near a church come Sunday mornings. But I don't believe that makes me any less dear to God, or any less near to Him, either."

Her words weren't making a lot of sense—it was like she was talking in circles. "What is it you're asking me?"

"I'm talking about faith, about believing those things that are written in the pages of the Bible, even if you don't fully understand them. My father used to tell me that the test of faith is not holding fast to those teachings when everything is going well, but holding to them even when the world around you seems darkest."

He couldn't let that pass unchallenged. "You're actually setting your *father* up as an example of faith?" He knew he'd said the wrong thing, even before the hurt flashed in her eyes.

But she recovered quickly, and her chin came up. "None of us are perfect, and God doesn't demand that we *be* perfect—only that we repent when we fail and continue striving to do what's right and good."

She made it sound easy, he thought bitterly. And why wouldn't she, when it seemed to be part of her nature to see the good in every situation?

How would she feel if she'd faced the ugliness that he had?

And what kind of God would be capable of forgiving him what he'd done?

He was glad to see they had arrived back at his office. Without another word, he held the door open and indicated she should precede him.

* * *

Daisy stepped inside, still troubled by Everett's words. He was missing so much if he didn't build that personal relationship with God.

The silence between them stretched, threatening to become awkward. How were they supposed to interact with each other now that they were engaged?

Daisy pasted on a smile. "Time for me to get started on lunch." She headed for the stairs, then paused as something else occurred to her.

"Is something wrong?" Everett asked.

"I was thinking, now that we're engaged, it doesn't make sense for you to continue to pay me for cooking your meals."

Some of the tension eased from his face. Had he worried about what she'd say? "That's entirely up to you. I certainly have no problem continuing to pay you for the next two weeks, but you're right, in short order, we shall share equally in all that we own."

Something else to get used to. She was just starting to enjoy the idea of having money and belongings of her own. "True. But that brings up something else. I want you to know I don't expect you to share in the cost of my new stove and the other things I'll need for my restaurant." She fingered her collar. "Which means I'd better start looking for another job once Miss Winters returns."

To her surprise, he drew his brows down at that. "Surely you don't still intend to pursue that restaurant idea of yours?"

Daisy stiffened. "What do you mean?"

"Now that you'll be my wife, there's no need for you to find another means to support yourself. I should be able to provide financially for our household. Isn't that the reason you wanted the restaurant—to find a reliable source of income?"

"Only partly." She took a deep breath. "I like to cook and bake, especially when I can cook for folks who appreciate it."

"Be that as it may, I don't see the need to invest the kind of money it will take to open a restaurant if we don't need to. At least not immediately. You can indulge yourself in the cooking you do for our household."

Is this what marriage to him was going to be like? Having him dismiss her thoughts and ideas out of hand if they didn't conform to his own? "Weren't you listening to me? I just said I didn't expect you to invest in my business. That's why I'm going to be looking for another job."

"Don't you think taking care of our home will keep you busy enough?" His tone indicated he was getting irritated.

"I'll manage. And don't worry, I won't skimp on your meals or the housekeeping if that's what you're worried about."

"Daisy, this is foolish. What do you hope to accomplish by wearing yourself out with all this unnecessary extra work?"

"It's something I want to do, something that'll be all my own. Just like this newspaper is all your own."

"Reporting the news is my profession, not a hobby."

So much for him believing in her as a businesswoman. "Are you telling me I *can't* do this?" What would she do if he said yes?

"No, of course not." He moved toward his desk. "Look, there will be enough adjustments for both of us with this upcoming marriage. Why don't we give ourselves a couple of weeks to see how things go and then discuss this again."

She took a deep breath, then nodded. "That sounds fair. But I warn you, I'm not going to just let this drop."

His cynically amused expression was back. "I didn't for one moment believe you would."

Later that morning, Daisy opened the oven to check on her cobbler as Abigail snagged one of the peach slices that hadn't made it into the oven.

"I think we should make some changes to this place after the two of you are married," the girl said thoughtfully between bites. "Or even better, *before* you get married."

One thing about Abigail: she seemed to have an endless supply of ideas. "What do you mean?"

"It would only make sense to take down the wall between the two living quarters. I mean, there's no need to keep separate spaces once we're a family."

Daisy paused in the act of closing the oven. She'd expected Abigail to mention new curtains or pictures for the walls, but nothing on this scale. She straightened and gave the girl a pointed look. "There's no need, as you say, but there's no pressing reason to change, either."

"But just picture it." Abigail rose and walked to the wall in question. "If we tore this out, we could transform your kitchen and sitting room areas into a proper parlor."

Abigail spread her arms to encompass her brother's sitting room. "Once we did that, we could turn this area into a dining room, big enough to accommodate guests."

Daisy smiled. Whatever Everett lacked in imagination, his sister more than made up for. "Planning dinner parties, are you?"

"It'll be nice to entertain our friends occasionally, don't you think? For instance, in Everett's letters he mentioned the Sunday lunches at the Barrs' home. Wouldn't you like to be able to repay them for their hospitality?"

That thought did evoke wonderful images of cozy gatherings with family and friends. Could she and Everett build that kind of home together? Is that something he even wanted?

Abigail stood and studied the other end of the living quarters with a finger to her cheek. "And don't you think the bedchambers are rather small? I mean, not tiny, but wouldn't you like something grander for you and Everett to share?"

Daisy shifted uncomfortably and turned back toward the stove. This was something she and Everett hadn't discussed yet. Everything had been so businesslike to this point, but they *were* getting married. Did he expect the two of them to share a bedchamber? Was that something *she* wanted?

"We could take the wall out between Everett's room and mine," Abigail said excitedly. "That would make one nice-size bedroom for the two of you. And if I moved into one of the bedchambers over on your side, that would give the two of you more privacy, as well."

Daisy was still mulling over the whole question of what Everett might or might not be expecting after the wedding. But she realized Abigail was waiting for her response. “That all sounds good in theory, but it also sounds like a lot of work and expense. I don’t think it’s something we should undertake right now.”

“Now you sound like Everett.” Abigail’s tone made it clear she hadn’t intended that as a compliment.

It was time to rein the girl in. “Be that as it may, there are enough other things that’ll need attention between now and the wedding. There’s no need to add to that list unless absolutely necessary.”

She saw the argument poised on Abigail’s lips and quickly added, “Why don’t we find something else to talk about?”

“Oh, very well.” Abigail returned to the table and rested her elbows there while she watched Daisy. “If I haven’t told you so already, I want you to know I’m very excited that we’re going to be sisters.”

Daisy smiled. Now, there was a subject she was in perfect agreement with Abigail on. “Me, too. I always felt cheated not to have any brothers or sisters.”

“I was beginning to despair that my brother would ever marry.”

“Oh, come now. He’s not so old as that.”

“He’s twenty-seven.” Abigail said that as if it were ancient. “But it’s not just his age. Everett always seemed too cynical to allow himself to fall in love.”

Daisy was surprised—did Abigail really see her brother that way?

“But I can see now he needed just the right woman to come along and capture his heart,” Abigail continued with a happy smile. “It’s ever so romantic that he proposed so quickly after he met you. Tell me, was it love at first sight?”

Daisy hesitated. How much should she say? It seemed

cruel to disillusion the girl. But she couldn't lie. "Abigail, please don't overly romanticize this. My engagement to your brother is more practical than romantic."

Abigail waved that aside. "That sounds like Everett, but don't let that worry you overmuch. I think in this case he's just letting himself believe that because it's what he's comfortable with. I see that little spark between the two of you, even if he won't admit it's there."

Spark? Now who was just seeing what she wanted to?

But while they were on this subject, there was one more thing Daisy felt compelled to say. "Abigail, I want you to understand that, while we both know I'm not the kind of girl your brother wanted in a wife, I promise to make him the best wife I know how to be."

Abigail sat up straighter. "I know nothing of the sort. You're exactly the kind of woman he wants *and* needs. And deep down, he knows that—he proposed to you, didn't he?"

Daisy felt she was getting in deeper and deeper. "Yes, well, I think it may have had more to do with me being convenient than anything else. But I've prayed about it, and both of us are committed to making it work."

"Well, if he's not head over heels in love with you now, he soon will be." Abigail gave Daisy a surprisingly mature look. "I know Everett can be stuffy at times, but he truly is a good man with a kind heart. You'll be there now to make sure he doesn't take everything so seriously—including himself."

Daisy moved to the stove while she contemplated Abigail's words. She was so lost in thought that she didn't realize Everett had joined them until he spoke up.

"What is that dog doing in here?"

Daisy started and glanced over her shoulder. Sure enough, at some point Kip had stepped across the threshold and was now blissfully allowing Abigail the honor of scratching his side.

"Don't get all stiff and grumpy," Abigail said. "I lured him over here. After all, he'll be part of our family soon, too."

Everett's frown deepened. "That dog is *not* family."

"Don't be so stuffy. Of course he is. He's the family pet. And since Daisy will be moving over to this side after the wedding, and the whole place will then be one home, it seems ridiculous to let Kip have the run of only one half of it."

Daisy cast a quick glance Everett's way to see how he reacted to Abigail's statement, but could detect nothing except displeasure with his sister.

Finally, he gave a stiff nod. "Just make certain he doesn't make a mess."

"Of course." Abigail shot a triumphant look Daisy's way as she moved to the cupboard to collect the dishes for their meal, and Daisy was almost certain she saw a quick wink.

A moment later, as Abigail set the table, she assumed an innocent expression. "I was just talking to Daisy about some changes I think you should make to the place."

"Were you, now?" Everett's tone was dry. "Something more than allowing that animal to impinge on my home, I take it."

"Uh-huh."

"Well, you may as well tell me before you burst from holding it in."

Abigail explained her grand plans while Daisy busied herself at the stove. When the girl mentioned the bedroom idea, Daisy again glanced Everett's way, but again saw nothing more than an indulgent, long-suffering attitude toward his sister. Did that mean he'd taken it as a given that they would share a bedchamber? Or was he just good at hiding his reactions?

As uncomfortable a topic as it would be, she'd have to find a way to bring up the subject of future sleeping arrangements soon.

"So what do you think?" Abigail finally asked.

"I think, as usual, you are dreaming big and not giving any thought to what it takes to make those dreams a reality."

Abigail seemed undeterred. "That's what dreams are for. But you do agree it's a good idea, don't you? We'll be one family after the wedding, which means there won't be any need to keep the quarters separate."

"True. But there's no burning need to make any changes right away, either."

"Except for your bedchamber."

"Abigail, must you be so indelicate?"

The girl's only answer was an unrepentant grin. Then she continued on as if he hadn't interrupted. "It wouldn't take much to accomplish the changes, and I think you really should take care of it all before the wedding."

"Do you, now? And how do you propose I pay for all these grand plans of yours?"

"You can use the money you'd set aside for Miss Haversham's fees to take care of it. And we need to get new furnishings, as well. If we order a few essential items right away, they may have time to arrive before the wedding."

"I daresay we'll disagree on our notions of what constitutes essential."

Daisy set the meal on the table then, effectively silencing the siblings for the moment. But once they were seated and the blessing had been said, Everett turned to Daisy. "What do *you* think of my little sister's grand plans?"

Daisy tried to keep her tone noncommittal. "It sounds rather ambitious."

"That's my sister—she dreams on a grand scale."

Abigail pointed her fork from one to the other of them. "I can hear you, you know. And why would anyone want to limit their dreams to the mediocre?"

Daisy couldn't argue with that philosophy. Her own dreams of opening a restaurant might seem overly ambitious to some.

Everett still kept his gaze on Daisy. "Even so, perhaps we can do some of what she suggested."

That capitulation, the second from him in less than thirty minutes, caught Daisy by surprise. "Oh?"

Abigail's response was much more vocal and enthusiastic. "You mean it? Oh, Everett, that's marvelous. I do believe love has softened you a bit."

Daisy started. Love? Abigail couldn't be more wrong.

But Everett held up a hand. "I said we'd see about doing *some* of it. It would obviously be inappropriate for us to remove the wall between the two living quarters before the wedding."

"But—"

"That's not negotiable," he said firmly. "But, assuming Miss Johnson is amenable, perhaps we can move you over to her side of the building and work on enlarging the bedchamber over here."

Both looked to her for approval.

"Oh, Daisy, please say yes."

Daisy was still trying to figure out what he might be thinking. But she quickly nodded. "Of course. But I warn you, the bedchambers on my side are not nearly as nice as the ones over here. For one thing, there's no furniture in the extra bedroom."

Abigail dismissed Daisy's concern. "That's not a problem. I can move my things over there. In fact, I'll need to clear the room out, anyway, so the walls can come down."

Everett passed the bread platter to Daisy. "As for the rest, I suppose we can see about ordering a few more furnishings, as long as we agree on a budget and you stick to it."

Abigail clapped her hands. "This'll be so much fun. I have some fabulous ideas for what we can do."

Everett gave his sister a pointed look. "I think it would be more appropriate to let Daisy take the lead."

Abigail cast a chastened look Daisy's way. "Oh, of course, I only meant—"

"We can do it together," Daisy interjected quickly. "I would love to hear your ideas."

"You may live to regret that statement," Everett said dryly. "But I shall leave the specifics to you ladies. I'll work out a budget for you this afternoon."

Abigail turned to Daisy. "The wedding is in less than three weeks, so we should start planning right away. How quickly can I move in with you?"

The girl certainly didn't waste time. "As soon as you like, I suppose. It's clean, but like I said, there aren't any furnishings to speak of."

"As soon as we're done with lunch, let's go look it over and figure out how we want to arrange things."

Everett frowned at his sister. "Don't nag at Daisy—it isn't ladylike. And your wrist hasn't healed yet, so don't try moving any furniture yourself. You two figure out what you want moved, and I'll either take care of it or hire someone who will."

Abigail apparently knew when to give in gracefully, so she merely nodded and turned her attention to her meal.

Later, just about the time Daisy finished the dishes, Constance topped the stairs.

"Oh, hello," Abigail greeted her friend. "Have you heard about Daisy and Everett's engagement? Isn't it wonderful?"

"It certainly is." The girl smiled shyly Daisy's way. "I offer my best wishes, Miss Johnson."

"Why, thank you, Constance." Daisy dried her hands on her apron. "If you girls don't mind keeping an eye on Kip, I need to speak to Abigail's brother."

"You mean your fiancé," Abigail corrected archly.

Daisy controlled the urge to roll her eyes. "Yes, him."

"While we're watching Kip, Constance can help me plan my move."

Constance gave Abigail a frown. "You're moving?"

"Not far…"

Daisy left the two girls chattering as she removed her apron and headed down the stairs. She was relieved to find that Everett was alone.

She cleared her throat, and he looked up questioningly. "Yes? Have you already finished planning my sister's move?"

"I left Abigail and Constance to it. Your sister seems

quite excited about it, though I'm not sure I understand why."

"Abigail is always up for an adventure, no matter how small."

Daisy smiled, then quickly remembered her mission. "I was wondering if I could discuss something with you?"

He set his pen down and gave her his full attention. "Of course. What is it?"

She took to fiddling with her collar. "I'd prefer to discuss this somewhere we're less likely to be interrupted, especially by the two girls upstairs." Her cheeks warmed. "It's of a personal nature."

It was all she could do not to squirm under the look he gave her.

But he nodded and stood. "I see. And where would you suggest we have this discussion?"

"I thought perhaps we could take a walk." She hated the nervous tentativeness. "But if now is not a good time for you to get away, we can—"

"No, no. I can spare whatever time you need." He crossed the room to retrieve his coat. "Have you let Abigail know we're going out?"

Daisy nodded.

"Very well." He held open the door. "Shall we?"

As they stepped onto the sidewalk, he paused. "I'll let you decide on the direction this time."

She pointed south. "This way, I think." As they set out, she explained her choice just to make conversation. "There's an open field past the schoolhouse where Kip and I take a lot of our walks. It's also where I gather berries."

"I know the place."

"There's an old log near one of the trees that makes for a nice bench, and we could sit comfortably while we talk." It would also allow them to be openly visible, as propriety dictated, without worrying about interruptions.

They strolled along in a not uncomfortable silence, for all appearances just enjoying the sunshine and fresh air. And after a moment or two, Daisy managed to relax.

When they reached the spot she'd described, however, all that peace fled, leaving her edgy and uncertain.

Everett handed her down, but remained standing. "Now, what is this matter you wanted to discuss?"

She wasn't quite sure how to start. "It's rather indelicate."

That earned her an amused look. "Thanks for the warning. Now that I am suitably prepared, you may continue."

She cleared her throat, then decided it would be best to dive right in. "Based on our earlier discussion, it's obvious Abigail assumes you and I will be sharing a bedchamber after we're married." Her cheeks were on fire, but she was determined to keep her voice steady. "It's something we haven't discussed, though. I mean, I'd like to know if that's what you want."

There was no flash of shock or surprise in his expression, which indicated he'd probably anticipated her question. "I have no objections."

His tone held that amused edge she was coming to really dislike. And she wasn't about to let him off that easy. "That wasn't my question."

He spread his hands. "I suppose my expectation is that we treat it as any other marriage." He raised a brow. "However, if you are averse to that, or need time—"

"No." That had come out more emphatically than she'd intended, and her cheeks burned hotter at the look he gave her. "I mean, I've always wanted a large family, but I don't, I mean, if you don't—"

He touched her shoulder. "Daisy, it's okay."

This was the first time he'd called her by her first name. She rather liked the sound of it.

But then, as if coming to himself, he pulled his hand back and tugged on his cuff. "To be more precise, I believe that our sharing a room would be the best course of action, for a number of reasons."

Dare she ask him to list those reasons?

"However," he continued, "if that makes you uncomfortable—"

"No." This time her tone was more assured. "I agree that it makes sense to keep up appearances since that's the whole reason we're going through with this." Is that what she really meant? "I just didn't want you to feel as if you'd been backed into a corner. At least, not any more than you already had by circumstances."

"It's quite considerate of you to concern yourself with my feelings, but, my dear Miss Johnson, when have you ever known me to do anything I did not want to do?"

Far from an endearment, the *my dear Miss Johnson* made him sound more distant than ever. Not that she was looking for endearments.

She shook off that thought and went back to the conversation at hand. It seemed he'd already forgotten he'd been forced to propose to her. But, since he was being particularly pleasant, she wouldn't bring that up.

He tugged at his sleeve. "I understand we haven't

known each other long and that this is not a union either of us desired."

She hoped her mental wince didn't show on her face. At least now she knew for certain how he felt.

"So I understand that you may need time to become comfortable with the idea of our marriage. If I may be somewhat indelicate, as well, if you were obliquely referring to our sharing more than a room, you can rest assured that I am willing to give you some time in that arena, too."

Now what did he mean by that? Was he offering to sleep on the floor? She was mighty tempted to ask him to elaborate, but then chickened out. "Very well." She stood. "Thank you for your time. I think I know where you stand." But did she really?

"There is one more thing," she said impulsively.

"And that is?"

"Do you think it would be okay to use first names when we are addressing each other?"

She saw something flash in his expression, but couldn't identify it before it disappeared. Had she overstepped some line of propriety again?

Then he smiled. "I think that would be quite acceptable." He offered her his arm. "Shall we, Daisy?"

As they headed back to town, Everett replayed their conversation, and her expressions, in his mind. He knew he hadn't handled that as well as he should have, but he wasn't quite certain where he'd gone off track.

Of course he wanted her in his bed. He was a man, and she would be his wife. And if he were being totally honest with himself, somehow, over the time he'd spent with her, she'd gone from being an annoyance to something much dearer. He didn't love her in the romantic sense; it wasn't in his nature to do so. But without him really noticing how or when it had happened, he'd begun to enjoy her company, to feel the need to protect her, to want to gain her trust and more.

And that thought scared him more than anything else in his life had up until now. And he wasn't ready to examine just why.

He should have known she'd tackle that particular issue head-on, the way she did every problem she faced in life. Daisy wasn't one to shy away from something just because it was uncomfortable or difficult. It could be a trying trait for those around her, but he was coming to admire her for it, as well.

Was he as honest and courageous when facing his own trials? He didn't like the answer to that question.

Because the fact that he was determined to hide his newly discovered feelings for Daisy was proof that he did not.

Chapter Seventeen

The next morning, Abigail ventured out for a walk. When she returned, she had a large parcel with her.

Daisy cast a stern eye her way. "You're not supposed to be carrying anything heavy."

"Now you sound like Everett. Don't worry. This isn't very heavy, and besides, a nice young man carried it all the way from the mercantile to our front door for me."

Not surprising. Daisy wondered if Everett was prepared for the fact that his nearly grown little sister would be attracting more and more attention from the youths of her acquaintance.

"Anyway," Abigail said with an airy wave of her hand, "look what I found at the mercantile." She quickly unwrapped her parcel and lifted out two colorful lengths of fabric. She draped each over a kitchen chair, then stepped back to give Daisy a better view.

Daisy wiped her hands on her apron and moved closer. One of the fabrics was exactly what she would expect Abigail to select. It was a sapphire-blue with thin, yellow, vertical stripes—very soft and pretty. The other, which drew her interest more strongly, was a bright, sunshiny-yellow with sprigs of vivid red, blue and purple flowers scattered across it. “They’re beautiful,” Daisy said, stroking the yellow print. “Are you planning to make some new dresses?”

“No, silly, this is for curtains.” Abigail touched the blue-striped fabric. “This one is for my room. Blue is my favorite color.” She gave it one last pat and looked up. “Now that I’m moving into a room that’s not cluttered with Everett’s miscellany, I wanted to do something to make it my own.”

Daisy pointed to the more colorful fabric. “And this one?”

“That one’s for your room,” Abigail said with a very pleased-with-herself smile. “I couldn’t resist. It was so bright and cheery that it reminded me of you. I hope you don’t think it was too presumptuous.”

Daisy was touched by the gesture. No one had done such a thoughtful thing for her since her mother passed away. “Not at all. The fabric is exactly what I would have picked myself. Thank you.”

Abigail grinned. “You might want to wait to thank me until we have them up in your room. I still have to do the sewing. And with this bandaged wrist, I won’t be at my best. Too bad we don’t have a sewing machine here like the one at Miss Haversham’s.”

Daisy pulled her hand away from the fabric. “If it’s too much trouble—”

Abigail waved her protests away. “Not at all. It just means I’ll be slower and not able to do any fancy stitchery. But I’ll just forgo the ruffles and pleating and make these curtains straight and plain for expediency’s sake.”

“I’m sure they’ll look lovely.”

“The only thing I’ll promise is that they’ll look better

than those dull window shades we're using right now." She straightened. "I won't keep you from your cooking any longer. I have some measuring and cutting to do."

She gathered up the fabric. "By the way, I didn't see Everett downstairs when I walked through. Do you know where he went?"

Daisy shook her head, aware of how little she knew of her husband-to-be's daily routine. "Out running some errands, no doubt. I'm sure he'll be back in time for lunch."

Everett sat quietly at the kitchen table as his sister and Daisy discussed cosmetic changes to his home. He was trying to come to terms with the fact that that's how things would be for him from now on. So much for the peaceful bachelor life he'd enjoyed all these years.

But for all of that, he was glad to see the two had developed a close relationship. Perhaps Daisy wasn't as refined as the girls his sister was accustomed to, but there were some things Abigail would do well to learn from his future wife.

Future wife. He was still having trouble getting used to that concept.

A sudden lull in the conversation gave him the opportunity to change the subject. He cleared his throat to grab their attention before they could launch into something else. "I'm glad you found something to keep you occupied, Abigail. It might interest you to know that I have prepared another pastime for you, as well."

"Oh?"

Why did she look so apprehensive? "I finally unloaded the boxes of books I had in the storeroom. They are now all neatly stacked in your library area next door.

So, sister of mine," he said with mock formality, "once you are done with your curtains, if you want to spend some of your abundant spare time cataloging and preparing those volumes for use in your library, you have my permission."

Abigail popped up from her seat and gave Everett's neck a hug. "Oh, thank you! Does this mean you approve of my idea now?"

"It means I'm resigned to the fact that you're not going to give up on it. And that you need some way to occupy your time so you won't get into further mischief."

She grinned unrepentantly. "So true. I'll start bringing my own books down, as well. I'll have the library ready for business in no time."

Everett gave her his sternest look. "You'll do nothing of the kind. Set whichever of your books you want to add to the library over there." He indicated a small table near the sofa. "I'll carry them to the bottom of the stairs for you as I have the time."

"That seems a bit—"

He didn't let her finish. "I don't want to catch you carrying anything down either set of stairs. Not until your wrist heals completely—do you understand?"

She huffed. "I understand my brother is a worrier."

He wouldn't reward her flippancy with a smile. "Abigail."

She gave an exaggerated sigh. "Yes, yes, I understand."

He didn't have a lot of confidence that she would follow his rules, but he planned to keep his eye on her.

"Another thing—I don't want you to take this as a sign that I'm resigned to having you stay here indefinitely. After the wedding, we will revisit the discussion of your return to Miss Haversham's."

Abigail lifted her chin defiantly. "Discussion, of course, is always an option."

He decided to let that remark go. When the time came, they both knew she would do as he instructed.

Then Abigail changed the subject. "I'm going to work on the new curtains this afternoon, but tomorrow I'll walk over to Constance's and see if she still wants to help with the library."

Was his little sister finally learning patience? There was a time when she'd have hopped up right then and there to recruit her friend to help with her latest scheme. Perhaps Daisy really was having a positive influence on her.

Later that afternoon, Abigail drifted downstairs and sat in the chair in front of Everett's desk. With a sigh, he set down his pen. Between Abigail and Daisy, he was hard-pressed to find two uninterrupted hours back-to-back. "Is there something I can do for you?"

"I think I should go ahead and move over to Daisy's quarters today. You can't get started tearing down that wall until I'm out of there," she explained. "And the sooner you do that, the sooner we can get it ready for after the wedding."

Everett still wasn't certain how he felt about having workmen invade his home, much less letting Daisy and Abigail loose to decorate it. With Daisy's flamboyant sense of color and Abigail's adventurous spirit, he could imagine the havoc they would wreak in his orderly inner sanctum.

But the die had been cast, and he couldn't turn back

now. “That’s all very well,” he told Abigail. “But you can’t start carting things over to Daisy’s place without her permission. You can talk to her in the morning.”

“Why don’t I go talk to her now?”

“Because she spent the day cooking and cleaning up after us. It seems reasonable to think she would want some time to herself right now.”

“Pish-posh, Everett. Why must you always try to be reasonable? I’m certain Daisy is like me and enjoys having people around her. Besides, she’s practically one of the family now. She won’t mind. And if now is not a good time for my move, I’m sure she’ll say so.”

“Don’t try to cajole her, Abigail.”

“I won’t.” Abigail gave one of her customary airy waves as she popped out of her chair. In a heartbeat, she was out the door.

Everett stood and headed for the stairs. He had no doubt that Daisy would agree to his sister’s plans—it didn’t seem to be in her nature to refuse such a request. Which meant he was in for several hours of moving Abigail’s furnishings and belongings.

Chapter Eighteen

Just as Everett had predicted, Abigail had him rearrange her things a number of times until she pronounced herself satisfied. She also had him hang her newly constructed curtains in both her room and Daisy's.

He wasn't certain what he'd expected to see when he stepped into Daisy's bedchamber, but he found himself surprised by the almost monastic simplicity of it. The bed was covered by her bedroll only—there were no sheets or coverlets, and no pillows. A small braided rug sat on the floor next to the bed, and two large crates served as tables. One held a Bible and lamp, the other a hairbrush and a small wooden horse. Her clothing—what there was of it—hung on pegs on the wall across from her bed.

If he'd expected her to be embarrassed or apologetic, he was mistaken in that, as well. While he hung the curtains, she explained to Abigail, with some pride, how she'd made the mattress herself, as well as the braided rug that served as Kip's bed, and how the wooden horse was carved by her father and given to her as a gift when she was six.

She truly seemed content with what she had.

Was that part of the secret of her ever-present optimism? That she could find contentment in whatever her circumstances?

Could it really be so simple?

The next day, Everett contacted Walter Hendricks, the local carpenter, to take a look at his place with an eye toward doing the proposed remodeling.

"It seems a straightforward-enough project," Mr. Hendricks said. "I don't recommend taking the entire wall out, but we should be able to take down a good three-quarters of it to open up the room. My boys and I should be able to get it all done—tearing out and smoothing over—in about two and a half days."

"When can you start?"

The man rubbed his chin. "I have another small job ahead of you, but I should finish it up in the morning. Is tomorrow afternoon okay?"

Everett nodded. "The sooner, the better."

Mr. Hendricks gave him a knowing smile. "Don't worry. We'll have it all done before your new bride is ready to settle in."

Everett made a noncommittal response, and the carpenter, with a tip of his hat, took his leave.

Everett moved to the window to check on Daisy. Today was her laundry day, and she was hard at work. He thought about bringing her something to drink, but saw Abigail step outside with a glass in her hand.

It appeared his services were not required.

He headed downstairs, noting how unusually quiet the place seemed, leaving him free from distractions.

Except the memory of last week's laundry day and how it had ended.

* * *

Daisy brushed the back of her hand across her forehead, pushing the damp tendrils out of her way. It was only mid-morning, but already she felt wilted. Still, the chore seemed easier this second time around. Not only did she know what to expect now, but she'd learned from some of the mistakes she'd made last week.

One other thing that made the job feel less of a drudgery was Abigail's frequent visits, bringing her lemonade and passing the time with her easy chatter. The girl even offered to help with a few minor tasks, but Daisy quickly dismissed that notion. She didn't feel it would be right to accept full pay from her customers if she didn't do the work herself.

Though she enjoyed Abigail's company and appreciated her efforts, Daisy missed having Everett checking up on her the way he had last week. He *had* come out here first thing this morning, of course, before the last gauzy wisps of darkness had fully disappeared, to check that her tubs were all situated in a manner that would make them easy to drain later. She'd tried thanking him, and he'd merely said he wanted to avoid a repeat of what had happened last week. And that had been the last time she'd seen him today. Had he been too busy to bother, or merely too disinterested?

Daisy pushed those thoughts aside. Hadn't she told both Abigail and Everett that she wanted to handle this job on her own? She couldn't really fault him if he took her at her word, could she?

That back-and-forth argument with herself kept her mind occupied through the rest of the day. By evening, when she'd brought the last of the clothes in, separated out the items that needed ironing and folded the rest,

Daisy was ready to focus on something different. She quickly freshened up, then went upstairs to find Abigail working on a sewing project.

"The *Gazette* goes out in the morning," she told the girl, "which means your brother will be working to get it printed tonight. I'm going over to lend him a hand."

Abigail immediately set her project aside. "What a great idea. I'm coming with you."

When they entered Everett's office, he was already printing the first page. "I know your hand is better," Daisy said by way of greeting, "but I thought you might want some help, anyway."

He looked up with a frown. "That's not necessary. I know you've had a hard day, and I have everything under control here."

The hint that he might be concerned for her welfare, maybe even had checked on her without her knowing, lifted Daisy's spirits. But it didn't dissuade her from her purpose. "Be that as it may, since we're to be married soon, I'd like to learn as much as I can about the family business."

Abigail grinned. "Family business—I like that. But since I'm not any good at this sort of thing, I'll take care of supper. I baked some fresh bread earlier. It's not as good as Daisy's, but it's passable. Why don't I prepare some sandwiches and bring them down here so we can eat picnic style. Then I'll watch Kip and keep you two company while you work."

Everett didn't raise any further objections, and they had a surprisingly pleasant evening. Abigail tried to teach Kip a few tricks with results that had Daisy laughing and even drew a smile or two from Everett. As with the laundry, Daisy found the job of typesetting much easier this second time around. And she and Everett developed a comfortable rhythm working together.

When Daisy headed home that evening, she was accompanied by Kip and Abigail. It somehow felt wrong to leave Everett all alone in his place. Of course, that was just as he had been before she showed up. Perhaps it was how he preferred it.

But when she lay in her bed later that night, she thought about how good it had felt while they were all together earlier. If she were a betting person, she'd wager that even Everett had enjoyed himself. Almost as if they were a true family.

The family they would be in actuality in less than two weeks. She lay there, letting that thought flow through her, settle in her mind. And in her heart. For the first time, it didn't seem so far-fetched that this was the man she'd build her life with.

Perhaps God had known what He was doing, after all.

Everett had waited until he heard Daisy's door close before he'd closed and locked his own outer door. Then he'd quickly climbed the stairs and listened for sounds that they were all upstairs. He heard the faint sound of Daisy's laughter, no doubt in response to something his sister had said.

Now, before he could retire, he had to disrupt the orderly arrangement of his bedchamber and get the room ready for tomorrow's demolition work.

While he shoved and slid various pieces of furniture to the far side of the room, he wondered at his mood. He had lived alone for most of the past dozen or so years. Why did it suddenly feel lonely over here?

Then his thoughts shifted to how deft Daisy was becoming at typesetting. He had to admit, she'd make a good partner in the running of his newspaper business. If that was something he wanted to continue.

Which, of course, he didn't. Someday soon he would get the break he needed and return to his place as a reporter in a big city.

In the meantime, though, there were worse things than being married to a woman who took a genuine interest in his work.

And on that thought, he turned down the lamp and climbed into bed.

Daisy was finishing the dishes the next afternoon when Walter Hendricks showed up with his two sons in tow. Predictably, Abigail made quick friends with the two Hendricks brothers, especially Calvin, the older son.

But once the work began in earnest, the girl quickly distanced herself from the noise and dust. "I have an errand to run," she told Daisy. "I won't be gone long."

Sure enough, when Daisy returned from her afternoon walk with Kip, she found Abigail waiting for her, her eyes sparkling with excitement. "I borrowed the furniture catalog from Mr. Blakely," she told Daisy. "I thought we could figure out what furniture we'd like to order."

Caught up in the girl's enthusiasm, Daisy eagerly pored over the catalog with her. But she was still uncomfortable with spending Everett's money, regardless of how he felt about it. She had to keep reining in the less-concerned Abigail. One item that hadn't been on her mental list, however, caught her eye. It was a large chaise lounge. The piece had simple lines but was topped with a wonderful-looking plush cushion. If she placed it in their bedchamber, it would give her a not-so-obvious alternate sleeping accommodation. At least then she wouldn't have to worry about which of them would be sleeping on the floor.

Abigail enthusiastically approved of her choice. "I knew you had a touch of the frivolous romantic in you. I was afraid for a moment that you were going to be thoroughly and boringly practical."

Abigail also insisted they order a sewing machine and some updated laundry equipment. Despite her frequent flights of fancy, the girl had a practical head on her shoulders.

After much back and forth, Daisy and Abigail finally had a list of items they both could agree on.

Abigail shook her head sadly. "I do think you're taking my brother much too literally on this budget business, but I'll defer to your wishes." She plucked the list from the table and linked her elbow with Daisy's. "Let's go place our order. The sooner we do, the sooner the pieces will arrive."

Daisy held up a hand. "Not so fast. We should discuss our selections with your brother first."

"But he said we should order whatever we wanted as long as we stayed within his budget, which, thanks to your stubbornness, we did."

"Yes, but since we *are* spending his money, to furnish and decorate *his* home, I'd like to make sure he doesn't have any objections to anything on our list." Everett had such elegant taste in everything, she was afraid she'd made some glaring mistakes in one or more of her choices.

But Abigail had no such qualms. "It's your home, too, and I assure you, Everett will be fine with whatever you decide—especially since you're his bride-to-be."

If only Abigail knew how little weight that really carried. "Still, I must insist."

Abigail gave in with good grace. "Oh, very well, if it makes you feel better. Let's see if he can look it over now."

"I think we should wait until he closes his office for the day."

"There's no telling when that will be. And what can it hurt to check now? If he's too busy, he'll certainly let us know."

Daisy didn't doubt that for a moment. Still, she was hesitant to disturb him.

Abigail, however, was already headed for the stairs. Almost before her feet touched the ground floor, she started in with melodramatic emphasis. "Everett, Daisy and I have selected the barest minimum of furnishings needed to make our combined quarters livable."

Everett leaned back in his chair. "Have you, now?"

"Yes." Abigail rolled her eyes. "And it wasn't easy because Daisy insisted on being positively frugal—quite a trying experience."

"If she succeeded in reining in your extravagance, then my hat is off to her." He turned to Daisy. "You didn't let her run roughshod over you, did you?"

"Not at all."

"Good. Then I take it you're headed to the mercantile to place the order."

Daisy smiled. "Actually, if you have a minute I'd like your opinion before we place the order."

"I'm sure it is perfectly acceptable."

Did the man ever give a direct answer? "Still, I'd like you to take a quick look. I wouldn't want there to be any unpleasant surprises for you once the items arrive."

"And time is of the utmost essence," Abigail added dramatically.

He gave Daisy a quizzical look, then stood. "Well, in that case, I suppose I'd better have a look. I'm having trouble concentrating on my work with that infernal racket upstairs, anyway."

They spread the catalog and their list out on his desk, and Everett stood between them as they looked it over. Daisy let Abigail point things out to her brother and explain exactly why each item was a must-have purchase. But several times he interrupted his sister to turn to Daisy and get her opinion. Was he just being polite? Or did he really care what she thought?

When Abigail got to the chaise lounge, Daisy saw Everett give her a quick, speculative glance, but he didn't say anything. She tried to keep her expression neutral, but wasn't sure if she'd succeeded. Had he guessed the reason she had included it in her order? And if he had, what did he think about it?

In the end, Everett found himself surprised by the list. The practical items far outweighed the decorative. What had happened to all that colorful exuberance she tended to use in her own place? Had his strictures about sticking to the budget boxed her in too tightly?

When Abigail bemoaned the fact that Daisy had vetoed the purchase of a small dressing table for her use, something she insisted every young woman *must* have, Everett turned to his bride-to-be. "Do you agree with my sister over the importance of this item?"

Daisy shrugged. "A dressing table is a nice item to have, but I've gotten along for quite some time without one, so I think I can manage a bit longer. The other items on the list are much more important."

Everett studied the list again. "I believe there are items here that we need regardless of any renovations, so they should not be counted against the budget." He met Daisy's gaze again. "That means there are funds to cover the addition of the dressing table."

Daisy's eyes widened in surprise.

"And a chair for it, as well," Abigail added quickly.

With a nod, Everett scribbled the additions to their list.

He did, however, say no to the fine-woven rug his sister thought would add just the right decorative touch to the room.

As the two ladies headed out toward the mercantile, Everett slowly returned to his desk. The chaise lounge on the list had caught his eye, especially when his sister artlessly explained how Daisy had picked it out without any prompting from her.

He had a pretty good idea why his future bride had selected it for their bedchamber. And if that's where she planned to spend her nights for the time being, then so be it. He'd told her he'd leave the sleeping arrangements to her discretion, and he was a man of his word.

If he was feeling a twinge of disappointment, then he would deal with it the way he dealt with every other disappointment in his life.

He would bury it and move on. Dwelling on disappointments and troubles only made one weak.

Chapter Nineteen

Daisy found that she actually enjoyed having Abigail living on her side of the dividing wall. Not only was the girl's chatter a welcome distraction from her own thoughts, but Abigail began to add touches of color and charm to the entire living space.

Cheery squares of fabric would appear as cloths to cover the crates she used as a table, and bits of bric-a-brac popped up in strategic locations.

"You don't mind if I put this chair in here rather than in my room, do you?" she'd say. "The light in here is much better to read by than the light in my room."

Another time it would be, "These curtains didn't work out as well as I thought they would in my room, so I put them here in the sitting room."

Abigail also began to treat the two living quarters like they were already one, going back and forth between them as if the invisible barrier Everett erected at the adjoining door didn't exist.

And random pieces of furniture from Everett's side began showing up in her place, as well. A footstool here, a wooden chair there—suddenly Daisy's place was looking much more cozy.

But she wasn't comfortable with Abigail's cavalier kidnapping of furniture from Everett's domain.

She finally put her foot down. "You need to stop bringing all these things over here."

Abigail's expression was one of wide-eyed ingenuousness. "All I'm doing is some simple rearranging of the furniture to make things more comfortable for the two of us. Don't you like it?"

"Don't pretend you don't know what I mean. Your brother and I aren't married yet, which means right now this is not part of his home, so you shouldn't treat it as if it were."

"It will be soon enough. I'm just getting a little head start." She waved airily. "But if you want me to stop rearranging until after the wedding, I suppose I can wait."

Daisy wasn't fooled. The girl hadn't offered to undo what she'd already done, just not do any additional encroaching.

Everett, however, seemed to either not notice or not care that pieces of his furniture were disappearing out from under him.

As observant as the man was, she suspected he was deliberately turning a blind eye to his sister's redecorating efforts. He was quite good at these subtle ways of showing how much he cared for her. Why couldn't he be more open about it? It would mean so much to Abigail.

And to Daisy, as well.

Chapter Twenty

On Sunday, as they strolled home from the gathering at the Barrs' home, Abigail complimented Daisy on her Sunday dress. Daisy, aware that Abigail was wearing yet another gown that was making its first appearance in Turnabout, smiled and gave the girl the history of the dress.

"How wonderful. I can tell from your tone that you must have loved your mother very much."

"I do. And I miss her very much, too."

The girl's expression turned wistful. "You're lucky. I don't remember my own mother much at all." Then she smiled. "But having an older sister like you will be almost as nice."

Daisy gave the girl's arm a little squeeze. She'd grown to love Abigail, to feel like she really was a sister. It was comforting to know that it was mutual.

Then Abigail cut her a speculative look. "But speaking of dresses, have you given any thought to a wedding gown?"

It was obvious Abigail didn't consider her current attire suitable.

But Daisy didn't have any other options. She grabbed the side of her skirt and spread it wide. "Why, this one, of course."

"Oh, but it's your wedding. Surely that warrants a new gown."

Daisy shrugged, trying not to let the words hurt. "I'm not much of a seamstress, and even if I were, there's not much time before the wedding."

"But isn't there a dressmaker here in Turnabout? I'm sure she can take care of this for you. And if she's too busy, I can work on it myself. Please, let me help you select a new dress. I've been told I have a very good sense of style."

"I'm sure you do, but—"

"Please. It'll be fun."

"Better let her do it," Everett added dryly. "My sister considers herself a great arbiter of fashion, and she does enjoy having a new subject to work with."

Suddenly realizing that the garment she wore for her wedding would reflect not only on her, but on Everett and Abigail, as well, Daisy's resolve weakened. "If you really think I should..."

Abigail jumped on Daisy's capitulation. "Oh, this will be fun. We need to find just the right pattern to accentuate your lovely figure and height. I have some catalogs we can look at this afternoon."

As Abigail quickened her steps, Everett turned to Daisy. "I'm afraid you're in for a long afternoon of poring over pictures and discussing the advantages of one style over another."

She smiled. "I don't mind. And it was very sweet of her to offer to help."

"For all her faults, my sister is a very giving person." He studied her carefully. "But don't let that hold you hostage or make you feel you must give in if you disagree with her choices."

This time Daisy's smile was genuine. "Have you ever known me to not speak my mind?"

Daisy and Everett parted at Daisy's front door. By the time she reached the second floor, Abigail was exiting her room with two catalogs cradled in her arms.

Daisy immediately rushed forward. "Here, let me take those. Your wrist is not quite healed yet."

"You're turning into as much of a fussbudget as my brother." But Abigail handed the books over without arguing. "Why don't we go over to the other side so we can spread these out on the dining room table?" Without waiting for Daisy's response, she sashayed to the adjoining door, signaling for Kip to follow her.

Everett sat on the sofa, reading one of the papers he had mailed to him from various cities. He looked up and nodded a greeting, frowning at the dog before he went back to reading.

"I'd prefer not to have anything too fancy or frou-frou," Daisy warned.

"Oh, I agree." Abigail opened the thicker of the two catalogs. "I think something with fairly simple lines would be best. That's not to say it won't be elegant, though. And it should have lace insets at the neckline and collar." She pointed to one of the pictures. "Oh, here, what do you think of this one?"

Daisy looked at the picture Abigail pointed out and was immediately captivated. The gown was truly beautiful. It had a gently scalloped neckline inset with lace that formed a throat-hugging collar. The bodice was embellished with tone-on-tone embroidery and beadwork. The long, fitted sleeves ended with a tapering point at the wrist.

"Oh, Abigail, it's beautiful, but it's much too fancy. The embroidery work alone would take hours and hours."

"True, but we can do a simpler version and still get the same effect. I'll help the dressmaker if she hasn't the time." She turned the page. "We'll keep looking to see if we find anything we like better, though. We have all afternoon."

In the end, Daisy didn't see anything she liked more than that first dress. She turned back to it and stared wistfully. Could she really have something this lovely?

Abigail had no such doubts. "You're right—this is the one. Now let's talk about colors. Of course we'll have to work with whatever selection the seamstress has on hand—I don't think she'll have enough time to order anything. But I'm thinking a soft shade in the blue or green family would work best with your coloring."

Daisy nodded. She was calculating costs in her head. If she used all of her laundry money and some of the earnings she'd managed to set aside from her work for Everett, she might just be able to cover it. She'd have to start saving all over again, but neither Everett nor Abigail would have cause to be embarrassed if she wore this dress.

As if reading her thoughts, Everett spoke up from across the room. "Sounds like you've made a decision. You can speak to Miss Andrews tomorrow. Tell her to bill me for her services."

Daisy stiffened. She might not have much to bring with her into this marriage, but she could take care of her own wedding dress. "Thank you for the offer, but I'll handle this myself."

He raised a brow at that. "Does it really matter whose money we pay with? Soon there won't be any yours or mine—it'll be ours."

Did he really mean that? "Nevertheless, we aren't married yet. I'd prefer to keep things separate until we do."

He shrugged. "As you wish."

Daisy eyed him suspiciously. He'd given in a bit too easily. But then Abigail reclaimed her attention with animated discussions of trim options, including types of lace, beads, embroidery and other embellishments.

Daisy realized she'd have her work cut out for her if she was to keep it simple.

The next morning, Abigail insisted on accompanying Daisy to the dressmaker's shop. "I love to look at fabrics and patterns," she said by way of explanation. But Daisy suspected she didn't trust her to pick out the proper fabric by herself.

Hazel Andrews greeted them with reserved enthusiasm, but warmed considerably when she saw the picture of the dress they wanted her to make. "It's been some time since I had a gown of this caliber to work on. Not since Mrs. Pierce quit ordering new dresses." She studied Daisy with a critical eye, then nodded. "It has the perfect silhouette for you."

"We were thinking something in blue or green would be best," Abigail said.

"I agree. With an ivory trim perhaps." The dressmaker's eyes lit up. "Oh, and I have the perfect fabric for such a gown. I've stored it in the back for just such a special project as this. It's a lovely blue-green shot silk that will complement your eyes and look quite elegant."

Daisy quickly spoke up. "Please keep in mind that cost will be a factor. And that this dress will serve as my Sunday dress after the wedding. Perhaps we need to consider a more sensible fabric."

Hazel and Abigail exchanged glances, then the seamstress gave Daisy a placating smile. "Let me fetch it for you to look at before you make up your mind."

When the seamstress came out with the fabric, Daisy felt her resolve weaken. It truly was a lovely color, with a subtle sheen that made it seem almost fluid.

She touched it reverently, then pulled her hand back. "It looks mighty expensive. Perhaps you should show me something a little more practical."

"Oh, but it's your wedding dress," Abigail argued. "You should forget practical. And this fabric is perfect—you know it is."

Daisy cast a longing look at the fabric, then shook her head. "What else do you have that would be suitable?"

The seamstress didn't move. "This fabric is not as expensive as you might think. And for your wedding dress, I'm willing to give you a discount."

Daisy tried not to get her hopes up. But when the seamstress named her figure, she was pleasantly surprised. It would take most, but not all, of her carefully hoarded funds, but she *could* afford it.

And since Everett was so opposed to her restaurant idea, there was really no rush in replacing her funds.

During lunch, Abigail chattered away about the dress. Daisy figured Everett must be bored, so she filled in the conversational gaps with questions about what kind of stories he was working on for the next paper. And her interest was genuine. Even though he pretended disdain for the kind of news Turnabout provided him with, he always managed to give them a fair and interesting treatment. She liked his way of reporting, the way he found the tidbits that spoke to him and focused the light on them.

When the meal was over, Abigail jumped up. "Sorry I can't help with the cleanup, but I promised to meet Constance downstairs to work on our library as soon as lunch was over." She turned to her brother. "You'll help Daisy in my place, won't you?"

Daisy quickly protested. "That's not necessary, I—"

"Of course I will."

His response caught her by surprise. She'd never seen him wash dishes. But she supposed he must have before she came along.

As he carried a stack of dirty dishes from the table to the counter, Everett cleared his throat. "Is there anyone you'd like to invite to the wedding, other than the locals, I mean?"

What a thoughtful question. "I can't think of anyone."

"Are you certain? I understand your not wanting your father around after the way the two of you parted but, even if this is to be merely a marriage of necessity, I thought you might want to have some of your other family or friends around."

"That's very considerate of you, but unnecessary. I don't think my grandmother would be interested in coming. And Uncle Phillip and his wife are pretty much under her thumb. As for friends, my friends are all here.

Traveling the way we did, I didn't have much chance to make friends on the road."

She spread her hands. "So there you have it. What about you?"

"Abigail is the only family I have that matters. As for friends outside of Turnabout, I'm not certain anyone I left behind in Philadelphia would travel over a thousand miles just to see me get married."

She smiled. "Then it seems we have similar circumstances. But we have the friends we've made here to witness our marriage vows, and I'm quite satisfied with that."

He nodded agreement, then cut her a sideways look. "I don't know what kind of relationship you wish to maintain with your father, but if you decide you want him here to walk you down the aisle, then we can try to find him before the wedding.

Did she want him here? She loved her father, but she didn't like him very much these days. "It might be best if I just let him know about the wedding after the fact."

"Whatever you decide, I'll support you."

She was touched by that statement, by the implied concern. "Thank you, but even if I wanted him here, I'm not sure I'd know where to look."

Once Everett headed downstairs, Daisy's thoughts turned back to the issue of her father. Ever since Abigail arrived, she'd been trying to help Everett see how very important family was, how he should cherish the time he spent with Abigail, despite any other irritations or concerns he might feel.

Was she willing to follow her own advice?

Feeling convicted, she headed downstairs to ask Everett for his help in sending a telegram—in fact, a series of them—to whichever towns her father would be most likely to be visiting right now. He might not get the news in time to attend her wedding, but he'd be passing back through here in a few months, and she didn't want him to be surprised by her new status.

Halfway down the stairs, she paused as something else occurred to her. She should ask Everett for a sheet of paper, too. It was past time she wrote to her grandmother and at least attempted to mend fences there, as well.

Much to Abigail's delight, the furniture they'd ordered arrived two days before the wedding. Daisy instructed the deliverymen to place the sewing machine in her sitting room and the laundry equipment in her storeroom. The bed that had been ordered for Abigail went into her room. Everything else was carted up to Everett's living quarters.

Abigail dragged Daisy into Everett's much-enlarged bedchamber to help with arranging the new furnishings in just the right places.

Daisy felt uncomfortable as she entered what, until now, had been Everett's private domain. "I really think Everett should have some say in how the furnishings are placed."

"Don't be a goose. As if my brother gives a fig for such things. That's the lady of the house's responsibility."

Daisy raised a brow. "At the moment, that's still you."

"Don't be tiresome." Abigail nudged her arm. "We both know I'm just a placeholder for you. Now let's get to it. If we're quick, we can get it done before Everett comes up for lunch. Believe me, he'll be glad to have it all taken care of without having to be bothered with it himself."

Daisy wasn't so sure of that. She knew how organized Everett liked to be, how he liked his things arranged just so. But she supposed he could always rearrange things if he didn't like what they came up with.

As they worked, Daisy was especially careful about the placement of the chaise lounge, situating it beneath the window of what was formally the spare room. That would give them enough space between their beds for some semblance of privacy, if that was what they wanted. She also placed a small trunk nearby that would be perfect for storing the bed linens when not in use.

The dressing table and other items of furniture she let Abigail have some say in, and the girl happily tried several arrangements before she pronounced herself pleased.

When it was finally arranged, Abigail stepped back with a pleased smile. "Won't Everett be surprised when he sees what we've done?"

It was obvious how much Abigail craved her brother's approval. Why was it so hard for Everett to see it?

"Let's hope he's *pleasantly* surprised," Daisy said dryly.

"Oh, you know my brother." Abigail waved a hand airily. "It takes him a while to adjust to new things, but he'll come around in time."

Not the most encouraging of reassurances, but Daisy accepted it as the best they could hope for.

"I suppose we must wait until after the wedding to move all of your things in here, but perhaps there are one or two items you'd like to add now to give it a more womanly touch."

Daisy immediately balked. She wasn't ready to intrude on his domain just yet. "I don't know. That seems a bit presumptuous."

"Nonsense. Everett needs to get used to sharing." Abigail took Daisy's arm and gave it a gentle tug. "Come on. I'll help you pick out some things."

Despite her reluctance, Daisy allowed herself to be swayed by Abigail. In the end, they settled on one of her mother's stitch-work pieces and the toy horse.

When they stepped back and studied the final effect, Abigail smiled. "The perfect hint of a woman's touch to offset my brother's somber decor." She turned and gave Daisy an impulsive hug. "Oh, I'm so happy for Everett. You're going to be so good for him."

Daisy certainly hoped the girl was right.

When Everett came upstairs for lunch, Abigail insisted he view the newly furnished room. Daisy stayed in the kitchen, letting Abigail do the honors.

When they came back out, Abigail's face fairly glowed.

"I told you he'd like it," she said to Daisy.

"Who am I to question the taste of two such well-traveled ladies?" Everett said with a straight face.

Daisy felt her own spirits rise. Was Everett actually learning to unbend enough to tease his sister?

Everett's conscience was troubling him, had been for a number of days. Daisy deserved to know his background now, before they were married. But would she go through with the wedding if she knew? Because it was vital, if they were to salvage her reputation, that the wedding take place.

That was his dilemma.

But this morning he'd decided he couldn't in good conscience *not* tell her.

So that afternoon, when Daisy stepped out of her building to take her dog for a walk, he was waiting for her.

"Oh, hello." She looked understandably surprised.

"Do you mind if I come along on your walk?"

"Not at all." She gave him a speculative look but didn't ask questions.

They strolled along in silence for a while, until he finally spoke up. "I think you have a right to know who it is you're marrying."

Daisy smiled. "I know exactly who I'm marrying—Everett Fulton, newspaper man, good neighbor, respected citizen of Turnabout. A man who is perhaps too much of a stickler and takes himself too seriously, but who has a good heart, is a loving brother, and has a strong sense of what is right and honorable and does his duty without question."

Her words took him by surprise. Was that truly how she saw him? But he pushed that question away. "What I mean is, you have a right to know my background, where I come from, so to speak."

She nodded solemnly. "I would love to hear your story, but only if you really want to share it with me."

He took a deep breath. He hadn't spoken of this to anyone before. Even Abigail didn't know the full story. "My father is a member of the English nobility, born the second son of an earl to be more exact."

His admission took Daisy by surprise, but it made sense. English nobility—no wonder he seemed so aloof at times. But he was waiting for her response. "Does that mean you're a member of the nobility, as well?"

"Not exactly." His smile twisted. "You see, my father never married my mother. She was an actress and considered quite beneath him. Which means I was illegitimate."

Daisy wasn't sure what to say to this. But he didn't give her time to respond.

"Father set her up in a nice cottage at his country estate, and when I came along, he saw that I had tutors, nice clothes, ponies—everything the grandson of an earl should have. But I knew from the outset that I was illegitimate and had no real standing in the family. In fact, I was a bit of an embarrassment and was kept hidden away in the country."

"Oh, Everett, I'm so sorry."

He shrugged. "No need to be. As I said, I led a very easy and privileged life. My mother often returned to London to continue her acting career. I was left in the care of servants, and they all catered to me quite nicely."

This was somehow so much worse than what she'd endured from her grandmother. Daisy tried to match his matter-of-fact tone. "How did you end up in America? Did you get tired of being ignored by your parents?"

"Nothing so noble. When I turned twelve, my father's older brother died in a boating accident, making him the heir apparent. It became his duty to take a wife in order to provide the family line with a legitimate heir."

It all sounded so polite, so sterile. Is that where he got his notions of what marriage was all about?

Without any conscious decision, they had arrived at

the same log in the same field where Daisy had questioned him about sleeping arrangements.

Everett handed her down then continued his story. "Father's new wife was understandably loath to share her husband with a mistress and his by-blow. So Mother and I were shipped to America, along with the funds to make sure we would be provided for. He even hired someone to make certain we settled in nicely."

Everett didn't sound particularly grateful.

"As luck would have it," he continued, "Mother was already carrying Abigail when we set sail. However, she didn't discover this until we were well underway, and eventually my sister was born after we arrived in America."

"What happened to your mother?"

"She married a playwright who drank too much and spent all her money. She died when Abigail was five."

She placed a hand over his. "I'm so sorry."

"Again, there's no reason for you to be. By that time I was on my own and making enough to get by. I'd been worried about Abigail for some time—the home my mother made for her was not the most nurturing of environments. When Mother passed on, I got her out of there—my stepfather didn't object—and I scraped together enough money to enroll her in Miss Haversham's school for girls. And I've managed to scrape up enough to keep her there ever since."

Daisy straightened. "My goodness. Your sister has been at that school since she was five?"

His posture took on a slightly defensive cast. "It was the best thing for her. We had no other relatives, at least none we could count on. And she certainly couldn't live with me, not in the places I was living back then."

"And now?"

"What do you mean?"

"Now you have a nice home. You're about to have a wife. Don't you think this is a good place for her now?"

"There's nothing for her here."

"There's you." *And me.*

"I don't want to talk about that right now."

Daisy wanted to shout at him that he never seemed to want to talk about it. But she could sense there was more to his story, and that it wasn't an easy thing for him to tell it. So she pulled her thoughts back to the conversation at hand. "Do you ever hear from your father?"

"Not directly. Up until I turned twenty-one, his man of business sent me a letter with a small stipend each year on my birthday. He never acknowledged that Abigail was his. And for all I know, he was right. But he supported her, anyway. Because all the money he sent me went directly to Miss Haversham's to help pay Abigail's tuition."

That sounded just like him—not one to take a handout from the father who had rejected him.

"Last I heard," he added, "he had inherited the title and had two sons and a daughter by his wife."

"Your half brothers and half sister. And you've never met them?" That seemed so sad to her.

He merely shrugged.

She straightened and met his gaze. "Now I know your story, and it doesn't change any of those things I said about you."

Was that relief flashing in his expression? Had he truly been worried about how she would react?

But then his expression closed off again. "There's more." She saw his fist clench at his side. "I debated about whether or not to tell you this part."

Chapter Twenty-One

Daisy saw the uncharacteristic uncertainty on Everett's face, and she braced herself. Whatever was coming was going to be worse than what he'd already told her. She said a quick prayer that she would react properly.

He reached down and plucked a blade of grass. "It is at the heart of why I left Philadelphia last year. I did something I'm not very proud of."

"Oh?" She knew he tended to be hard on himself. Perhaps it wasn't as bad as he thought.

"I told you I was a reporter for a large newspaper there, and left because the editor and I had a major disagreement. What I didn't tell you was that he was right to fire me. I would have done the same thing in his place and not lost a minute of sleep over it."

Goodness, what in the world had he done? Still, she held her peace and let him do the talking.

"I had a lead on a story, a very big story, ripe with the kind of notoriety that sells newspapers. I'd gotten wind of rumors that a prominent local politician had taken a mistress and that the woman bore him a child.

This man was married, mind you, and he and his wife had two children."

Given what she'd just learned of his own history, she could see where such a story would have captured his attention, reporter or not.

"When I looked deeper, I found snippets of information that indicated he had covered up his affair by sending the woman and child to England." His lips curled in a self-mocking smile. "You can just imagine the irony of such a story falling in my lap. I checked the facts, and they seemed solid. And such was my fervor to expose this dishonorable dignitary that I didn't keep digging and checking as thoroughly as I usually do."

Her heart sank as she got an inkling of where this was going.

"Based on my reporting," he continued, "my editor published the stories and sold tons of papers. Everyone was happy as could be, except, of course, for this politician and his family, who kept protesting his innocence. Naturally, no one believed him—after all, they'd read the truth in a respected newspaper. So, in order to get himself and his family away from all the harsh public attention, this cheating politician gathered his wife and daughters and set sail on their private yacht for a getaway. Unfortunately, they were caught up in a storm, and the boat capsized. The politician and one daughter drowned. The wife and other child survived."

She placed a hand on his arm to show her sympathy for both the victims and him. "How awful."

He seemed not to notice her gesture. "A week later, the story I had written proved false. The carefully crafted lie and so-called proof had been engineered and fed to me by one of his political opponents. Someone who knew it was a story I couldn't resist."

"Oh, Everett, I'm so, so sorry."

"Because of my lack of objectivity, a good man and his family were publicly raked over the coals. And my actions, no matter how indirect, led to his death and that of his daughter." He stood and looked down at her. "I just thought you should know what sort of man you were yoking yourself to before it was too late for you to back out."

With that, he turned and left her there.

Daisy felt at a loss as she watched him leave. What he'd done had had terrible consequences. But she could see that he was hurting, that he was filled with remorse and self-loathing. She should have said something, done something to comfort him. But she'd failed him.

Father above, Everett is a man in need of forgiveness, both from You and from himself. I know You will forgive him if he but asks, but how can I help him to see that? Please, help me find a way.

Everett walked into his office and sat at his desk shuffling papers, but was unable to concentrate on any of it. Telling Daisy had been the right thing to do, the honorable thing. But that hadn't made it any easier.

She now had to choose between marrying a man who had done this truly unforgivable thing, or live with a tarnished reputation. What was she thinking? It had been cowardly of him to leave so abruptly, but reliving that nightmare had scraped his feelings raw, and he couldn't bear to see loathing or rejection in her eyes.

He had attended the funeral, had seen the politician and his daughter laid to rest. The sight of those two caskets had been convicting. The sight of the grieving widow and surviving daughter had wrenched something deep inside him.

He'd stood in the back of the crowd, not wanting his presence to bring further pain to this family. But somehow the widow had seen him. For one endless moment, their eyes had locked across that cemetery lawn and he'd felt her pain. When she finally looked away—turned her back on him—he'd walked away.

Would Daisy turn her back on him, as well?

His door opened and Daisy marched in, her dog at her heels. Her eyes were flashing with some strong emotion and he surged to his feet, bracing himself for the worst.

"It wasn't very gentlemanly of you to walk off that way without me."

He tried to read her expression. "My apologies."

"Apology accepted." She lifted her chin. "I just wanted to let you know that I ran into Adam on my way here and, since I haven't heard back from my father, I asked him to walk me down the aisle Saturday. He agreed."

Was that her way of telling him she intended to go through with the wedding? But did that mean she'd just taken the better of two unappealing options? "Adam is a good choice."

"Glad you approve." She smiled. "And for the record, though he is remarkably thickheaded and obtuse, I think my husband-to-be is also a good choice. Those things I said about him earlier still stand."

And with that, she spun around and walked away.

Everett slowly sat back down. She was going through with it, *wanted* to go through with it. The flood of emotions surging into him almost made him dizzy. There had been no loathing, no rejection in her eyes when she looked at him. There had been anger, yes, but something else, too, something amazingly like affection.

How could that be? Deep down he knew he wasn't a very likable person, even when one didn't know his secrets. Yet she saw something good in him. What was it she had said about him? *A man who is perhaps too much of a stickler and takes himself too seriously but who has a good heart, is a loving brother, has a strong sense of what is right and honorable, and does his duty without question.*

He wasn't sure he really was that person, but suddenly he very much wanted to be.

Daisy's wedding day dawned bright and clear. The sky was dotted here and there with wispy clouds that posed no danger of rain and only served to intensify the blue of the sky behind them.

Daisy stood at the back of the church with Adam and Reggie, waiting for her cue to walk down the aisle. This was it. In a few short moments, she would speak the vows that would tie her life irrevocably to Everett's. It was a scary thought, but exciting, too.

At least she was properly attired for the occasion—Everett would have no reason to apologize for her appearance. She looked down at her skirt, gently touching the luxurious fabric, admiring the scalloped hem and lace trim.

The gown Hazel and Abigail had created for her was just about the finest she'd ever seen, much less worn. And that included gowns she'd seen in her grandmother's drawing room and in Abigail's catalogs.

Abigail had played the role of sister of the bride with relish. She insisted on arranging Daisy's hair, piling it all up fancy with a few ringlets cascading down. And there was a coronet of flowers in her hair. The girl had also picked a bouquet of lovely wildflowers, along with roses from Reggie's garden.

She felt like a princess. And an impostor.

Everything about today would be perfect, if only she was marrying someone who loved her. Was this truly the answer to her prayers? Or was it rather the penance she must pay for not listening to Everett's concerns over their use of that door?

Everett had been so good about not making her feel he was angry or unhappy with the circumstances that had brought them to this. But she knew he had to feel some amount of frustration.

Would they be able to get past that?

Reggie was keeping an eye on the preacher, looking for the signal that it was time to start. Then, as if picking up on Daisy's nervousness, she turned and gave her a smile. "You look mighty fine, fine enough to fit in in my grandfather's parlor back in Philadelphia. Don't you agree, Adam?"

"That, she would. In fact, I can only remember one bride who looked lovelier." He winked at his wife, and Daisy was surprised to see a faint blush stain Reggie's cheeks. Would she and Everett ever share those kind of special moments?

Reggie looked into the sanctuary again, then turned with a smile. "All right, they're all set."

Daisy's heart stuttered, as if she'd been caught in the act of something improper. Adam tucked her arm under his elbow and smiled down at her. "Shall we?"

She pushed away the last minute wave of panic, and nodded.

Adam's smile took on an understanding edge, and he patted her hand. "Deep breath. Smile. Eyes straight ahead. You'll do fine."

She smiled gratefully, lifted her head and signaled she was ready.

All heads turned to face her as she stepped into the aisle, but Daisy's gaze sought and then locked onto Everett's. She saw his eyes widen just a bit as he took in her appearance. His obvious approval gave her a little boost of confidence.

Then Adam gave her arm a squeeze, and they were moving forward. The walk down the aisle seemed both infinitely long and unbelievably short. Then Adam was releasing her and handing her off to Everett.

The cynicism that seemed a natural part of his expression appeared to be curiously absent now. Instead, it was replaced by something softer yet stronger at the same time. She responded with a shy smile.

When he took her hand, there was a moment of connection, of intense awareness, that almost made her jump. She could tell he felt it, too. Was it because of the occasion? Or something more?

His hold was warm, strong, possessive. But as before, there was protectiveness and tenderness, as well. She was suddenly filled with a sense of peace, of *rightness*. This was meant to be. Did Everett feel that, too?

Reverend Harper's words broke the spell, and both Everett and Daisy faced forward. But she remained acutely conscious of the man at her side, and the warm comfort of his hand holding hers so protectively.

She stood through the entire ceremony as if watching it from a distance, as if it were happening to someone else. The only thing grounding her was the feel of his hand holding hers.

To her surprise, Everett had a ring to place on her finger at the appropriate time. As he slipped it on her finger, she stared down at it, a simple gold band with a small, square-cut, blue stone set on prongs. She was enchanted by just how perfect it was, how very right it looked on her finger.

She looked up and found Everett watching her, and for once there was no guarded quality in his expression. Just warm encouragement, and something more primitive that she didn't quite understand but didn't fear. And that was the very best wedding present he could have given her.

When the vows had been recited and Reverend Harper pronounced them man and wife, Everett bent down to give her a kiss. It was sweet and warm and altogether breathtaking. And over much too soon.

Then they were turning to face the congregation. The first person Daisy saw was Abigail, and she was surprised to see the girl had a tear trickling down her cheek, but her smile was beautifully joyful.

Then Everett was leading her down the aisle in firm, sure steps. And from every side, Daisy saw smiles of shared happiness and approval.

Had this marriage had the unexpected effect of giving her a firmer standing in the community?

She pushed that thought aside—that wasn't the kind of thing one should contemplate about one's marriage.

As they stepped out on the church steps, Daisy blinked a moment in the brightness of the sunshine. Then she blinked again in surprise. A flower-festooned motorized carriage was waiting for them, with Chance sitting in the driver's seat.

Reggie had offered to hold a reception for them at her home after the wedding, and Daisy would have been fine with making the short trip there on foot. But such a thoughtful, romantic gesture from Everett caught her off guard, and her pulse quickened in pleasure at what he'd done. When she turned to thank him, though, it was obvious from his expression that he was as surprised as she was.

Before Daisy could say anything, Abigail rushed up and gave Daisy a hug. "We're truly sisters now. I'm so happy." Then she stepped back. "Do you like the conveyance? I thought you should be transported from the church in style."

"It's very thoughtful. Thank you."

"Yes, thank you, Abigail." Everett turned to Daisy. "Shall we?"

The reception was set up in Reggie's beautiful and expansive backyard. To Daisy's surprise, there was a grand turnout. She and Everett greeted guests as they arrived until Daisy felt she must have shaken every hand in town.

As Everett circulated among the guests, his gaze kept drifting back to his wife. There was no trace of the peddler's daughter in her today. This Daisy would fit in any society ballroom or parlor. It was partly the dress, of course. But it was more than that. There was a sort of natural grace to her, a genuine friendliness that shone through from within.

Perhaps fate had dealt him a winning hand, after all.

He was making his way to Daisy's side to offer her

a cup of punch when Reggie waylaid him. "I'm ready to photograph you and your bride. I'll fetch Daisy if you'll find your sister." She pointed toward a large oak that shaded one side of her lawn. "I've got the camera set up over there."

Everett finally tracked down Abigail. She and Constance were chatting with Jack, who was keeping an eye on Kip and Buck. By the time they reached Reggie, Daisy was already there.

Reggie had set up her camera so that the tree would serve as a backdrop for the picture. "Let's get a photograph with just the bride and groom first," she instructed. "If the two of you would stand right there."

She fussily arranged Daisy's dress, having her hold her flowers just so. Then she stood back, studying them. A grin teased the corners of her mouth. "You are married now. You can stand closer together. And don't be afraid to hold hands."

Everett didn't need to be told twice. Holding his wife's hand had become one of his favorite pastimes.

"Perfect. Now if you'll just hold it there for a few minutes… Okay. Now you'd mentioned wanting to get a picture of the two of you with Abigail."

Daisy nodded. "Yes. A family picture."

"In that case," Abigail interjected, "Kip should be in the picture, too."

Everett frowned. "That animal is not part of the family."

"Come now," Reggie said, "posing with an animal will be just like old times for you."

"What's this?" Abigail looked from Reggie to Everett.

Before either Reggie or Everett could elaborate, Daisy jumped in. "I'll tell you about it later."

With a nod, Abigail stood between the two of them, with Kip right in front of her.

A few minutes later, Reggie straightened. "Beautiful. I'll deliver them to you as soon as they're ready."

Daisy was glad when the reception began to break up. It had been a lovely gathering, but she was ready to return home. Except she was also a little anxious, too. At least Abigail would be there to act as a sort of buffer, to keep things feeling normal and familiar.

But to her surprise, Abigail gave her and Everett farewell hugs.

"You two go on without me," she said. "I've already packed a bag, and I'll be spending the night at the Harpers' home with Constance. And Jack has volunteered to keep an eye on Kip for you tonight, with his parents' permission, so Kip is staying right here. That means you will have the house entirely to yourselves."

Daisy couldn't quite make herself look at Everett, who remained maddeningly silent. "That's very sweet of you, but it's really not necessary," she said weakly.

"Of course it is." Abigail gave her an arch smile. "You two may not have been able to take a honeymoon trip, but as newlyweds you should have some privacy on your first night together." She made a shooing motion with one hand. "So go along, and I'll see you at church tomorrow morning."

Any further protest would raise brows, so Daisy merely nodded. Would Abigail's absence make this first night easier or more awkward?

And what in the world was Everett thinking?

Chance and his motor carriage were still there, waiting to take them home. Chance stepped forward and doffed his hat as he gave a sweeping bow. “Shall we be on our way?”

Daisy would have rather walked—anything to slow things down a little. But Everett handed her up, and within minutes they were stepping down in front of their home.

Now what?

Chapter Twenty-Two

Everett took her elbow—there was that spark again—and led her to the door. He opened it, and Daisy preceded him inside.

It was only four o'clock in the afternoon, so it was nowhere near time to retire for the evening. Daisy didn't know which was worse—waiting for night to fall, or how she was going to feel when it actually *was* time to retire for the evening.

She gave him her best attempt at a smile. "I'm going upstairs to change out of this fine dress and back into my everyday clothes. Then I'll see about fixing us some supper."

He released her arm. "Don't rush the meal on my account. I'm not very hungry at the moment, and there's some paperwork down here I need to get to."

Is that how he planned to spend the afternoon of their wedding day? But she merely nodded and headed for the stairs.

Daisy opened the door and stepped into the bedchamber she was supposed to share with Everett now.

She'd been in here before, when the new furniture arrived, but somehow it looked and felt different now.

Her belongings, meager as they were, were all here—thanks to Abigail.

Her mother's Bible lay on the bedside table, and her silver hairbrush, which had also belonged to her mother, was on the dressing table. The dressing screen stood discreetly in what had once been a second bedroom.

The sight of her everyday shoes on the floor right next to Everett's seemed almost unbearably intimate.

A few minutes later, when she hung her dress in the wardrobe, she studied Everett's clothes hanging neatly there. His things were so refined, so impeccable. And her clothing, with the exception of this beautiful gown, was sadly lacking in comparison.

It was just one more reminder of how mismatched they were.

To give him credit, however, Everett hadn't made her feel unworthy, at least, not lately.

She quickly pulled out one of her serviceable homespuns. She was who she was—no point wishing she was someone else. Time for this Cinderella to head back to the kitchen.

Everett hadn't watched Daisy as she climbed the stairs earlier, but he'd been very aware of her every movement. He knew this was difficult for her, but she seemed to be holding up well. His wife was a woman of strong character.

His wife—it was really and truly done now. It might not be the marriage he'd planned for himself, but he could already see there was much to like in this arrangement.

As for this sudden awkwardness between them, it was normal for a new bride to be nervous—that had to be all it was. Because surely she knew she had nothing to fear from him. He intended to let her set the tone for the physical part of their relationship. More than likely, she planned to sleep on the chaise tonight. But he was confident that in time she would grow more comfortable with him and the idea of sharing the marriage bed. After all, she had said she'd like to have children.

He determinedly pushed those thoughts away and tried to focus on his paperwork. But later, when she called him up to supper, he realized he'd gotten very little accomplished.

During the meal, Everett tried to engage her in idle conversation, but was only partly successful. Though she responded to his comments, she seemed nervous and her gaze more often than not slid away from his. He'd never seen her so flustered before.

Finally, he decided there was only one thing he could do to settle her nerves. He cleared his throat. "I have some things I need to finish downstairs. Don't wait up on me."

Her gaze flew to his and held, her eyes widening in surprise. Was there a hint of disappointment mixed in with the relief? Or was that just wishful thinking?

Whatever the case, it would be a very long evening.

Once he left, Daisy finished cleaning the kitchen, still unable to recapture that sense of peace she'd had earlier. He'd noticed, she was sure. No doubt that had been responsible for his eagerness to leave the room once the meal was over.

The house felt so empty without Abigail and Kip.

Perhaps, when those two boisterous beings returned tomorrow, things would feel more comfortable, more normal again.

Finally, the last dish was dried and put away, the table was wiped down until it practically sparkled, and the floor was swept.

There was nothing left for her to do but retire for the night. And perhaps the quicker she got to it, the better. The thought of preparing for bed with Everett in the room was enough to spur her to action.

Daisy entered the bedchamber and quickly went through her nightly rituals. When she was ready to retire, her gaze shifted from the bed to the chaise and back again. This was it—time to decide where she would sleep tonight.

The need to make this decision had been lurking in the back of her mind all day—which no doubt accounted for the state of her nerves—and she still wasn't certain what to do.

He was leaving the choice entirely up to her, and she knew he wouldn't press her. What did she want to do? What did *he* want her to do?

Father above, I don't know what I should do, or even what I want to do. I would like to be a proper wife to my husband, but I'm not sure if he'd welcome me or think me presumptuous. And am I really ready to take such a step? We've only known each other a short time.

But is this a matter of time, or a matter of closeness? Because I do *feel I know his character.*

She turned to the bed, her pulse quickening. But her feet wouldn't take that first step.

Yes, she knew his character, but she didn't know his heart.

At the last minute her courage failed her, and she scurried to the chaise and quickly added the pillow and coverlet from the trunk. As she burrowed under the covers, she knew herself to be a coward.

And she suspected she wouldn't get a wink of sleep tonight.

Everett quietly opened the door, not sure what he would find on the other side. She'd left a lamp lit for him with the wick turned down low.

Her soft breathing told him she was asleep. And that she had chosen the chaise. He felt an unexpected twinge of disappointment. But he didn't blame her. He really hadn't shown her any of the tender emotions a sentimental woman like her would expect from the man she married. He wasn't sure he even had it in him to give it to her. The best he could hope for was that she would grow accustomed to him.

He prepared for bed as quietly as he could, accompanied by the sound of her soft breathing. Something about that sound got under his skin and quickened his pulse. It brought back the memory of the kiss they'd shared at the end of the wedding ceremony—sweetly chaste but firing a hunger for more, bringing out all of his protective, and possessive, instincts.

He'd promised to give her however much time she needed, but how many nights would it take before she was comfortable enough with their marriage to give up the chaise?

Perhaps sharing a few more of those kisses would speed the process.

As he slipped into bed, the sound of her breathing seemed to fill the room, a strangely seductive lullaby.

It was going to be a long night.

* * *

Daisy woke to find the sun already up. She couldn't believe she'd slept straight through the night. She bolted upright, but a quick glance at the bed across the room told her she was alone. It was neatly made, with nary a wrinkle visible. Had he even slept in his bed last night?

She made quick work of her morning ablutions, then dressed and stepped out of the bedchamber.

Everett was in the kitchen, stoking the stove.

"I'm sorry I overslept. I'll have breakfast ready in two shakes."

"No need to rush. We have lots of time before church service starts."

Daisy joined him in the kitchen and pulled out the skillet, taking a mental inventory of what was in the pantry.

As she counted eggs and measured flour, Everett moved to the adjoining door and opened it, and the inner door as well. He stood staring into Daisy's former living quarters for what seemed a very long time. What in the world was he thinking about?

Finally, he moved back toward the kitchen, but left the doors open. Obviously there was no reason to keep them closed now.

"I do believe Abigail was correct," he said. "We may not be here much longer, but opening up this wall while we *are* here would make sense."

Daisy's heart dropped. Was he still so determined to move away from Turnabout? Couldn't he see what a wonderful life they could build here?

A small furrow appeared on his brow. "Do you have some reservations? If you'd rather not, we don't have to change a thing."

"Oh, no, I think it's a wonderful idea. It would definitely make this place feel more like one home instead of two."

"But?"

She took a deep breath. "I just hoped you'd changed your mind about moving."

His jaw tightened. "You knew before we agreed to this marriage that that was my plan."

"I'm not accusing you of hiding anything. I just hoped you'd come to appreciate what you have here more."

"Well, that was a false hope."

She tried to lighten the mood with a change of subject. "I think we should celebrate our first morning as man and wife with a special breakfast. What do you say we add an extra egg to the skillet, and have some griddle cakes and strawberry preserves as well?"

Everett accepted her change of subject without protest. "That sounds good. And while you're working on that, I'll fix the coffee."

Just like a happily married couple.

Too bad it was all an act.

Chapter Twenty-Three

As soon as they arrived in the churchyard, Abigail left Constance's side and hurried over. She gave them both exuberant hugs and arch smiles before rushing inside to join the choir.

As Daisy walked into the church, the same church where yesterday she'd spoken her marriage vows, she had the feeling everyone was looking at her differently today. And she supposed she *was* different. She had a new name, a new status, a new family.

After the service, they again had their midday meal at the Barrs' home. Before they sat down at the table, though, Reggie led them into the study where the wedding pictures were displayed on a small table.

Daisy stepped forward eagerly and was immediately entranced by what she saw.

The first picture was the one Reggie had taken of her and Everett alone. Daisy couldn't stop staring at the way Everett looked in the picture, as if he were actually proud to be standing next to her. There was something reassuring and uplifting in the way his hand held hers so possessively. Was she just seeing what she wanted to? Or was it all really there?

She finally tore her gaze from that picture and looked at the other, the one that included Abigail and Kip. What a fine-looking family they made!

Daisy glanced up at Reggie. "These are beautiful. I can't thank you enough."

Reggie waved away her thanks. "You're quite welcome. It was a joy to be able to take these pictures for you."

Daisy glanced Everett's way and caught him staring at the pictures, but she couldn't read his expression. Had he seen the same thing she had?

That evening, Daisy stood in the kitchen, preparing a light supper. Abigail had disappeared with a vague comment about rearranging some of the volumes in her library. And Everett sat on the sofa, reading through his many newspapers.

She loved this feeling of domesticity, of normalcy, of *family*.

She glanced up, then blinked and looked again.

Everett was still reading, but one of his hands was absently rubbing Kip's neck. Did he even realize he was doing it?

She moved toward him, a soft smile on her lips.

He glanced up with an answering smile. She saw the exact moment when he realized what he was doing. His hand stilled, and his expression closed off.

"No need to stop." Daisy joined him on the sofa. "You both looked like you were enjoying yourselves."

"Yes, well—"

"You actually looked like you'd done this before."

"As it happens, I have."

That admission caught her by surprise. "You had a dog?"

"Once, a long time ago."

He seemed unwilling to say more, but she wasn't ready to let it go. "What kind of dog was it?"

"A hound." He shifted uncomfortably.

"And he was your pet?"

"Not exactly." He folded his paper and leaned back. "There was a kennel on the estate where I grew up. Hunting dogs, bred and trained for it. My father was fond of hunting, you see, and insisted everything be kept at the ready for when he wanted to indulge in the sport."

There was a hardness to his voice when he spoke of his father.

"As a boy, I liked to watch the trainers work with the dogs. I was allowed to do so, on the condition I stayed out of everyone's way. These were prize hunting dogs, so there was no question of me trying to make a pet out of any of them—that would interfere with their training."

It seemed now that he'd started talking, he couldn't stop. She wondered if he was even aware anymore that he was speaking to her.

"When I was nearly seven I noticed one pup, the runt of the litter, who had a bad leg. Something about the pup's refusal to give up appealed to me, and I took to slipping him scraps of food. I always suspected Wilkes, the man in charge of the kennel, knew about it, but if so, he looked the other way."

His smile twisted. "I even named the animal. Figuring a runt would need an impressive name to offset his shortcomings, I named him Samson. But I quickly shortened it to Sonny."

She smiled at that. It somehow made the little boy he'd been more endearing.

"The trainers mostly ignored Sonny, so I was able to play with him occasionally. Sonny always greeted me exuberantly and followed me around as if I was someone special. I was even able to teach him a few tricks."

He was quiet for a very long time, but Daisy could tell he wasn't finished with his story.

"One morning," he finally continued, "I went to the kennel and couldn't find him. I asked Wilkes where he might be. It seemed my father had arrived the prior evening for an unannounced hunting trip. He'd reviewed the new additions to the kennel, and when he saw Sonny's limp, he had the animal put down."

Daisy's heart twisted painfully, and she reached for his hand and squeezed it. "Oh, Everett, I'm so sorry."

Everett wore that cynical smile again. "No need to be. It taught me a valuable lesson. Animals are just that—animals. Coddling them serves no useful purpose."

He stood and gathered up the papers. "If you'll excuse me, I think I'll carry these downstairs. There are a few stories I want to summarize for Tuesday's paper."

She watched him leave, her heart breaking for him. What a terrible, terrible thing to have happened, especially to a six-year-old. No wonder he wouldn't unbend when it came to Kip—he was afraid of feeling that same hurt again. Did he even realize why he'd built that wall?

Well, there were cracks in that wall now, and she aimed to make sure she and Kip pushed right through them and tore that wall down.

* * *

After supper, Abigail decided to retire to her room early, to do some reading before going to bed.

Everett watched as Daisy worked on some mending to one of her shirtwaists. That reminded him—he'd have to see that she bought some additional clothing. There was no need for his wife to go around in nearly threadbare garments.

Threadbare was a good word for his own emotions at the moment. Why in the world had he volunteered that story? He had never once spoken of Sonny in all the years since it had happened, had nearly blocked it out of his own mind. Yet she had pulled it from him with no effort at all.

Such loss of control was disconcerting. He had to resist this pull she had on him, or he would lose himself entirely.

And he might as well start now. Because there was a matter that required immediate attention. He cleared his throat. "I have something I'd like to discuss with you."

Daisy looked up, a question in her smile.

"Now that the wedding is behind us," he explained, "it's time Abigail went back to Miss Haversham's school to finish her education. And I'd like for us to present a united front when I speak to her."

Daisy set her mending aside, giving him her full attention. "Do you really think this is for the best? She enjoys being here so much."

"Her infatuation with Turnabout and all things Texas will fade in time. But the sooner she returns to Boston, the less painful the break will be."

"I didn't mean being here as in Turnabout, I meant

being here as in being with you. She loves you, Everett, and she wants to spend time with you."

"There will be time for that once she completes her education."

"You're going to break her heart if you do this."

He expected these sort of melodramatics from his sister, but not from his wife. "Nonsense."

"Whether it's your intention or not, she'll see this as a rejection."

"Then we'll need to make it clear to her that it's not."

She gave him a steady look and seemed to be undergoing some kind of internal struggle. Finally, she straightened. "I never told you the full story of the time I spent with my grandmother—mostly because it's personal. But now I think I should explain it to you."

He leaned back, intrigued in spite of himself. "I'm listening."

"I guess I should start with some background." She fiddled with her collar. "My grandmother—Grandmère Longpre, as she had me call her—was what one would call a *grande dame.*" Daisy made an airy movement with her hand for emphasis. "She was the daughter of a wealthy and socially prominent New Orleans family. Her husband died long before I was born, but before he passed, they had two children together, my mother and my uncle, Phillip. I'm told the family had ambitious plans for my mother's future. They anticipated securing a marriage for her with the son of another prominent family to add to their already considerable consequence."

She grimaced. "Unfortunately, at least in Grandmother's eyes, before they could make it official, my mother fell in love with an itinerant peddler and ran off and married him. Grandmother promptly disowned her."

Everett was very familiar with being disowned, though in his case, he had never been properly "owned" to start with.

"So years later," Daisy continued, "when my mother took ill and had to return home, you can see it wasn't a decision she made easily." Her expression hardened. "And Grandmother made her pay for what she saw as the humiliation my mother had heaped on her and on the family name."

Everett guessed that Daisy, even as a very young child, had been made to pay, as well.

"As for me, I was viewed as little more than a mongrel half-breed child. I told you I spent much of my time in the kitchen—that's because I felt much more welcome there than in my grandmother's presence."

He wanted to comfort her but wasn't quite certain how. He moved to sit beside her on the sofa, and apparently that was enough. She touched his arm and thanked him with her smile. "I know, unlike how my grandmother felt toward me, you truly love Abigail and are trying to do what you think best for her. But, Everett, you need to let her see that. Or you risk having her feel like I did—unloved and unwanted."

He felt some sympathy for what she'd endured, but surely she could see this was different. "Abigail knows I love her."

"Perhaps. But she also needs to knows that you love being *with* her and that you care about what makes her happy—not what she can do to make you happy. There is a difference."

What did she mean by that? "That's not what this is about."

"Isn't it?" This time *she* touched *his* arm. "Perhaps I'm wrong. But if nothing else, Abigail needs to know, without a doubt, that she doesn't need to earn your love, because she already has it."

She stood. "Please think about what I said. And if you can find it in you, pray about it, too. I'm going to bed now. Good night."

Everett stayed where he was, thinking over what she'd said.

Sending Abigail back to school was the right thing, he was sure of it. But perhaps he did need to sit his sister down and make certain she really understood why he felt that way.

And even though he was certain Abigail knew how deeply he cared for her, he supposed it wouldn't hurt to tell her so.

Everett knocked softly on their bedroom door. When there was no answer, he quietly opened the door so as not to awaken her. To his surprise, however, Daisy still sat at her dressing table, brushing her hair.

And what glorious hair it was. It was the first time he'd seen her hair unbound, and he definitely liked what he saw—thick, wavy tresses, the color of fresh-planed oak, rippled down to the middle of her back.

He tore his gaze from her mesmerizing hair, and their eyes met in the mirror. He felt an almost physical connection stretch between them.

Slowly, he moved forward, and their gazes never wavered.

He held out his hand for her hairbrush. "Do you mind?" His voice was thick, nearly unrecognizably so.

Her eyes widened, but she silently handed him the brush.

He began to draw it through her tresses, enjoying the soft feel of it, the way it seemed almost a living thing in his hands, playfully reflecting the candlelight, coyly sliding through his fingers. He inhaled the faint rosewater and lavender scent and thought he'd never smelled anything so fragrant.

As he worked, he was aware of her watching him in the mirror, of the increased rhythm of her breathing, of the warmth radiating from her.

This woman, this *lady,* was his wife. She was a gift, not a burden. Why had it taken him so long to see it?

After a time—heartbeats, minutes, hours, he had no idea—she took the brush from him and stood, facing him.

He took her chin in his hands. "You are so lovely," he whispered. "You are even more beautiful tonight than you were on our wedding day."

"No one's ever called me beautiful before," she whispered.

"And yet you are, strikingly so."

Her eyes had a luminous quality, but he saw no fear in them. He bent down and very gently kissed her. This kiss was different from the previous one they'd shared. What had started as gentle exploration suddenly turned into something much more. Her arms went around his neck and clung to him. Everett's own pulse jumped, and he tightened his hold on her.

Everett felt an exhilarating mixture of victory and capitulation. He felt an urgent need to protect her and claim her and cherish her, all at the same time. At this moment, if she'd asked him to walk through fire, he couldn't have refused her.

He lifted his head, but she gave a little whimper of protest and tugged his head back down. He didn't need further encouragement.

When they finally separated, he took her hand and led her to his bed. To his joy and relief, she not only went willingly, but wearing a shy smile on her face.

Chapter Twenty-Four

The next morning, Daisy hummed as she made breakfast. Today she felt well and truly married. And she had hope that their life together could be as marvelous as God intended for a proper marriage to be.

Everett had said such wonderful things to her last night, had made her feel so cherished and special. She hadn't known he could be so gentle, so tender.

Then she grinned. He would probably be affronted by such descriptors. But the cynic had a soft side, and she'd seen it now.

She heard Everett exit the bedchamber and glanced over her shoulder to give him a smile. "Breakfast will be ready in two shakes."

He returned her smile with a very self-satisfied one of his own. "No need to hurry on my account. I'll have a cup of coffee while I'm waiting."

Abigail padded into the kitchen from the other side of the building, Kip trailing behind. "Something smells good. Do you need any help getting it on the table?" Then she looked from one to the other of them. "Well, you two certainly seem in a good mood this morning. What's going on?"

Daisy felt her cheeks grow warm, but tried to keep her tone nonchalant. "And what's not to be happy about? It's a beautiful day outside, and we're all healthy and well provided for in here. Besides, aren't you opening your library this morning?"

Suitably distracted, Abigail began chattering excitedly about her plans for the library's opening day.

But Daisy caught the look Everett gave her, the one meant only for her, and the happy humming continued in her soul.

Everett headed downstairs right after breakfast, the smile still on his lips. Who would have thought being a family man could feel so fulfilling? Daisy, with her generous heart and sweet courage, had definitely opened his eyes to the good things to be found in his current situation.

Maybe she'd been right about other things, as well.

But for now he needed to put aside all those less-than-productive musings. He had a lot of work to do—the paper was scheduled to go out in the morning.

Everett worked steadily until midmorning, when Lionel stopped by to deliver the bundle of newspapers that had come in for him on the morning train.

Once he was alone again, Everett absently sorted through the various editions, more focused on the sound of Daisy's humming than the headlines. He decided it had a happier-than-usual, very satisfied ring to it this morning.

Then he straightened as he found an envelope addressed to him mixed in with the papers. He opened it, and immediately his focus narrowed to what he held in his hands. This was it—what he'd been waiting for all these months—an offer from a large newspaper concerning a reporter position. They wanted him to spend three weeks working on staff with the understanding that, if they liked his work, the job was his.

Which meant the job *was* his. He knew he could pull this off.

St. Louis might not be the location he would have chosen for his comeback, but it was a good, solid step on the road there. Finally, he could get back in the game and take his rightful place. He could shake the dust of this backwater from his shoes.

He climbed the stairs, wanting to share the good news with Daisy. She might still have a few qualms about moving, but surely she'd be happy for him and get over that soon enough.

He found her alone in the kitchen. Abigail was no doubt in her library.

"Oh, hi," she said when she saw him.

There was a new softness in her smile, a lightness in her tone that made him feel ten feet tall. They were closer now—surely that would make it easier for her to understand. "I have some good news."

Her smile broadened. "What is it?"

"The editor from the *St. Louis Banner Dispatch* has asked me to try out for a reporter position."

He hadn't truly expected her to jump for joy at the news, but neither had he expected the flash of utter dismay he saw in her expression before she suppressed it.

He tried again. "This is what I've been waiting for. It's not Philadelphia, but it's a definite step up from Turnabout."

She made a sharp gesture with her hand. "Don't say it like that. There's nothing wrong with Turnabout." She took a deep breath. "And anyway, bigger doesn't necessarily mean better."

He ignored that comment. "Accepting this position will mean we can move to a city with many of the amenities Turnabout is lacking. And I can return to being a reporter, not a typesetter and press operator."

Her expression turned wistful. "But we're happy here, aren't we?"

He took her hands, hoping the physical connection would help her understand. "And we can be just as happy in St. Louis."

She didn't pull away. Rather, she gave his hands a squeeze of her own. "Think about everything you'll be leaving behind—dear friends, a home that we've made our own, the *Gazette.* The people in Turnabout have come to expect the newspaper twice a week. Not only that, some folks have even said they're looking forward to that restaurant I want to open someday. How can we leave all of this behind?"

Did she truly understand so little about him? "We'll make new friends. Someone else will step up to take over the *Gazette.* I'll even train them. And we'll live in a finer home—one that you can furnish and decorate however you like."

Her lips set in a stubborn line. "I don't want a finer home. I'm happy with this one." She took a breath. "Say we do move—then what? Is St. Louis just another stepping stone for you? As soon as you find a more prestigious job in a bigger city, will we move again?"

Best to get this all out now. "Perhaps. But moving

is nothing new to you. I don't understand why you're being so stubborn about this."

"I told you before we ever got married, I left my father partly because I wanted to set down roots."

"It's not as if we'll be itinerant drifters. The only time we'll move will be when we can improve our situation."

He felt her stiffen at his use of the phrase *itinerant drifters,* and she slowly withdrew her hands.

"Improve it by your definition, you mean."

"By any reasonable person's definition."

"So now I'm not a reasonable person?"

"In this particular instance, no."

He saw her struggle for control as she took another deep breath. But her next words were said civilly enough. "And what about Abigail? Will you keep uprooting her, too?"

He frowned. "Of course not. As we discussed yesterday, she'll go back to Miss Haversham's to finish up her education. Once she's graduated, she will, of course, live with us until she finds a suitable husband."

Daisy's eyes narrowed suspiciously. "A *suitable* husband? What does that mean?"

"It means that her husband should be a man who can take care of her and provide for her both financially and socially in the manner that she deserves." This conversation seemed to be going down all the wrong paths.

Her expression settled into one of sadness and disappointment. "You still don't understand, do you? Being happy isn't tied to things or to status. It's tied to loving and being loved."

Everett tried to take back control of the conversation. "The matter of my sister's future husband is one we can discuss at another time. Of more immediate importance is the fact that I've already decided to take this position. I'll leave for St. Louis on tomorrow's train and go through the three-week trial period. Afterward, once the offer is official, I'll come back to settle affairs here and take you and Abigail away from this place."

She met his gaze steadily, her lips set in a firm line. "And if I don't want to go?"

Would she really take such a stand? But he couldn't let her see how desperately he wanted her to accompany him—he would never beg, not even of her. "Then that will be your choice. I've already made mine."

Daisy returned to the stove as Everett stiffly marched down the stairs. How could her world have changed from such sweet joy this morning to such bitter disappointment now?

How could Everett be so blind to what was right in front of him? There was such richness and sweetness to this life if he would but take hold of it. Did his ambitions, his need to prove himself someone far superior to the castoff his parents had treated him as, have that great a hold on him?

If only she could believe that this move would be enough to satisfy him, to make him content to finally settle down. But she had seen the hunger for bigger and better in his face as he talked about what the move meant to him.

God, I know I should praise You in life's valleys as well as its mountaintops, but sometimes it's just so hard to follow through on that. Help me to see Your purpose in this, or if I can't, to at least make peace with the circumstances by remembering it is in Your hands.

The prayer settled the churning in her gut somewhat, but there still remained one big unanswered question.

Should she stay or go?

Predictably, Abigail did not take the news well. She protested that she'd just opened her library and it was already doing well. She warned that she would run away again if Everett sent her back to school. She pleaded that she couldn't bear to leave her new friends. And she cried over the idea of being separated from Daisy and Everett.

But to Daisy, the most telling of her protests came when she asked Everett what she had done to make him want to send her away.

Through it all, Everett kept saying it was what was best for her and that if she could stick with it for just one more year, then she would be done with it once and for all. He also pointed out that learning to finish what one started was a valuable lesson that would stand her in good stead throughout her life.

Daisy found herself caught between the two of them, though her heart was in Abigail's corner. She did her best to comfort the girl and promised there would be lots of correspondence and that the number of visits, in both directions, would increase.

Everett raised a brow at that, but she looked him straight in the eye, silently challenging him to contradict her.

In the end, he shrugged and let her promises stand.

That evening, they worked together to get the newspaper ready to go out. While they still worked smoothly together, Daisy found none of the joy in it that she had before.

When she saw the small notice he'd made for the front page, stating the printing of future issues of the *Gazette* would be temporarily suspended, she protested. "I think I've learned enough to get the *Gazette* out for you while you're away."

He raised a brow at that. "I appreciate the offer, but it's not really necessary. I'll start putting out feelers for a new owner—I know several individuals who might be interested. Once I return, we can settle the matter and then the paper can resume."

"I *want* to do this. Granted, I won't be able to put out as substantial an issue, and my articles won't be as well crafted as yours, but I can manage to get something acceptable out." She raised her chin up a notch. "Wasn't it you who said running a newspaper is making a promise to your patrons that they can count on you to deliver what they want to read about, week in and week out?"

He studied her thoughtfully. "Are you sure?"

"Yes. And Abigail can help me. It'll give her something to occupy her mind with these next couple of weeks." *And me, as well.*

After another long moment of silence, he nodded. "Very well. I'll change the notice to indicate it'll be an abbreviated version while I am away."

Feeling she'd won a much-needed victory, Daisy went back to work, determined to quiz him on all of the aspects of his job she was still fuzzy on. That, too, would give them something less emotional to focus on for the rest of the evening.

Chapter Twenty-Five

Everett left his hotel room and headed for the *Banner Dispatch* office. The latest copy of the *Turnabout Gazette* had arrived yesterday, and he'd pored over it. Daisy was doing a surprisingly good job keeping it going. And her voice was coming through loud and clear in the stories. It was almost as if she stood beside him discussing these local happenings. The stories she printed had more of a down-to-earth, colloquial tone than the stories he'd written, but he knew that they would be all the better received by the locals for it. There was less outside news in it than what he normally included, but what she did include was handled well.

She'd included a letter, and here, too, her voice shone through. It seemed Mrs. Humphries, mother of six, was expecting again, and Lionel, down at the train depot, had hired Noah Foster to help out. She also reported that Eileen Pierce, a widow with something of a notorious reputation, had stopped by to see if Abigail would purchase some of her books to place in the library. That had given him some pause, but Daisy, in her typically generous fashion, had said it appeared the widow needed money but was too proud to ask, so she'd given Abigail the money to make the purchase. There was also some personal news.

Her father had arrived in Turnabout a couple of days ago. All of Everett's protective urges surfaced, and he keenly regretted that he'd not been by her side to face the man.

But there was no hint that this had been a difficult encounter for her. In fact, she'd invited her father to move into the spare bedroom at their home, with the understanding that he was welcome to stay, so long as he didn't drink or gamble. Still, Everett knew how deeply Daisy loved the man, which meant she could so easily be hurt again.

But soon this interview period would be over, and he could be with her again. Tomorrow would mark the end of the three-week trial run. And all indications were that he had succeeded. He and the senior editor had had a long talk when he arrived about what happened in Philadelphia. Everett hadn't attempted to sugarcoat any of what had happened and his own culpability. But he'd also assured the man he'd learned from that mistake and that it had made him all the more zealous to get to the truth of a story.

Afterward, he'd been given a number of assignments—everything from covering minor social events to major breaking stories. And in every case he'd come through with flying colors—that wasn't braggadocio, that was fact. He'd enjoyed those assignments, enjoyed being part of a larger newsroom again, enjoyed pursuing stories that were meatier than births and barn raisings, enjoyed the satisfaction of seeing his byline on a front-page story.

He'd also been in touch with Miss Haversham, and she had assured him that she was prepared to accept Abigail back right after Independence Day. Additionally, he'd found a nice townhouse that would be just right for him and Daisy to move into. The kitchen was furnished with a new stove, and the place had electricity and all the other amenities to be found in a big city. It even had a nice backyard that would be perfect for both her dog and her kitchen garden. In time, she could not only grow accustomed to it, but enjoy making the place her own.

Yes, everything was coming together perfectly.

So why wasn't he more excited?

This was exactly what he'd hoped for and worked for since leaving Philadelphia, and it had happened faster than he'd dared believe it would.

But all of Daisy's talk of friends and community and setting down roots had insinuated itself into his mind, into his very being. For all of his worldly polish, it was something he'd never had before, something he hadn't really thought he'd needed.

Yet these past few weeks, when he'd come home to his empty apartment in the evenings, he'd had lots of time to think things over.

One of the things he realized, surprisingly, was that he missed having some messiness in his life, the kind of messiness Daisy and Abigail were so good at. Routines and orderliness were all well and good, but they were rather sterile and uninteresting if there was nothing to shake them up occasionally.

Another quite profound understanding hit when he realized that every time he sat down to a meal, he found himself pausing, waiting for Daisy to offer up her prayers of thanks. Those sincere, conversational, personal prayers, along with her everyday examples of forgiveness and grace, had also made their way into his being, had rekindled a spark he thought long dead. He found himself longing for the kind of relationship she had with God, the kind of relationship that was close and personal, not tied to some vague theology. And he was making progress with that. He'd begun reading his Bible again and offering up his own prayers.

Then other, smaller awarenesses hit. He found himself missing that daily chess match with Adam and the greetings on the street from people who really knew him. He found himself saddened at the thought of Abigail not being a part of his day-to-day life, at not being nearby when Adam and Reggie welcomed their new baby into the world. And if he were to be honest with himself, a small part of him even missed putting out the *Gazette* twice a week. When had his world changed? And why hadn't he noticed it before now?

There was a question he needed to answer right now, though—while he was almost certain Daisy would follow him, did he really want to pull her away from everything she'd built for herself?

A peace settled over him as he realized the answer to that question.

So what was he waiting for?

Chapter Twenty-Six

Daisy was making notes on the latest story she was writing for the *Gazette.* This one would feature Abigail and Constance and the great work they were doing with the lending library. Everett was due back in two days, and she wanted to make certain he wasn't disappointed with the job she'd done in his absence.

She didn't want to think about what would happen afterward.

His letters had been filled with news of the places he'd seen since he'd arrived in St. Louis, and the sites that she would enjoy visiting when she moved there. He even mentioned the many fine restaurants she could visit. And he'd told her of a townhouse he'd found that they could move into, pending her approval. At least there was that.

He was trying to do what he could to make this move more attractive to her. That showed he wanted her to be happy.

As for her dream of opening a restaurant, he'd never lent much credence to that, anyway, so it hadn't factored into his plans for their new life. And she'd already resigned herself to shelving that dream even if they stayed here, hadn't she?

She'd done a great deal of thinking and praying on the matter since Everett left. And she'd finally decided that she would make the move with him and do it cheerfully. It did no good to mope and pout. This was his dream, and it wasn't right of her to try to sour it for him.

Her only worry now was how to convince him to reconsider his plans for Abigail. The girl had definitely blossomed in the time she'd been here. And she loved her brother so much—did he see that?

Leaving would break Abigail's heart, and Constance's, as well. Every time the two girls discussed how to turn the new library over to Constance alone, tears began to flow.

On that score, unfortunately, she could see no happy ending. Even if she convinced Everett not to send Abigail back to Boston—which she was determined to do—Abigail would still be moving to St. Louis and away from Turnabout.

Daisy pushed that unhappy thought away. She tried to focus instead on some of the blessings that had come into her life these past weeks.

First, she'd received an answer to the letter she'd written her grandmother. Except it had come from her aunt Marie. Uncle Phillip's wife had informed her that her grandmother had passed away two months earlier.

Daisy had felt an unexpected sadness at that news. While the two of them had never been on friendly terms, her passing meant that there would never be a chance for them to mend fences.

But the rest of the letter had proved to be warm and gracious. Aunt Marie wished her every happiness in her marriage and assured her that both she and Uncle Phillip would be delighted to have her and Everett come visit whenever they liked.

Almost immediately after the letter arrived, her father had shown up. She'd been shocked at his appearance, for the first time realizing he was getting on in years. And the kind of life he'd been leading was taking its toll.

She wanted to provide him with a home and the care he needed, but how would Everett feel about that? Surely she could convince him that there was room for her father in this new life he had planned for them.

And perhaps one more…

Reggie walked in just then, a sense of purpose in her step.

Daisy smiled, ready for a distraction. "Is there something I can do for you, or did you just come by for a visit?"

"Actually, neither." Reggie had a look of concern on her face. "I noticed a commotion at your place when I passed by, and thought you might want to check it out."

"A commotion?" Daisy was already heading for the door. "Did something happen? Are the girls okay?"

Reggie gave her a reassuring smile. "They're fine."

"Then what is it?"

"It would be best if you saw for yourself."

More puzzled than ever, Daisy quick-stepped to her place and pushed the door open. She stepped inside to see both girls and Kip staring at her with expectant expressions.

Daisy looked around, but didn't see anything out of the ordinary. "What's going on? Reggie mentioned something about a commotion."

Abigail made a sweeping motion toward the back of the building. “It’s over in the storeroom. You should go take a look.”

There was something odd about the way the girls were looking at her. She slowly crossed the room, glancing back at them just before she reached the doorway. Their smiles reassured her it wasn’t anything serious, but she still had no idea what was going on.

Daisy reached the doorway, then stopped dead in her tracks.

Everett stood there, an uncertain smile on his face. “Hello, Daisy.”

Her mind immediately started racing. What was he doing home already, and why was he here instead of at the newspaper office? Had he not gotten the job?

She stepped farther into the room, then halted again when she noticed what was behind him—a shiny new stove with a huge red ribbon on top of it.

“Everett, what? I mean, I don’t—” She took a deep breath, then gave him a huge welcome-home smile. “Hello.”

He moved aside and nodded to the stove. “Don’t you like it?”

“Of course I do. It’s the biggest, shiniest, most beautiful stove I’ve ever seen. But what is it doing here? What are *you* doing here? I thought you weren’t coming home until Thursday.”

“I got homesick.”

Homesick? For Turnabout? Or for her? Her pulse quickened, and she tried desperately not to read too much into his statement. “Did you get the job?”

“Mr. O’Hanlin offered me the job, and at a higher pay than I’d expected.”

"Congratulations." She tried to put as much sincerity into that word as she could.

"But I had to turn him down."

Hope leaped inside her, threatening to steal her breath. "You did?"

"I did. Because I realized something. Something you tried to tell me but that I wasn't ready to hear, until now."

She couldn't have dropped her gaze from his if her life had depended on it. "And what was that?"

He closed the gap between them and took her hands in his. "That it's not where you are that matters so much as who you're with. That family and community and roots that go deep are very important to a person's ability to thrive. And that one should never discount the dreams of others, especially those they love."

Love. Did he really mean that?

He stroked her cheek. "I know I've been arrogant and thoughtless and every kind of fool, but I hope you'll give me one more chance to get this right. I want to build my life with you right here in Turnabout. I want to turn the *Gazette* into the finest small-town newspaper there ever was. And I want to stand by you as you follow your dream to open that restaurant you want."

Daisy leaned her face into his hand as she looked into his eyes. She couldn't remember ever being happier. "Oh, Everett, I want those things, too—but only if I can share them with you. I do love you, you know, more than I can bear sometimes. And I've missed you so much these past weeks."

He gathered her in his arms and gave her the kiss she'd been longing for. It was a long, wondrous moment before they came up for air. They were both breathless, and she could feel the pounding of his heart keeping time with hers.

"Now," he said as he slipped his arm around her waist and led her toward the door, "before we forget where we are, let's go tell Abigail we're not moving, and neither is she." He gave her waist a squeeze. "Because family should stay together."

Daisy smiled at that. She had begun to suspect that their family would be increasing by one member early next year.

But she would wait until they were alone again to share her news.

God was so good. Who could have guessed when she arrived in Turnabout that He could bring forth so many blessings from such inauspicious beginnings?

Daisy knew in her heart that she'd finally found the place she'd always longed for, the place where she could feel she truly belonged.

It was right here in Everett's arms.

Epilogue

Daisy stood at the stove dishing up the last slice of meat loaf, along with some new potatoes and corn. The last of the rabbit stew had disappeared ten minutes ago. After she served this plate, she would be down to chicken soup and cold ham. She'd never dreamed so many people would show up for the opening day of her restaurant. It seemed almost everyone in town had walked through those doors this morning.

She'd just finished piling on a hearty helping of vegetables to go with the meat loaf when she felt a pair of arms snake around her waist. She let out a little squeak of surprise, then carefully set the plate down and rounded on her husband. "Everett Fulton! You almost made me drop this plate, and it's my last slice of meat loaf."

"I have faith in your dexterity, my dear." He leaned down and planted a kiss on her cheek. When he stepped back, one arm remained around her waist. "Last slice of meat loaf, is it? Far be it from me to say I told you so, but it looks like you're doing a booming business."

Daisy raised a brow. "That came about as close to an *I told you so* as you can get without actually saying the words." Then she smiled. "It's no doubt just the newness of it that's brought all these folks here today, but it *is* exciting, isn't it?"

He grinned down at her. "No more than I expected." Then his expression turned serious. "You look flushed. Why isn't Abigail in here helping you?"

"I look flushed because it's hot in here. And Abigail has her own business to attend to. I think she had six new subscribers to her library already this morning." Daisy was as proud of Abigail's accomplishment as she was of her own. And it was fun to see how the two businesses complemented each other.

"Besides," she added, "Pa has been helping me this morning. He's out front now, keeping an eye on things and refilling glasses as needed."

"Just promise me you won't overdo it," Everett said as he placed a hand gently on her stomach, as if to protect the precious new life growing there. "I can hire you some help if things get too busy around here."

She gave him an exasperated frown. "I'm healthy as a horse, and near as strong. I will *not* have you treating me like an invalid for the next seven months."

"Not like an invalid," he countered. "Rather like the precious person you are. And as the light of my life and the mother of our future child."

Everett watched as her expression went all soft and her cheeks flushed prettily. And just as he had every day since his return from St. Louis, he silently thanked God that Daisy had come into his life.

Because of her he had a family now—a true family. People he could love unconditionally and who he knew truly loved him in return.

And that was all the status he needed.

* * * * *

SPECIAL EXCERPT FROM

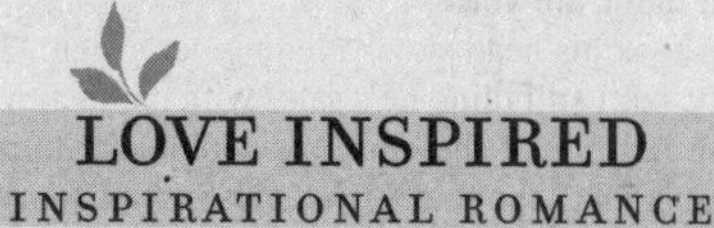

Suddenly a father after a toddler is abandoned on his doorstep, Corbin Beck has no idea how to care for a little boy. But town troublemaker Samantha Alcorn is looking to turn over a new leaf...and hiring her as his live-in nanny could solve both their problems.

Read on for a sneak preview of Child on His Doorstep, *the next book in Lee Tobin McClain's Rescue Haven miniseries.*

"I'm sorry I was distant before. That was just me being foolish."

Samantha didn't ask what he was talking about; she obviously knew. "What was going on?"

Corbin debated finding some intellectual way to say it, but he wasn't thinking straight enough. "I got turned upside down by that kiss."

"Yeah. Me, too." She glanced at him and then turned to put a stack of plates away.

"It was intense."

"Uh-huh."

Now that he had brought up the topic, he wasn't sure where he wanted to go with it. For him to go into the fact that he couldn't get involved with her because she was an alcoholic... Suddenly, that felt judgmental and mean and not how he wanted to talk to her.

Maybe it wasn't how he wanted to be with her, either, but he wasn't ready to make that alteration to his long-held set of values about who he could get involved with. And until he did, he obviously needed to keep a lid on his feelings.

So he talked about something they would probably agree on. "I was never so scared in my life as when Mikey was lost."

"Me, either. It was awful."

He paused, then admitted, "I just don't know if I'm cut out for taking care of a kid."

Her head jerked around to face him. "You're not thinking of sending him back to your mom, are you?"

Was he? He shook his head slowly, letting out a sigh. "No. I feel like I screwed up badly, but I still think he's safer with me than with her."

She let the water out of the sink, not looking at him now. "I think you're doing a great job," she said. "It was just as much my fault as yours. Parenting is a challenge and you can't help but screw up sometimes."

"I guess." He wasn't used to doing things poorly or in a half-baked way. He was used to working at a task until he could become an expert. But it seemed that nobody was an expert when it came to raising kids, not really.

"Mikey can be a handful, just like any other little child," she said.

"He is, but I sure love him," Corbin said. It was the first time he had articulated that, and he realized it was completely true. He loved his little brother as if the boy were his own son.

"I love him, too," she said, almost offhandedly.

She just continued wiping down the counters, not acting like she had said anything momentous, but her words blew Corbin away. She had an amazing ability to love. Mikey wasn't her child, nor her blood, but she felt for him as if he were.

If he loved his little brother despite the boy's issues and whining and toddler misbehavior, could it be that he could love another adult who had issues, too? He was definitely starting to care a lot for Samantha. Was he growing, becoming more flexible and forgiving?

He didn't know if he could change that much. He'd been holding himself—and others—to a strict high standard for a long time. It was how he'd gotten as far as he had after his rough beginning.

Corbin wanted to continue caring for his brother, especially given the alternative, but the fact that Mikey had gotten lost had shaken him. He didn't know if he was good enough to do the job.

Samantha's expression of support soothed his insecurities. He wanted love and acceptance, just like anyone else. And there was a tiny spark inside him that was starting to burn, a spark that wondered if he could maybe be loved and fall in love, even with a certain nanny.

Can saving a kidnapped child bring danger to this K-9 cop's doorstep?

Read on for a sneak preview of Tracking a Kidnapper *by Valerie Hansen, the next book in the True Blue K-9 Unit: Brooklyn series available August 2020 from Love Inspired Suspense.*

Traces of fog lingered along the East River. Off-duty police officer Vivienne Armstrong paused at the fence bordering the Brooklyn Heights Promenade to gaze across the river at the majestic Manhattan skyline. Her city. Her home.

Slight pressure against her calf reminded her why she was there, and she smiled down at her K-9 partner. "Yes, Hank, I know. You want to run and burn off energy. What a good boy."

The soft brown eyes of the black-and-white border collie made it seem as though he understood every word, and given the extraordinary reputation of his breed, she imagined he might.

"Jake! My baby! Where's my baby?" a woman screeched.

Other passersby froze, making it easy for Vivienne to pick out the frantic young woman darting from person to person. "He has blond hair. Bright green pants. Have you seen him? Please!"

LISEXP0720

"I'm a police officer," Vivienne told the woman. "Calm down and tell me what happened."

The fair-haired mother was gasping for breath, her eyes wide and filling with tears. "My little boy was right here. Next to me. I just… I just stopped to look at the boats, and when I turned to pick him up and show him, he was gone!"

Vivienne gently touched her shoulder. "I'm a K-9 officer and my dog is trained for search and rescue. Do you have any item of your son's that I can use for scent?"

The woman blinked rapidly. "Yes! In my bag."

Vivienne watched as the mother pulled out a stuffed toy rabbit. "Perfect."

In full professional mode, she straightened, loosened her hold on the dog's leash and commanded, "Seek."

Hank circled, returned to the place at the river fence that the woman had indicated earlier, then sniffed the air and began to run.

The leash tightened. Vivienne followed as hope leaped, then sank. The dog was following air scent. Therefore, the missing child had not left footprints when he'd parted from his mother. Someone had lifted and carried him away. There was only one conclusion that made sense.

The little boy had been kidnapped!

LISEXP0720